C◍LLIDER

CHRIS
HEJMANOWSKI

FISCHER PRESS, LLC.

Collider is a work of fiction. Names, characters, organizations, places and incidents portrayed in this novel are products of the author's imagination or are used fictitiously. Any resemblance to actual events, locales, or persons, living or dead, is entirely coincidental.

Fischer Press, LLC

www.chrishejmanowski.com
www.colliderbook.com

Library of Congress Control Number: 2012941144

ISBN 978-0-9857180-0-8

Cover Design by Ryan Schinneller

Printed in the United States of America

To Grace, my little G.O.T.U.

Acknowledgements

My thanks to all who helped me produce Collider; my publishers ABC Book Publishers, Inc. and Fischer Press, my editor Kathy, and my advisor and agent Kim Benton. To my parents, Gregg and MaryAnn, thank you for giving me all that I have. Your support and encouragement, regardless of my successes, has made all the difference. To the Stevens family, your encouragement and promotion in this entire process have been invaluable. Thank you for all your optimism. And to my wife Tracy, who's continued interest in this project and unconditional confidence in me, motivate me daily.

COLLIDER

In 1905, Albert Einstein published three world-altering theses, the greatest of which was his Special Theory of Relativity. Years later, in 1915, he furthered human understanding of the mysteries of the universe with the publication of his General Theory of Relativity. In this paper, he used a figure known as the cosmological constant. This integer served to balance all the known forces in the universe. It was a move that was, at first, ridiculed by his peers. Yet years after his death, this universal constant was proven to be valid. In reality, it represented a force so powerful as to push everything we can see in the cosmos away from everything else. This universal expansion, initially believed to be steady, has been shown in recent years to be accelerating, and in every direction. The nature of this force, this dark energy as it has come to be known, remained one of the greatest mysteries of the known universe. Until now . . .

"Reality is merely an illusion, albeit a very persistent one."

- Albert Einstein

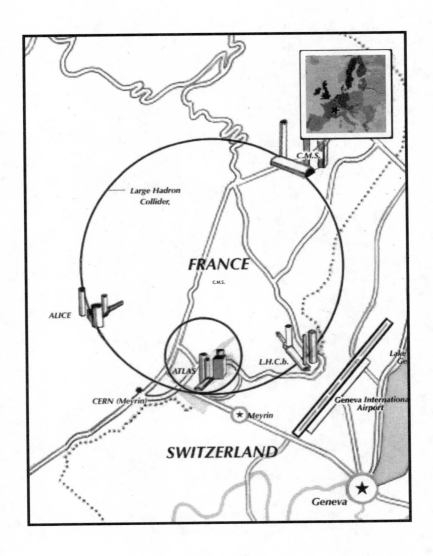

CHAPTER 1

The ships below looked like tiny grains of rice as he gripped the thick cold rail with both hands and leaned out over the water. Each passing car or truck vibrated Fin's lightly muscled frame in concert with the bridge he balanced on. The wind buffeted his thin cotton shirt like a tattered flag as he peered over the edge of the concrete and steel structure. Two hundred feet below, the blue-gray waters of the San Diego Bay passed quietly by. Fin stared beyond his own feet at what could be his end and couldn't help thinking how much his life had changed from just six months ago. Rachel was still alive then, and they had a thriving family. He was the point man for CERN, the European Organization for Nuclear Research, in a legal battle that captivated an international audience, and his career as a particle physicist had been flourishing. But now, in the aftermath of his wife's death and the decay of his own religious and scientific faith, Fin was desperate for some understanding of this shattered life.

Closing his eyes and taking a deep breath, Fin searched for the courage to let go. His thick shock of dark hair danced wildly in the wind as it whipped by. Standing here at the precipice of his life, he wasn't sure what he believed in any more. If there was a God, why would He take his young wife from him; and if there wasn't, well then there was no loss in jumping.

Just let go and it will all be over, he told himself.

Another massive eighteen-wheeler shot past him, temporarily blotting out the early afternoon daylight and shaking the bridge violently. The wake of the semi blasted the right side of Fin's body with road grit. Turning quickly to avoid it, Fin's feet slid forward off the ledge, forcing him to catch himself briefly with both hands. His full 155 pounds jolted downward beneath his strained shoulders and pulled his left hand from the rail. As he swung wildly, Fin struck his face on the metal bars and bounced away from the structure. His right hand snapped open, and for a brief terrifying moment he fell freely toward the water until his hand blindly found a hold again on the thin lower rail. Coming to rest beneath his grasp, Fin could taste the salty blood streaming from his nose.

Below him the water had lost its blue tint. It was gray and moving faster than before. Fin lunged for the rail with his left hand but missed, instead finding a thinner bar below it. He kicked frantically, whipping the air with his feet and trying to raise himself up.

Eva! Fin's pupils dilated with the warmth of panic washing over him. It was as if his daughter hadn't existed for him until this very moment. *How could I have done this? Eva doesn't deserve this, how could I be so selfish?* Eva's mother had already been taken from her, and it was Fin's job now to ensure his three-year-old felt safe and loved, not abandoned.

Fin's grip slowly loosened beneath his weight. Cold and aging steel covered in bird droppings proved a poor choice of surfaces to wager his life on.

How could no one have seen me fall? Didn't anybody care?

Fin shot another glance below him. The ships were gone, and, where only moments ago there had been calm waters, there were now whitecaps. The wind had risen. It pushed him repeatedly away from the girder that crossed his chest, leaving him to slam back when his weight proved too much. A body length or so below him was the lower ledge of the massive box beam that supported the road surface.

Swinging his mass in unison with the wind, Fin launched himself beneath the bridge. His feet contacted the safety of the fourteen-inch ledge as his knees and chest and face met the upright iron wall of the beam. Clinging to the rough surface, Fin pressed his body against it as flat as he could to keep from falling backward. He stood for an instant, frozen in this position of relative safety, while just a misstep behind him was the unobstructed drop to the water below. The ledge was not an even one. Rather, it had a downward slope preventing the collection of rain and other unwanted items. Fin mashed himself against the beam with greater force. He couldn't keep his feet from sliding toward the edge, and his heels crept outward with a sickeningly unstoppable momentum. Although he desperately gripped the insoles of his shoes with his curled toes, his feet continued to slip. His knees slammed into the ledge as his face and chest bounced off the vertical surface. A cold rush of terror shot through his chest as his center of gravity dragged him backward. His mass shifted beyond the safety of the ledge. Spinning his arms wildly, Fin fell back into the open air.

Leaving his life behind, Fin plummeted toward the bay. He felt the wind shift from his face to his back as something pushed him toward this demise. The arches beneath the bridge looked like an immense cathedral as he rushed past them. Below him, the water was churning, and what Fin initially took to be his own approaching shadow now looked to be a growing dimple in the water. Fin accelerated downward toward this point, which now became a swirling vortex of deep green.

How could this be happening? Rocketing downward, he felt

the mist from the water already soaking his clothes and his face.

Sitting upright in Eva's bed, Fin woke covered in sweat, with his chest heaving and their nightly book still resting on his lap. Lowering his head, Fin took a deep breath.

"What the hell does this dream mean?" Fin whispered to himself.

Almost nightly now, it had become more intense with each occurrence. After Rachel's death, Fin's nights had initially been devoid of any dreams, but in the last few weeks this one had thrived like a weed in a barren field. Every night the dream seemed as new as it had the night before, and with each exposure, he was drawn closer and closer to the water before he woke. Fin missed Rachel, but his fear of abandoning Eva was overwhelming. He'd go through hell for his little angel before he'd let that happen.

Fin glanced at his watch, 3 a.m. He quietly left Eva's room and walked past their kitchen toward his darkened bedroom. A long day of teaching loomed ahead of him before he'd have another opportunity to meet with Father Moriel.

CHAPTER 2

Mara Salvatrucha, or MS-13 as the FBI and their rivals know them, enjoys the reputation of being one of the most violent gangs in U.S. history. Life had cast Azazel Guevara well for membership in this clan. Born a son of immigrating Salvadoran guerrillas, Azazel joined the gang to find a respect he never had in his native El Salvador. Covered in tattoos, at five-foot-nine he was shorter than his fellow Salvatruchan brothers, but thicker and far more dangerous. Azazel's criminal family, now a growing syndicate of terror, had initially been protectors of Salvadoran immigrants in LA. They quickly made their mark through violent crimes, and MS-13 murder scenes became known for their machete executions.

Azazel fully embraced this criminality, now grown to include drug and gun smuggling, contract killings, human trafficking, and police assassinations. He found his greatest pride in the ability to lure fresh youth into the organization. At the age of twenty-eight, Azazel was one of the oldest and most feared members in the local faction of MS-13. He had lived in the area for over fifteen years, and had a great deal of influence on the younger members of the community—an influence he wielded aggressively at tonight's meeting.

There were no windows in this meeting pit; it was lit only by a single unshielded bulb hanging from the center of the ceiling. Azazel liked preaching in this abandoned paper mill because it gave him a feeling of gritty determination. "We're shrinking," he told the younger male crowd assembled for tonight's meeting. "We're getting squeezed by the fuckin' monkeys that used to run this city. We need new blood, loyal blood, to continue what our people started," Azazel added, prowling the concrete space. The room's brightly lit center faded past its occupants to reveal the dark imperfect concrete at its edges.

His pace quickened, his gaze stopping occasionally to meet the eyes of the meeker members of the thirty or so gathered. "We need to be visible if we're gonna be the top gang, the number one Hispanic gang. We need more press, more blood, *mas grande huevos!* The puercos ain't afraid of us, the other gangs ain't afraid of us. They all need to show respect." Azazel had a surprise for his family tonight. It was a gift he was saving for the crescendo of his rant.

In the MS-13 culture there were only three ways of gaining membership into the group, and hopeful applicants had their choice. In the first ritual, called a beating-in, the incoming member was beaten—without mercy or rules—for thirteen seconds by the gang. The torrent of kicks and punches was successful if their new brother or sister was left unconscious. Often, the night's activities resulted in the death of their pledge, but those who survived earned the respect of the group. The second choice for initiation was an act of random and unprovoked violence, which must result in murder. This was known as walking the line. Azazel had chosen this form for his initiation since it came most naturally to him. The sheer anarchy of the deed was what enticed most prospective members. These acts served to heighten the growing dark mythology of MS-13. The final convention, reserved for women, was known as a sexing-in. This was to be their special treat tonight.

Their prospective member was a 20-year-old prior runaway

named Maria Ramos. She was a slim and shapely young Latina who had come to Azazel's attention a year earlier while whoring herself on a corner in MS-13 territory. After having his way with her, Azazel tried to convince her to come and work for him. As was expected, Maria refused out of fear of what her pimp would do to her. One week later her pimp's decapitated body turned up off the Santa Fe freeway, near the Metrolink station platform. With him out of the way, Maria willingly came to work for Azazel. In the weeks that followed, his appreciation for her grew after she had beaten a customer nearly to death with a hotel phone when he refused to pay.

Azazel slithered to the door. Out in the dimly lit hallway waited the women of the gang, where they were relegated during meetings like this. "Send her in," he ordered. Turning back to the room he added, "Hombres, we're going to end tonight with a sexing."

Maria entered the room. "You know what to do," Azazel stated. She slowly undressed. Dropping her robe to the scarred floor, the harsh light cast long shadows over her dark flawless skin. With her long hair draped over her breasts, she stood naked before the men of the gang. Knowing what atrocities Azazel was capable of, the more senior members retreated to the room's dark periphery, hoping to leave the junior members to suffer the consequences of their leader's newest perversion.

"What the fuck are you doing?" Azazel spit his words at them through gritted teeth. "She's asking for your approval, all of you. If she's to be one of us, then we handle her like all the rest. We show her the same treatment, the same love as all the rest, no mercy!" Azazel stood in the shadows of the room, his facial expressions unavailable outside the arc of the solitary bulb. "Begin, and I'll *tell* you when it's over."

The cheering began slowly, a cacophony of growls and screams to further inspire the sport of the evening. The first member hit Maria hard from behind, driving his shoulder into the center of her back, knocking her to the ground. Azazel withdrew further into the shadows, allowing his disciples to practice their craft unhindered. He stood silently watching Maria search the room frantically for his eyes from where she lay. One by one, with senior members first, they violated her. Maria fought back, kicking and biting, scratching faces when she could. Deep curls of skin accumulated beneath her fingernails with each act of defense. Her initial look of entitlement when she entered the room was gone now, replaced with one of panic. Shoving her face into the coarse cement as she was penetrated, the last of any assumed favoritism was forced from her. There was no love or pleasure inherent in this, simply violence for its own sake.

She was his, and Azazel was pleased to see that she now knew this too. He glanced down at his watch.

Eight o'clock, where the hell is he?

Azazel exited the room, stepping over the women where they sat on the dank hallway floor awaiting their newest sister. Making his way up the dark tunnel, the echoes of Maria's continuing baptism faded as he neared the surface. He hit redial on his cell phone and stared up at the night sky, waiting for the network to connect.

Pick up your goddamn phone, Salvador. Three rings later, their financial officer's voicemail ended Azazel's wait. "Where the hell are you? I told you tonight was important. You and me need to talk, hermano." Slamming the phone shut, Azazel shoved it back into his pocket and headed down the tunnel.

The screams had subsided, or at least Maria's had. Azazel

entered the room, allowing the light from within to spill out over the anxious crowd anticipating his entrance. Their candidate lay semiconscious in a slick of crimson. Azazel stood in the doorway with a small upward curl at the corner of his mouth. "Now," he growled, "it's over."

Maria was Salvatrucha.

CHAPTER 3

Fin had been driving from the UC Davis La Jolla campus, where he was an associate professor in the physics department, down to Chula Vista three to four times weekly to talk with Father Moriel. Today he had taken the long way for his daughter, Eva. She loved the view on the drive over the Silver Strand Boulevard causeway. They would often roll down the windows of their silver Volvo to smell the salt air and spot dolphins or seals playing in the cool southern California waters. Lately though, Fin could barely get himself to look over the edge of the bridge as they crossed.

"Cancer is a tool of the devil, black and natural. It was Rachel's ultimate cross to bear," Father Moriel said to Fin, shifting uncomfortably in the hard wooden pew.

Up until now, Fin's only experiences with the stages of grieving had occurred with his mother's death last year, as well as his father's fourteen years earlier. After Rachel died, he passed through the denial stage earlier than Moriel had expected. Fin moved quite comfortably to anger, one directed toward God and Rachel alike. Tonight both men shared a pew in the quiet church while Eva played in the vacant aisles.

"It doesn't make any sense." Fin said quietly through clenched teeth, his upper body muscles all tensing in unison. "If she had lived, all our friends would have said it was a miracle, and our prayers to the Lord had been answered. But she died, and so now they try and feed me rhetoric like, 'It's

God's will,' and 'It was meant to be!'" Fin had been angry in the last few weeks, but today's mood was different, darker and more invested in its own despair.

The church was dimly lit, with only the candles in the sacristy lighting the nave where they sat. The auburn ceramic tiles of the church floor and dark wooden pews reflected their deep gold light.

"We're not meant to understand the big picture, you know that," Father urged. "Anyone can have faith after surviving a traumatic event, or the birth of their child. It's at its most rare and spiritually valuable in times like these . . . when it *has* no rational basis."

Father David Moriel was a short portly man of Italian descent. He was profoundly intelligent. Having received an undergraduate degree in biology from Hartwick College in New York, he went on to earn master's degrees in both theology and genetics at Boston College. He was unique among his fellows in his scientifically influenced religious beliefs. He had his own theories pertaining to the conjoining of the two vastly different schools of thought on the origins of man. His mixed background was both a blessing and a curse. He possessed an approachable, rational side his parishioners appreciated, but his scientific nature was his greatest cross. He battled his own doubts in what the church expected him to believe, often having trouble embracing what he could not prove. His faith was something he struggled with daily, something he longed to find proof of. Moriel saw the same struggle in Fin, he understood the need to continue their talks, which often strayed into theoretical physics, mathematics, and genetics.

Father Moriel had an unusual habit of closing his eyes when attempting to make a point. At times he would leave them closed for entire sermons—sermons which were often eloquent but very disjointed. Rachel and Fin joked that if they were quiet enough, the entire parish could escape during these periods, and Father would never be the wiser until he opened his eyes. They once talked their friends into coming early to Mass just to secure the front two rows of pews on both sides of the church. During the sermon the group rearranged themselves entirely. This innocent stunt earned Fin the nickname of *Sapientone*, or "Smartass" in Italian.

Fin had stopped listening at this point. Instead he was watching his daughter playing with the dancing shadows cast by the prayer candles. She was giggling as she ran in and out of the pews, being careful not to step on the larger tiles. Her long black hair reflected the red light just like her mother's had.

"She's too young to understand where Rachel's gone," Fin said. "She asks for her mother at the strangest times. Sometimes it's interesting, but other times it's just odd."

"Like when, Fin?"

"She'll ask about her during dinner or in the middle of the night when she wanders into my room from hers. I usually take her into bed with me and just hold her until she stops asking and falls asleep." Fin often cried himself back to sleep on these nights as well, but that wasn't information he was ready to share. "We were finally finding our peace. How could He have done this? *Why* would He have done this? And with a three-year-old left behind," Fin asked as they sat in the pew in the front of the darkened church. Holding his head in his hands, he continued softly. "I don't know what the hell I'm doing. Rachel made all the doctors' appointments, all the playgroup arrangements. Christ, she even knew how to tell when Eva had to pee!" He seemed exhausted and emotionally laid bare. "I don't know what I'm doing Father," Fin added under his breath as he stared down at the floor.

"She looks happy Fin, and healthy. Obviously you're doing something right. It's not supposed to be easy, at least not at this early stage. It's only been a few months." Fin remained fixed in his posture. After a long pause Father added, "Have you been dreaming?"

"No. Well, a few recurrent nightmares, but nothing really." He didn't feel like being psychoanalyzed tonight. "Usually I fall asleep, and six hours later I'm awake, as if nothing existed in between," Fin answered in disgust. "When I close my eyes, I can't even picture Rachel's face. I've got to look at old photographs just to see. . . ." He turned away from Eva's direction as his eyes began to well up. He'd cried in the beginning a lot, openly at first in front of his daughter, feeling that this was both natural and healthy for her to see. But she was too young to understand, and it only seemed to frighten her.

"In the beginning, I'd wake up in the morning ignorant of her death, only to have the entire weight of this depression come flooding back in one big wave. Now I just wake with the immediate sense of her absence weighing on me."

"Have you been keeping yourself busy as we've discussed?"

"Not in a healthy way. I spend idle time wrestling with my own thoughts in an endless circular fashion. Feelings of loneliness trigger my Catholic guilt, which leads me to wonder if I missed early signs like her slight weight loss or a small decrease in her energy level."

"Fin, you can't blame yourself. God's will . . ."

"Since she was an ER physician, I wonder why changes in her health, no matter how insignificant, didn't tip Rachel off to her disease. I roll from guilt to being angry at Rachel that she put me in this position, and then very quickly back to guilt. I feel like I'm spending what little energy I have left trying to keep things normal for Eva, a task I know I'm failing miserably at."

"Your doubts seem to be growing stronger. I'm worried about you both, Fin."

Fin sat, staring at the floor between his feet. He welled up again. Moriel had a talent for skipping all the bullshit and poking those he cared for right in their emotional wound. Most times folks appreciated it, but tonight it was just pissing Fin off.

"Why bother? Really, what's the use in having faith if all you get in the end is a swift kick in the throat? Something that makes absolutely no sense, benefits no one, and serves only to strain the already weak relationship we have with this . . . absentee landlord deity of ours." Fin sat quietly for a moment, trying to make sense of the feelings that were fermenting in his head. "I just don't give a shit anymore, not about all this anyway," he whispered, gesturing quickly around the church without lifting his head. "I think that I, we, should get going, Father. It's getting late. Eva has to get to bed and I don't think I can get anything more out of this tonight."

"You feel like this is all you will ever have, but we have no idea what the Lord's plan holds for us," Father added as they rose. "I'm not suggesting that you get over Rachel's death, not in the least. But you owe it to Eva to have faith that you will. We're all destined for something. You just need to be spiritually ready to recognize it when the time comes."

Fin sensed a mounting claustrophobia, as if the church were closing in on him. Rising to is feet, he collected their coats and hastily made his way toward the door with Eva. She squirmed in his arms and repeated the word "candles" over and again. "Not tonight, Honey, maybe next time," he told her. "Besides, I'm not sure Mommy is even noticing."

"When are you planning on coming back to continue our discussions, Fin?"

Fin continued toward the back door without turning to acknowledge Moriel's inquiry. "I'll be back in a few days, just like always, Father. Don't worry, I'm not thinking of offing myself yet." With that he kissed Eva on the forehead and excused himself.

Six thousand miles away, buried deep in the earth beneath a sleepy Swiss town and far from the sight of prying eyes, a leviathan was stirring. Its bloated coils laid through miles of black soil held within their waking the secrets of the universe, promising to deliver humanity's next great hope for understanding their own salvation.

CHAPTER 4

"Man, this place smells like shit," Sal muttered to himself. He hated coming here. He could smell tonight's venue over a half mile away. Azazel had found this abandoned paper mill while looking for a place to stash guns and drugs. Over the years it had evolved into their primary meeting place.

"It's bullshit leaving a gang meeting smelling like you spent the afternoon in a friggin' outhouse," he had told Azazel. But the location was perfect—remote, dark, and very soundproof.

The xenon lights of Sal's Benz did a poor job cutting through the fog, but he'd been coming to meetings here for so long that he hardly needed them on. The old gravel parking lot was a lunar landscape of potholes now, but he managed to avoid them all on his way to the gully. The entranceway to the plant, closed more than twenty years ago, provided them the cover of recessed parking. A failed attempt to demolish the plant in the late seventies now gave the local faction of MS-13 their hole. Sal checked himself before he left his car. He knew that all the risks he had taken in the last few months would be shit-down the tubes from just one careless moment.

As he descended into the pit, the smells changed. "Damn, what *is* that? It's like BO and Clorox." His voice echoed off the dank tunnel walls.

Azazel was walking toward him up the tunnel. "Where the hell have you been? I told you to be here at eight. This is getting to be a pattern, Mutt, and one that I don't like."

"Relax, I got caught up in some business. Nothin' major." Sal never stopped walking. He dismissed Azazel's suspicion with a shrug of his shoulders, all the while shaking his head. He moved past his rival on his way to the pit. The girls were busy gathering up Maria, who was now awake and sitting against the far wall of the room. Propped up with her knees drawn to her chest, she was still naked, but partially covered in a colorful blanket that was wonderfully out of place in this shit hole. Her head was slumped down between her knees and a small pool of fluid still lingered around where she sat.

"Christ! Somebody get her cleaned up. And get her something more to put on." Sal had grown to hate these rituals, not to mention this place. It was cold and damp, and these gatherings almost always ended in some sleep-disturbing act of hatred. Collectively, it all made this place feel evil.

Over the years, this lifestyle had worn him down. Sal was tired of the incessant scheming and murdering, but he kept his opinions to himself. He had seen the consequences that trivializing gang traditions could bring upon someone, and there never seemed to be an end to the fury. It seemed there was a beating-in or raping-in of a new soul on the heels of nearly every death from rival gang violence. The foul smell of tonight's activities was bad enough, but the site of this bloody and abused woman was making him physically sick. Sal turned to walk out of the room before embarrassing himself.

"Where you goin'?" Azazel moved to block the doorway.

Sal stopped; slightly surprised that Azazel was taking this tone with him in front of the group. "Come on, vato, let's step outside to discuss this."

Azazel stepped forward into the pit and placed a heavy hand on Sal's chest. "You been missing a lot of shit lately . . . *Vato!*"

Azazel had proven himself to be unpredictable and dangerous over and over, and he loved to display it. "I asked you a fuckin' question man! I only seem to see you at the money meetings, never for the fun. What's the matter, Mutt, you need some encouragement?"

Sal knew what that meant. "Who do you think you're talkin' to? We're in this together, hermano, don't forget where we come from."

Salvador Jose Cabrera was a fellow El Salvadorian, but a year younger than Azazel. He was roughly five-feet-ten inches tall and muscular, but lanky. His thick black hair, now braided in tight cornrows that clung to his scalp, highlighted his deceptively young face. His eyes were his most striking feature. They were two different colors, one blue and one brown, prompting Azazel to give him the moniker 'Mutt.'

"Just because we came from the same place don't mean we're at the same place." Azazel jibed, following Sal up the tunnel as they moved toward the surface. "You owe me the life you have now. *I* saved you after your parents were killed. You'd still be the immigrant orphan of a schoolteacher if it weren't for *our* "family.""

Sal spun around to face his mentor, just close enough now to the surface to highlight the finger he stabbed in Azazel's direction. "Watch it. I sought you out, remember."

"Things aren't always as they seem, hermano."

Sal locked eyes with his old friend for a moment, considering Azazel's comment. His otherwise normal life was derailed ten years ago when his parents were both murdered in their home. After local government failed to prosecute those responsible, Sal decided to deal with matters on his own. Seventeen at the time, this college-bound student spent nights walking the streets, getting to know the local gang culture—bar scene after street fight after petty drug deal. He learned that his parents' murder had occurred in MS-13 territory at the hands of a rival gang. Sal had no violent history to speak of but had one common tie with his would-be saviors . . . he was a fellow El Salvadorian.

"Whatever. This is getting us nowhere." Sal turned again to move up toward the open night, thinking to himself. *This common bond isn't my vaccination against the violence, it's a curse.*

The rival gang bragging about his parents' murder was an upstart. It was rumored they were a splinter of the 18th Street Gang. Split from one of the oldest gangs in L.A., this new faction numbered less than two dozen. The safe house they were using was easy to find for the Mara Salvatrucha gang, and late one night it was stormed by a dozen MS-13 members. They quickly cleared the house, killing everyone inside, everyone except one.

With the air still pungent with the stench of the massacre, Sal was led into the kitchen. Sitting on the floor, leaning up against the pantry, was a man breathing heavily, with two blood soaked bullet holes in the belly of his white T-shirt. "This is the cerdo who pulled the trigger. We wanted you here for this." The young man, in his early twenties, sat in a confluence of his own blood. Propped against the cupboard, he supported himself with one hand while the other clutched at his bloody abdomen.

Azazel raised his 9mm in line with the man's head. "It's time to pay for your sins."

Sal stopped him short of firing. "Give it to me," he'd commanded. Feeling the heft of the weapon for the first time, Sal raised it to the side of the man's head. With emotions he'd pent up for months, Sal pressed the gun firmly into the executioner's scalp. "Scared?" he asked through his tears. "I bet they were too. Fuck you!"

The brash pop of the single round startled him. There was no struggling, no twitching. The body just slumped to the floor, lifeless and faster than he had expected. He would never forget how the bright red blood and brains contrasted against the dirty white linoleum, an image made only more horrifying by the complete silence after the shot was fired. Azazel was impressed, and with his true family gone, Sal was now considered a brother.

Standing in the "pit" tonight, squaring off as they were, all ears pricked to hear their confrontation. Sal knew that, if pushed, Azazel could order his execution, but he also knew he was needed. He had become the financial brains behind the local clique and without him they'd just be another group of street hustlers. He knew where all the money was invested, had all the passwords to the online accounts, and had all the signatures needed for transactions. For the time being, Sal was safe inside his own financial relevance.

"Move, I'm not feeling well."

Azazel followed Sal up the remainder of the tunnel and out into the fog. "Maybe you didn't hear me, vato, you need some encouragement? Huh? We're struggling to keep this family together and you're out 'taking care of business.' Man, this *is* business. Tonight was business, business that you should be at!"

Sal stopped again, this time keeping his back to Azazel. "Where do you think your Lexus came from? Where do you think your friggin' fifty-five inch LED is from? If I take the part-time green your bitches and shit bring in and turn it around into this lifestyle, then you got no business riding me. Back the fuck up!" Sal had never spoken to Azazel like this before, and their relationship was either maturing or dissolving. Sal wasn't sure, but either way it was about to change drastically. He stood there, fearfully waiting Azazel's next move.

"Damn, you're a little tense tonight, hermano. You *do* need some encouragement. Take a day or two off and I'll call you for some festivities, but don't forget who gave you your tres puntos." Azazel placed his hand on Sal's left shoulder, digging his index finger into the gang marking he bore beneath his shirt.

For an instant they locked eyes, the pressure beneath Azazel's finger burned Sal's flesh. He winced slightly, withdrawing a bit. He wanted to say more to smooth the moment over, but felt it was time to take this posturing for a ride. Still, he'd never pushed Azazel in this way before and had only seen bad things come from those who did.

The men knocked fists, signifying that all was good between them. But it wasn't, and Sal knew it. It had not been all right for some time now. He turned to walk to his car, a slight chill running up his spine as he turned his back to Azazel again. Opening the heavy door of his CL Class, Sal dropped into the thickly upholstered driver's seat. Gripping the steering wheel tightly, he started the car and quickly pulled away. Departing the parking lot, he reached around behind his seat to check for his bag. He had one more appearance to put in tonight.

CHAPTER 5

"'It was the greatest blunder of my life,' Einstein once told a friend. He felt this way until the end of his days. The cosmological constant, as he called it in 1916, was a mathematical move that haunted the master to the end."

Fin was relieved that he could not see his audience in the glare of the stage lights. He didn't like the scrutiny of new situations. As a young man, he had been set apart from his peers because of his intelligence, often resulting in a hallway spectacle between classes. A skinny, knobby-kneed teenager, he'd have his books flipped out of his grasp while walking down the stairs or his glasses knocked off his face in the hurry of midday class change. He learned early to move quickly between classes, keeping his head down and avoiding eye contact. This, and a keen sense of humor, he found, were the best ways to minimize hostile encounters. Making jokes at his own expense, putting himself down and getting a laugh before someone else seized the opportunity, became a staple of his youth.

"No one in the diverse field of physics enjoys such an immense degree of fame or respect as this patent clerk who changed our lives forever. Who else do you know whose name is used in everyday conversation? It's used as either a compliment regarding superior intellect or a sarcastic remark to cut down some complete numb nut." A wave of laughter rose within the darkened auditorium. Fin paused, hoping to garner some credit with his young audience.

Fin had been trying to put last night's talk with Father Moriel out of his thoughts. The conversation had served only to depress him further, mostly because the one thing keeping him afloat in these last few months was no longer proving therapeutic. In the past, when Fin had felt down, his only salvation had been his work. That was what he was blindly hoping for today.

"So, one of the greatest analytical minds of our time doubted himself so greatly that in the last decades of his life he all but removed himself from the frenetic pace of discovery that had defined it. In 1905, Einstein simultaneously released three history-changing theories whose nuances we're still uncovering today in our experiments." Fin casually walked around the hardwood stage as he spoke. He found that if he kept moving, his anxiety about being in front of a crowd remained manageable. "His papers on the photoelectric effect, the special theory of relativity, and the theory of Brownian motion give us the technology today for our plasma televisions, cell phones, and laser pointers." He shined his laser pointer around the ceiling of the auditorium for effect.

Fin didn't fit the typical image of a physicist. An overachiever in everything he did—compensation for an ugly duckling complex as a younger man—Fin had been an athlete in college. He stood five-foot-ten and weighed about 160 pounds. At 36 years old, he'd done his best to retain his athletic physique, despite his busy schedule. His square jaw, thick dark hair, and rough good looks belied his deep intellect.

"But Einstein's masterpiece, as many see it, was his theory of general relativity, which was published in 1920. In it, he constructed for us the fabric of space-time. He showed humanity how mass, gravity, and time are unified in one beautiful symphony of mathematics. But Einstein was a deeply religious man, a man who strongly believed that God's eloquence in science was paramount. He was once quoted as saying 'Subtle is the Lord, but malicious He is not,' although I prefer Einstein's later personal translation of 'God is slick, but He ain't mean.'" Again Fin paused, allowing a few chuckles to settle in the darkness.

As with many previous engagements, today he wore his glasses to convey a more intellectual appeal. He was highly regarded in his field as a particle physicist and had gained fame in academic circles as a member of several elite think tanks. Fin often found himself amidst those who were responsible for very renowned projects. As a result of this narrow scope of fame, he was frequently asked to speak at colleges and universities. His goal at these talks was to scout for worthy graduate students who could push the envelope of physics the way Bohr and Friedman had. Fin's talks often focused on his work with CERN, the Europe Organization for Nuclear Research, and the development of the Large Hadron Collider.

"What Einstein believed was that God would not be malicious enough to hide important facets of our reality in a way that rendered them undiscoverable. His theory took into account all of the matter and energy in the universe, something that no one in his time was even remotely prepared to do . . . but he was, and he did. His calculations revealed to him that the universe should either be expanding or contracting, but that wasn't consistent with an eternal universe as laid out in the Bible. It was also not a predictable or an eloquent summary of his theory, and this troubled Einstein greatly. So to satisfy this religiosity, he proposed the cosmological constant."

Fin liked to identify with his idol. He, too, strived to find harmony between his desire for universal understanding as a scientist and the belief in God as Creator of the universe. His views were both shared and cultivated under the tutelage of his graduate school advisor. But his sense of peace with this balance became nearly impossible to perpetuate after Rachel's death. His feelings of anger and doubt had grown during his conversations with Father Moriel. Now his thoughts took him back to those discussions. He suddenly realized he'd been standing quiet and still on stage for a conspicuously awkward amount of time.

Staring out into the lights, Fin managed to mutter, "I'm sorry, where was I?" He adjusted his wire-rimmed glasses before continuing. "Einstein realized that with all the mass and gravitational forces in the universe, eventually all would have to either expand to the point of complete heat loss, or collapse onto itself, incinerating everything. Again, not a notion in keeping with the eternal biblical construct. In the absence of a better explanation, and ignoring his own calculations, he invented this numerical brace . . . the cosmological constant. It was a number just large enough to balance all that he had surmised while keeping the heavens in place, a static universe. He had once said 'God does not play dice with the universe.' His friend, Niels Bohr, responded to this statement in a letter reminding Einstein to 'stop telling God what to do.'" Again, a small chuckle rose from Fin's listeners.

"These were planets, solar systems, and galaxies all hanging in the balance of Einstein's equations. His colleagues were mathematical giants who perceived their surroundings as numerical enigmas pregnant with God's secrets. For Einstein, this journey could end only with the predictable understanding of all things, the order and stasis of the universe as God had intended it." Fin's audience, the seeming embodiment of selection bias, was now hanging on every word. He felt like he was home telling Eva a bedtime story.

"This idea of a cosmological constant was not received well by Einstein's peers, and it was even brought to his attention several times that his inclusion of this integer did not keep with his own calculations. Out of his deep desire to remain true to what he believed in, he rebuffed these challenges. In 1929, Edwin Hubble, using his theory of redshift of light, discovered that the universe truly was expanding. This is a Doppler-based theory about light waves, and with it Hubble was able to calculate that objects were moving away from us and not stationary as Einstein had suggested. As stars or other light objects move away from us, the light waves that they emit are spread out, kinda like the sound waves from a retreating train. At the front edge of these objects, the waves would theoretically bunch up. The trailing waves, being more spread out, appear in the colors of the lower end of the spectrum . . . in this case reds, or infrareds. The larger the shift, the faster the acceleration. Only later did scientists discover, using slightly more sophisticated means, that the rate of expansion itself was increasing. All of this was in direct contrast to Einstein's theory." Fin paused for a drink of water, noticing a few students asleep in the front row.

"The real kick in the pants was that after all the years of beating himself up, it was discovered in the early nineties, decades after Einstein died, that not only was the universe expanding, it was accelerating." The venue was quiet; most students understood what was coming next. "The cosmological constant was real and relevant after all, and it was not only propping the universe up, but forcing it apart at an ever increasing rate. So the new mystery was, and still is, why? Why is this happening, and what's causing it? With all matter accounted for, what forces are pushing us apart faster and faster? What keeps our reality propped open? It's measurable, its effects are observable, but we can't see it, and the best reason that the greatest scientific minds can come up with is 'Dark Energy.' Something right out of science fiction—that's what we're trying to prove, or disprove, at CERN."

He'd done it. In one little ad lib talk he'd snatched the attention of those most interested in the field by giving them the CliffNotes to science's deepest quandary.

"Thank you for your attention, now . . ."

Fin was abruptly cut off by his faculty host as she stood to face the audience from the front row.

"Dr. Canty will now take any questions that you may have," she stated.

"*Shit*," Fin thought. He could feel his mood melt under the hot lights.

He was hoping there wouldn't be any questions. This was meant to be a rousing call to the field, not a goddamned show-and-tell. If the friggin' kids found it boring, then this field wasn't for them. If they found it stimulating, then they could talk with their advisors about grad school. He looked at his watch. He had one hour to pick up Eva at day care. "Okay," he said, "let 'em rip. Yes, you up front . . ."

Twenty-five minutes later, and eleven questions into the session, his patience was wearing thin. Most of the queries were focused on the pop-sci aspect of what CERN was attempting to do. What if you create a black hole or what if the anti-matter you find destroys us? Questions that any self-respecting scientist would have discovered their own answers to long before this little get together, not to mention questions he'd already had to deal with on a much grander stage. "Where have all the sharp minds gone? Not a single valuable question among them," he thought to himself.

Fin took a deep breath, "I have time for one more question this afternoon. Yes, the young man who slept through most of my talk."

"What do you think of his choice?"

"What choice, son?" Fin snapped, his irritation bleeding through in his tone.

The young man cleared his throat, obviously embarrassed now. "Einstein's choice to ignore his scientific intuition and risk his masterpiece for his faith."

The room was silent. Impressive. He'd picked this kid because he'd been asleep. So where the hell did he come up with this question . . . and for the last one of the day too. Fin just stared at him, unsure of what he was feeling. Pausing to give this one a little more thought, he realized he was beginning to sweat—his palms, now his forehead—he was beginning to feel the heat of the lights. This one simple question seemed to tie up so many purse strings in his own imposing bag of anxieties. Rachel's death, his career, and now raising Eva on his own, they'd all been gradually suffocating him. It had all been forcing him to question his own faith, a faith that for so long he had considered unshakable.

"I think it was his greatest stroke of genius," Fin blurted out, a little more forcefully than he anticipated. "His math told him one thing, his heart and faith told him another . . . and in the end, in some unfathomable twist of fate they were both correct. What does this number represent? What is this thing, this stuff that holds it all together in a way we can't see? We may never know, but as human beings we're obligated to look and that's where you come in." He pointed to the young man who had asked the question. "This field needs introspective young minds—minds that twist problems and solutions into shapes that are imperceptible from the common vantage point. If you think that's you, then your education's not yet complete."

There was no way he was going to find a better ending to this outing and it was time to go. He thanked the crowd and his hosts and smartly excused himself. Stiff-arming the pressure plate and throwing open the auditorium door, Fin jogged out into the daylight, pleased with his theatrical conclusion. He was late to pick up Eva. "Father's gonna get a kick out of this tomorrow," he thought.

CHAPTER 6

Sal pulled into the parking lot of St. Angelo's Pizzeria. It had been about two hours since he left the "hole." The fog was worsening, but he hoped that would only provide more cover. His hands were shaking.

"What the hell am I doing?" he kept thinking.

This was either the dumbest thing he had ever done, or the infancy of his proudest moment. He had grown so ashamed of himself over the past two years, the life of destruction he found himself in was so far from what his parents had intended. This was the only way. Weeks ago he had sent an e-mail from a bogus account to the local FBI field office. After explaining the central role he played in MS-13 as the money man, he expressed his willingness to cooperate with any ongoing investigations . . . as long as they would provide some protection for him. Initially, several days passed and he was beginning to get pissed that his offer, one that put him in overt danger, had fallen on deaf ears. But five days ago he had received an answer. He had been instructed to choose a place to meet and to come alone. He had chosen the location but the Bureau had chosen the time, 1 a.m. on Tuesday.

It was now five minutes after the hour and he was beginning to wonder if he had been set up. MS-13 had some pretty lofty connections, not to mention the possibility that they had discovered his intentions after that first e-mail. The longer his mind raced around the thought of leaving or staying, the more certain he was that this meeting was a bad idea.

"Stay calm, all good intentions require faith," he told himself. It was something his mother used to preach. He took a big breath and let the weight of his chest slowly force the air out. This meeting needed to happen. Exhaling forcefully again, he relaxed his hands on his lap. He closed his eyes and allowed his chin to slump to his chest. It had been such a long day, spending all morning and the better part of the afternoon collecting copies of all the faction's financial records—their bank accounts, on-line investments, bonds, and even a few off-shore accounts that he had set up. All the accounts had been under various aliases, but all were established with his handwriting and counterfeit identifications. It had taken years to build this network of money laundering and he had become very good at it. It was proof of the syndicate's evolution into an unstoppable force of organized crime.

On the backseat floor, an old blanket covered a small lump. Lifting the corner of the blanket, he stared at the Batman backpack that lay there. It was his from grade school and it was all he could find in the house on such short notice. Sal had fed it all the paperwork he would use against MS-13 and hoped that its design was innocuous enough that no one would suspect it contained anything so condemning.

Sal was startled by a firm rap on his driver's side window. Turning quickly, he saw several figures walking toward the front of his car. There was already another dark sedan pressed firmly up against his rear bumper. The man at the window flashed an ID, giving him a glimpse of his photo with the holographic gold and blue badge of the FBI. "Are you Salvador Cabrera?"

As Sal opened his door, there were now two other men

standing around his car, with at least two more off in the immediate distance. "Yes, sir," he said, quickly trying to get an accurate count of all the agents. "I sent the e-mail."

"You'll come for a ride with us then," the agent added, in a statement rather than a question. Stepping aside, he motioned Sal toward a blacked out minivan that had pulled up a few yards away.

As they walked toward the vehicle, Sal's thoughts were of all the financial records stashed in his car. He had placed them all in the bag thinking the entire exchange of information would take place tonight. Though the notion of telling the agents had occurred to him, he had a generous handful of the bargaining chips, and if they were not ready to lay theirs out, then neither was he. After Sal climbed into the van, the door slid closed with a solid thud and, without any of the outside agents joining them, the vehicle departed.

They drove for about ten minutes sitting in darkened silence. "Where are we going?" Sal finally asked. There was no answer. "Hey, where the hell are you taking me?"

In the third row from behind him came a woman's voice, a sound he wasn't expecting. "We're going to talk," she said in a soft voice that would likely be calming in any other situation. "I'd like to lay some ground rules first," she continued.

Sal had not seen any of the faces of the agents in the van and had no idea how many people were with him. "I ask the questions, you provide the answers," the female agent added calmly. "If they're answers that meet my approval, we'll continue. If they're not, please remember that all I need to do is drop you off in the middle of your turf and MS-13 will take care of the rest for us. Do we understand one another, Mr. Cabrera?"

"Yes, Ma'am." *Shit*, he thought, *I guess there's no turning back now.*

"Let's begin . . ." Over the next forty-five minutes Sal was driven throughout the city, being asked questions about his involvement in MS-13. All the while, the lights in the van were left off and the driver managed to avoid any direct overhead street lights. After they had established his history with the local faction, the agent focused more intimately on the financial contributions Sal brought to the table. "Tell me about the money."

"Well, there's a lot of it," Sal answered. "Most is invested in legitimate assets - stocks, bonds, futures, and some real estate in a few areas. What isn't invested is just kept at a safe house for immediate use to purchase, you know, goods. There's not much that's just loose cash though, maybe twenty or twenty-five grand."

"What amounts are we talking about, Sal?" She'd begun using his first name more and more. Although he knew this was just a tactic to calm him and get him to open up, he *was* feeling more relaxed.

"There's about 600 thousand in the market, mostly in index funds through online investment firms. There's also about three hundred thousand in I bonds. Azazel . . ."

Sal froze. *Shit!* Had he lost his friggin mind? How the hell had he let his guard down that much? Not only was he naming names, but he was giving them to this mystery woman in the order of the most senior man first!

As if hearing his thoughts, she continued, "It's ok, Sal, I don't intend to burn you." She hesitated, "At least not as long as you cooperate with us. Please relax and go on."

He took another deep breath. "Those in charge don't put

too much of the money in one place. It was my suggestion, a practice I put in place just in case someone ratted. I've also begun to purchase some land. Most of it's here in the U.S., but there are small amounts in Mexico and in Central America, too. In more than one location we've leased the land out to some large and legitimate corporations, like pharmacies, grocery stores, and auto dealerships." Sal was not sure where to go from here, since he already felt he was spewing too much.

He could feel the woman staring at the back of his head and it was beginning to rattle him. They had been driving around for almost an hour now and Sal still had not seen anyone's face. A growing claustrophobia fueled his urge to quickly glance behind him, a motion that was interrupted by the agent's next question.

"How are these assets controlled?"

"By me. Every week I let, uh, Azazel, know what we've got and where it all is." *Well, almost all of it*, he thought. Along with the caches Sal had spent all these years building for the gang, there were several secret ones he had built just in case he ever decided to run. He had never kept any record of those transactions, and other than his own personal knowledge there was nothing linking him to them. If he had to run, only distance was going to save him. The money he had accrued was the only thing that would afford him that distance. "I move it around on occasion, but for the most part I merely add to what's already there."

As they returned to the parking lot where the adventure had begun, she continued. "Does anyone else have access to all these assets besides you?"

"No, but a few months ago Azazel began talking about bringing in a new member to assist me, but I haven't heard any more about it. He told me he eventually wanted this member to have full access in case anything happened to me, because no one else would understand all the documents and accounts." That had been the move that prompted Sal to act. This new kid would have to be bright and very driven. If this newbie, or anyone else, discovered what he'd been hiding, Sal would be killed.

"How did you feel about that decision?"

Sal paused, this seemed an odd question. "Well, I'm not sure. From a business sense it's solid. But no one in MS-13 likes to hear 'just in case something happens to you,' you know? I like my significance, it keeps me alive."

The van came to a stop a few yards away from his car and the sliding door opened automatically. His hostess relieved him with a final statement. "I think our partnership is very promising, Sal. I look forward to our next talk. You'll be hearing from us. I'll assume the same e-mail address will work. In the meantime," she leaned forward in her seat, quietly breathing her words into Sal's ear. "Stay out of trouble, and don't fuck this up."

As the door slid closed and the van departed, he thought, "*Don't fuck this up . . . hell, that oughta be easy.*" All he needed to do was keep lying to the most dangerous gang in America, while he snuck around behind their backs ratting on them to the Feds. Heading toward his car, he suddenly remembered the bag he had left behind. Sal jerked the door open and lifted the blanket. A sudden chill in his chest drained the blood from his face.

"Shit!" He had already fucked things up.

CHAPTER 7

Morning dew, that clean warm smell mixed with just a hint of strawberries. That's what Rachel's hair used to smell like. It was such a comforting aroma, and he never even told her that. Fin hated going to bed alone on the nights she had a late shift in the ER. She would come in like a thief, taking her shoes off at the door and walking through the house in her socks. Leaving all the lights off, she'd sneak into the bathroom, shower, and then try and slide into bed undetected. Even if she managed to get that far without waking him, her scent always betrayed her. That same aroma cast a halo over Eva after her bath.

Bedtime books were Eva's favorite nighttime ritual, and Fin enjoyed it as well. Books were a staple in Eva's day that helped maintain some normalcy. He had tried to change the stories, but found she was happiest if they stuck to a few dozen books over and over again. For his own sanity, he would vary the endings a little. After Eva's teeth were brushed, she was tucked in. Eva had always been a good sleeper. He and Rachel had avoided lying with Eva at night, not staying too long in her room, even when she was in her crib. But after Rachel died this became a difficult routine to maintain. To make matters worse, Eva had transitioned to her "big-girl" bed only a couple of months before her mother's death. Slowly, over a few weeks, Fin had begun to lie down with her for a little bit each night. He told himself that it was for her sense of security, but deep down he knew that it was just as much for his.

There was not much talking tonight after her books. Eva was sleepy, and Fin hoped that she would drift off early. Lying in her bed holding her, his mind wandered to their future. How would Rachel's passing change the woman Eva would become? What the hell was he going to do when she was in her early teen years?

The room was dark and peaceful and he was finding some respite in the scent of his little girl's hair again. Eva probably wouldn't remember her mother's smell or voice. These were the things that he would make sure he told her about. Imagining their future without Rachel, Fin's vision began to blur with his tears.

"Why are you sad, Daddy?" Eva asked suddenly.

Surprised that she was awake and not sure where this was leading, he answered, "I'm okay, baby, just go to sleep."

"Are you dying?" she added without pause.

"No, baby, I'm fine." He hugged her even tighter. Closing his eyes forcefully, he hurt even deeper to think that, despite his best efforts, she thought he too would leave her.

"Am I dying?"

Truly surprised, Fin sat up a bit. "What? Of course not, baby. You're fine, too." Before he could begin to worry about what that meant, she once again set everything right.

"Then we're fine and you shouldn't be sad anymore." Eva rolled her head to the side and kissed her father on the cheek. Then she closed her eyes and fell asleep.

Fin felt as though she had rescued the entire night from his malignant worry. In one single uncluttered exchange, this little creature had taken him through the emotional gauntlet, only to leave him completely at peace.

"Just in time my little GOTU." That's what he and Rachel used to call her, their "gift of the universe," their G-O-T-U. It seemed that whenever they found themselves far off track, arguing up in their proverbial trees, Eva would ground them. She would say or do something that seemed so arbitrary, but was so flawlessly placed that they couldn't deny the folly of their disagreement. Nor could they deny the unmistakable gift in her simple words. She was always there, in a way that neither of them could be for one another. It had seemed miraculous to Fin that this tiny child, who was brought into the world through the love he and his wife felt for one another, took care of them emotionally in ways no one else in their lives could. Lying there, his thoughts led him off to sleep, resting in the serenity that his daughter had given him.

Fin was jolted awake by the harsh ringing of the phone. He looked at his watch. It was two in the morning, and Eva was sound asleep. He rose and exited her room, taking special care not to wake her.

"Hello?"

"Hello, Fin?" said a familiar voice, the delay in the transmission gave away its overseas origin.

"Edvard, is that you?" Edvard Krunowski was a fellow particle physicist and the current Director at CERN. He had been integral in recruiting Fin onto the planning team for their current Hadron Supercollider project. Edvard, the prodigal son, who had returned to the Europe after nearly thirty years of professorship in the United States, had also been Fin's graduate school advisor. "You sound anxious, old friend, what's troubling you?"

"Troubling? Just the opposite, Fin. We're finding something wonderful . . . something that we did not expect!" His thickly accented voice almost sang the news.

During the past twenty years, CERN had constructed a sprawling underground monstrosity that spanned the borders of France and Switzerland. The intent of this project—the largest and most expensive scientific experiment in the history of mankind—was to discover what physicists had for decades been trying to wrap their heads around . . . dark matter. The machine had been turned on for the first time several months ago, and its initial startup had been plagued with electrical problems. For the foreseeable future, it was only supposed to be undergoing calibration testing.

"You're running operational spins? I thought that wasn't supposed to happen for at least a few months!" Fin exclaimed in an excitedly disapproving tone. "What's she showing?"

Three hundred feet below the Swiss town of Meyrin, this most massive of machines was designed to find the most elusive and minuscule particles that were theorized to date. Through its twenty-seven-kilometer-long, three-meter-wide tunnels ran vacuum tubes, the coldest and emptiest places in the galaxy. The use of liquid helium–cooled superconductor magnets permitted scientists to steer opposing beams of protons. Accelerated around the circuit to near-light speed, these particle beams were fated to obliterate one another in a head-on collision. Fin knew the theories well; some were his. These interactions could very well reveal Higgs-Boson particles, or even the mysterious dark matter, the invisible stuff that seemed to hold galaxies together.

Fin had theorized that, although these antimatter particles by their very nature did not interact directly with everyday matter, they should still leave detectable traces of their fleeting existence. He postulated that these particles originated from another place, possibly another dimension. The analogy he had often used with his students was that of two columns of marbles traveling toward one another.

"Every action has an equal and opposite reaction—the law of conservation of momentum," he would remind them. "Energy and matter should be conserved. If we are assuming this dark matter, these antimatter particles, share our common space, then they too should exert detectable forces." At this point only a select few of his students were usually still tracking, but his enthusiasm often overwhelmed his ability to notice. This was what got Fin most excited. Once he was on a roll, it was hard to stop him.

"In other words, if we slam a bunch of stuff together from this direction, then an equal amount of detectable stuff should come out in the opposite direction. Like the marbles."

The detectors in the Collider were designed to do just that, detect the scattering particles that made up our world as they shattered against one another in these vacant spaces. With these patterns of dispersing "marbles," the software was written to exclude all known patterns and forms of matter. What remained, the "weird stuff" as Fin often put it, was the stuff left for the software to analyze. This realm of outliers should be rare, or even new, material to particle physicists. Though it was seemingly invisible, it too should be symmetrically balanced in its scattered motif. If in the infinitesimally small fractions of a second after the particle beam collisions, this matter and antimatter debris coalesced to form even just a few particles of antimatter, they would in theory create gaps within the observable patterns of marbles to be measured by the detectors. Their very exposure would be the effect left behind by our inability to see them. They should show up as the absence of marbles within the observable patterns.

Still standing in his darkened kitchen, Fin pressed the phone to his ear, waiting for Edvard's answer. "Are you sitting, my friend?" Edvard asked. "We're not seeing any absence of matter at all." He stopped.

"What? How the hell is that important? Ed, did you call me in the middle of the night just to tell me that you have nothing exciting to tell me?" Fin grumbled.

"Fin, we're not seeing an absence of matter, we're seeing a surplus." His answer was met by silence on the other end. "Fin, are you hearing me? The detectors are registering more matter after the collisions than before the collisions." The line crackled. "We're not sure if it's new stuff or not, but it sure is more stuff than we started with."

"Are you sure . . ." He was cut off, the delay in the call made it difficult to time the conversation.

"You should come out here, take some time away. I know it's been hard, but you need a break. The last few months have been exceptionally difficult ones, and not just because of Rachel's death. You were instrumental in defending our work here at CERN, and the scientific community owes you for it. Your testimony at the state level made you a hero to your peers."

"Yeah, and it simultaneously made me public enemy number one for those who felt our work there was the modern-day equivalent of sacrilege."

"I agree, and that's why in the morning I'm going to phone your department head and let him know of our recent discovery. Your absence from this place has been felt, and it would help all of us to have you out here. My son would love to see you and Eva again."

The countryside there had been one of Rachel's favorite places. He could sure use a break from all this routine. Fin was tired, and the events both at home and politically over the last few months had exhausted him. "I'm not sure about this, Ed. I've been spending a lot of time trying to maintain some normalcy for Eva."

"Well I think that this would be a marvelous place to feel normal again. She'd love it, Fin."

"I've also been spending a lot of time, well, I've spent time, talking with a friend of mine. It's helped me get through all of this."

"Who?"

"Father Moriel." Fin cringed slightly; he knew how strong Ed's dislike was for the Catholic priesthood.

"Fin, they're just the foot soldiers. The Catholic Church is the corporation that sucks the true meaning from religion. You're wasting your time there. Come out here, Fin. You and I together will discover the real roots of our religion."

"Are you sure about these measurements? I mean, the collider is hardly calibrated fully."

"I'm sure, we're sure. I think this is the beginning, my friend. We're going to use this machine to see into God's plan like we never imagined! Go back to bed, Fin. We'll talk more tomorrow, but think about my offer." He paused. "Remember, Fin, Nobel prize . . . Nobel prize!"

The line went silent. Fin hung up the phone. Maybe this was what they needed. Maybe he needed to immerse himself into his science to find his religion again. Edvard had always believed that only through physics could man come to understand God. Maybe this was their new beginning.

CHAPTER 8

Fitful. That was the best way to describe the sleep he'd had, if you could even call it sleep. Sal lay in bed staring up at his blank ceiling, thinking of the dreams that owned him last night. That goddamned bag—since that bizarre interrogation, all of his well-laid plans were unraveling. This development had left him stripped of any leverage he'd had with the FBI. The only tool he owned here was the information they needed, and now they had it. How the hell did they get it? How'd they even know it was there, or what it contained . . . and wasn't it illegal to search and seize property without a warrant? Frankly, the whole thing made him angry, and the more he ruminated about it, the more he thought that maybe he should send off another e-mail chastising the Bureau for their unprofessionalism. He'd trusted them with this information, placed his life on the line and they screwed him. He got up out of bed and went to his computer.

"Dear FBI,"

He stopped and looked at his greeting. "Dear FBI, what the fuck is that" he muttered to himself in disgust. This whole situation had reduced him to a fourth grader. "Deep breath, Salvador." He mumbled aloud to himself before trying again.

"Ma'am,

I am writing to request another meeting and to discuss my collection of data that you and your men now possess. It is useless to you without my interpretation of it. Please contact me regarding our next appointment.

v/r SB"

With one soft click his thoughts were on their way. He felt a little better. At least he wasn't being a total patsy. Sal sat there, just staring at his screen, barefoot and in his underwear, scratching himself in an early morning sort of way, when a new message appeared in his inbox.

It was from Azazel. Dropping his head back and once again staring at the ceiling, Salvador took a sanitizing deep breath, its long exhalation terminating in the expletive of his choice. "Shit," he whispered. Hesitating, uncertain what malevolence it brought with it, Sal opened the phone.

"Call me," was all the message said.

Though the FBI was interested in his help, and hopefully in helping him, he did not have time to dick around with their timetable if Azazel was going to continuously test his loyalty. And that's just what he loved to do. Sal had witnessed this before. It started with some typical gang activity, harmless by most standards, and then ended in some heinous illegal act that shackled you to the faction for an eternity. These festivities usually culminated in a rival gang murder or even a cop killing. Even if you were not the trigger man, Azazel always made sure you were on the hook, and that you knew it too.

Sal knew that he would have to accelerate his plans now. The financial information with the Bureau would have to be sorted out, and then he'd need to disappear. Hopefully they'd do a better job concealing his involvement and whereabouts than they had done with previous cases. MS-13 had had no difficulty finding those in hiding, despite the FBI's witness protection program.

Sal wasn't sure how he would manage after abandoning this house either. After his parents' murders, he couldn't bring himself to leave. This morning Sal was content to just sit at his desk and stare down the hallway toward his parents' vacant bedroom. He'd never realized what a sanctuary this house was, with the soft creaks of its hardwood hallways, the low ceilings that once had seemed so lofty to him, and all of his parents' things scattered about that made this place a home. He'd grown up here, and it was still home to him.

Sal had gone into their room often since their deaths and even cleaned out their dressers and closets once or twice, only to put everything back where he'd found it. He could find no reason to move on, and had never intended to stray so far. It had just taken him so long to awaken from his prodigal ways. If the change was going to happen, though, he needed to keep those who threatened his redemption close. MS-13 was not an assemblage given to speculating; if there was a fear that a member might bring the organization down, they were immediately targeted for elimination. It often came from those with whom they were closest—and usually without any warning.

A soft humming sound pulled him out of his daydream. He retrieved his cell from his coat pocket, "Shit!" It was already two in the afternoon.

"Azazel, what's up?" he asked in the most morning-like tone he could muster.

"Vato, you 'member those festivities we talked about? Well, I got some fun for you and me. Maria brought in some new blood and we're gonna have ourselves a little fiesta tonight." Azazel paused, "You there, Mutt?"

"Yeah, I'm here. Sorry, I'm just still half asleep. When's this all going down, and where?" Sal was thinking about his own hopeful agenda and the timeframe for the next meeting with his mystery FBI lady.

"Tonight, and we're counting on you. Don't disappoint me."

Sal had anticipated more discussion with his FBI contact before he had a chance to "fuck it up" as she'd so elegantly put it. These evenings of fun often resulted in gunfire and sirens. Some stupid arrest would certainly ruin everything, not to mention the fact that he could be killed. But he had no choice, after the other night's exchange he had to save face. "Can you be a little more specific?" Sal ventured.

"You just meet me around seven at the hole and we'll go from there." After a faint click, the line went silent.

To Salvador, Azazel's voice, which had once tasted of salvation, now seemed just a saccharine reminder of his own failure. He had often wondered how he'd ended up in this hell, following the false guidance of such a lunatic. Sal had been so lost those first few months after his parents' murders, and Azazel had given him such hope for revenge, as well as a sense of belonging in the absence of his own family.

Gang colors were a must at these functions, but he decided instead to wear one of his father's favorite El Salvador football jerseys under his coat. Wearing his father's clothes made him feel a part of something invincible. That simple Salvadorian royal blue and white jersey gave him a feeling of self-worth that he had long ago shed. He slowly felt his thoughts pulled back to that day of discovery.

Salvador had been returning home, excited, from an afternoon of car hunting. He was hoping to afford a reliable used car, but something with a little style. He was also hoping to become a little less dependent on his parents, especially if he were to continue school. Excited to tell his father of the '88 Buick GNX he'd found, he burst through the front door. As he entered, he nearly tripped over their bodies. The images of his parents lying there in their foyer still haunted his latent eyes, a waking nightmare he'd sickened himself with so many times. They lay in such a haunting ritualistic way, both lying on their backs in a small pool of blood with their arms outstretched. They were placed next to one another, but in opposite head-to-toe fashion. Their left hands clasped together, and held fast with dried blood. In the flesh of each of their conjoined palms was carved a small cross. Sal had nearly fallen on them in his despair, with a blind hope that there remained just a single breath of life left to steal. He remembered wanting to call for help, but being unable to tear himself from them for fear of missing a fleeting opportunity to say goodbye. It felt like an eternity before he made it to the phone, and when the paramedics arrived, he couldn't even recall what he had reported. The police had assumed robbery was the motive for the crime, but so little of value had been taken from the house. They had expressed to Salvador this was something they had seen before, and it was indicative of local gang killings. The particulars of the crime scenes were the sort of clues not given easily to the press. There was always the fear of copycat murders, which only served to muddy the waters for the investigators. They preferred to keep the juicy bits of the murder undisclosed.

That day's investigation of the crime scene was as far as the police had taken it—at least that's how Sal remembered it. There were never any suspects or leads, and certainly no hope for avenging their deaths. Weeks had passed without any news, at which point he had long ceased attending classes. It had taken MS-13 to explain to him that his parents were singled out because of their heritage, just as it had taken MS-13 to help him reclaim their dignity.

That seemed like a lifetime ago, and sinking into this downward spiral again was not going to help solve anything. Forgiving himself the misplacement of the morning, he decided to get this day over with so he could concentrate on the other more important issues at hand.

As he prepared to leave today he noticed there was one new message in his inbox. It was from his nameless co-conspirator at the Bureau. "For this meeting you pick the time, and I'll pick the place. We appreciated all your candor and hope there is more to the collection you've given us so far."

"Man she's got balls," Salvador uttered with a slow disbelieving shake of his head. "I didn't give you shit lady, you stole it."

"*Let's meet tomorrow night at midnight. Just let me know where.*" He sent his message into the ether. Maybe this was all going to actually work out. Now he just needed to get through tonight's gauntlet.

CHAPTER 9

Azazel had just hung up with Sal, when his phone began ringing again. "Yeah?" Azazel answered.

"Mr. Espiritu, my name is Job. I have a situation I'd like you to take care of for me."

"Who the fuck is this, and how did you get this number?" Azazel rarely received calls from people outside of his very small circle of business affiliates.

"We have some mutual interests, and a mutual acquaintance."

"That don't answer my question, Mister."

"I have a good deal of cash, and your deeds have become nearly indiscernible from those of your competitors on the 11 o'clock news these days. I was hoping we could make a business arrangement." The male voice on the other end of the phone was deep, with a rich baritone quality commanding attention.

"I'm listening . . ." Azazel hoped the pay was high and the task straightforward.

"We have an individual we'd like terminated. We were hoping you were our man."

Halfway across town, the morning had seemed to crawl by for Fin. After dropping Eva off at day care, he had navigated his way to work through the tangle that was Southern California's sunup traffic. From his office at the University, he e-mailed his department chair, informing him they needed to discuss some big news, or at least what could be big news. He had hardly been able to sleep after the phone conversation with Edvard last night, and for the first time in months it was because of something good. His mind raced with the possibilities of what this new data could mean. He tried to keep his child-like excitement in check, but the last few months had left him desperate for something positive.

Throughout his career, Fin had learned to take news of scientific breakthroughs with a grain of salt. These revelations were often not scientifically replicable, and were frequently the result of a human mathematical error. Fin continued to remind himself that this was a very distinct possibility, more so than the likelihood of their new information being valid. They would have to run further calculations with variations on the detection software. Achieving the repetition of these results reliably again and again would take time, quite possibly a lot of time. Physics was a field that yielded magical results when done well, and they needed to be sure they took the necessary steps this time to do it that way. Simple miscalculations had been the seed of so many costly mistakes in science. All too often, he and his colleagues had involuntarily fed these mistakes to the media on a silver platter. They were front page results that set people of scientific prominence up for phenomenal successes or professional bankruptcy, and in many of these cases arrogance outweighed intelligence. Fin had used countless examples over and over with his students to emphasize the need for attention to detail. "In the end," he would preach, "a simple check of one's math can save all those involved from profound embarrassment—not to mention saving taxpayers millions of dollars."

He was staring out his office window thinking of this scenario when his secretary threw open his office door.

"Edvard's on the conference line, and Jim wants you in his office."

Jim Purcell was a big meaty guy who loved life. He loved it in a booze-and-broads kind of way. He and Fin had first met as undergrads and struck up an unlikely friendship. Over the years, they had risen through the same scientific meat grinder that had led Fin to his current position. Purcell, however, was not into existential research in the way some of his colleagues were. He was appointed to the position of physics chair only after Fin turned it down. Fin felt being chairman would prevent him from pursuing other, more romantic, scientific aspirations, like the one that would be grabbing everyone's attention today.

"What've I missed?" Fin blurted as he entered the unusually full conference room. "I'm sorry," he said as he paused in the entry way "I didn't know you were having a meeting." He wondered if he'd barged into the wrong room.

"Ah, Fin. Glad you could make it, Dr. Krunowski e-mailed me last night asking me to gather everyone up this morning. He's on the phone and has some exciting news to share with us." Purcell gestured toward the empty seat at the head of the table.

Fin had been expecting Purcell, and maybe a grad student or two, not the chairs of every university department.

"Sit down, Fin," a familiar voice boomed over the conference pod in the center of the boardroom table. "I was just telling our colleagues of our conversation last night." Edvard was one of the best spin artists Fin knew. He could sell shit to a pig farmer and had an unrivaled ability to excite those around him about things they barely understood.

"How much have you shared with them?" Fin pulled out

the one remaining chair at the table and sank into the soft dark leather.

Jim Purcell interjected, "We're just starting, Fin. Please continue, Dr. Krunowski."

"We've been collecting this data now for a little more than a month and have run multiple variations on the detection software to look for inconsistencies . . . and we've found none. Our data supports an increase in matter, not just mass mind you. The ever ubiquitous 'E equals mc squared' allows for particles of increased mass, but not for the creation of *new* matter."

Fin understood this principle well, but it was one that escaped many of his bioscience colleagues present in the boardroom today. "Edvard, let me stop you for a minute." Fin leaned into the table as he interrupted. "I just want to unfurrow a few of these brows around the room. What Dr. Krunowski is referring to is the principal of mass-energy equivalence. In his famous formula Einstein infers that mass and energy are merely different manifestations of the same thing, where mass can be turned into energy and vice versa."

Fin turned on the electronic blackboard, its e-ink surface flickering to a warm off-white from its static black sleep mode. He wrote down $E=mc^2$ while he spoke. "Energy equals the mass of an object multiplied by the square of a constant, which is the speed of light." Every gesture he made left behind a ghostly green line as he began to draw out his thoughts on the pressure-sensitive board. Selecting a new color, he drew for his audience the various mathematic derivations of Einstein's most famous equation.

"If you rearrange that same equation, you get 'E' divided by 'c squared' equals 'm.'"

$$E/c^2 = m$$

Since the speed of light is a constant, as long as you increase the energy in a system you produce increased mass." His board looked like a physics caricature, with variously colored numbers and letters all vomited haphazardly on this blank screen. Excited about his rapidly reached conclusion, he turned. Most brows remained furrowed despite this highly animated clarification. Returning to the board, he waved his hands over his creation, effectively erasing it.

"Precisely," countered Edvard. "In the Hadron Collider we are dealing with protons whizzing around a huge track and then slamming into one another at nearly the speed of light. We're trying to create new and exotic particles that we're pretty sure exist but that we've never actually seen."

Fin continued at the board, leaving huge colorful arcs in the wake of his arms. "The speed of light and the mass of the protons are constants we cannot change. So, the only variable that we can control is the speed at which these particles slam into each other . . . that's our 'E'." Finally, he saw a few bulbs in the room come on. "The higher we make our 'Energy,' the greater the 'mass' we can generate. Particles with larger amounts of mass as an outcome would not be a big surprise, in fact we were hoping for that. But, and this is the whole point, no one expected to generate extra matter."

"Exactly." Edvard's transmission crackled as it escaped the conference phone. "When we add up all the variables, the speed of our particle beams—our 'energy'—it is not enough to produce the amount of matter we're measuring. Somehow we've got more than we started with."

Fin stood for a moment, silently appreciating their combined, unrehearsed explanation to his fellow scientists. He never worried about demonstrating his intellectual prowess to these self-appointed equals. It was one of the things that Rachel had found most attractive about him . . . confidence in the absence of hubris. "Though this is not what we expected to find, it is certainly a discovery that merits much further evaluation. It may open up new possibilities of a unified theory." Fin walked back to his seat, savoring the looks of enthusiasm around the room.

"As it was Dr. Canty's theories in part that helped us to make this discovery here at CERN, I'd like to request his presence during this time of initial discovery." Edvard paused, knowing the communal knowledge of Fin's recent loss also played a role in granting him a sabbatical.

Purcell looked to Fin for input. "How do you feel about this proposal?"

"I think my presence there would be helpful. Not to mention that this is all very exciting and good PR for the university's science departments, especially in light of the last few months."

"I think in order for us to feel we're not missing anything here in Geneva, we need to have our full collective present to bend the numbers." The spin was complete; the salesman had used his pupil as an unknowing participant in the deal. With Edvard's last request, the transaction was finalized.

"Pack your bags," Purcell added. "With the holidays coming, you'll have until the first of the year away. I'll have the departmental secretary arrange for your flights. Time and money permitting, you'll leave the day after tomorrow, if that's ok with you."

Fin felt for the first time in months that he was getting his due. One of the foremost physicists in the world was requesting his presence as a member of this elite body of scientists at

CERN once again. It was quite possible their discoveries could help human understanding of the physical world, the biggest leap since the turn of the twentieth century.

"Absolutely, it's alright with me, Jim. Thank you for understanding." He rose from his seat and thanked everyone present, giving special thanks to Edvard. Walking down the corridor to his office, Fin could hardly recall even exiting the board room. Twenty-four hours ago he was suffocating himself in his sorrow and guilt, physically unable to foresee any alternative future for them. It was truly amazing how one day had changed his entire outlook. He felt like he'd just lost his virginity, though he'd probably keep that analogy to himself when he visited Father Moriel this afternoon.

CHAPTER 10

After clarifying with his secretary where their airline tickets were to be e-mailed, Fin departed campus for the day. Harboring no intentions of returning to the building tomorrow, he said his goodbyes to all those at work that he'd miss for the holidays and left. He wanted to pick up Eva and start his long drive down to see Father Moriel early to beat traffic. The autumn air hung heavy with the smell of rain, and he hoped that it would hold off until they arrived home later this evening. Driving toward her daycare center a few miles from the campus, his mind raced with all the preparations he'd have to make before leaving the country for so many months. He'd have to leave someone in charge of the house, as well as his car. The last thing they needed was a dead battery after ten weeks of long-term parking fees when they returned to the States. He was almost giddy with the thought of seeing the Geneva countryside again, as well as being in the company of family friends.

The process of picking Eva up from daycare had grown its own rituals. After her mother's death she had begun again to cling and cry in the mornings. This was a habit that Fin thought they had defeated months earlier. Despite her young age, both her teachers and Father Moriel felt that this was a reaction to her mother's absence. Fin's inclination was to come into the room and stay longer, but Eva's caregivers insisted that she would do better if she learned for herself through repetition that he would always return for her. It had taken a few weeks to accomplish, and only further added to Fin's guilt, but she'd come to realize that her daddy would never leave her. The procedures at pick up time however had become very specific. He was to be against the wall opposite her classroom and crouched down, but not sitting, to receive a running hug. After this, he'd pick her up and carry her to the car. On the few occasions that he'd forgotten or, heaven forbid, had been sitting on the floor, he'd been given a good three-year-old scolding. Today he was committed to those rituals. Fin informed the caregivers in Eva's room they'd be gone for a few months, and that they'd see her again after the New Year's holiday. Walking out to the car he could hardly contain himself. "Baby, how'd you like to go on a big adventure with Daddy?"

Since they were ahead of schedule and the traffic, he decided to take their favorite way down to Chula Vista. He opened the windows so that they could smell the salt air and hear the birds. Eva giggled at the sight of the pelicans cruising along next to the bridge, surfing the drafts rising up from under the structure. Fin had a children's CD playing and Eva was singing along with her songs. He cast a long glance at the water below. The normal boats were missing and the waters looked unusually rough.

He was deep in thought about the events of the last few months. In mid-March of 2008, a small group of concerned citizens in Hawaii—referring to themselves as "Activists Rebuking CERN for its Heresy," or ARCH—had filed a lawsuit in Hawaii's U.S. District Court requesting an injunction against CERN's proceedings in Geneva. They had hoped to prevent the full operation of the Large Hadron Collider until after year-long workups were completed. These workups were intended to test both the instrument's hardware and software, as well as produce a full environmental assessment. ARCH claimed the very existence of the planet might be in danger if these experiments were allowed to continue. Their lawyers, appointed for them at no charge by the American Family Christian Association, argued in their opening statement that "the small black holes, the very entities that these physicists have portrayed on the Discovery Channel as galaxy-devouring behemoths, are to be conjured up right here on Earth. All of this money and time has been spent, and will continue to be spent, only to further drown creationism in a sea of scientific confusion." In the wake of these proceedings, Fin had been chosen by CERN to head a small group of scientists to refute these claims. In doing so, he had nearly singlehandedly saved the agency.

It had started to rain while Fin was in his trance, and he was jolted back to the present by joyous screams coming from the back seat. Eva was getting wet, and she loved it. "Damn!" Fin muttered as his hand shot for the window controls. "Sorry, baby, Daddy didn't notice it was raining this hard." He turned on the windshield wipers. They were only a few miles from the church now, and he would take care of her wet clothes when they arrived.

"Daddy? Are we there? Is this our trip?"

"No, baby, we're just going to see Father. Would you like to light some candles for Mommy tonight?" Fin just wanted to get her into the church and changed out of those wet clothes. "Let's go see what Father's doing," he said as they pulled slowly into the parking lot. The rain was coming down in sheets now, slowly washing away the daylight. Fin grabbed Eva's change bag, then loosed her from her car seat. He ran, covering her with his coat, to the south transept door. The church was bathed in incense, likely lingering from the mass Father performed earlier. It was peaceful and quiet inside, just the way Fin liked to think of this sanctuary. They found Father Moriel busy in his office.

Moriel rose from his desk, casting his usual friendly smile at them as they entered. "Oh my, you're soaked," he blurted. "Hi, Eva! I hadn't realized how the weather had changed. Is it supposed to last long?"

"I dunno. I didn't even know it was going to rain at all today." Fin said, setting Eva down to give Father a hug.

"I'm supposed to make my monthly pilgrimage into Mexico this week. I detest driving in bad weather, especially with that car. I'm not sure what legs it's got left, Fin." He retrieved a towel from the top drawer of his bureau and handed it to Fin.

"Hopefully the storm won't last too long. We're leaving too, the day after tomorrow." Fin took the towel from his friend. "There's been an exciting breakthrough in our research at CERN, and the University has approved me for a short sabbatical."

Moriel turned with a look of surprise on his face. Fin's tone of voice was one he had not heard in this place of worship since before Rachel's death. "Fin, you'd better be careful my friend, you almost sound as if you've found some hope in something. He sat back down at his desk while Fin finished changing Eva into some dry clothes.

"You know, Father, I'm not sure if I want to go into too much detail right now. I feel contented for the first time in a while, like I've got my feet back under me and I'm a little afraid of upsetting that delicate balance. I'd like to keep this feeling to myself for a bit." Fin sat down opposite Father. "Let's talk about you for a change." Eva had walked over to Father and offered him something she'd been playing with.

"What's this, darling?" He took the small shiny metal object from her and held it up for Fin to see. "What's this?" he repeated for Fin's benefit.

"Huh. I've not seen that for years." Fin had tilted forward in his seat to take the object Moriel was now passing to him. He held it up to the light to take a closer look at it. "It's a pin, an award actually, that I won in my doctoral fellowship, it's called the 'Singularity Citation.'"

Eva had returned to her father holding out her hand. "Mine, please," was all she said.

Fin handed the pin back to her. It was a flat bronze pin, an oval, and roughly the size of his palm. It had a single ray etched through its center projecting upwards to the top of the pin. "It was something given to me by the director of CERN for my work used in their detectors."

"Thank you again, baby." Moriel expressed his gratitude to Eva with a smile and a small chuckle as she again brought him her treasure.

"Well, it seems as though she wants you to have it, Father." Eva had returned to Fin and begun eating the peanut butter and jelly sandwich that he'd packed for her dinner. They'd spent quite a bit of time in the car getting here, and Fin had been trying to get some food into her before she got too tired to eat. "What's the deal with your car?" Fin asked as he hauled his little princess onto his lap.

"Oh, it's just getting old. The Church appoints me as the liaison to these folks, but then expects me to perform a miracle with this old machine in getting there every month. It's time for something more reliable, but I just don't see where it'll come from." Father was most intrigued to learn how this news of CERN's discovery had changed Fin's outlook. He desperately wanted to explore this renewed interest in life but knew it was best to leave it alone for now. If Fin was happy, that was enough. "Who will look after your belongings here, Fin?"

"I was hoping that you would, Father. I mean, if that's ok with you. I see no reason we couldn't switch vehicles as well. My car's just gonna' sit in the pay lot for the duration, and it'll do better to have someone starting it daily." Eva was finished eating and had begun to grow sleepy in Fin's arms. The soft glow of the office lights reflecting in her blue eyes evoked her mother's beauty. Fin felt blessed to have her with him. She had become his everything, the single most inspirational reason for all he did. "You could take it tomorrow on your trip, and then you wouldn't have to worry about getting stranded," he said, while he continued to watch at Eva. "I'll take yours and just leave it in the lot. We'll figure something out when I get back." His words trailed off as they both realized Eva was asleep. He finished in a whisper, "I just need to switch out her car seat before we go."

Father gave in to his curiosity. "I may not get a chance to speak with you at length for some time. I don't get many chances to talk hard science with folks any more— you're the last vestige of my scientific past. At least give me some indication as to what you've found."

Fin hesitated. "All I can say Father is that our search for answers into God's mind has revealed, at first glance, only more mysteries and questions . . . ones that open up avenues of thought that no one had explored in the past." He paused, looking down at Eva sleeping again. Dropping his voice a few decibels, he continued, "to be honest with you, I'm a little scared to believe the good news."

Moriel gave him a quizzical look. "What in the world is

that supposed to mean?"

"Well, what if we get all the way out there and there's something wrong with my math . . . or with the machines that were built using my calculations and theories?" Fin closed his eyes and took a deep breath. He continued through a wavering voice, "I'm worried that this good news is only an illusion, and when these clouds shift they'll bring only more rain. I don't know if I can dig myself out from beneath again."

Father stood up and walked around to sit on the front of his desk. "Fin, as long as I've known you, I've been amazed at how strong your belief in yourself and your family was. Only after Rachel's death have I seen that waiver, and for the first time since then I see that belief again. Your new hope from this good news is not the fluke—this doubt in yourself is. Never be afraid of your faith . . . especially in yourself."

Fin began to feel that heat behind his eyes again, only this time it was for a positive reason. "I think we'd better get going so I can get her to bed."

Running out into the rain, Fin was struck by the worsening torrent. He quickly moved Eva's seat from his car to Father's. They'd be home within the hour and he'd put her right to bed . . . she was down for the night now. Fin thanked Moriel and gave him keys to the house as well.

Father escorted them back to the car with his umbrella. "Be safe and I'll expect a call from you within the week. I'm anxious to hear what's developing. I hope what the next few months bring not only helps you to move forward with your family, but also with your faith."

Pulling away, Fin watched a rain-soaked Father Moriel and St. Pius XI parish retreat in his borrowed rear view mirror. He felt a bit of desperation as he drove on. Father's friendship had come to mean so much to him and Eva. Focusing on the road through the increasing rain, a blinking red light caught Fin's eye in the lower edge of the windshield.

"Dammit." He muttered to himself. In all their haste they'd forgotten to move Father's electronic toll tag from his car. Without the device, Father's border crossing would be painfully prolonged. Fin was already stuck in the quagmire of traffic that this dark rainy night promoted, but he knew that this would be easier to remedy tonight. Putting on his turn signal, he began looking for an opportunity to get into the left lane. He'd have to turn around at his next opportunity.

CHAPTER 11

This place was not so ominous during daylight hours, but as the light faded, it took on an entirely different feel. There were very few cars in the gulley, which made Sal a little anxious. With a good representation of the gang at these afternoon meetings, it was often difficult to mobilize everyone in an organized fashion. However, these small hungry packs usually meant a mission, some sort of mobile chaos.

These little excursions that Azazel and the crew loved to plan lived at the very heart of Sal's uneasiness with MS-13, and he was beginning to think that they knew it. Despite the daylight above, his surroundings quickly faded into darkness as he passed down through the tunnel toward the pit. The smell of the atrocities that had been celebrated down in these bowels never faded—they only seemed to deposit themselves in some sort of aural sediment. All the cries and screams, all the rapes and beatings, were indistinguishable from one another now. Sal had been so numb for so long, he wondered if he'd ever have the strength to lift this cross from his back fully. He continued down the tunnel toward its unforeseeable end. He knew there to be others here, though there was no light coming from the pit. Sal navigated his way into the room with his remaining senses, his hands reminding him of the surroundings he refused to commit to memory. He could feel someone or something else in the room and hear its breathing. It was slow and shallow and seemed to be coming from directly in front of him in the darkness. There seemed to be more than one.

"You made it, and on time too," said a soft female voice. He froze, feeling a chill of fear in his chest. Unable to see, he let his fear of the faction's omnipotence steal his courage. He wanted to run, but the voice's familiarity made him uncertain.

"Of course I'm on time. Who the hell are you and where's Azazel?" With his bravado wavering in the dark, Sal hoped that he was wrong in his assumptions about this familiar female voice. His eyes were beginning to adjust. There were several others present with them as well. He winced in pain as the shards of light suddenly cast out the darkness. "What the hell are you all doing down here . . . and who's the gringo?" In the back corner of the pit stood Azazel with Maria kneeling at his side. There were a few other MS-13 members present as well as a man that Sal had never seen before.

"We were enjoying the absence of light, appreciating the darkness, as Azazel put it. We . . ." Azazel placed his hand on Maria's shoulder, preventing her from finishing her thought.

Sal thought she had a very kind voice, one that did not befit her reputation. It was also unnervingly familiar to him, and it would seem that Azazel had noticed that.

"We were waiting for our last guest, and now that you've arrived we can continue with the festivities." Taking a few steps forward into the direct glow of the light, Azazel gestured toward the stranger. "This is John, he wants to be Mara Salvatrucha, and I've decided to let him pledge our growing fraternity. He has chosen to walk the line. Tonight we will see what's in his heart."

"Wait a minute, we're supposed to vote on this shit!" Sal walked toward their leader. "Since when are you making all the important decisions by yourself? And since when are we adopting white boys, especially ones his age?" Sal stabbed a finger toward their guest. "This ain't no fuckin' kid, Espiritu!"

"Maria and I made this decision together. We felt it was in the best interest for the group." Azazel turned toward Sal, but remained uncharacteristically calm. "Tonight's events are not only to welcome a new member, but to relight the spirit of another—you, hermano."

"I don't need relighting, but thanks. Who is this, and where the hell did he come from?"

Azazel put his hand on Sal's arm. "Relax, vato, he's a friend of the cause."

"What cause? This is gettin' fuckin' weird man. I don't recall ever discussing new members or the fact that your new sidekick here was going to help rule the roost either!" Sal yanked his arm out of Azazel's grasp.

Azazel's jaw tightened. "We've gotten too far from our roots, man, it's time to shove the fear back into their hearts!" The tiny room was starting to fill with his energy as he began to inject his rising fury into their newest sacrifice. "We need to show them and ourselves that we're not to be fucked with any more, that if we want it we take it! Our guerrero pequeño is going to take us there." He clasped hands and, shoulder to shoulder, firmly slapped backs with the newbie. He returned his attention to Sal. "You need to be with us on this, Mutt."

Sal felt like he had been set up by the school bully. His loyalty was being directly questioned and he could either open his mouth and reveal his weakness, or keep it shut and play along. He had no choice. "When do we move?"

Walking up the tunnel toward the waiting cars, Sal couldn't help wondering if he'd survive tonight. The tension between him and Azazel was more palpable than it had ever been, but he was eerily calm, despite having his authority directly questioned in front of the group. Azazel was his oldest confidant in the clique, a fact that was starting to make Sal very uncomfortable. "What's the plan? How many cars are we taking?"

The sunlight was beginning to disappear as the tunnel delivered its members to the surface. "We'll take two." Azazel said gesturing toward two other members of the group.

"I'll ride in Maria's car." Sal offered.

"No. These guys can take Maria's, and the five of us will ride in mine." Azazel's Lexus 470 had no problem swallowing eight passengers comfortably.

"Well, then what about the newbie?" Sal offered.

"John will ride up front with me." Azazel walked over to the driver's side of the vehicle.

Climbing into the middle row, Sal found himself sitting next to another younger male member of the gang, Maria sat behind them both in the third row. Azazel remained outside the car with his door open.

Growing anxious, Sal asked "What's the plan Espiritu?"

Before Azazel could enter the car, his cell phone rang. Moments into the conversation, he and John exchanged a knowing glance. With a subtle tilt of his head, Azazel beckoned their new recruit, and the two men walked away from their passengers.

Who the hell was he talking to? thought Sal. All of his contacts are here already. Tonight was already going poorly, and he was increasingly certain that he was not going to get out of this one without a fight. The sun had already dropped below the cityscape and Salvador's eyes had yet to adjust to the darkness inside the car. While they were down below, threatening clouds had congregated and their progeny were already beginning to fall lightly. Azazel had walked briefly to Maria's car while on the phone, and their pledge stayed loyally at his side.

John was tall, about six-foot-two, Sal figured, with a thin build. His light blond hair was in stark contrast to everyone else's at the gathering tonight. This new arrival had really shaken Sal up. Not only were announcements like this unusual, but allowing members beyond the teen years to pledge was unheard of . . . not to mention men in their late 20s! Sal watched them both through the rear tinted window of the Lexus. Azazel seemed to be mostly listening, which was not commonly the way his phone conversations went. In a bizarre move, Azazel briefly handed the phone to this gringo, who ended the conversation after a few moments and handed a closed phone back to Azazel.

When they returned to the car, Azazel had something larger than his phone in his hands. He approached the Lexus from the rear and opened the hatch. Sal did his best to keep an eye on him, but he couldn't make out through the rain spotted window what he was loading into the car. Whatever it was, it made very little impression on the large vehicle. Walking around the driver's side, Azazel got in and shut his door, while their trainee got in from the other side.

"Our young hopeful here will find his prey out on our roads tonight," Azazel announced. "We're headed to find ourselves a rider."

Sal knew that Azazel liked the spontaneity that a carjacking offered. It was the random selection of their victims, the naked violence involved, as well as the split-second decisions needed to emerge from the pursuit unscathed that kept him enthralled. The usual plan was to troll the streets, sometimes for hours, looking for a victim that "felt" right. They would either flash their high beams repeatedly to irritate the driver or just ram their front bumper into the victim's vehicle at a stop. Either way, when the driver or passenger exited their car, the kill was on. The new member was charged with dispatching the innocents— if they were really ballsy they'd take care of the remaining occupants of the vehicle as well. Nothing was ever taken from the victims; this was not a robbery. It was a tool to instill terror into the populace. It also served to both inaugurate and incriminate their plebe. But tonight was to be different.

"Do we have a basic area we're gonna' sweep tonight? I mean, who's following who and where are we going?" As he spoke, Sal heard a sound that brought him both clarity and terror.

From the darkened third row behind him came Maria's soft and calming voice. "I think we should lay some ground rules first."

CHAPTER 12

Sal's thoughts were being continually derailed by his fear. Shit! He was being marked and he was just sitting here waiting for it. How could he not have recognized her voice, that calm sultry questioning . . . or was it the same voice? Calm down, he had to collect himself. It was still possible that he remained the sole conspirator. There was no way to be certain. How could they have found out? Sal tried to unclench his fists and take a few deep breaths again. The darkness gave him the shroud he needed to think. If he showed too much angst, he'd likely blow everything and get himself killed just the same. He'd play the game as long as he could, ignoring his emotions and reacting only if he needed to.

Azazel's next words provided the support to sustain Sal's belief. "Let's get out into the suburbs first, then we'll start looking for our target." He shot a quick look at John before turning onto 5 South to head out of the city. "Remember, be swift but careful. Our success tonight depends on their fear." Their applicant nodded quietly, staring straight ahead as his mentor spoke. "They're chicken-shits, and they'll hardly believe what they're seeing. They'll run scared, and by the time the cops get there we'll be fuckin' gone."

Azazel had his crazy eyes tonight. That usually meant that he was out for his own gain and heaven or hell help the poor son of a bitch that didn't play along with him. "I had another dream last night," he told his passengers. "Tonight will set it all in motion. It will bring about the beginning."

There was a long silence after he'd spoken. "The beginning of what?" asked their recruit.

"The beginning of my part in His plan."

John still didn't seem to understand. Sal rested his head against the window and closed his eyes. He didn't understand either, but he didn't care anymore; he just wanted out. He'd been hearing about this dark demon orchestrating Azazel's actions for years now. The newbie seemed nervous, and Sal hoped he would stop asking questions, for his own sake.

Sal had seen one pledge lose his nerve in this final approach only once, and Azazel had needed to finish the job for him. They'd all piled back in the car, but on the way home they'd taken a detour. Azazel had stopped the troupe at a local park, where the newbie had been forced out. Espiritu had told him that because he'd failed his task, he'd have to suffer a "beating in" if he still wanted to be Maratrucha. The 11 gang members present had beaten him for almost ten minutes, and when it was over their prospect was dead. At the following meeting, Azazel had focused on the boy's failure and told the gang that weakness like this only bred further disgrace. He'd threatened that it would not be tolerated and over the next few months there had been several purging deaths, as he liked to refer to them. A leaner, more vicious clique had emerged.

The rain was pounding the street tonight, carving halos around the headlights of oncoming traffic. "This storm should help us tonight. It'll provide a great cover." Sal's attempts to sound enthused made him nauseous. He couldn't reconcile allowing some innocent person's death just to maintain his illusion. An illusion he was not even certain was still whole.

"There!" John blurted, smiling as they exited the 5. "That's the car we're after!"

Sal leaned between the two front seats. "What do you mean 'the car we're after'? Is this a hit? We don't walk the line with a hit. What the hell's going on?" Sal spun in his seat looking for some clarification in the faces of the others.

Several cars ahead of them was a small red Ford. Azazel jerked the wheel violently, swerving and nearly hitting two other cars while crossing lanes to catch his objective. There were still several cars between them, and he'd have to be creative to make this work.

"Shit! You're gonna' fuckin' kill us . . . watch what the hell you're doin'!" Sal's anxiety was boiling over. This son of a bitch was doing this just to force him out in the open. "Since when do the plebes dictate which vehicle we're to go after?" He couldn't let this happen, no matter what it meant for him. Leaning forward he firmly placed a hand on Azazel's right shoulder, and then his whole world was thrown sideways. The car was filled with bright orange air bags and the dust from their ballistic deployment. Azazel was slammed into his side window, crushing the glass beads forcefully into his skin and out into the rain. Sal was thrown against his junior brother and up against the opposite door. Their car spun wildly into the intersection and hydroplaned into the path of oncoming traffic. Something heavy flew forward and hit Sal in the head, then it fell at his feet. Looking down, Sal felt his heart skip a beat. Staring up at him was the caped crusader. It was his grade-school backpack! He quickly shoved the bag under his seat with his foot.

"What hit us?" Maria asked in a breathy tone. She'd been thrown forward and was picking herself up off the floor in front of her seat. "What hit us?" she asked again. "Did you run that light just to catch that goddamn car? You crazy bastard, you almost killed us!"

Azazel's unbelted body lay slumped over the steering wheel, motionless, while their front passenger tried in vain to open his door.

Looking out his window, Sal could barely make out a garbage truck through the rain. It was turned slightly sideways underneath the light. Traffic whizzed all around them.

The passenger side of the car had been crushed, pushing the rear door inward and rendering it useless. The junior member sitting next to Sal was quiet, still upright in his belted posture. With his body held in restraint, his head was twisted in a grotesque and unnatural pose, his neck and skull obviously broken.

Before Sal had a chance to react, their target vehicle had returned and pulled up alongside theirs. It stopped just a few feet away, facing his side of their SUV. The driver exited the car, leaving his headlights on to illuminate his approach through the rain. He ran up to the shattered window.

"Is anyone hurt in there?"

Azazel remained slumped over the wheel, his shirt bloodied and torn across his back from the broken glass. Under the changing red and green hues of the traffic light, Sal leaned into the front to check his pulse. It was weak, but present. He turned to confront the voice at the window, but a deafening muzzle blast over his right shoulder jolted him instinctively back into his seat. His right ear ringing, Sal opened his eyes wide in an effort to overcome the flash blindness. The man in the window disappeared in a heap beneath the shoulder of the Lexus. Their front seat passenger had completed his inaugural task without any concern for their escape, and for a moment all occupants of the vehicle sat motionless. Forcing himself to focus, Sal moved quickly. Collecting his backpack from under the seat, he threw open the door and stepped over the body next to the vehicle. Their victim was lying face up, his eyes were wide open and a growing streak of darkness stained the puddle he lay in. A generous flap of the man's skull lay agape where the bullet had exited the side of his head. Sal froze, and for an instant he swore they made eye contact. A chill ran up his spine before he hastily continued on. Running through the rain, Sal prayed no further shots would be fired as he fled. He slid behind the wheel of the idling car, closed the door, and forcefully merged with departing traffic.

Through the rain, Sal was able to make out the green and white sign for 5 South. Cranking the wheel hard to the right, he coerced the little car as it fishtailed, crossing several outside lanes to enter the freeway heading into Mexico.

"Holy crap, holy crap, holy crap . . ." he kept muttering under his breath. *They had my bag . . . they knew all along.* The little car jerked to the right, crossing a deep puddle. *It was Maria in that van two nights ago. They've been watching me . . . I'm next to be killed.* Sal had to focus. He was about fifteen minutes from the border, but he had no idea how he was going to make the crossing without getting stopped. If he made it across, he could continue south down Mexico Route 1 into the Baja Peninsula. There were small parcels of adjoining land in Todos Santos he'd purchased over the years with the gang's money, but he'd still have to make it there. The land was one of the secret stashes he had lined up for just such an escape but never figured that it would be under such dramatic circumstances. A golden wave of light flashed over the dash as he passed under one of California's Amber Alert signs. *The system was up and active.* With the blood draining out of his knuckles as he gripped the wheel, Sal had to force himself to stay focused.

Coming up on the next sign, he increased the speed of his windshield wipers to give himself a clearer view of its announcement. Craning his neck out over the steering wheel, he was able to make out the message as he shot beneath it. They were looking for a silver four-door sedan and not the red little Ford Fiesta he was hurrying away in. He breathed a small sigh of relief. He'd finally caught a break, but how the hell was he going to make the border crossing? He had less than ten minutes to figure something out.

Sal began to pray, something he'd not done in a long time. He asked for this one favor and in return promised full penitence. He'd never again fail to live up to the responsibilities laid before him, and swore to face adversity in a way his late parents would have expected . . . if only he could get past this one insurmountable hurdle. Traffic thickened and the toll plaza loomed large in his tiny windscreen. Sal continued to pray.

As Sal approached the crossing, he was ushered far to the right by a drenched figure in a bright yellow poncho. Through the cascade of rain blanketing his window, he followed the undulating caterpillar of traffic as it crawled toward the gates. Slowly passing beneath the towering roadside lights, Sal drove in and out of the dark and lighted bands that crisscrossed the pavement. He made his way diagonally toward a single ostracized lane at the far limits of this stockade. Sal continued to pray for salvation from this trap, while obediently following the ever diminishing congregate of vehicles. Fully expecting to be pulled from his car by waiting police at any moment, he couldn't help but wonder if he'd made it this far just to fail within sight of his freedom. Sal swallowed hard. He neared the California state line, watching another yellow poncho-clad figure interrogate the occupants of the vehicle in front of him.

The small car shuddered as he released the clutch and crawled ahead into the gate. Exhausted and submissive to his own fears, Sal reached for the window crank and slowed under the shadow of the toll. With a firm rap on the roof and a small twinkle of red light on the dash, he was waved through forcefully and without question. Nearly stalling the car entering Mexico, he could hardly believe what had happened. Glancing backwards in his mirror as he left the toll, Sal let out an exasperated laugh. His prayers had been answered.

As he drove off, a small noise caught his attention. He listened for a quiet moment, and then heard it again. Sal turned on the overhead dome light while peering at the reflection of the back seat through his mirror. In the far left corner he was drawn to a small pair of eyes looking back at him. In his surprise, Sal nearly drove off the side of the road. This entire time, he had not been alone.

"What's your name, sweetie?" he asked.

Over the sound of the road and rain came a soft but confident reply.

"Eva."

CHAPTER 13

The last thing he recalled was a searing flash of light with an inference of pain. After that there was a brief moment of angst. What would she think? Who would take care of her? Then . . . a peace he had only once read about.

Blue was his favorite color. Somewhere in his teens he'd decided it was green and then orange . . . but really it had always been dark blue. He was aimless in a sea of this hue. Drifting slowly in the absence of falling and besieged with an out-of-body quiet that was like the precipice of sleep, Fin could feel the warmth of watching the cold blanket of snow fall and smother his school day to come. His grandfather's wet kisses and the weight of his dog on his legs in the morning. The touch of his mother's hand after he'd cried and the heat of her love in her words that followed. The smell of cologne in his father's deep hugs.

It all rushed at him gently, preoccupying his consciousness with a peacefulness that drew him in. Steadily, his singular motion slowed to an ebb and flow, back and forth as if nearing the shallows. Back and forth, it repeated until his weight returned to him through a heaviness from his chest to his back.

Fin opened his eyes. It was too dark to see his surroundings at first, but he could hear the sounds of lapping waves and the call of loons. Through his blurred vision it was difficult to make anything out clearly. Tilting his head back, he saw the inverted silhouette of trees lining the shoreline behind him come slowly into focus. Staring straight up, he saw the black sky was full of stars. They seemed out of place to him, without any recognizable constellations or familiar patterns. Fin rolled over and put a knee down in the cool water. Slowly he rose to his feet.

"How was this possible?" he thought. Fin looked out over the lake where his family had vacationed when he was a boy. The nighttime scene was just how he remembered it.

Their 31-acre retreat here in Maine was purchased in its undeveloped state, just as nature intended it. Fin was only six when he and his younger brother helped their father and grandfather erect the lodge that would serve as their refuge from technology and the growing monotony it was breeding. That first summer they divided up the structure into bedrooms upstairs and their large family room downstairs. They collected granite to construct the mantle and fireplace, with a chimney rising out through the roof in the center of the room. Choice trees were earmarked for clearing, and then left for the winter's ice fishermen to be felled for firewood. The family sent what wasn't burned to be milled for the flooring and cupboards.

Fin walked up the bank through the thin ferns. The land sloped up gently for the first seventy-five yards from the water, then rose aggressively up the mottled granite mountain side. The trees were thick and towering. Only timber that was either old and rotten or otherwise in the way had been marked for removal before they began their construction. At the base of the rise, the family had built their fishing hut. It was a single-room structure with a loft, constructed on stilts to protect it from the winter's ice slabs. It had room for everyone to warm up after ice fishing, and to spend the night if they desired. The loft allowed everyone to share a common space, something his father loved. Behind the shack was a clearing between the foundation of the shelter and the base of the mountain, left for the sliding snow during the colder months. As he passed, Fin could see the scars and pock marks in the tin sheeting that covered the foot of the hut from the years of rocks and trees that had fallen against it. Its age had only strengthened its character.

Straight ahead was the well-worn path leading up the hill. At the top rested their cabin on the rise overlooking the lake. Ascending toward the point where the wooden decking began, Fin could hear the loons continue to call. He stopped and looked down at the first board of the walk. On it was carved all the names of the family members who had made this haven possible. He wondered how everything seemed to be as he remembered it.

This wooden path was a labor of love, one that he and his brother had constructed to ease their aging parents' trip to the water. It took three seasons to complete and they were careful in trying to use only the trees felled in clearing the way for the base. The foundation, especially some of the original segments, was anchored at regular intervals into the granite outcroppings. Fin stared ahead into the dark forest. It had been years since they had replaced any of these boards themselves, but they looked as fresh today as on the day they had been laid. This retreat had been in the family for almost 30 years, but after his parents died, he and his brother decided to sell the property. They were living on opposite coasts, both with obligations that kept them from attending to the place the way they used to. It was a decision that he had regretted ever since.

Fin walked the planking, weaving in and out of the gigantic stands of ash and pine, trying to catch a glimpse of what he knew to lie above on the ridge. Initially, only the light from the stars lit his way up the path. In the cool night breeze the tree tops swayed, coaxing him further with their snaps and creaks, the same ones that had scared him as a child. Fin began to see lights through the trees further up the rise. Moving quickly, he jumped the dark ferns and underbrush between the unboarded turns of the walkway. He doubled his pace, hoping that an answer to this mystery might be waiting for him at the summit. Fin emerged from the woods into the clearing. He turned and glanced back over his serpentine route. Standing silently at the southern edge of the top seven acres, Fin marveled at the beauty of the lake and the valley it filled almost 200 feet below. The water served as a flawless mirror for the moonlight from above. Fin stared up at the dark night sky, again struck by how different it looked tonight.

Behind him the main house stood just as he remembered it, with large sliding glass doors on both the first and second floors overlooking the water. The lights were on upstairs, casting the dim shadow of the balcony railing onto the groomed lawn at his feet. The scent of a wood fire he had been following curled from the stone chimney above him. Approaching the house, he could see most of the lights were on, and then unexpectedly one of the downstairs lights went out. For the first time a sense of fear swept through him before he cautiously walked on toward the back terrace. As he reached for the handle on the sliding glass door, Fin thought he caught a faint whiff of Old Spice. The sound of a snapping twig pulled his attention sharply left. Fin froze as a long shadow stretched over the lawn from around the side of the lodge. As the individual rounded the corner of the building, Fin could feel his blood chill. Standing not ten feet away was a man Fin had not seen for almost fifteen years.

"Fin," said his father tearfully, "I've missed you, Son."

CHAPTER 14

The scent of his father's cologne, buried in the strength of his hug, gave Fin a feeling of safety he'd not felt since Rachel left. He was crying like a baby, and the more he tried to stop, the more cathartic it became. Those months of emotion poured forth to the one individual Fin could only wish he had been there for him.

Unable to wrap his mind around what was happening, Fin stammered out the words amidst his sobs: "What are you doing here, Dad? How are you . . . how's this possible?" He pulled back. Searching for answers in his father's face, Fin refused to let go of his arms.

"Fin, it's you that's finally here, I've only been waiting." Jack Canty was a slender man, taller than Fin but with a similar build. In his twilight years his drive had not dwindled. He was the kind of man who had insisted on doing all his own home improvements, no matter how long it took. Many an afternoon in his later years had been spent sneaking out into the garage to work, only to be chastised by his wife when she found him up on the roof doing repairs or mowing the lawn. Jack had aged well. The athletic build he owned after college had never fully left him, and he'd slid gracefully into the role of a distinguished grey-haired gentleman. That was how Fin saw him now.

Fin's lip curled in unison with his furrowing brow. "What? Waiting, I don't get it." His sobs slowed, allowing his sentences to pass unbroken. "You've been here at the lodge all these years?

Man, is Mom gonna be pissed," he added with a self-satisfied chuckle, wiping a tear from his face.

Jack smiled, staring into Fin's eyes.

"What's going on Dad? Really, where am I?"

"This is difficult for most folks the first time they hear it, Son. It'll seem to be the least likely explanation . . . but it's true, Fin." Jack paused knowing that his son's passion for facts would cloud his acceptance, making his transition difficult. "You've died, son."

Fin stared at his father vacantly while thoughts and questions swirled in his head. "I died? When? How?" Fin dropped his hands to his sides. He gaze wandered as he tried to retrieve any memories leading up to this moment. "That can't be, I don't remember anything . . . and I don't feel any more enlightened. I mean, where are all the answers, the secrets of life that we're supposed to learn? I had all these questions . . . about life's meaning, the universe. What about all the unanswered astrology and physics questions I have?" His gaze fell to the ground again as he tried to recall anything that might add reality to this new dimension.

"That's the way it is for most of us," his father said, dipping his head to regain eye contact with Fin. "It'll come to you, Son, you just have to be patient and give it time."

"When? How much time?"

"We're not given the answers when we get here, Fin, that's not the way it works. This place is the next step, not the final destination. In fact, I'm not sure there is a final destination."

Fin stood dumbfounded, still overwhelmed by the night's events.

Jack gestured toward the lake. "Look how peaceful it is here. Who knew I was actually purchasing a slice of Heaven all those years ago?" He laughed out loud. "Your mother says I've gotta stop using that one." With his arm around Fin's shoulder, he motioned for them to head inside.

The lodge was just as Fin remembered it from his childhood, brightly lit with beautiful hardwoods and touches of Appalachia thrown in all around. In between the intricately colored throw rugs, the honey-yellow beechwood floors reflected the light cast by the oil lamps. The main room flowed smoothly into the kitchen area, separated only by a teak-covered bar his father had spent countless hours laboring to perfect. Fin sat down on a well-worn stool, searching the room with his eyes and trying to take it all in.

Jack sat in the kitchen, opposite his son, on the kitchen side of the bar. They'd had many meaningful life discussions over the years, right here in this very spot. "Death does not grant us omniscience . . . at least it doesn't seem to."

"Is that for everyone, or just what you've witnessed?"

"Always the scientist—this is not evidence based here, Fin. But after a while here, one learns to, well, feel how it all goes."

"I don't understand." Fin's shoulders dropped. "I've never been good at feeling my way through."

"Just as it was in the last life, things here are earned through effort, though our depth of discovery and understanding seems to exist on a higher plane." Fin refocused his attention as his father continued. "It seems our nature is to understand what we can't see or feel only after we move on to the next phase."

"And this is the next phase?" Fin asked sharply.

"Sometimes you have to lose what you had to understand what you've gained," Jack continued, at the risk of overwhelming his son. "The sense of your own perfection, the freedom you had in life before marriage, that was lost after you had a family. But only then, after the void in your life was filled, did you come to realize that hole had even existed. It took your daughter's love to reveal the 'pit' in your soul that it filled."

Fin's eye twitched and he rubbed it vigorously for a moment.

Jack paused and took Fin's hand. "Her love helped to complete a picture that never seemed imperfect until she was there."

Again Fin rubbed his eye. A vague feeling of restlessness came over him before it vanished without leaving any emotional residue.

"You're given the vantage point and the tools in *this* life to move beyond the restrictions of the physical world of the last life. What brought us here, as well as what we bring with us, provides the foundation for the answers we're all looking for." Jack stopped for a moment, noting Fin's confused look. "Look, all the parts of our lives that we wasted time on, the things that were trivial to each of us, are no longer a part of our existence. Here, we have the ability to focus on the things that matter most to us, the things that truly drove us onward but were only obscured by this . . . trivia," he said, rolling his hand through the air as he finished. "Imagine what you'll accomplish here, knowing that you're not alone and that, as we move on, we'll always be together."

"*Are* we alone here?" Fin asked, looking around the room.

"When you woke by the water, did you notice anything, well, wrong?" Jack asked, redirecting the conversation.

Fin had to think for a minute. "You mean besides waking up in the water at a camp that I've not been to in almost 15 years?" he said sarcastically, growing just a little more anxious. "Well, my vision was blurry. I could barely make out my surroundings at first. The trees were unclear and I couldn't really see across the lake . . . but that seemed to only last for a couple of minutes."

"We all have a period of adjustment when we arrive. It's different for each of us."

"How so? Did you experience this too?"

"For me, it was my hands. I had no trouble seeing things clearly, but I couldn't feel anything. It took an eternity for me to be able to do so. Only then could I feel the touch of your mother's hands in mine. We're all different, and we all take our own time before we fully accept this place. It may take a while before you're able to see what you need to see."

"What do you mean, what I 'need' to see?"

"We're all seeking something greater, something larger than ourselves to belong to, to exist for. But for most of us, that something is just beyond our perception, just out of reach because of our own doubts or imperfections. It's that something that's most important to us, whether or not you fully recognized it before. This place seems to highlight whatever that something is, no matter how much you may have avoided it before. In time, you'll recognize yours, too."

"How is it that we both ended up at the same place? I mean, what are the chances? Does everyone end up where their loved ones are?" Fin's skepticism was regaining its focus.

Jack smiled. "No, Son, they don't, but where else could you have ended up?"

Fin just stared across the counter at his father, unable to come up with a reasonable alternative.

"Seldom will you encounter a force in nature to rival human will, and it's stronger in some than in others. Its ability to create is unrivaled, and we're lucky that way . . . our whole family is, Fin."

Fin remembered the question he'd asked before his father had shanghaied their conversation. "Dad, are we alone here?"

Jack rested his elbows on the counter. "I've never talked with God, if that's what you're asking, Fin. I'm not sure where He is, or what He is for that matter. All I know is that we didn't end up here together by chance."

"That's not entirely what I meant."

Jack hesitated briefly, raising his eyes to meet his son's. "No, Fin, we're not alone. Everyone's here."

CHAPTER 15

The smell of formaldehyde was not an unpleasant one, but the thought of what it was preserving was what bothered Father Moriel. It all reminded him of the meat packing plant his father used at work back in Minnesota when he was a kid. The sterile-looking stainless steel drawers covering the walls complimented the county morgue's eighty-year-old grey marble floors. Together, they made for a very unfeeling place in which to see old friends for the last time.

Detective Tom Graves broke the mounting silence, "I'm sorry, Father, after we located the car, Dr. Canty's car, you were the obvious choice to identify the body." They both stood silently staring at the olive green plastic bag that contained the remains of tonight's victim. "This need only take a minute, but you can take longer if you'd like, sir." The sound of peeling back the bag's heavy zipper and its thick plastic hide resonated off the surfaces in the room, giving the act an even greater sense of finality.

Father just stared in disbelief, his breath becoming visible in the cold air. Living in gang-infested areas, and being involved in northern Mexico, he had been asked to identify bodies in the past, but never those of close friends. "That's him. That's Fin Canty." Graves gave him a minute to offer a prayer before drawing the bag closed and shutting the drawer.

Taking a purposeful breath, Father continued. "Ok, I'm ready." He looked up at the detective, trying to choke back his anticipatory tears.

"I'm sorry Father, ready for what?" He wasn't sure what Catholic ritual he had forgotten since high school. Tom Graves had been raised in a household where he was taught to respect the beliefs of others, despite differing religious affiliations. He understood what a difficult time this was for loved ones. The police were often in a rush to apprehend those responsible and were likely to seem callous to the grieving family and friends of the victim. It was a true challenging situation, but one that he had begun to master.

"I'm ready to see her, too," Father said, feeling his emotions rising in his throat, the heft of his sadness almost unbearable.

"Sir, I'm not sure what you were told, but there is no one else." It had been a little over two hours since the incident, and much was still unknown.

"Fin's daughter, Eva. He has a three-year-old." Father was starting to get agitated.

"We're aware of that sir, but we don't know the child's whereabouts at this time. There were no one else at the scene."

The contents of Fin's wallet had given the police the information regarding the auto they thought they'd be searching for, his silver Volvo. Only after a patrol car serendipitously discovered it in the church parking lot did the full implications of tonight's events begin to reveal themselves. The Amber Alert system had only just been updated alerting drivers to the correct vehicle, Father Moriel's little red Ford, within the last twenty minutes, and so far there were no leads.

"Are you sure, Father?"

"I just saw them two hours ago. She was definitely with him in the car . . . I helped him put the car seat in." His conflicting emotions were quickly coming to a head. Moriel was pleased there was no body to identify, but that opened up all kinds of fears regarding her whereabouts, as well as her safety. "How is it that you don't know where she is?"

Ignoring this last question, Graves turned to leave. "Follow me Father." The two men exited through the restaurant-styled doors into the waiting area and continued directly outside beneath the front walk lights. Graves pulled his cell phone from his coat pocket and dialed the precinct.

Father could hear the phone ringing through the receiver, and after only two rings he abruptly grabbed the detective's wrist.

"What is it, Father?"

"Hang up for a minute, son. Who did you say your people thought were responsible for this crime?" Father had been turning in for the night, in anticipation of his trip to Mexico the following day, when the police had knocked on his chamber door. The overwhelming news of his friend's murder, infused with the initial accusatory questioning, had made him forget all the finer details of the event.

"The observers said that it seemed a random act of violence, one that we often associate with gang initiations. The SUV involved had been seen racing recklessly through traffic just before being struck by the garbage truck. Why?" The detective still held the ringing phone to his head.

"Likely a Hispanic gang, no doubt. Yes?"

"Odds are good, yes. Again, sir, why?"

"My car was equipped with one of those automatic toll things," he said, frantically spinning his hands in the air. "You know, to cross the border with!" Father was suddenly gripped by an undeniable certainty of where Eva had been taken. He could hear the voice on the other end of the phone pick up. "Detective, I think I know where they went."

It had been over an hour since they'd introduced themselves to one another. Sal had introduced himself as Uncle Sal, and Eva had been silent since. They were about 50 miles into their journey down the Baja Peninsula, traveling on Mexico 1 on their way toward Ensenada. El Banco de Mexico and El Primero Banco, two of Central America's largest banks, had branches there, and Sal had forged accounts for the gang at both of them. It had also been his practice for some time now to open separate accounts, secret accounts known only to himself, in either the same city or at the same branches as the faction's laundering accounts. In this particular location, he'd done both. He'd chosen to split his secret stash at both institutions, right along side the faction's money. In recent years, most of the Mexican-owned banking corporations had been bought out or been aggressively taken over by the coalescence of predatory banks from larger industrial countries. This had encouraged the development of the Baja Peninsula into a highly competitive industrial player—a change that had allowed Sal's ill-gotten money to grow more securely. It also laundered his funds further, as the initial deposits were into small locally owned banks. The transition of his funds into legitimate international corporate banks had only given additional credence to the identities he had conjured up for their deposits. Now all he needed to do was show up with the correct identification and signatures and withdraw the money . . . he hoped. He realized that it was only a matter of time before they'd begin looking for the correct vehicle and track it across the border into Mexico. It was still unlikely that they knew who he was, unless they'd caught Azazel and the rest of the members in the van. Knowing the MS-13 hardiness, he assumed if the car was still drivable, they weren't there when the cops arrived. This could cause problems in the future, but for the time being it would help him.

He'd been glancing at his rear view mirror every few minutes to watch what his little stowaway was doing. Eva had been vigilantly keeping an eye on him, and to his surprise she didn't seem scared.

"Where's my daddy?" she finally asked, having never taken her eyes off Sal.

Sal had little experience with children, especially little ones of such innocence, and he had no idea how to answer her question. He felt like the Grinch trying to come up with a convincing lie for little Cindy Lou Who. Hiding behind his parents' deaths all these years, Sal had consciously avoided facing the destruction that gang violence had caused people. He'd always told himself that it was only members of other gangs who had been hurt, but the blatant disparity between that and seeing Eva here in the car with him was ghastly.

"Is he with my mommy?" she asked before Sal could concoct an answer.

"Where is your mommy, sweetheart?" His conscience was beginning to throb.

"She's with God," Eva said pleasantly.

"Oh Christ," Sal muttered to himself, closing his eyes briefly. "Yes, Eva, that's where he is. He's with God and your mommy now. And," he added, "I'm sure he will always be watching over you."

That answer seemed to sit well with her. "Will I get to see them soon?" she asked. "I want to see Mommy on our trip too."

She smiled as she watched out her window.

Sal didn't know what she was talking about. He figured this was just three-year-old stuff. He was, however, relieved that there was no crying, not yet anyway. "What trip is that, sweetie?"

"Daddy and me were going on a trip tomorrow. Is this it?" She seemed comfortable with the plan as she understood it, and Sal didn't feel it was in his best interest to upset her.

"Yes, sweetheart, now just relax and I'll tell you more about our trip as we get there." As the car rolled on, the drone of the car's engine and the road noise lulled her back to sleep. Sal kept glancing back at her. She seemed so peaceful and innocent. He wasn't sure how the hell this had happened, but it had. He promised himself that, no matter what, he would always do right by this little girl, whatever that meant. Fate, or God, had placed her in his path for a reason. His conscience had been misplaced for so long, it was comforting to make a difficult decision on behalf of someone else. He would not fail her. He could see the early morning lights of Ensenada approaching. The wrecking yard would be opening soon.

Sixty miles north, at the border, the grainy security camera footage was being combed. A large-scale man hunt would begin soon.

CHAPTER 16

Moriel woke. The hound's-tooth pattern on the ceiling of the Volvo played tricks on his tired eyes, momentarily seeming acquire extra dimensions. He rubbed his eyes forcefully to eliminate the illusion. He had been asleep for the last few hours in the driver's seat of the car, and his back pain had awoken him just in time. Jim Purcell was early for work and was walking through the parking lot with determination as Moriel brought his seat upright. He opened the heavy leather-covered door and swung his legs out, his 52-year-old back reminding him where he'd slept last night. He had only begun to adjust to a world without Fin Canty, but the rest of Fin's close friends were still unaware of his absence.

"Dr. Purcell, sir, I need to talk with you," Moriel called to him as he strode across the main lot toward the Applied Physics & Mathematics building. Father Moriel was not a man who enjoyed giving bad news, but when it needed to be done, he felt that, if possible, the only way to do it was face to face. "Sir, I'm sorry to bother you, but I have some news, some terrible news."

Jim Purcell was generally an inwardly focused individual, and this morning was no exception. He continued to power his way toward the front door of the science building while barely acknowledging Moriel. "Certainly, Father, but I've not been to mass for quite some time, so any salvation issues should probably be directed toward my wife," he retorted with some self-satisfaction.

"Fin Canty was murdered last night." Father's words stopped Purcell in his tracks.

"What did you say?" Purcell's voice now held an unsteady degree of anger, and his demeanor toward this stranger changed with their new degree of intimacy. He turned to face him directly. "Father, please, what did you say?"

"Dr. Purcell, I am so sorry to be the one to bear the news, but Fin was a very close friend of mine as well, and I didn't want the police to be the ones to tell you. Last night around ten o'clock, he was . . ." Father's voice began to shake. Up until now, he'd not spoken these words to anyone who hadn't already known, and hearing them come out of his own mouth seemed to cement the night's events. Jutting his lower jaw forward, he exhaled forcefully through his quivering lips and began again. "He was shot and killed in what the police believe was a gang murder. Eva's missing."

Purcell stared at him in shock. "I just spoke with him yesterday afternoon. We had a meeting, one that was the beginning of something huge for him. He was supposed to be leaving this morning to fly with Eva to Geneva." His unwillingness to believe what he'd just been told was growing with each word. "Father, are you sure we're talking about the same man?"

"Jim, we met last December at Fin and Rachel's Christmas party. You and I talked only briefly. We spoke about your beliefs on Darwinism versus creationism." Father put his hand gently on Purcell's forearm. "I wish to God there was some mix up regarding his identity, but I identified the body myself only a few hours ago. I'm certain it was . . . is Fin."

"This is surreal." Purcell looked as if he was going to be sick. The color had nearly drained from his face in the bright morning sunlight. "I think I need to sit down. Can we go to my office so we can talk?"

Purcell led the way into the building and up the flights of stairs to the third floor. No words were spoken. He was going through the same process Moriel had suffered less than ten hours ago. Unlocking the door, he made his way with Moriel across the department waiting area and entered his office. Purcell gestured across the well-appointed room toward a comfortable chair. "Please, Father, have a seat." Never redirecting his gaze, he dropped his coat on the floor near the hat rack and made his way over to the small bar near the window overlooking the science courtyard. "Can I get you something to drink?"

"Yes. I'm not usually a drinker, this this morning I think I'll have bourbon if you've got any." Father sat quietly for another five minutes or so while his Purcell prepared their drinks and took his seat behind the large leather embossed desk that sat between them. Accepting his drink, Father said, "Tell me how you met Fin."

"We met in college, I knew both him and his wife for years. Hell, I knew them when they were dating. I was the one who helped Rachel put Fin back into his bed, drunk on his twenty-first birthday . . . after he threw up all over her new shoes." He paused, "My God, I can't believe this. Where do the police think Eva is? Do they think she's . . ." He hesitated again, not sure if he could tolerate the word most appropriate for the question. "You know, alive?" He finished his drink in one swallow.

"There seems to be evidence that she was taken in my car into Mexico. The police are . . ."

"Your car? What were they doing in your car?" Purcell's staccato delivery cut Father off cold.

Father could see Dr. Purcell was used to having someone

to blame for the things that went wrong in his life. He accepted his tone as an expression of their shared feelings of powerlessness. "He brought Eva by my parish, St. Pius, last night to tell me of his good news and pending trip. His last few months have been hell, as you know. This turn of events seemed to be a true blessing for him—both of them, actually. It really seemed to change his outlook. He was leaving his car with me for safekeeping and instead took my old jalopy for their brief ride to the airport."

"I'm sorry, Father. I just can't believe this is happening." Purcell paused, looking down into his empty glass. He turned and walked to the bar to pour himself another drink. "Another?" he asked Father. Purcell returned to his desk and handed the fresh drink to Father. He glanced down at his watch; it was already 8:00 a.m. "Shit," he muttered under his breath. "I'll have to call Fin's contact in Geneva."

"You mean Dr. Krunowski?"

"Yes." Purcell regarded Moriel with a little surprise before continuing on. "It's already 5:00 p.m. there." Purcell suddenly looked exhausted to Father Moriel. "I should try to catch him before he leaves the institute for the day." As Purcell sat down again the phone began to ring. Hoping there would be no one on the other end he'd need to share the news with, Purcell answered it. "Hello." A booming voice caused him to wince uncontrollably. "No, Edvard, Fin did not leave already. Edvard, Ed . . ."

Purcell had maintained eye contact with Moriel initially, but now he closed his eyes to answer Edvard. "Ed, I have some very difficult news."

Father took this opportunity to explore Purcell's vast office. There were numerous academic degrees and awards posted throughout, but what captivated his attention most were the photographs intermingled with them. Many were of Purcell and Fin, obviously dating back to their college days as physics majors. As he sipped his drink, Father couldn't help but wonder how profoundly Fin's death would affect not only his friends, but the ever more complex field of physics. He had only been half listening to Purcell's conversation, but had heard his own name referenced several times. Now there was an unusual pause in the conversation, which drew his attention back to the desk.

"Please Father, help yourself to another drink if you'd like. Edvard's got me on hold, some emergency call he's gotta take, I guess. Hello, yeah I'm here . . . no go on." Purcell's gesturing glance waved Moriel over toward the bottle.

As Father contemplated a third drink, the cell phone in his coat pocket began to vibrate excitedly. He excused himself, allowing Purcell some privacy to finish bringing his friend into the grieving fold. He stepped into the office waiting room to take the call. He didn't recognize the number listed on the phone's front screen.

"Hello, Father Moriel here."

"Father, this is Agent Rivera. I'm a local FBI field agent working on many of the gang-related violent crimes in the SoCal area. I was hoping to have a word with you." Her voice was very soothing. "I'm sorry for your recent loss, and I understand that the local police have already questioned you, is that correct?"

He could hear other conversations going on in the background. "My dear, it sounds like you're in a cave. I'm afraid that this is a bad time, can we talk at another time?" He had hardly slept last night, and what sleep he did get was certainly not curative.

"I understand, Father, but often rapid pursuit of the matter, even during these initial difficult hours after a crime, gives us the information we so desperately need. Is there a good time that we can meet?"

She seemed genuinely interested in getting the information—something Father knew was not common with "routine" cases. Out of loyalty to his friend, and his desire to find Eva alive, he agreed. "Of course, any time in the next day or so will be fine. I'll have matters to attend to for the family of the deceased. I'm sure you understand."

After Fin's body was identified, the police notified Fin's only living immediate relative, his brother, Liam, on the East Coast. Father was upset he was not available for the family in that moment. He called Liam back shortly afterwards, consoling him and offering to help in any way he could.

"I'm currently finishing up another case, one that may be related, and I was hoping to stop by your church tomorrow morning. Would that be alright?" Agent Rivera asked.

"That sounds fine, my dear. I'll expect you sometime around 10 a.m. then. Our morning service is at 8:30, but I have another at 11:00." Father added.

"I wouldn't worry about that, Father. We'll only need a bit of your time. Thank you, and we'll see you tomorrow." She hung up before he could add anything further.

Putting the phone back into his pocket, Father listened at the door but didn't hear anything. He opened the door and saw Purcell holding the phone to his ear with one hand while holding his head with the other. Purcell looked up quickly and motioned for him to come in. "Ed, hold on a minute, there's someone here I want to introduce you to." Purcell gestured for Father to resume his seat near the desk. Purcell pushed a button on the phone, and then replaced it in its cradle. "Ed, are you still there?"

"Yes, I'm here. Did you say you wanted to introduce me to someone?" The voice coming over the speaker phone was vaguely familiar to Moriel, though he couldn't place it off the top of his head.

Purcell interjected. "Father, please say hello to Dr. Edvard Krunowski, Fin's former advisor and . . ."

". . . the current director of CERN. Hello, sir, I'm Father Moriel. I was good friends with Fin Canty . . . and his family. I'm sorry for your loss. Your voice sounds familiar, I wonder if we might have met at some point."

"Perhaps, Father. Fin told me of how you often spoke since Rachel's passing. He was a dynamic man and will be missed very much by his brethren on this side of the pond. I am truly at a loss for words to express the shock and sadness I'm feeling over his death. This facility owes its ability to operate to the legal work Dr. Canty was involved in. As you're both aware, Fin was instrumental in the collection of supporting evidence for CERN's cause. His work as the spokesperson for our scientists and CERN at the hearings showed that the reactions we're now causing were occurring tens of thousands if not millions of times daily within the earth's upper atmosphere, and thus far there has been no ill effect on this planet. Thanks to Fin, the request for an injunction was rejected by the U.S. District Court of Hawaii, and actions to bring further federal bearing on the case have been denied based on the overwhelming evidence he provided. Fin simultaneously became a hero to his peers and public enemy number one to those who found our quest for scientific truth the modern-day equivalent of sacrilege."

"We all appreciate what Fin did for the field, Ed," Purcell added, as he rubbed his eyes.

"We were to have the holidays together, here with Eva. I understand there are few leads as to her whereabouts. Is that true?"

"Yes, I believe so. As a matter of fact," Father added, making eye contact with Purcell while he spoke. "I was just contacted by the FBI regarding all of this. I'm going to meet with one of their field agents tomorrow morning."

"Thank God," Edvard added remotely. "We can only pray that they find her well. I was just asking Jim when this occurred. Do you know what time this all took place, Father? I ask because we've had some strange developments in the last 24 hours here, too."

"I believe it was around 10 p.m. last evening." It was becoming easier to talk about, a point that saddened Father even more. "What developments have you had?"

"I don't know how much Fin told you, Father, but the research we're doing out here is providing some very interesting findings for the field of physics. Our collider was initially just yielding particles of increased mass, simple muons and neutrinos coupled with photons. It became evident, however, that we were ending up with more matter than we started with— extra stuff, as we discussed before, Jim. Now, with the machine running for as long as it has been, we're starting to see more complex compounds."

"How long has the machine been running?" asked Purcell.

"Total? For about three days now." Edvard paused, waiting for a rebuttal that never came. "We realize that by our design the machine was never intended to run for that long this early on, but the data was changing. At first the matter just showed up as an overload for the detectors. We've had to reprogram the Tier 1 and 2 computers to accept and analyze larger debris. Then, last night around 0400 hours, oddly enough around 10 p.m. your time, the reconfigured software began identifying these new compounds. Amidst the helium nuclei that were roaming Atlas and CMS, we found something else."

"Atlas?" Father was doing his best to follow the conversation.

"Sorry, Atlas is one of the main particle detectors at the Large Hadron Collider here at CERN. It's our main tool in our search for new particles derived from the high energy proton collisions." Ed paused before continuing on. "This something else we've detected, though there's very little of it, is carbon!" Ed's voice was climbing in octaves, his excitement oddly contrasting the news of Fin's death.

"I don't understand. What's the importance of all of this?" Between his lack of sleep and the emotional stress of the last twelve hours, Moriel was beginning to have a hard time concentrating.

"Well Father, in a star, hydrogen atoms are flung at one another in a very hot and dense arena. During this main sequence, their nuclei fuse to form helium. This process gives off the light and heat we feel here on Earth. As the star or sun ages, it runs out of this fuel to burn. What's left is a celestial body that now contains only helium atoms, and the star becomes ever smaller and denser beneath the weight of its own gravitational collapse. The increased density causes this star to begin burning the only fuel it has left . . . helium. In doing so, while the star re-expands, these helium atoms begin fusing and thus give off more light and heat, but this time they result in the production of carbon atoms. It's a simple process of addition, really."

"So you're saying you've created a sustained locus of cold fusion?" Purcell asked with incredulity.

"That was our first assumption as well. But you see, we're detecting no heat; nor has there been any additional change in the energy of the system. We're not sure how or why this is happening, but it is definitely happening. However, that's not the strangest thing about all of this." He stopped, leaving his audience momentarily unsure whether they'd lost their connection. The line crackled and Ed continued, "I'm sorry. I just wish Fin were here for this."

Father interjected, "I have some understanding regarding scientific things like this, and I have to ask, has anyone attempted to date this carbon?" Father was beginning to understand the implications that his physicist friend was postulating.

"Not in this case Father," Purcell added. "I'm not sure if the age of the carbon would even be relevant. It's a long story, but the newly formed nature of this carbon precludes the use of that test anyway."

Edvard laughed forcefully. "Very good, the idea occurred to us as well . . . and normally I'd agree with you, Jim. You see, the real riddle here has to do with just that point. It hinges not on the fact that we're getting carbon, though that's odd in its own right. Rather, the mystery here is the fact that the carbon we're finding *can* be dated."

CHAPTER 17

"Where is the girl?" Job was pissed. The hiss of his voice could be heard around the room through the small cell phone speaker. "I gave you very specific instructions on where the target would be and what to accomplish . . . to say that I'm disappointed would be an understatement. This was not supposed to happen." Maria stood over the bed where Azazel lay, still recovering from the accident two nights ago. She was not accustomed to dealing with their latest financier. "Your uncharacteristic pause leads me to believe you are surprised I know of your failure already."

"I'm sorry, sir, we did the best that we could under the circumstances." Her reply was weak, uncharacteristically so for her. She was aware of the large sums of money at stake, as well as the fact that Job's agenda—whatever it was—had been compromised. Azazel had told her of the importance of getting this right. "It means the difference between us stayin' just another Salvatrucha faction or risin' to the top as the center of our universe. We got a chance to run it all," he had told her. The payoff for this job was enough to secure their longevity, not to mention the potential for additional business from Job. After a long pause she continued. "We have a lead, and have already arranged our next step."

"Sweet whore, perhaps you do not understand the reach of those I represent. Their wealth is immense, and the depth of their influence stretches the breadth of centuries. For you to fail at this task is to become obsolete. I certainly hope for your sake that does not happen." His words portended a fate worse than Maria had previously understood.

Inside certain circles, distrust of the scientific community had grown over the years, and the work being done at CERN had only added to it. Small groups of recreational astrologists, as well as fringe religious fanatics, had fueled public concern over the catastrophic, world-ending, yet fictitious possibilities that they claimed could emerge from CERN's work. Terms such as "God Particle" and the "Mind of God" had been thrown about in the press with purposeful abandon to foster doubt and alarm in the public psyche. Bit by bit, this grassroots affair had gained both form and momentum. The news groups that had initially heralded the project as human domination over the mysteries of the universe changed their tune once the wealthy right-wing Christian groups began threatening to withdraw their funding. News agencies that had once touted the scientific prowess of those responsible for CERN's achievements were now airing stories asserting that the scientific community wanted to create black holes and rips in the time-space continuum. They had begun to portray CERN's endeavors as a means to discover the inner workings of the universe with a total lack of concern for physical and religious consequences. With a longing for fame, these allied communities had sown the seeds of distrust that had grown into a full-on assault, questioning the motives of any scientist involved in such projects. Unfounded fear regarding the unraveling of God's architecture had gained the attention of some very powerful groups . . . which is where Job found relevance.

"My dear, my displeasure is shared by all those involved, I assure you . . ." Job hesitated, like an irate father choosing his words carefully. "Azazel was not to make this move without my authority. I strongly suggest you find her and complete the deal before I do so by other means. Please pass my concerns to your counterpart, I want her found." He spoke with a deliberation that came from wealth and education. "If your cohorts cannot convince me of their competence in this matter, you will be removed from our plan . . . we cannot afford any more mistakes. I will call you again soon." The line went dead.

Maria closed her phone and placed it quietly on the nightstand next to where Azazel still slept. His condition was slowly improving, though breathing deeply still came with some difficulty. MS-13 was a lot of things, not the least of which was an organization of professional drug traffickers. Their movement of prescription pain killers had become second only to that of the FDA in volume country-wide. The corporate network that the factions had created gave them access to a virtual pharmacy. Over the last few days, the use of Percocet, as well as Valium, had alleviated a great deal of Azazel's pain and allowed him to sleep more comfortably. In his narcotic stupor, his state of awareness flowed without borders into and out of consciousness. His dreams had grown more vivid, as when he used drugs before, his prophet had visited him many times.

"This can yet be salvaged. Find the little one and send her to me. Then you will join me, and together we will yoke her innocence to our cause and devour the one who searches for her." In the red and golden light that shone through the swirling dust, the image of his oracle rose beyond his ability to focus. Staggering beneath the ever broadening figure that faded into the dust above, Azazel awoke in a cold sweat with a renewed hunger to complete his mission. Maria was still sitting at his bedside. Wincing, Azazel took a slow and deliberate breath.

"Remind me again of our plan tomorrow with the priest."

CHAPTER 18

"I left the telescope set up just as you had it." Jack had followed his son up the spiral stairs to their favorite rooftop hangout. "Things are certainly different here, though I can't explain why or how honestly. I don't remember all their names, but I never see the constellations that I used to see." He continued while handing his son a cup of coffee.

"I've noticed." Fin added with an air of distraction as he peered again into the heavens with his newly rediscovered toy. "From our lowly vantage point way out on the Orion Spur, we have an unobstructed view of the universe. On a clear night without any light source to interfere with viewing, one can see billions of stars in the sky from this roof." Tonight however, something was different. "There don't seem to be any fewer of them. It's just that they're all . . . different." The earliest memories of time spent with his father were those lying in their back yard staring up at the tapestry of light. Jack Canty had taken the time to teach his son the names of all the major constellations. He even bought Fin his first telescope, though Santa got all the credit for it. Running through the center of this lifeblood of their earliest father-son connection, was a shimmering ribbon of distorted light that stretched from horizon to horizon. The Greeks called it Galacos, the milky stripe that filled the night sky. On one of these nights lying in the grass, staring heavenward, Jack taught him that the portion of the Milky Way we see is the spiral arm of our galaxy that lies a few thousand light years closer to its core.

Fin was hooked. The night he learned that this massive object was swirling around in space with us was the night he decided that, whatever he ended up doing in life, it was going to have something to do with these stars. He was floored to learn that we, as passengers on this humble spaceship Earth, spend our lives traveling at thousands of miles per hour circling tens of light years from its bulging center. The pattern of these celestial discoveries had remained unchanged for a millennium, just as when the Greeks first named them. However, the sky that Fin was staring at tonight was not the one he recalled with such intimacy.

Standing on the observation deck that he and his father had built so many years ago, he marveled at the pattern of stars that were out tonight. "I can't pick out a single constellation that looks familiar, and the Sagittarius Arm of the Milky Way isn't even there. *Nothing* seems familiar here." He swept the clear night time sky slowly and purposefully just as his father taught him when he was little, stopping every few degrees to reassess what he was examining. The luminescence of these simple stars shared the same frame with nebulae and super nova that were far closer than he was used to. Close enough to pick out details with this simple refractive telescope. "It's like we're floating around inside an entirely different galaxy."

"I brought you a blanket in case you both get cold. Enjoy yourself up here." Before Fin could question his statement, Jack excused himself to the floor below.

Fin continued sipping his coffee while peering out at this alien landscape. He desperately wanted to make sense out of where he was, and out of this new sky. Why would God make the sky different? It didn't' make any sense, what would be the point of taking the time to change something so basic when most people would never even notice. If this was heaven, it should be familiar and comforting.

Bending over the optics of his telescope, Fin suddenly became conscious of someone on the roof with him. He felt the warmth of familiar fingers in his hair. Standing quickly and turning to face this new apparition, he caught a whiff of a favorite perfume. He found himself looking into the deep blue eyes he remembered. Rachel's skin was just as soft and flawless-looking as he recalled, and her smile was brighter than anything his telescope could show him. The warmth of their love flowed through him again with the meeting of their lips, her body pressed firmly against his. Placing an open palm on the dainty small of her back, Fin pulled her femininity into him. The soft fragrant skin of her slender neck was still the erotic zone he had come to appreciate in their college years. Rachel closed her eyes and tilted her head toward the night sky. It was a warm night and they slid down to the crumpled blanket left for them. No words were spoken in that first hour, only the physical exchange of their love out under the stars.

"Where have you been this entire time?" Fin asked as they held one another afterwards. "I don't recall even wondering why I hadn't seen you."

"I've been right here, only you weren't ready to see yet." She rested her head on his chest, letting her arm drape across him while playing with his hair.

"I don't understand that whole thing. I mean, why would God keep us from seeing the things that are most important to us?" he added with a degree of frustration, while he ran his fingers up and down the center of her back. They lay wrapped in the warm blanket, their legs intertwined with one another's.

"Why does it have to be God who makes those decisions?"

"Who else would it be?"

"Maybe it's us who make it that way. What were you so enthralled with when I walked up here?"

Taking a minute to let Rachel's last statement sink in, Fin answered, "The sky, well, the star pattern actually. It's not like anything I've seen before . . . what was that last thing you said?"

"Wrong hole?"

"Very funny. No, the other thing."

"Oh, that. Maybe it's *us* who make it that way . . ."

Fin rose to his feet, cutting her thought short. Still naked, he walked back to his telescope.

"Nice, you might want to tuck that thing in before you hurt someone . . . or yourself from the look of things."

"Uh huh." Fin's attention was consumed again by the stars.

After a few seconds of waiting for an answer Rachel continued, "May I ask what I said to give you such an urgent desire to leave a beautiful naked woman lying here all by herself?"

"Huh? Oh, sorry, babe. 'Us, maybe it's us' . . . that's what you said. Since I arrived here, or died, or however you want to put it, I've been noticing that things are just as I'd hoped, or needed maybe."

"That's how they've always been for us. It's how we've always tried to make them."

"No, I mean that things aren't as some omnipotent being would lay out." He was peering at the night sky again through the telescope, this time with renewed vigor.

"We're strong-willed people, we've always had the luxury of things turning out well for us," Rachel added.

"I've always regretted losing this place, the cabin, the connection with the family, but here we are. It's where I ultimately ended up . . . as did my Father and you. This telescope, it's the most advanced one that my father ever bought for me, a Newtonian reflector on a Dobsonian mount. It's the only one that I can take true measurements with, and it just happens to be here. There doesn't seem to be anything magical about this place though. If I fall, it hurts. When I drop something, it breaks. When I'm tired, I sleep. Everything seems to follow the same general laws of physics we're used to. The wind blows, sound travels, and water is wet, and I can't breathe beneath it. And so far I've not seen anyone fly! So why is it that the night sky is so vastly different?" He was talking almost at a feverish pitch, one that Rachel was accustomed to. It often happened when he was on the verge of a discovery, or at least when he felt that the next puzzle piece was just beyond his reach. "Maybe God has less to do with all this than we thought."

"What are you saying?"

"Well, maybe all of this is because of us?"

Sometimes her participation in these physics discussions was feigned, but this time Rachel's curiosity was piqued. "Ok, I'm listening. Go on."

"What if we have more to do with creating our reality than we give ourselves credit for? What if our reality bends to conform to *our* will, versus us conforming to the reality we're forced into? Think about it. We as a species seem to consistently discover a new rule or loophole in the physical world to accomplish our next goal and overcome the next hurdle. The laser, powered flight, organ transplant, genetic engineering, HIV treatments...There's always a solution . . . always. Maybe the power of prayer is not so much our Lord hearing and answering, but more the strength of the collective will involved in altering our reality."

Rachel remained lying on her back, staring up at the stars as he spoke.

"I have to do some work, take some measurements, and calculate a few things here. Do you remember what I wanted to name our first child if we had a boy?"

"Of course I do, it was Edwin. Thank God that that never came to fruition." Rachel had propped herself up on her elbow at this point and was still hoping to lure her husband back for round two of their reunion.

"Well, the namesake for that idea was the astrologist Edwin Hubble. One of his greatest contributions to physics was determining that the universe was actually expanding. To do this he used what he called the redshift." Fin turned to look at his audience. Rachel was still staring up at the stars and the soft curves of her bare breasts were highlighted by the faint blue glow from above. Fin's words stalled out as he gazed at the heavenly body in front of him and wondered how he had gone on without her. Her long shapely legs stretched out before her all the way to her pointed toes. Her firm flat stomach made it almost impossible for him to focus on what had grabbed his attention previously. The growing pause in his explanation dragged Rachel's focus back to her husband.

"What? Go on, I'm listening, and you just ...stopped." Rachel realized what had derailed his train of thought and smiled. "I promise that we'll get back to that. Just finish your thought before you drive me mad."

"Sorry, babe." Fin returned his gaze to the barrel of his telescope. "Using his theory about light waves, Hubble was able to calculate that objects were moving away from us and not stationary as Einstein had suggested. He paused, staring out at the lake that lay hundreds of feet below. "I wonder what that rate is here."

"How long would that take? You know, to figure out that number?" Rachel pitched her head back, her long black hair draping over her shoulders and onto the deck.

Fin got the point. Watching Rachel stare up at the night sky, he felt free again, and accepted. It was the same feeling he'd had when they were dating, falling in love. She was the most beautiful woman he'd ever met, and the first to find his intellect and passion for science attractive. Being called names and getting picked on as a child, his skinny legs and knock-knees with glasses too large for his face, all those years in grad school feeling like an outcast, his theories and dreams often landing him at the fringe of his discipline—it all melted away when he was with her. She was Fin's turning point, the source of his confidence, and the muse for his scientific creativity. Still, he couldn't help but feel that there was a significant hole in this reality. Something plagued his soul by its absence, although he couldn't put a name to it.

Fin's right eye began to twitch ever so slightly; he blinked rapidly before squinting hard and rubbing it. In this moment, he chose to accept this reality as it was served. For once, he would enjoy where he was, and the companion he'd craved for so long.

All these feelings and calculations could wait. After all this was eternity . . . right?

CHAPTER 19

The little red Ford had likely already been discovered on the security cameras at the border. It should have taken the cops only a few hours to figure out what happened and what car they were really looking for. Azazel and his pupil had seemed to know exactly what vehicle their target was in, as well as precisely where it was going to be. That didn't sit well with Sal. Thus far, he felt fortunate there had been no run-ins with the locals, but he knew that it was only a matter of time before that all changed. He'd have to ditch this ride soon for another, if he hoped to make it all the way.

This case was likely now regarded by the authorities as a murder-kidnapping so it was only a matter of time until the FBI would be involved, and Sal had already had his fair share of that scene. They'd be looking for this car, and for that reason alone he'd have to disguise it well enough to avoid its discovery regardless of what he did with it. The sun was nearly up over the coastal city of Ensenada when he spotted a local auto supply shop opening up just ahead. This would be their first stop on the way home.

The usual drab and institutional approach toward city servant offices had been abandoned at the 31st Street precinct station. Inside the station was an enormous circular room sloping inward toward the center from the outer edge like a terraced garden. All desks and offices were oriented around this central depression, where dispatching and the control booth sat. The offices of the most senior members, including detective Tom Graves, were placed at the outer perimeter of this tempered Holodrome of justice.

On any normal day, Graves looked out of his glass office down onto the worker ants as they digested all the fodder that helped to grow their investigations. Tonight, however, he was working on less than six hours of sleep in the last two days, and this scene only served to feed his caffeinated mania. Often praised for his excellent police work and chastised for the poor use of his subordinates, Graves did not feel comfortable with anyone else doing his work for him.

After the discovery of the mistaken vehicle ID, the correct information had been posted to the Amber Alert system. Since then, there had been the usual deluge of calls, only this time many of them pointed to a coherent scenario– an escape to Mexico.

Like most cops, Graves hated surrendering his investigation to outsiders, but in the case of a pursuit that crossed international borders he had no choice. It was the FBI he'd have to share his jurisdiction with this time.

"I don't give a shit where they've gone to. I just want to make sure that I keep my hand in this!" Graves could feel his growing hostility toward the FBI agent on the other end of the line. "Dana, if this case drags us into Mexico, then so be it. I only need you and your team for manpower. I can't muster the bodies or international resources to push this manhunt into another country at this point."

"I understand that Lieutenant, but your tone of voice is

not going to alter the fact that I now own this investigation. I suggest that you change, and lighten up if you still want to be included as this plays out." His FBI counterpart was no stranger to the way that these cases made competent cops feel, nor was she blind to the strain that their now defunct two-year relationship was already placing on this case.

"Stop calling me 'lieutenant' dammit. My men reviewed that border tape and distributed the stills to the precincts both north and south of the border hours ago, and so far we have nothing." Their relationship had grown serious over the three years they were together, but in the end their work had created a rift that they found impossible to overcome. This conversation was proving a painful first step in reconnecting. Graves waited for the soft voice on the other end to reply before continuing his demands.

"Lieutenant . . . Tom, I fully understand your frustration, but if you'll let me continue, I think I may be able to share some new information with you about the search." Agent Dana Pinon was a well-respected law enforcement professional, one who had worked many missing persons cases in the SoCal area before. "Your posting of the images has already broken open a lead. I have a few agents in the Ensenada area who seem to have missed our culprit by only a few hours."

"Goddammit! Are you kidding me? How the hell did that happen?" Graves was standing now, growing more impatient as he paced behind his desk.

"I don't know, but it doesn't mean the trail is cold either." Her voice remained calm despite Graves's growing alarm.

"We're running out of time here, Dana. That little girl might already be dead, or traded, or worse!" He knew that the longer this chase dragged on, the more likely it was that they would never find Eva alive. The drug trade was flourishing in Mexico, not to mention its fair share of human trafficking as well. Graves took a slow deep breath, and then resigned himself to hear the rest of the story. "I'm sorry, please go on." He sat back down at his desk and rested his head on the high back of his black leather chair.

"Thank you." Dana knew these cases rarely turned out well if they were not solved in the first few days. "It seems that our gang-banger has some skills. The car was found in a pile in a wrecking yard, but only after it was glossed over several times by both the local Mexican police, as well as our own men. The red Ford that we were looking for was not exactly the same car that we found.

"What do you mean?" Graves was confused.

"Well, for starters the Bureau had a hell of a time locating it. There were no eye witnesses, and initially it seemed our suspect, and the car, had simply disappeared. There's very few surveillance cameras in that area of Mexico, but the few that were found gave us nothing ...until a wider sweep of the area gave us a few minutes from a camera inside an auto shop ...our perp has a penchant for a creative flare. The car had been hastily painted to look rusted out with orange spray paint. Our suspect painted over the leading edges and bottoms of the door, as well as trunk lid. He also applied peel and stick window tint to the back windows, removed the hub caps and covered the rear bumper with stickers. The wheels that remained he also painted orange. Prints so far have revealed both multiple sets of adult prints as well as a single set of smaller children's prints. There's no blood thus far and the owner of the scrap yard says that the car was sold to him by a male fitting this suspect's description. The plates were missing but the engine block numbers were a match. He also said that a little girl was with him and seemed fine . . . that was about five or six hours ago."

"So where are we now?" Graves had zoned out for a second. It had been almost a year since he had heard Dana's voice, and it was bringing back emotions he hadn't expected to feel today. Snapping himself back to the present, he caught the most important pieces . . . girl alive . . . gone for about five hours . . . and the whole shit sandwich was taking place somewhere in Mexico.

"The owner of the scrap yard says our suspect asked to borrow the phone and then he and the little girl left in a taxi about 15 minutes later. He did mention he took the time to put in the little girl's car seat before he left." She paused while she let her counterpart digest that piece of information.

"This case is getting weird Dana. There's still the other vehicle that was involved, the SUV that got away. So why did this guy take the victim's car and flee?"

"I know, nothing here makes any sense. It certainly doesn't follow any gang crime I've investigated before." Her voice sounded sad.

"It's the motive for this whole picture that's still eluding me. If this were just another case of gang violence, or initiation, or whatever, why would this guy be caring for this little girl?" The two suffered a few seconds of silence. "I have a better feeling regarding her safety, though," Graves said with a slight lift to his mood. "So what do we know after that?"

"Not much. We're tracing the phone calls from that shop, but this is Mexico and it might take a bit. We're trying to find out what cab company he called, and then we'll know where it took him. I have several agents at that shop right now waiting for further news from the telephone company. They're recruiting local law enforcement to set up a reasonable perimeter around the city. Look, why don't you get some sleep and I'll call you when I know more."

Graves took a deep breath. Dana's voice was very soothing. "Thanks, Dana. I'll look forward to hearing from you."

More than 100 miles away, in an Ensenada district normally reserved for tourists, a man wearing a new suit strolled out of local department store into the bright afternoon sunlight. He was holding hands with a little girl dressed in a beautiful new pink and white dress with ruffles. They were each wearing new shoes and had an air of money about them. They also had two large shopping bags, one for each of them and full of basic, but new, clothing items.

Their stop at the local bank had been put off a little longer than Sal would have liked, but they had needed to stop to get Eva something to eat. He had also neglected any potty stops, which was nearly catastrophic. The little dance in the cab that was accompanied by the three-year-old chant, "I gotta poop, I gotta poop," suddenly opened his eyes to the new issues that, as Uncle Sal, he'd now have to be aware of.

At the bank his paperwork and signatures had matched spot-on with those they had on record. The forged identification he used worked without issue, and Sal withdrew the full twenty-five thousand dollars that he had stashed at that branch.

They walked out into the parking lot, and following the audible report of a few electronic chirps, they loaded both their belongings and themselves into their newly purchased silver Chevy. The main artery out of Ensenada overlooked the road they'd taken coming in. It was getting closer to late afternoon and the traffic was starting to pick up as those leaving work departed.

"Whee! Look at those pretty lights, Uncle Sal!" Eva pointed energetically as she gazed eastward out her window toward the road that had led them into the city. Off in the distance, in a small parking lot on the edge of town, there were multiple police cars with their lights flashing. The lot was in front of a well-known local restaurant, but the police were likely not interested in the cuisine. Instead, their interest was focused on the car that Sal had transferred his old plates onto just a few hours ago.

"Just a few more hours, little lady, and we should be there," Sal announced contentedly. Buckled securely into her car seat, Eva continued to eat her crackers and watch the glistening Pacific in the late afternoon sun. Four and a half hours after their unscheduled stop, with the old car ditched, the police temporarily occupied, Sal's wallet full, and new clothes on their backs, they were on their way south again to Todos Santos.

CHAPTER 20

The young lady he'd spoken to on the phone yesterday was younger than Father Moriel had imagined her to be, but she was very professional and quite put together. Agent Rivera, as Maria had introduced herself, was dressed in a black business suit with a skirt that was hemmed just below her knees. She had a Hispanic accent that was more obvious in person than it had been over the phone during their previous conversation.

"Thank you for the tea, Father. Now then, if you don't mind, sir, I have some questions about the deceased as well as the missing little girl. Can you give me some background information about your relationship with them?" They sat in the first pew to the left of the altar, with the morning sun shining through the great stained glass window over the balcony and casting a halo of colored light around them. Father placed his right arm up over the back of the bench as he turned toward his interviewer.

"Well, Dr. Canty and his family were friends of mine. I have . . . I had known him and Rachel, and their daughter Eva for many years."

"How long, sir?"

"I guess for about eight or ten years now. Recently he'd been coming to talk with me more often due to his wife's untimely death, amongst other issues." He glanced up toward the stained glass Christ with his last statement.

"How was he dealing with his loss?"

"He'd been having a very difficult time reconciling Rachel's death, as well as his own recent notoriety. But if you're asking if he was suicidal, that's ridiculous. He loved his little girl—and besides, he was murdered."

"How did she die . . . his wife?" She had not taken her eyes off the priest since they had first met. Azazel had warned her not to trust a man of God in his own house. Azazel's dreams had been coming more frequently now and he seemed a man possessed to her. He was convinced that the timing between their earthly instructions from Job and his own visions, as he called them, was not coincidental. Ever since Maria's initiation night, Azazel's behavior had become more unorthodox, and mysteriously ritualistic. He'd been spending far more time "praying" in the dark. He was up all night and slept during the daylight hours. His recent obsession with finding this little girl and bringing her to the master had superseded even Job's instructions. Through all of this, Maria had been finding it harder and harder to follow him. She was starting to understand why Salvador had fled. She owed everything she had to Azazel, which was only half of why she was still there. Mostly, she was afraid of what might happen if she betrayed him.

"She had cancer, my dear. Rachel died almost five months ago today, which makes this entire event that much more tragic. That poor little girl, out there somewhere without her mother or her father to look after her." Father removed his glasses and rubbed his eyes. "I've been worried sick, and losing quite a bit of sleep these last few nights. Fin was on the verge of another of his scientific breakthroughs with CERN."

"I'm sorry, Father, this must be very difficult for you." She thought the priest showed a hint of frustration in his voice.

"As you may not know, there was quite a bit of controversy

surrounding his employment there. Fin was involved in a great deal of their research, as well as their legal defenses, but he was convinced that he was doing God's work."

"Father, I'm curious to know your theory as to why, or rather how, Dr. Canty was killed. Do you believe that it was random gang violence, or something more?"

"Fin was not likely to forge enemies of his own accord. He and Rachel were very non-confrontational people. The powers at CERN used him to put a face to their work, a face to their communally assigned malevolence."

Maria caught Moriel's glance. "You seem to have some anger toward this CERN. Do you think their work is evil, and they were using Fin to present a more pleasant face to the world?"

"No, but I do think that the general public felt their work with the collider was malevolent, and those at CERN who wanted to safeguard their careers were only too happy to make it Fin's job to change that perception. However, after Rachel's death, all of those issues seemed to fade into the background. Eva became his first priority."

"Do you feel that any of this may have played a role in his death?" She wasn't sure just who or what she was probing. This entire issue had her curiosity. "It seems that Dr. Canty, a recently widowed father, was not a man who would have enemies enough to do something like this to him." Maria was interested in why there'd been a hit placed on this otherwise harmless man of science.

"It took Fin's career and his involvement with this project at CERN to uncover his enemies." Father turned away and sat back in the pew facing the altar. "A few months before Rachel's diagnosis, Fin became part of an international lawsuit against

CERN. The university had given him time off to travel abroad to act as the spokesperson for the scientists and their endeavors."

"I don't fully understand, Father. How would that make him enemies?"

"This was a big case, a watershed case with religion versus science at its heart. Those forcing the issues argued that these were godless men of science aiming to kill God and prove math and physics ruled our universe. Rachel's illness came on the heels of this unwanted new fame. The stress on Fin was immense, and his increasing notoriety only made it worse. The press portrayed him as the angry and godless scientist. He was suddenly the spokesman for what had been until then a faceless threat to the public." Moriel paused. "I am not a believer in coincidences, my dear. Everything happens for a reason. We all have greater purposes in life." Moriel shot a lingering, almost meaningful, glance toward Maria. "Sometimes this greater purpose is not readily apparent, but when the Lord makes it known, one has an obligation to fulfill His work."

Maria regarded him carefully. He did not look as haggard as she had thought he should for a man with such little sleep, especially on top of such profound worry. "Where do you think our perp took . . . Eva, right? That's her name?"

"This should all be old news to you Agent Rivera. Didn't your boss—or bosses—fill you in on all of this? I've already been over these facts with the Bureau. As a matter of fact, it was your people who told me that their, or rather my, car was found abandoned in Mexico. Ensenada, I think." Father watched the young woman write these facts down hastily. "It's imperative that we find her, my dear." Father's last statement had caught Maria's attention, and she lifted her gaze up from her scribbling to briefly make eye contact with him. He was about to speak again when his office phone rang. "Please excuse me while I answer that." Moriel stood and retreated to his office.

As Maria watched him walk away, his portly frame waddling back and forth on his short stocky legs, she reached into her handbag and ran her fingers down the barrel of her gun to the stock. She wasn't sure whether it was Azazel's words that were giving her a false sense of suspicion here or if it was something else about this priest that made her feel uneasy. The old man was not as distraught as she expected him to be.

"Hello, Father Moriel." He stood over the desk leaving his back turned to the open doorway and his guest. "Why yes, actually one of your agents is already here doing just that right now."

Maria was able to make out the beginning of the conversation before there was a long pause.

"I see. What would you have me do then, Agent Pinon?" Father held the receiver to his ear for a few lingering moments after the line went silent. Placing the phone back on its base, he heard the door to the south transept slam shut. Returning to the enclave he found the church to be empty.

The midday sun was still shining through the church's large circular stained glass window. Shafts of light cast through the image of Christ highlighted the meandering dust particles as they made their way to the granite floor. The purple and green hues gave the great hall a peaceful quiet. Moriel returned to the first pew and sat quietly to reflect. He pondered what his next move should be as he awaited the arrival of the FBI.

Six thousand miles away, Edvard Krunowski sat at his dimly lit desk reviewing the recent reports of the main collider's spectral scans. He could hardly believe the success that they'd achieved thus far, but this picture was far from fully developed. He regretted not being honest with Fin before his death. If he had told him the full nature of what they were finding, Fin would never have let him move so fast so soon . . . and so carelessly. These recent carbon results had been observed before, but not like this. These amounts were far greater than what they had found in their preliminary tests. And even though the concept of the increasing complexity of matter was not entirely new, it had never rendered the carbon 14 isotope before. The increase in matter itself had been sudden, too, and far too contemporaneous not to be significant. Yesterday's conversation with Jim Purcell had been a disappointing and frustrating one, and Edvard already missed the spirited discussions he'd had with Fin. Their similar views of physics intertwined with their belief in creationism had provided the spark that forged their early relationship. And aside from all of Fin's intellectual expertise, these beliefs had also served as the primary basis for his involvement in the Hadron Collider at CERN. Edvard had known that he needed to surround himself with like-minded individuals if his extraordinary theories and goals were to be ultimately realized. Even after he'd explained the significance of datable carbon to Jim Purcell, Jim still did not fully grasp its monumental importance.

"You are still not hearing me, my friend," he had said several times during their long-distance phone conversation. "The dates of the carbon-fourteen are nothing monumental. They're only on the order of the last few hundred years. In the world of radioactive dating, this figure is well within the accepted range of error. The real relevance here is that there *is* carbon-fourteen, and that carbon-fourteen is only able to be dated if it comes from a source that was previously living. It can't just be the end result of atomic fusion that's occurred in the emptiness of some multibillion dollar pressure cooker. The source needs to have existed within the life cycle of all things."

All of these findings were beginning to confirm Edvard's lifelong notion that the afterlife may hold the missing links to physics' "theory of everything." These recent discoveries were encouraging him to push harder for what he knew was needed next.

The Lord's divine plan was in the details, and Edvard was ever more convinced that these details were beginning to reveal themselves to him.

CHAPTER 21

The apartment was unfamiliar . . . maybe it was his grand-mother's from long ago. Fin lay on his back on the gold-colored carpet, the entire series of events playing out in a pleasantly disjointed fashion. The warm sunlight of early afternoon shone through the front window where a little Christmas tree sat on its stand. From the open archway leading into the room, came the sound of a small child laughing. Fin turned to see Eva running toward him with her arms outstretched and smiling. She jumped just inches before reaching him and landed in his arms, nearly bouncing away as she flopped onto his chest. He rolled over, playfully pinning her to the ground with raspberry kisses to her neck. To Fin this innocent scenario felt unreal. Rarely, if ever, had he been able to discern a dream while in the midst of one, but this time it was different. With all the alarm of a man about to be dragged from his loved ones for execution, he grasped Eva and sat up.

"This is a dream! Quick, baby, give me kisses!" Amidst his frantic attempt to hoard as much affection as he could before he woke, he was suddenly aware that this sweet encounter with his daughter was ending. How had he not longed for her until now? He kissed her soft little cheeks over and over again trying to make the most of this fragile moment. She giggled continu-ously, squirming beneath the weight of his affection. With one last soft kiss on his lips, he woke, calling out loud for her. "Eva!"

Lying in bed next to Rachel, he could still feel Eva's warm

little lips on his. Staring up at the blank ceiling, Fin's heart was racing as a sudden feeling of desperation overwhelmed him.

"Baby, what is it? Did you have a bad dream?" Rachel had woken on hearing her daughter's name aloud.

"Where's our little girl? What's happened to her?" All his memories of her were returning to him, both viscerally and emotionally. "How the hell could I not have felt this . . . this chasm before?" Fin was already out of bed, searching the room for his pants. "Is she here, too? Where is Eva?" He sat back down and began dressing.

"Fin! It's the middle of the night, honey."

"Where is our little girl? Is she here with us?" His frantic search began again.

"She's not here, Fin, she's still . . . there. Baby, sit down *please*. Let's talk, we have nothing but time."

"What is there to talk about, I've got to . . . remember." Fin's words trailed off as he stood—half dressed—silhouetted in the night's light shining through the window.

"What is it, Fin?"

Frozen and staring out at the lake, Fin verbalized the images as they flashed across his memory. "There was a man with, with one blue eye and one brown. Oh Christ, I was shot and she was with me!" Sitting back on the side of the bed he began to cry.

"It's not your fault, baby. There's nothing you could have done to change this." His body shook rhythmically as he sobbed. Rachel pressed her body against his bare back, resting the side of her head against his neck as she held him.

"How could I have not felt her all this time?" The pain of her absence flooded over him in waves of growing hopelessness.

"We have no control over when we leave, or who we leave

behind. You didn't do anything wrong, and you couldn't have done anything differently either." She could feel his body shudder again and again as he finally felt what he had for so long been unable to see.

Angrily shrugging off her embrace, he stood up quickly. "How the hell can you live with yourself, not knowing where she is or if she's ok? She's our little girl!" His sadness and despair had again broken free of its chrysalis.

"That's not fair. You have no idea how I feel!"

Those last few hours were coming back to him now. He remembered leaving the church and even planning for their upcoming trip. He recalled running into the rain toward the accident and leaving Eva alone in the car. "I left her, I told her I'd never leave her and I left her." He was manic, walking in circles in their small bedroom.

"Everyone comes in their own time, and there's nothing we can do about it." Rachel was trying to calm him down. "You're starting to see it all, Fin, but that doesn't mean you're ready to understand it yet."

"Are you saying that you understand all this?" He was turning slowly with his arms outstretched. "I've been here for God knows how long and I'm just now realizing that our most precious possession is alone. That I've abandoned Eva in the middle of an intersection with a murderer in a rain storm, on her own!" He continued dressing. "I've got to figure this God forsaken place out. I've got to know, to understand. I can't just sit here happy and stupid like everyone else, waiting to see how this all turns out." The uneasiness that he'd been feeling all along now had a name, and Fin finally felt like he had a purpose. "Heaven is where you go to find peace and happiness, not to be confused and separated from those you swore you'd always take care of. This isn't heaven." Fin stormed out of the room. Heading for the roof, he fired off his last retort. "This is only one step closer to Hell."

Rachel sat with her gaze fixed on the open door. With each passing day Fin had been spending more and more time pondering the night sky. Their life was becoming like it had been before, when Fin was obsessed with running calculations and taking celestial measurements. That's what Rachel had to look forward to now—Fin's all-consuming desire to understand what this place was.

There was no point trying to fall back to sleep. With the morning sun soon making its appearance, Rachel slowly dressed and headed downstairs.

Jack was already awake and making coffee. "His mother was the same way, you know, frantic when she realized that we were here alone. Wait 'till he sees *her* for the first time." He rolled his eyes and continued to grind the coffee.

"I'm worried about him, Dad. He's more anxious with every passing day."

"He's never been dead before either." he added with a chuckle. "He's not like you and me, sweetheart. He needs to know why," Jack said, opening his eyes wide with raised eyebrows. "He needs to understand it all. He's always been that way, and death does not necessarily change who we are. After a while he'll calm down, once he's able to feel what we all feel. Still . . ." he continued, "I can't say that I'm totally in disagreement with him. Something doesn't feel right about this to me either."

Rachel trusted Jack's opinion as her own father's. "What do you mean, 'something doesn't feel right?'"

"I dunno. When I first arrived, there was that period of

adjustment, just like I told Fin. But after a time, I was able to feel it all again, the love, the warmth. But above all, I was able to feel every*one*, no matter where they were. Like I said," he paused again, looking up at Rachel, "something just feels different here. . . . "

"I have some news! I think I've uncovered something important!" Fin proclaimed as he exploded into the kitchen. The sun was beginning to rise over the lake and the last of the stars had faded into the palate of the dim morning light. "Everything is expanding at the same rate here, too." He was out of breath and still in his pajamas.

"Baby, what are you talking about?"

"The stars . . . the supernova . . . all of it! It's all moving away from us at the same rate of acceleration as our own universe, or the last one—home—whatever! You know what I'm talking about." They were both staring at him. "Before we were all dead! Come on, you know what I mean!"

"We don't, hon, really. Calm down and . . ."

"Don't tell me to calm down. Listen!" Fin was frenzied, almost unable to sit still.

"Over the last few weeks, I've been measuring the rate of expansion of the gas shell about that supernova in the eastern night sky. I've also been keeping tabs on the stars that seem to move along with us in our galaxy here. Using their redshift, I was able to roughly calculate the rate at which these objects were moving—relative to us, that is. Everything in our neck of the woods is staying constant, just as I'd expect it to, but the most alarming thing is that the objects outside of this galaxy are accelerating away from where we are. And here's the kicker . . . "

His right eye was beginning to twitch again, something

that Rachel was becoming increasingly aware of.

"The rate of expansion here is the same—all objects outside of this galaxy appear to be moving away from us, and from each other, at the same rate as they did back home!" Fin was thrilled with himself for deducing this and was expecting far more in feedback than just blank stares. "Einstein's cosmological constant holds its value here, too. What I'm saying is that 'heaven' seems to be following the same astrophysical rules that we know our own universe to follow, and likely for the same indescribable reasons!"

"So, are you saying that we're still in the same . . . universe?" Rachel didn't know what else to call it. "Could we just go home if we could find a wicked-fast spaceship?"

Fin shrugged off her smartass remark. "I don't think so, no. Nothing out there looks familiar, nothing. Even if we were on the farthest side of the known universe, there should be some subtly familiar constellations regardless of the angle of viewing, but there aren't. It's all different."

"Maybe we're in a black hole and it just looks that way." Without looking up, his father offered a weak grin and raised his eyebrows, hoping that what he said was somehow intellectually relevant.

"I thought of that, too, Dad." Jack raised his chin and puffed his chest out slightly, pleased with his contribution to the morning's conversation. "But we aren't."

"Shit." Jack muttered as he went back to fixing morning coffee.

"If we were in a black hole, or at its singularity ...a place in space-time where matter is infinitely dense, we wouldn't see the night sky as we do. It would be a thin line of light, and likely one that would have vanished as we passed the event horizon."

"That's all theory though, right?" Rachel had always played devil's advocate to Fin's theories. He appreciated it, and it was the primary reason he bounced all of his ideas off of her. "No one has ever witnessed the inside of a black hole, nor will they."

"Exactly! All of these differences would themselves only be possible if we'd somehow managed to avoid being torn apart by the massive tidal forces leading into one. Or if, once at its center, we'd survived the crushing gravity and astronomical levels of radiation." Fin sat down at the bar. He'd been fidgeting since he'd walked into the room. He tried to steady his hands but was only able to occupy them by continuing to tap his fingers on the bar. "We're not in a black hole, that I'm sure of."

"Well, it's all very interesting, Son, but what does it mean?"

"Well," Fin said cautiously, "I do have a theory . . ."

The authorities were never able to establish the identity of the man who ran the red Ford through the Mexican border. Therefore, there had been no interest in the property he'd left behind. Azazel waited a few months to let any interest that may have existed fade away before ordering several of his junior members to scour the house for any clues to Sal and the little girl's whereabouts. They had moved into his house like rats infesting an abandoned building. As had become customary with most of his activities, Azazel entered the home at night. Arriving in the foyer he crouched, placing his palm on the familiar altar he'd left behind years ago. He claimed the forsaken home as his own and had Salvador's desktop computer raped for any information that could help locate him.

"Azazel, we need to talk." John had become a prominent

figure in the faction, due mostly to his strong ties to Job, who had appointed him as the chapter's link to all efforts related to righting the botched hit. Job had forced this change down Azazel's throat as punishment for so profoundly screwing up the assignment to begin with. Job had also made it clear that all transactions were to be carried out between himself and John, without interference by the gang, if they desired any degree of continued monetary backing.

"What?" Azazel was sitting at his desk with his back to the door. He had moved into the largest bedroom, the one that used to belong to Sal's parents. Their clothing and all other belongings had been thrown into the basement shortly after he moved in. Azazel's appearance had changed over the last few months. He'd lost a great deal of weight and looked gaunt, nearly dead. His skin was pale and he'd taken to shaving his head.

"We've nearly finished going through the information we were able to obtain from the house. There's not much."

"You disturbed me for that?" Azazel was still in charge, and was as feared as he'd always been. Since the disappearance of Sal and the little girl, his anger had become more explosive.

"I said that there's not much. I didn't say that there was nothing." John moved a little closer in the darkened room, remaining careful not to threaten Azazel's space. "It seems that there were a few e-mails that were deleted, but I was able to salvage them from a section of the hard drive that was only partially overwritten. The messages were exchanged with some banking institutions in Mexico. Espiritu, there were a few that were not on the registry that we found in his bag." John held out the printed evidence.

A smile was growing on Azazel's face. "Now that's something worth my time. Go on . . ."

CHAPTER 22

"What are you saying, Fin? That this isn't heaven?" Jack had stopped what he was doing, his frustration with the conversation mounting now.

"No, Dad, I'm just saying that maybe heaven isn't what we thought it was." Fin could feel the Catholic disapproval coming from across the counter. His father didn't like his faith tampered with.

"Well, what is it then?" Rachel added, as she walked over to the large sliding glass doors to watch the weather move in over the valley. She'd been acting very distant all morning, especially now as she stood with her back to the men.

Resting straight armed on the countertop, Jack urged again, "Don't keep us wondering, Son. What's your theory?" He was looking over the bar at the two of them as they stood conspicuously separate in the room.

Staring at Rachel, Fin wondered if their earlier argument in the bedroom was beginning to play itself out. "Ok, hear me out." He sat back down and turned his attention to his father. "Let's start with what's closest to home. Our galaxy, which spins like a pinwheel, doesn't expand. Within these galaxies, the stuff at the farthest edges spins with the same speed as the stuff right next to the center. By design, that rate should be slower toward the edges because of the decreased pull felt that far from the super massive black hole that resides in the center of these pinwheels. There's not enough visible material in these monstrous bodies to account for the gravity that holds them so tightly together. The only explanation for this is that there's additional material—dark material—that we can't see."

"How do you even know that this invisible stuff exists? If you can't see it, how can you even say it's there?"

"Well, we can see its effects, Dad. When the mass of a body is great enough, it can bend the one thing that escapes all else—light. That's called gravitational lensing, and it tells us this matter is there. When the light from a distant source encounters massive objects, it bends around its gravitational field, kinda like a tennis ball rolling across a suspended sheet that's holding a basketball at its center. That tennis ball may have the velocity to pass the larger ball, but only after its path conforms to the depression in the sheet that the basketball makes. Around these galaxies we can observe the nature of this event, and the degree of lensing that we see has actually allowed mapping of this matter that's otherwise invisible." Fin took a sip of his morning coffee before continuing.

"Now, for almost a century, we've known that all of the galaxies have been flying away from one another, but we don't know why. The galaxies themselves remain constant entities, but their distance from all the other galaxies in the universe is increasing, like dots drawn on the skin of a balloon as it's blown up. When all the matter and energy is added up, there isn't enough by a factor of ten to account for this expansion. Somewhere, somehow, there's a repulsive force in the universe that's forcing all these galaxies away from one another at an ever increasing rate. Einstein's idea for a cosmological constant provided enough energy to keep all the matter from collapsing back on itself under the force of gravity. In reality, this force is actually larger than he anticipated, and it's driving everything apart. No one knew what this figure represented. Hence, a dark *energy* was assumed to provide this repulsive force." Fin's right eye continued to twitch. He rubbed it vigorously.

"What's been done to look for this stuff?"

"A lot, Dad. The attempts in the past have varied from silly to monumental. The most recent effort has been the large Hadron Collider in Geneva." Fin subtly cocked his head to the side as he looked to Rachel. "As a matter of fact . . .," he added, pausing, "the night before I arrived here, I received a phone call from Edvard Krunowski."

"I never liked that man." Rachel turned back from the window to face him. "I know he was a friend of yours, but I never trusted him." Fin had come to regard her initial impression of folks as gospel because she was rarely wrong about them. "What did he want?"

"He wanted Eva and me to come out to visit them. It was regarding new developments there with the machine." Fin had stopped talking and was staring out toward the lake. There had been a frost on the ground that morning, and the rising sun had begun to succeed in its effort to melt it. His eyes began to well up again with the thought of his daughter back there without them. Fin pulled himself back and continued despite the quiver in his lower jaw. "Ed said something about increased matter in the collider. They'd been registering the production of matter versus its destruction or conservation. He referred to his theories and said something about the two of us being able to see into God's plan like we'd never imagined." He shook off the apparitions of Eva that were trying to hijack his waking vision.

"So what you're saying is that the man who threw you to the wolves, the man responsible for crucifying your career in the name of CERN, who hadn't contacted you since the trial in Hawaii, suddenly calls you out of the blue with earth-shattering news that is nothing if not good for *his* career. All just before you were randomly attacked?" Rachel had taken a few more steps toward him, facing him now with her arms crossed in front of her.

"What are you saying? That Ed had something to do with my death?"

"I'm just saying that I never liked that man. I've always had a funny feeling about his motives. That's all."

"There's a big difference between being a prick and a mob boss." Fin concluded sarcastically. "Anyway, Dad, we have this number—the cosmological constant—and we keep it in our equation to not only prop the universe up, but give it the oomph it needs to affect the motion and speed of entire galaxies as they move away from one another. Over the centuries, this number has appeared to be getting bigger, albeit by minuscule amounts, but it keeps getting bigger nonetheless. We've always just assumed that it was a function of our increasing mathematical accuracy and not an actual increase in the cosmological constant . . . , but I've never been convinced of that." With his fingers tapping, Fin stopped to take a sip of his coffee.

"Why's it increasing, the cosmopolitan constant, or whatever the hell you called it? What's the significance there, Son?"

"Well, Dad, I'm not sure. No one is, really. By measure, the dark energy accounts for about seventy percent of the Universe. Einstein's greatest blunder, it seems, has turned out to be the most dominant force in the cosmos. And it's getting stronger all the time."

Fin had been blinking deeply to try to stop the muscle twitches that had been quickening. He was having a hard time concentrating, between the lack of sleep the night before and his growing anxieties regarding his daughter. He'd found an overwhelming sense of guilt clouding his thoughts.

"Where does this leave us, literally?" Rachel asked, once again involving herself in the topic.

"Well, if we follow what we can see and measure, we can assume that we're not in the same universe we once lived in, but another one entirely. A place that every single one of us prayed we would go to when we died—a new and completely separate reality—heaven."

"So you *do* think this is heaven then?"

"Well, yes, Dad, but let me finish." Fin was getting excited again. "If this new universe has the same rate of acceleration, along with the same cosmological constant, one can assume that this place is being affected by the same dark energy and dark matter."

"Maybe God just found a formula that worked, and thought 'why not use it here too?'" Jack was still staring at him from the kitchen.

"Possibly, Dad, but that's not the whole of it. What if this dark matter really isn't that dark." He stopped to make eye contact with them both. "What if it was everything that we're seeing?"

"Babe, you already said that we can't see it, only measure it."

"I know, but what if all that we see here serves as the dark matter for all that we were seeing there?" His words rendered the room quiet for a moment.

"You're referring to heaven." Jack was suddenly enthralled with what Fin was suggesting. "You're saying that . . ."

"I'm saying that this place and all that we can see *is* that dark matter." The room was still, as all three of them contemplated this possibility. Fin's twitches were coming subtly faster now. "It's quite simple, actually. We live in four dimensions normally. We have the three directions that, say, a bird travels in. Up, down, and then straight ahead. Other than this X, Y, and Z, there's the fourth dimension, time. These are the only four that we register as we go on about our lives. Within these four dimensions exists everything that we see and know. But now we have an entirely new place, this place, to add to the 'everything' we knew of. What if heaven is an alternate dimension? What if this reality exists, and is overlapped right on top of our last one. What if these two dimensions pull on each other across these barriers but without any other sort of physical interaction, just like the theory of dark matter? Each one would then serve as 'dark matter' for the other, keeping the whole system in check."

Fin stretched his neck. A small dull ache had begun to develop behind his left shoulder. "Subtle is the Lord, but malicious He is not." he added under his breath.

"What did you say Son?"

"It's just something that Einstein said once. Maybe the details aren't intentionally hidden from us after all. Einstein believed that the Lord provided all we needed to understand our universe."

"Dad, you said to me when I arrived here that it may be in our nature to see or feel what we can't appreciate fully only after we've moved on to our next phase in life. Maybe this is just the next phase, and we only need to be patient enough to get here to discover the rest of the facts about our lasting mysteries."

Rachel turned suddenly from the window that she'd been staring out of. "I do think about her you know." The sudden change in subject took both men by surprise. They sat staring wide eyed at her as she continued.

"It's not like I just wrote her off. I knew she was with you." This conversation had obviously been building in her head since their argument earlier. "She's my little girl too, and I miss her every day." With her last statement, tears of regret began to fill her eyes. "I never went on without her! I died, Fin. What was I supposed to do?"

"I'm sorry. I know you still love her. I'm just not sure what to make of all this," Fin said, gesturing around the room. "I just don't understand how you could be so happy without her, so seemingly oblivious?" That last statement felt harsh and he tried to put his arms around her, but she took a step backwards.

"After I got here I couldn't appreciate movement. The days seemed to stand still, and people vanished and reappeared to me without explanation. I was lost, without a sense of time and where my loved ones had gone, and that included you. I wasn't ready to leave you, either of you , Fin, and for what seemed like an eternity I just waited for you to arrive . . . the same way we're now waiting for Eva to arrive."

"I miss her, and I haven't been able to think of anything else since that dream." His twitch had stopped, as had his fidgeting. "I promised to always be there for her. She's the strongest and brightest little thing I've ever known. Every time I close my eyes now, I see her smile and her big blue eyes. I don't understand, or even care to understand, why it took me so long to see this. But now I do see and feel her absence and something just isn't right." Rachel could see the pain behind his eyes. "She's so innocent, and so happy. She didn't understand what it meant to be alone until you were gone. She became everything to me after you left." He looked at his father. "Everything." Rachel began to cry softly.

Jack placed his hand on Fin's as it rested on the bar top. "Stop, Son, that's enough." He looked into his son's eyes. Jack paused as he made eye contact with both of Eva's parents. "I don't know why I know this, but I do. Eva isn't here, Son."

"I know that Dad, what I'm saying is . . ."

"No, Fin. What I'm saying is that she's not going to be here . . . ever."

CHAPTER 23

8 months later . . .

The days were long, and mostly warm. Softly rolling hills, covered largely with green grasses and palm trees that waltzed with the brine wind blowing easterly off the ocean. Speckled with islands, the water's shimmering zirconium face smiled back at the sun, giving the rainbow-colored fish a home fit for Poseidon. The horizon was a blue ribbon that stretched miles in either direction. Sugar smooth sand lined the beaches, running effortlessly under the gentle waves. This was the place that Eva and Sal now called home.

These few acres of paradise in Todos Santos were the part of the dream that Sal had longed for, open and clean. It had been months since he'd worried about being discovered here in their haven, not just by the faction, but by all of MS-13. It had been even longer since he'd had any contact with those he had for so long yearned to be rid of, and he was finally enjoying some respite from his sleepless nights. He was beginning to find relaxation here with his new family, but he also knew that this was the time when the cancer could return.

On this plot sat their two-bedroom bungalow, its ceramic floors and bamboo blinds keeping them cool during the day. Eva sat at the breakfast table, as she did most mornings, in pink pajamas and her booster seat eating her cereal. Today the gulls and pelicans playing in the surf had stolen her attention. They rose slowly above the chaos of the waves, searching, then diving with total abandon. Headlong and full of hunger, they'd rush toward their target. Eva stared out the window at this aerial ballet while she ate and giggled periodically. She had blossomed wonderfully in this new environment, taking to Sal in ways that he hadn't expected. She seemed genuinely comfortable in his arms and had been sleeping without difficulty for weeks now. Her eager mind had been soaking up the new language with an ease that most adults only dreamt of. They read books every night, just like she said her Daddy did, and took walks on the beach during the day, looking for new seashells. She also took to Sal's grandmother, her new Abuela.

"Good morning, Nana." Sal could hear her slippers quietly slapping against her bare heels as she came down the hallway toward them. He was drinking his morning coffee as she walked into their midst wearing her blue housedress.

"Buenas dias mi familia. How's my little one doing this morning?" She placed her soft arthritic hand gently on the side of Eva's head and pulled her into a kiss.

"Good, I think. She's finished nearly her entire bowl of cereal already. How'd you sleep last night, Abuela?" Sal asked, smiling widely for Eva's benefit.

"I was going to ask you the same thing. Any more nightmares?"

Sal turned away from her to wash his hands at the sink. "I haven't had any for weeks."

She waited patiently. They may have been apart for years, but she still knew her grandson well. "Do you want to tell me the truth now?"

"I told you before . . ." His voice rose sharply before he caught himself. Disrespect for one's elders was something that he'd sworn not to pass on to Eva. "Lo siento, Abuela."

"I hear you some nights, walking around the house after being woken by them. If you don't want to talk about it, I understand, but please don't lie to me about what you're going through."

He gently ushered her toward the hallway and out of the range of little ears. "It's complicated, Nana. I was involved in a great many things that I'm not proud of after Mom and Dad were killed. You know that." He shamefacedly dropped his gaze from her eyes.

"That's in the past now, Nieto."

"Not the least of which was destroying this little one's last hope for knowing or remembering her parents. I was too cowardly to do the right thing before it was too late, and now she's stuck here with us, without her real father."

"You did not take her father from her, and had you tried to stop this you may have been killed too. Besides, there's nothing complicated about it. At least there doesn't need to be." She softly wrapped her hands about his wrists. "I understand that you were a part of things you wish you had not been. I'm sure you also wish your parents weren't taken from you either, but they were and you're here now. You have a responsibility to Eva to do the right thing by her. That's where you are now, and that's what matters most."

Sal turned from her and returned to Eva. He stopped walking when he reached the ceramic tile of the kitchen and smiled at Eva, making eye contact with her while she ate. "Keep eating, baby, then we'll go outside and play." Maintaining his physical presence in Eva's morning, he whispered to his grandmother, "If I had only remembered that and thought about others first, done the right thing no matter how difficult it may have been, then maybe this beautiful child would be home with her father eating her breakfast with him . . . and not here with us."

"But it didn't happen that way, and you have to live with that. Catholic guilt is something of an acquired taste." She had been introducing their religion into the conversations more and more lately. She was bothered by the fact that this aspect of his life was so desiccated. "We're not born with it, but it's hard to shed once it's found a hold. If you don't deal with it, it'll eat you up and you'll never find the redemption you need. Everything happens for a reason, Salvador."

Sal walked to the sink to rinse his coffee mug. The shadow of the yellow drapes framing the kitchen window flickered across his hands. *Tio.* That's what was inscribed on the mug in red glaze. It was a gift from the pottery group that his grandmother belonged to, fired and given to him just after they'd arrived this past Christmas. This small community where he'd chosen to settle his little family had welcomed them without reservation. Sal turned off the running water. "What are we going to do for her preschool?" He maintained his gaze into the stainless steel sink.

A relieved smile crept over his grandmother's face. "So you're going to stay. That's a good sign." She shuffled past Sal to the table to pour herself a cup of coffee.

"It's been almost a year, and so far nothing. It still scares me to let my guard down, but at some point I've got to for Eva's sake." He turned from the sink to watch Eva blowing bubbles in her sippy cup full of milk. "For the sake of giving us all a normal life . . . you know?"

"Well, that decision is up to you, dear. She's your responsibility. I'm just here for support." She sat down at the table next to Eva.

"I think that I want her enrolled in Santa Maria's program." He had not been back to the church since he'd arrived here. His guilt had crippled him, and as of yet he didn't feel that he'd earned Eva's forgiveness, or his own. It was going to take a lot more sacrifice to accomplish that. With each passing day her purity both invigorated and punished his soul for his past sins. He had no idea when he'd feel that he'd earned her company, but it certainly had not occurred in the few short months she'd been under his watch.

"Good. I think that's a decision I can support. Now what about you? Confession is a fine way to start getting absolution for your sins." She took a sip of her coffee. "Eva, baby, do you want some fruit?"

"First things first," Sal said, casting out the gloom of the earlier conversation with a newfound hope. "Let's get Eva taken care of and then we'll worry about me."

"Life's short, Salvador. Eva loves you, and I know you cherish her too. You'll do what's right . . . I believe in you."

"If you'll finish your breakfast with our little princess, I have some online banking business to attend to. After that, we should be comfortable and never have to wave our fingers through the flame of that world again." He kissed his women on their heads as he departed, lingering just a little longer in the warmth of Eva's hair.

His grandmother grasped his wrist. "Sal, you will be judged by what you have done with the life you have left." She loosened her grip and patted his arm before returning her attention to Eva.

Azazel's dishonest nature and distrust of any establishment had been supplanted by an evil that was darker and more sincere. These pernicious visions had perverted his criminality. It was a vile wickedness now, flowing from a decaying soul. In the eyes of his followers, he had become a creature that slithered behind the light and existed only in the interposing darkness. "I don't want half-ass results and near misses, I want an answer, goddamn it! We've been watching this bait for months without any bites and I'm growing impatient." His interactions with John had devolved into meetings ripe with a growing mistrust of this appointed attaché. "I feel Sal's fucking happiness, and it makes my skin crawl! I want to watch him die, and He grows impatient."

John had begun to lose track of which "He" Azazel was referring to, as had many of the MS-13 disciples. At times he seemed lucid and spoke of the MS-13 mission as one that was financially driven according to Job. At other times, Azazel couched his desires in terms of instructions handed down to him by his drug-conjured demon. His path to this point was a long and twisted one, one leading him through many countries and consuming many friendships.

In the early 80's, at the age of 11, Azazel fled El Salvador with his younger brothers after the government-funded communist death squads killed nearly everyone in their home village. The growing civil war forced them to travel north through Central America to Mexico, staying either with friends or with family along the way. They settled eventually, with the help of their uncle, in Joya La, Mexico. It was a small town about three miles south of Tijuana. Azazel, the eldest, harbored the greatest anger of the three brothers and was often in trouble with local law enforcement. Even at a young age, Azazel was cunning, and street smarts came easy to him. He found his way into the local Mexican run-off drug trade very soon after his arrival in

Joya La. He'd made friends with a local group that trafficked in marijuana and would often sell to American college students partying in Tijuana. When he was 12, he met an older teenager who went by the nickname Conejo, or Rabbit. This young man told Azazel of the lucrative gang life in south central LA. Azazel's new friend had found himself in the midst of the FBI's effort to rid the Southwest of the growing influence of the MS crime syndicate. The U.S. government's early plan to deport all those connected with such organizations back to Central America served only as a free recruiting tool for the gangs. Azazel was enthralled by the vibrant pictures these stories painted in his head and the thought of a future in which he wielded the power to dispatch his own justice. One week after Conejo befriended him, he abandoned his family and entered the United States.

After arriving in LA, where he initially lived with Conejo in his uncle's basement, Azazel was initiated into the fraternity. Money was scarce, but violence was not. Within two years Azazel was closer to the local MS-13 members than he had been with his own family, sharing everything with Conejo like brothers. Azazel was first marked when he was two weeks shy of his 14th birthday. His first tattoo was across his back and read "EME ESE," Spanish for MS. Punctuated with three dots in a triangular arrangement, it was known to gang members as "tres puntos." These points represented the three places that MS-13 would lead you to: jail, the hospital, or the cemetery. All members bore the mark. At the age of 14, Azazel became an assistant to the local gang leaders. In a role often reserved for the older and more seasoned in their culture, he quickly declared his alliance to the association. He carried out tasks ranging from tracking monies related to local drug sales to traveling, sometimes as far as Virginia and New York, to attend meetings with the other growing MS-13 factions. He quickly became respected among the various cliques for his corporate knowledge of the organization and his ability to plan events that fostered fear and furthered MS-13's syndicate of crime. His ability to evade police and survive hostilities earned him the name El Espiritu, the Ghost.

Three years after his entry into the gang, Azazel was tasked with an operation that earned him his greatest street credibility and propelled him to the forefront of the LA clique. He planned and carried out the execution of his own recruiter, his *hermano*, Conejo. Certain members of MS-13 believed Conejo had conspired with local law enforcement in exchange for his release after circumstantial evidence had placed him at the scene of a double murder. His confessions were rumored to have brought down a more senior member of MS-13, another male who Conejo felt had shown him great disrespect when he had raped his girlfriend after getting her high.

In MS-13 culture there were few rules, but there was one essential law: *If you rat, you die.* As a result, at a preordained location, the remaining male members of the LA clique held a secret meeting. In this meeting it was decided that because Azazel was closest to, and most trusted by, Conejo, he was to be given the honor. The assassination was green-lighted.

Azazel told fellow gang members that the events had revealed themselves to him in a vivid dream in which a dark figure told him that, through his strength and will, he would be a leader. But this alone would not make him a *great* leader—only through the use of his rage was he to achieve this status. In this dream, the dark one told him, "Christ himself will witness your victory and remain silent. Your prey will die easily, passing to *Us* to consume." The dark figure had stood dimly lit by the sunlight from behind, Azazel told them, as if cast through choking dust. As the light faded further, the silhouetted form fading along with it, he was told, "You are my eyes, my hands, and my wrath. Your power will be great."

Azazel awoke after his dream terrified, sweat covered, and panicked. He was possessed with a visceral sense that he was not alone in his room, a feeling remained. He felt the guidance of something more powerful than himself and knew that his first act needed to be a defining one. Azazel's prophet had shown him the way to this end. Azazel's act went down in gang history as an unprecedented expression of brazen violence and bloodshed.

Contacting Conejo, Azazel asked for his assistance regarding a meeting with a man who would sell them a diamond ring for his woman, a girl Azazel wanted to make his. He told Conejo he was uneasy about the transaction, but reassured him it would be in the middle of the day at a safe location of their choosing. To underscore the audacity of his crime, Azazel arranged for the meeting to occur at a local church. The men arrived early and sat in the last pew, near the confessionals. The church was quiet, with only the elderly of the community knelt in midday worship. Over the balcony behind Conejo and Azazel, watching over the church from its mount, was the crown jewel of the diocese—a centuries-old circular stained glass window depicting the Living God in reflection. This masterpiece had been given to the church 80 years earlier, a gift from Pope Pius the XI for aiding the new Pontiff in his efforts to establish a Pax Christiana in the aftermath of World War I.

Sunlight shone through the stained glass, casting pastel colors through the face of the Savior onto those of Azazel and Conejo. Their location in the church allowed fellow gang members an undetected approach from the rear. The few witnesses who were present in the church fled quickly as MS-13 members asphyxiated their subject with a length of 550 cord. Azazel stabbed his friend 13 times in the chest before slitting his throat, nearly decapitating him. On his chest Azazel left a note that simply read "TRIADOR," affixed to his flesh with the same knife that had been used to stab him. Before fleeing, Azazel crouched as if in prayer over the body, marking his prey in tribute to his prophet. Conejo's bloodied and lifeless body was dragged to the altar and left under the illuminated gaze of the stained glass Christ. With his arms outstretched and his ankles bound with the cord he had been strangled with, Conejo lay at the foot of the altar, his blood trickling down the stairs. El Espiritu had been trained well by his brother—business is business. The killers were never identified.

John stood now, having moved a little further into Azazel's darkened room. Feeling the pressure from both sides of this business arrangement, he too was getting frustrated. "I understand Azazel, but I can't make this happen any faster than you can. Maybe you could ask your prophet where he is," he added sarcastically.

Azazel hunched his back and rose slowly to his feet. With the drapes drawn to keep out the early morning light, he seemed ethereal in his movements. With his fists clenched and arms extended at his sides, he began shaking, almost vibrating, with anger.

Through gritted teeth, Azazel spit his words. "Watch your tongue, or I'll cut it from your mouth. I want that fucker dead by my hand, vato. Do you understand me? Find him!"

John's cell phone began to buzz softly. Backing a few steps

away from Azazel, he answered it. "Hello?" His eyes opened wide and he nodded with a steadfast gaze in Azazel's direction. "I see, and what time this morning did that transaction take place? Thank you, I want to know exactly where that branch is."

"Make the call yourself." Azazel said as John hung up. "I want you to tell Job now. This needs to end." Azazel sat back down and turned to his shadowy desk. "I want this to be a small group. Two or three people tops. Figure it out, set up the move, and let me know when we're ready to leave. We need to finish this for Him."

John excused himself into the brightly lit hallway and waited for the door to close behind him. He dialed the number and waited.

"I'm listening." The voice on the other end of the phone was calm but resonant.

"Sir, I'm sorry to disturb you this late, but I wish to inform you that we've found her."

"You know what needs to be done. Don't let us down."

"Yes, Father. I won't fail you this time. Goodnight." The line went dead.

CHAPTER 24

The past several weeks had brought the season's first frosts. The normally soft green lawn had a stiffness to it that faded with the rising sun. These were the areas noticed by most people—the areas where the light conquered the darkness and drove away the cold. But where the sun failed to shine, in the darkness beneath the trees of the forest, the frost proved a worthy adversary for the gathering day. Fin's ability to see the spots of untroubled light had diminished under the weight of a growing awareness of areas of darkness and cold. In these places where the frost remained, the life it settled on suffocated just a little longer. Fin's world was becoming one less of relief and happiness, and more of darkness and suffocation.

Fin's aches and pains had become more pronounced, and he was beginning to move about like an arthritic old man. His muscle twitches were now accompanied by a rash that had begun on his back over both shoulder blades. The skin was mottled, as if bruised from being hit, and beneath it were small blisters that would rise to the surface and rupture daily. He picked at it constantly, hoping to find healthy skin beneath, but the overlying tissue at each of these sites refused to heal. Every morning he woke in pain, but worst of all was the heaviness of Eva's absence in his heart, and every morning he wondered how much longer he could remain here feeling this way. This morning was no different.

Rachel had been watching him as they sat silently at breakfast. "Baby, you've got to eat something. You're wasting away." Fin had been refusing nearly every meal with them. He stared straight ahead, his cheek twitching. Then he closed his eyes tight, hoping it would stop.

"I'll eat later. I think that I'd like to get out a bit today."

"Good!" Jack was coming down the stairs from his room, already dressed in jeans and a ridiculous red plaid flannel outdoorsman shirt. "I could use some help this morning cleaning up outside after the last few nights of wind. I think that there's some decent kindling lying around now, too." He loved feeling the chill of the air while getting his hands dirty with manual labor.

"That'll be nice Dad. How 'bout it Fin, are you up for that?" Rachel lifted her mood, hoping to buoy Fin's with it.

Fin had been staring mindlessly. He'd been in his head for the last few minutes and only aware of his own fantasies. "Sorry? . . . I'm sorry, what did you say?" Looking up, now he could hear his father's words echoing in his memory. "Sure, that'll be fine." He appeased his audience with a lame smile. "Let me just head upstairs to change first." Fin turned to leave his stool and involuntarily listed right, falling into the bar. Catching himself against the rail with his ribs, he winced.

"I'm ok, just a little light headed, that's all." He stood up and held out an open palm, signaling Rachel to stay seated. He steadied himself momentarily, taking a deep breath and staring at the floor. "There, just fine, see? I'll meet you outside then." At the landing he abruptly turned around.

"What? What did you say?" Fin looked at Rachel and his father. He seemed confused but more present emotionally than moments before.

"I asked if you were up for that." Rachel added a little concerned.

"No, babe, after that. What else did you say?"

"I didn't say anything, Fin. Are you all right?"

He closed his eyes and shook his head almost imperceptibly from side to side. "I'm fine, I've just not been sleeping that well. Maybe you're right, baby, I need to eat more. I'll go change. See you out there in a bit, Dad."

Jack called after him, "Dress warm, it's cold out there today."

"Always the mother hen." Hearing the door close behind Rachel and his father, Fin started up the stairs.

He had been feeling an unsteadiness in his step since he woke this morning, and a soft ringing in his ears lent an imbalance to his gait. This faint presence had grown over the hours into a more persistent noise, like a faint whisper, or maybe several whispers all at once. It was distant enough that Fin couldn't discern its meaning, if any were intended. At the top of the stairs Fin's footing betrayed him. He fell awkwardly against the wall on his right and jammed his elbow into the rail. "Shit!" He rubbed his elbow vigorously. With his anxiety over Eva's absence swelling, Fin's frustration rose more easily than usual. Though his legs and his vision told him one thing, his mind was convinced that the world was moving him in a different way.

With each step away from the ground floor the whispers became more insistent, and despite their unintelligible nature, they seemed to be growing closer. Though it was frustrating, these voices were comforting, almost soothing. The whispers gave Fin a sense of calm, one he hadn't felt in quite some time. Fin turned to his right again, this time using the wall to steady himself. Finding himself staring at a vanishing wisp of fog fleeing down the stairs, a momentary chill pricked the hairs on the back of his neck. There was a brief fruity scent in the air, and Fin turned around quickly, trying to follow this thing with his eyes and make sense of it. At the last step, the apparition hesitated, briefly taking on a translucent red hue on top and a bluish color toward the bottom. The color faded and the entire figure moved off out of sight.

Fin's feet were nearly useless as he stumbled down the stairs after this hallucination. He tried to convince himself that his lack of sleep and growing depression had finally pushed him over the edge, but he couldn't deny his curiosity about whatever this was. Fin struggled to reach the bottom of the stairs, the pain in his shoulder and the voices in his head both growing. He felt a hand on his shoulder. Spinning around he found his world had left him with no trustworthy sense of up. His brief but violent trip to the floor ended in unconsciousness, but only after the formless whispering grew to a shriek.

Opening his eyes, Fin found himself in the quiet and still entryway. He had no idea how long he had been out, though both the vertigo and the voices now seemed to be gone. Fin collected himself and, rising to his feet, he pushed open the door and stumbled outside. The cold stung his nose and quickly chilled his eyes to dryness. Fin blinked several times, forcing the facial twitches to surge into a drum roll of muscle spasms.

"You haven't changed your clothes. Fin, are you all right?" Jack was standing in the middle of the yard with a bright green wheel barrow next to him and a rake in his hands. "Son, you don't have any shoes on."

"Did you see that, Dad . . . or hear anything?"

"See what?"

Fin stood and stared off into the woods down the hillside. "Nothing, I guess." The pains in his back were coming in waves now. It was a dull torture deep in the muscles. He grimaced as he rolled his shoulders in a weak attempt to alleviate his growing anguish.

"Maybe we should go inside for a bit." Jack had dropped his rake and was moving toward him when Fin suddenly broke away and ran for the woods.

"Wait, I can still hear you!" Fin screamed as he tore off down the hill. The whispers were louder now, and they had almost reached a conversational level. Amidst the many voices, one rose above the rest. It was clearer and nearly understandable now.

"Fin, wait!" Rachel called as she and Jack took chase.

Fin barreled into the woods, avoiding the wooden walkway that led to the water 400 feet below. Fin ran through broken brush and fallen limbs. He could feel the stinging pain of the myriad thorns and rocks as they chewed their way into the flesh of his feet. Ducking and sliding, he was occasionally redirected by ghostly movement barely perceptible in his peripheral vision. The woods had attained an early evening darkness, with thick shadows cast amongst the vague shafts of light that broke through the canopy. The noises caused by the chilling wind no longer persuaded the trees into soothing song. Instead they reminded Fin of the frightening sounds from his childhood when he and his brother had played here. He came to the edge of a granite precipice. Sliding to avoid falling, he looked down toward the thinning tree line near the water. A shape, more human in form than the one he'd seen previously, walked slowly toward the lake. Fin's chest heaved with fatigue. The figure stopped and turned back toward his perch. It looked up and briefly appeared to recognize Fin's presence before continuing on.

Fin retraced his steps and found his way to the path leading to the water. Running down the wooden stairs he could hear his heart pounding in his ears. The muscle aches were now a distant reality as he flew effortlessly toward his goal. Reaching the bottom of the run, he spun toward the water thirty yards away, skidding to a stop in the frosted moss-covered mud.

"Hello. I know you're here." He yelled. "Eva?" Fin could still hear the whispers accompanying him, along with his own heavy breathing. He waited before continuing on. "I know that you're here, please talk to me."

He walked slowly toward the lake. With every great tree he rounded, he half expected to be confronted by this stranger, though "stranger" didn't fit the feeling he was having. The lake was covered with tiny wavelets that idly made their way to shore. Aided by the gentle breeze, the ferns covering the bank leaned away from the water's repeated arrival.

To Fin, the whispering had become a deafening noise. The dissonance of voices was nearly insufferable when added to the pounding symphony of the water and howling wind, as he perceived it all. Each wave sounded to him like a crashing boulder against the shore. He could feel the footsteps of his wife as she frantically approached the landing. With both hands covering his ears in agony, he turned back toward the embankment and attempted to yell above the din. "What is that?" Fin yelled to Rachel, crouching down at the water's edge.

"What is what, baby, why are you yelling?" The forest was silent save for the soft breeze and occasional crack of timber.

It was all building, gradually becoming louder and louder no matter what he did to try to stop it. Covering his ears, he could barely tolerate it, and despite knowing that she was talking to him, he could no longer hear anything Rachel was saying. The noise was pounding inside his head and he began to feel the vertigo again. Fin clutched his head in his hands and fell to one knee in the soft grasses near the water's edge. Just as the cacophony became nearly unbearable, it stopped.

The brief tranquility was filled with a single clear female voice that came from behind him. "A heaven not fought for is a Hell you'll endure."

Fin turned and looked up to see a figure silhouetted against the sun. "It's ok, Fin. I know how you're feeling, and I agree with you."

Fin stood slowly. She was wearing a red house coat with a pair of blue scrub bottoms, ones that Rachel had given to her for Christmas some years ago. "I've been calling to you, and I'm sorry if this is all coming too fast for you. Many things are about to change, and you need to be strong for Eva, Son."

Exhausted and standing with his bare feet in the cool water Fin was able to mutter only one word: "Mom!"

As she put her arms around him, the stillness that she had brought him began to crumble. Fin could hear the noises beginning again.

CHAPTER 25

Dana Pinon and her department had maintained an "open" status on the Canty investigation, as they did with most unsolved missing person's cases. "He's gone, or at least he's not in the area anymore." It was always difficult for those involved when a trail would go cold the way they often did, especially in instances like this when there was a child involved. "The last time I questioned Father Moriel was just before the Archdiocese—or the Bishop, I guess—decided to reassign him." Dana shuffled through the file as she held the phone between her ear and shoulder.

Graves's precinct had closed the case three months ago. Their assumption was that the FBI would continue to pursue any new developments should they arise. It was not in their best interest with their limited resources, both in materials and personnel, to pursue these issues beyond what was considered reasonable for a city precinct. And at this point, assuming that the little girl was dead was what seemed reasonable.

"We may have a new lead in this case . . . maybe." Graves continued on quickly. "What do you mean when you said he was reassigned?"

"The Archbishop decided it was best to provide him a new venue in which to preach."

"Do you have any idea where he was sent?"

"Somewhere in Mexico, I think. I guess that in light of his monthly missionary visits to Tijuana, the Church felt it was an obvious move." Dana kicked off her shoes beneath her desk before putting her feet up.

"Why wasn't I made aware of the fact that a key player in this case had been moved to another country?"

"It's no longer your case, Tom, and besides it's been a few months now. I was informed that he was going to take some time off in between to go visit Canty's remaining family on the East Coast before moving. I think he went back East to deliver the cremated remains and preside over a memorial service."

"Was he moved as part of the FBI's witness protection program."

"No, it was just in response to some advice we provided." Dana still found the sound of Graves' voice, even when the conversation was about work, comforting.

Graves paused. "Why was he relocated then?"

"We were tipped off to some gang activity targeting him and advised him, or rather the Church, to do so."

"What type of gang activity?"

"We had reason to believe that the same group responsible for the death of Fin Canty and the disappearance of his daughter was impersonating FBI agents to get more information from him. We think they were trying to find her. It would seem that this gang-related crime was not as routine as we had assumed it was. We never got any further with that lead."

"Why not?" Graves had come to know Dana's bull dog nature and was astounded she wasn't able to pull the knot out of that string. Despite her soft features and trim athletic build, she was packing the personality worthy of two good agents . . . and wasn't afraid to push a few buttons to accomplish the job correctly.

"Father Moriel was of little value in providing any useful

information. He couldn't seem to recall anything important about our suspect, other than she was a young Hispanic female in a dark suit." The sight of her long legs up on her desk as they stretched out from beneath her skirt had begun to distract the testosterone burdened minions outside her office. "They'd only met once after the murder, at his church."

"There wasn't any video?"

"The point of entry the individual took was out of line-of-sight of any surveillance cameras. That includes those both of the church and the surrounding neighborhood. Our suggestions were taken as high as the leadership of the Catholic Church on the West Coast. We felt it was in Moriel's best interest for them to remove him from an already inflamed situation before we had another death to investigate."

"You trusted him?"

"No, but we still had no choice in the matter. It was the right thing to do. Besides, we watched him closely for months without anything even slightly suspicious going on." Her breath drew short, "Tom, where the hell is this going?"

There was a brief pause as Graves reconsidered telling Dana over the phone. "We received a cryptic e-mail message this morning from someone claiming to be Father Moriel. According to his message, he thinks he may have found our missing little girl in Mexico."

The visions had increased in frequency over the last year. They were nearly every night now. Some nights they seemed to consume his sleep fully, and on others they were just brief tastes of colors and sounds. No matter what their form, they were distinctive enough that, with each waking hour, Job knew he was still being watched and his role had not been forgotten. There was very little communication, though the message had clearly not changed. Job knew he was not the only disciple, but the beast never gave him more than his own instructions. He told Job where to find Azazel, but that was it. He demanded obedience if their arrangement were to be honored.

Neither tonight's dream nor any of the rituals beforehand had been any different. Throughout the months since the failure in Southern California, the beast had demanded sacrifice. Human bloodshed was paramount in the rituals, although it mattered not what was the source. To suffer discovery would undo all that had been planned, which left only one avenue of appeasement.

The offerings could not be evident. They had to be in locations that pleased his master, but did not betray him. In the beginning, the pain had limited Job's most courageous efforts to small cuts over his own arms and legs, but that had evolved. Tonight's offering was enough to save his Catholic faith, if not his own flesh. He prayed God would not condemn him for this betrayal, and the discoveries promised to him by the beast would justify all he had done, assuring forgiveness in his success.

The blood ran down Job's chest, curling around the muscles of his ribs and into his left armpit as he lay within his emptied tub. He withdrew the number ten blade from his upper chest, its route from his clavicle downward distinguishing itself from the previous night's efforts by the mounting crimson path it left behind. The sacrificial cut was deep into the belly of the muscle, sending the fibers into spasm. He could feel the warmth of the fluid collecting beneath him, contrasted between the coolness of the ceramic basin that supported him and his own skin. Job's pectoral and deltoid muscles twitched with the intense irritation brought about by the stainless steel blade as well as from the growing blood loss. His body's immediate response to this intrusion had already caused a radiant numbness that had inoculated his elbow and little finger. None of this was new, and yet every night was an adventure in tolerance. Job lay in place for several minutes as the rivulets of blood coursed downward toward the open drain, allowing for the full intent of his actions to be known. All in the name of the Lord, the one true Savior, for whom Job risked and sacrificed all. "The Lord is good," he muttered, pulling the blade further through his flesh. "Ours is not to wonder why, but to accept the path we've been given."

After rising, he pressed a thick dressing to his chest, allowing the direct force to slow the bloodletting. These lacerations were deep, though surgically administered. The months had left him mottled with the scars of his offerings, each in various stages of healing, all across his limbs and chest. The wounds often closed on their own within days, though the pain never fully receded. After completing his sacrifice and cleaning up, he turned in for the night.

Some nights, the visits began, it seemed, even before he was fully asleep. They began with the noises and smells. There were many voices. Powerful whispers that seemed like restrained screams filling the background. None were fully discernible, but all were tormented and ever present. There was the stench of burning flesh, which reminded him of the seared animals that, as a young boy, he and his father had killed and cooked on their extended hunting trips. Only here it was far more pungent. Often what he wished to see was blurred by the uncontrollable weeping he experienced at the mercy of this foul perfume. His skin, too, burned when exposed to the acrid filth that hung in the air. As he fell asleep, it began this way again tonight.

"I desire the little one here with me. She will serve to draw her father in." The swirling gold and brown cloud that shrouded Job's tormentor shook with his baritone voice as it settled, partially revealing a towering creature he had never fully laid eyes on. Shuddering at its cloven feet, Jobs felt his will to run leave him. He sank to his knees at the site of this decaying monster. The beast's face was recognizable only by its burning orange sockets, which fixated on him as it spoke. The very fires of Hell seemed to cast this demon into silhouette.

"How do we know he will oblige?" Job averted his eyes and remained prostrate.

"It has already begun. When he arrives, his choice to forsake his own salvation will have already secured mine." The swirling winds slowed and the whispers faded briefly into the distance. "Send her to me. Do not fail me this time."

Job woke with a start, his chest stinging with fresh blood slowly finding its way through the bandage into his silk night shirt. His arm throbbed and his fingers had only grown more numb since he'd fallen asleep. He slid his legs over the side of the bed. These dreams had seemed so unreal many months ago, but now, despite their otherworldliness, they felt to him as real as his waking vision. The Lord God was testing him, and he would not fail. His allegiance to his Catholic faith was strong, and no matter what punishments were suffered at the will of this demon, no matter what he had to sacrifice, he would not fail his God. So much had already been sacrificed, that there was no turning back now. He would see to it that the world had proof of the afterlife, a proof he so desperately wanted.

Job walked slowly to the bathroom and opened the medicine cabinet. Taking off his pajama top he replaced the saturated dressing and went back to bed. He hoped the remainder of the night's sleep would be peaceful.

CHAPTER 26

Sal could feel the nails of the old wooden kneeler denting the flesh of his knees. Genuflecting in the back of the small single-room church, Sal relished the growing discomfort he felt in his knees. He wondered how he'd fallen so far from a penitent lifestyle. Gazing around the inside of the aging building, he marveled at its darkly stained wooden walls and ceiling lofted high with the rough timbers that held them there for so long. This house of worship epitomized the Catholic religion as it was eons ago. Built centuries in the past in humble fashion, the parishioners had taken loving care of its aging wooden structure, nurturing its existence as it had theirs. The exterior white paint, sun-bleached cleaner than the day it was painted, was peeling under the powerful slow effects of the salty air. The church sat atop a balding hill whose slopes of swaying grasses ushered the wind and birds up to their outlook. Within its simple steeple was housed the three hundred-year-old brass bell now tarnished green with time. And protected inside, relieved of the burdens wrought daily by man's evils, were the generations of locals who prayed together for their eternal salvation. This was the family that had welcomed him and Eva with open arms, and without any questions.

The streams of light cast through the modest leaded glass windows created areas within this place that were provisionally stained with their color. Within these patches of light, on the floor at Sal's feet, sat little Eva, quietly humming to herself. Sal had drifted away from the visiting priest's sermon, his attention instead pulled by her simple song and unwavering purity as she traced patterns with her fingers in the thin dust that layered the worn wooden boards of the floor. Next to him knelt his seventy-year-old grandmother, listening to the new priest's words. Sal knew that she was secretly thrilled that he'd finally returned to the church.

"*This is more for her than me*," he had told himself. It seemed to make it easier for him to relinquish some of his guilt and take this first step.

"*A reading from the book of Job.*"

The new Padre had been in town for only a few weeks, though Sal noted that his grandmother seemed to be drawn to him already. Several times throughout his homily, the two had made eye contact, and she seemed quite pleased at that. Sal appreciated his American accent, but this small rotund man's ability to walk amongst the people, preaching without having to read the word of the Lord was what struck him most. He felt very safe here. This warm family atmosphere was what he longed for, and what Eva needed.

"*For God watches how people live;*
He sees everything they do."

The priest's words echoed off the solid floors and walls, giving them an even more virtuous feel.

"*No darkness is thick enough to hide the wicked from his eyes.*

We don't set the time when we will come before God in judgment.

He brings the mighty to ruin without asking anyone, and he sets up others in their place."

Sal remarked at how Father had preached most of this gospel without ever opening his eyes; he seemed to feel the spirit and allow the words to just pour forth. But a chill came over Sal as he listened to the homily. A chill that he had previously managed to cast aside with the optimism that this place encouraged.

"He knows what they do, and in the night he overturns and destroys them.

He strikes them down because they are wicked, doing it openly for all to see.

For they turned away from following him.

They have no respect for any of his ways.

They cause the poor to cry out, catching God's attention."

"Let's go," he said softly, turning to his Grandmother. "I think that we need to leave here." They were standing now, having risen in between their periods of kneeling. Sal felt anxious, or guilty. Either way, the priest's words had struck a chord that was making him uneasy.

"Relax, everything is fine Salvador." She gestured toward Eva where she sat, quietly playing beneath the pew. "After communion we'll stay a bit and talk with Father."

"No. We need to get home." He glanced down at Eva. In the dust that surrounded her, she had scrawled a series of tracings, each one the same as the next, differing from one another only in their size or orientation. Some large, some small, but all were the same symbol.

Sal knelt down again and admired her work. He reached out and softly caressed her long black hair. "What are you drawing, baby." He asked her quietly.

At first Eva didn't answer. She carefully finished the figure she was working on then looked up at him. "My daddy."

Surprised at her answer he took a closer look at her scribbling. She hadn't mentioned her father for several months now.

Sal scrutinized her collage. The symbols were the composite of a circle with a single line emanating upwards through its center.

Over and over again she had inscribed these simple figures in the dust wherever her little arms could reach without smearing what she had already drawn.

The remainder of the parish joined Sal in kneeling. His anxiety was mounting.

"Ok, after communion, but then we leave. I don't want to stick around today," Sal whispered.

His grandmother looked disappointed. "I told Father that today he would get to meet you and Eva. He seemed very interested in meeting you both."

Sal hated to let her down. "I'm sorry, not today, maybe next week."

After receiving the Eucharist, their small family exited the back of the church, like part-time Catholics, before the closing prayer. Their drive home was nearly silent with only Eva talking. She was carrying on a conversation of her own with an unseen partner.

"Who are you talking to sweetie?" her Abuela asked.

"No one . . . am I going to see Daddy soon?" The two front seat passengers exchanged brief glances.

"It was inevitable, Sal." His grandmother spoke softly. "She's nearly four years old. We have to talk with her about it sooner or later."

"That's the second time today she's mentioned him." He

answered in mirrored tone. He was starting to feel more uneasy.

"Why do you ask, Eva?" Sal projected his voice into the rear view mirror. He was curious why this subject had lain dormant for so long and had only now come up again.

"He misses me."

Any reply to her triumphant answer was cut short by surprise as they entered their driveway. He was shocked to see the front door to their simple stucco house ajar. "Did we forget to close the door?" Sal asked rhetorically as he pulled up their stone drive. He regarded the home cautiously. Nothing else seemed grossly out of place.

He pulled to a stop a few yards from the front walk. "Wait here. I've been having a funny feeling all day." He grasped the door handle and released his seatbelt. Letting the belt slide over his left shoulder, he opened his door and put a foot down. "Just let me take a look around first, then I'll come out to get you two." He left the car running and disappeared around the back of the house.

At the back door Sal noted deep impressions in the wet sand. "Shit," he muttered under his breath. There had been some petty crime in the area as of late, small break-ins despite the limited extent of the community. The locals felt it was a result of the increasing numbers of tourists. Sal took a deep breath, trying to keep his anxiety at bay and not overreact to any of this. He unlocked the door and entered the back hallway.

He could hear the TV on, but that was something that was not uncommon. Eva had recently discovered she could turn it on and off by herself, and she often left it on as they exited the house. Sal felt his heart rate climbing and his adrenaline beginning to flow. He quietly closed the door behind him and melted into the bedroom immediately to his right.

176

The room was well lit and empty. There was no sign of any disturbance. He reached into his chest of drawers beneath his boxers and withdrew his nine mil. The rounds were in the clip which was kept separately from the gun for Eva's safety. Rising up onto his toes, he claimed it from the top of the sill that bordered the room. With one forceful motion he introduced the rounds into the weapon, driving the clip home with a hearty snap and forcing the release button out of its tunnel.

Sal paused for a moment, listening for any movement. Turning, he made his way heel to toe out into the hallway and down toward the main room and the breakfast area. As he slowly covered the ground toward the front of the house, he took the weapon off safety and drew back the slide, chambering a round.

Sal stopped as he reached the breadth of Eva's room on his right. Glancing in, he noted sand on the ceramic floor in front of her small throw rug. A sound of a chair dragging across the tile snapped his glance back toward the kitchen.

Could this be happening?

He had convinced himself that he'd been safe.

How could they have found me?

He was sure he hadn't left any trail for them to follow.

"Get control of yourself," he breathed. He reflexively flinched at another abrupt noise. This one seemed far bolder than the last.

"I never should have left the women in the car."

He took a deep breath and tried hard to swallow his anxiety. Sal burst around the corner aiming his weapon into the kitchen, his heart pounding in his throat.

"Mother fucker!" He lowered his gaze and dropped the weapon to his side. "Get out! Out!" A dirty little yellow dog cowered at Sal's outburst. It had somehow found its way into the house and was rooting through their garbage. It had made an absolute mess out of the kitchen. "Fuckin' mutt. Out!" The animal raised its head to acknowledge him as it moved toward the front door, tail between its legs. Making eye contact with him as it passed, the dog suddenly dropped its ears and averted its gaze toward the dark blur that consumed Sal's peripheral vision. Before he could react, Sal was met with a sharp blow across his temple. His perfect world blurred briefly before everything went black.

Moriel walked the length of the small church, shaking hands with all his new parishioners as he made his way toward the pew he'd seen the old woman sitting in. She had made such an effort to let him know of their situation that he couldn't help but expect to find the unexpected, Eva.

He'd not been able to glimpse any child sitting with them throughout the service, but he still had faith that he'd found her. In the hectic shuffle that is Catholic communion, coupled with the mass exodus often resulting from a long sermon, he'd lost track of them. Had he passed the pew where they were waiting? Had they gone already? She'd seemed so adamant that they all meet today. Something unusual caught his eye as he turned toward the foyer.

To his left, in a pew toward the back of the church, was a young Hispanic woman. She was kneeling down, not in prayer, but rather seemed to be inspecting something on the floor. She was softly crying, her body shuddering with each wave of emotion. Father watched her for a moment, her fingers tracing a pattern on the floor again and again in the golden afternoon light. He took a few more steps toward her.

Feeling his eyes upon her, Maria turned upwards toward Father. For a moment both froze, stunned in their unexpected reunion. Looking past her toward the floor, Moriel laid his hand gently on her shoulder. His brow furrowed as he focused on the patterns drawn in the dust beneath her.

Amidst her weeping, Maria confessed. "She was here. I've seen these images in Azazel's writings." She pointed toward Eva's tracings in the dust, her tears blurring the borders of the icons as they fell. "I missed them, Father, I missed them, and now he'll find her."

"My God," Father whispered as he crossed himself. Brushing against the small medallion in his breast pocket that Eva had given him so many months ago, he realized he'd seen this symbol before too.

CHAPTER 27

He woke where he'd fallen, but in an uncomfortably con-trived position. Sal's head was pounding and just moving his eyes seemed to make his vision blur. He was on his back with his arms outstretched to either side of him with his feet together. He recognized his position as that of his parents repose as he'd found them so many years ago. He could make out a figure pacing in short circuit just beyond his reach.

"You thought you could hide from us?" Azazel was seething with anger. "Did you think we wouldn't find you? Ey, Mutt?"

"What'ya gonna' do, Azazel, kill me for leaving?" Sal propped himself up on his elbow knowing full well this was Azazel's plan. His gun caught his eye, gleaming in the morning light by the door where it had fallen.

"You can try for it, hermano, but you'll never make it."

Sal sat up slowly, holding his head where he'd been struck. A knot was already beginning to form over his temple.

"I'm going to kill you *both* for leaving. Where is she?"

"Where's who?" He winced, settling back a bit.

"The little girl. I took care of the old bitch in the car already. She was an easy target while you were out. You're gettin' soft, Mutt. It's the little girl I want." Azazel stood over him, allowing Sal to get a good look at him now.

"What *happened* to you?" Azazel was gaunt, and his skin had taken on a grayish appearance, a nearly translucent cov-ering through which his veins seemed to scream for escape.

His head was covered with sparse patches of thinning hair that revealed a white scalp beneath it.

"Did you recognize the position you woke in? I only use that for special occasions . . . like with your parents." The pleasure he took in revealing this secret was betrayed by his vast smile. "I told you things weren't always as they seemed."

Sal's fury overwhelmed him. He rose to his feet with his fists clenched in anger and took a few unsteady steps toward his former friend. "You son of a bitch . . ."

From only a few feet away Azazel pointed his weapon, stiff armed, at Sal's face. "We needed more native blood. You slick white-boy wannabe's fall nicely in line with just a little coaxing. And that's all it took," he added with a smirk, "just a little coaxing." He drew the hammer of his weapon back, arming the firing pin with a muted click. "I'd watched you for a while, with your button-down shirts and school books. Your parents' execution gave me a little more practice at my craft, and something else too, something I wasn't sure I could count on. It gave me you, my financial expert . . . and a brother," he added sarcastically.

"I was never your brother you sick son of a . . ."

Azazel took a few steps forward, forcefully shutting Sal up by reducing his firing range. "I was lost then," he said as he pointed the muzzle of his weapon into Sal's face, "before Him, but not now. Since we've formed a team, my mission is clear. Now I'm going to finish what I started—I'm going to finish the Master's work."

The sound of a closing car door turned Azazel's head just long enough for Sal to swiftly cover the ground between them. The two men flew back as Sal's superior weight crashed them both into the far side of the coffee table, throwing its contents up into the air. Amidst the broken wood and glass, Sal frantically clutched Azazel's blood-splattered wrists as they both struggled for an advantage.

Sal forced Azazel firmly to the floor. Grimacing from the searing pain in his ribs, Azazel summoned every ounce of his strength to turn his opponent. In Azazel's emaciated state, Sal far outweighed and outmuscled him.

But slowly, as if by some sinister force, Sal's strength left him. He could feel the willingness to fight drain from his body. In his darkening stupor, he noticed it—the crimson liquid that bathed them both was his, and not his enemy's. The deep jagged laceration in his wrist left by the fractured glass was hemorrhaging his strength with each pulsatile ejection. He limply rolled off his attacker onto the floor. Desperately clutching his left wrist, he could feel the tepid jets of blood force their way through his fingers into a mist that was beginning to cover everything around them.

Azazel rose to his feet. Covered in his brother's blood, he raised his weapon again. "Adios, hermano."

Sal heard the sharp crack of a firearm discharge, but could feel only the chill of his own blood loss. He wondered if death brought a peace that prevented him from experiencing further pain. Opening his eyes, Sal was met with the site of his old friend staring down in disbelief at an expanding stain on his own shirt. Azazel was clutching his abdomen as he began to stagger backwards. Standing not five feet behind him, silhouetted by the open doorway, stood Eva. Her loose grip on Sal's weapon had given way to its recoil, and she had dropped it with a heavy thud onto the ceramic floor. Wisps of smoke from its spent shell drifted upwards from the barrel. Azazel unwillingly dropped to his knees and turned his attention toward Eva.

Sal lay in silent horror with his head propped uncomfortably against the side of the couch. Watching the events unfold, and unable to stop any of it in his weakened state, his vision faded as the warmth of his life poured onto the floor beneath him.

Azazel collapsed as aortic blood coursed through his fresh wound. Focusing his decayed spirit, he managed his last living act of evil.

In his dying moments, the last thing Sal heard was the snap of one final round leaving the muzzle of Azazel's weapon. As his soul departed, it did so with the knowledge that he'd failed in his promise to God. Sal's angel had become, in defense of his sins, an unrepentant sinner in her last minutes on earth.

CHAPTER 28

Clutching his chest in an agony that rivaled his own death, Fin stumbled into deeper waters. The pain he was feeling was a visceral one. Though nothing had physically happened to him, the sensation of having something penetrate his being was overwhelming. He regained his footing and stood. Now in only waist deep water, his family seemed to fade into the distance. He held out an open palm motioning for them to stay where they were.

"I can't stay." He called toward them as they seemed to recede from him. "I understand now what Dad meant. I can't stay here any longer." An insidious current pulled at his feet, one he had never noticed before in this lake. This latent river beckoned him to enter deeper waters. Walking backwards Fin continued, "I'm sorry, I love you Rachel, but I have to find her."

With tears falling, Rachel ran into the shallows of the lake after him. Her mother-in-law grabbed her arm. "Dear, you can't go where he's headed . . . your bond with Eva is not the same. Our souls are at rest, because they're whole, but not everyone's the same that way. Some of us have soul mates, and those mates don't have be our partners in life. Fin's soul was never whole here, and it can't remain here if it's not, Eva is Fin's soul mate ...she's the other half that completes his salvation. His fate lies along a different line from here, from us." They watched as Fin continued further out. Slowly sinking into his providence, he continued to make his way from them.

Fin had turned and was facing the open water. With the other side of the lake no longer visible to him, he could see only the water stretching out before him. Feeling his feet leave the soft, silty bottom, he began to drift. The water seemed rougher and warmer than it had from the shore, the waves occasionally washing over his face. The whispers had returned, though the voice of his mother was not amongst them. He knew they were calling to him, summoning him further, though he couldn't understand what they were saying. The waves were larger still, each one forcing his mass up and over its crest with a surge and a fall that drove him momentarily beneath the surface. Fin sputtered and coughed as he fought to stay afloat.

His perspective had been lost. He saw only a surrounding haze that was growing darker with each passing moment. Thoughts of Eva and her pain tortured him in his fearful state as he struggled to stay up, the water now forcing its way into his nose and down his throat. Fin coughed spastically as he remembered the nightmares he'd had after Rachel's death. His every effort to breathe was met with a deluge that suffocated him further. At first he held his breath, waiting for an opportunity to replenish the spent air that filled his lungs, but each attempt was met with a further wall of water that stoked his anxiety. Finally, with his searing lungs no longer able to tolerate the air hunger, Fin reflexively drew in a full breath. The stinging liquid rushed down his trachea and filled his chest, sending a wave of burning spasms throughout his torso. In his panic, he clawed at the surface of the water from below, managing to break the plane one last time. With his energy spent and his panic giving way to a compassionate indifference, Fin slipped below the surface for the final time.

From the shore, Fin's family watched in horror as he was

consumed by the torrent. The water seemed to rise up unnaturally around him in its effort to draw him under. From where he had vanished, a whirlpool began to take shape. At first evident only as a tiny dimple in the surface, this whirlpool grew as its anger dragged the surrounding waters around with it in an ever increasing diameter. A strong breeze began to blow offshore, seeming to obey the will of this expanding vortex, or perhaps the will of the victim it had swallowed.

Fin initially remained buoyant enough to see the choppy surface above him as he slowly sank beneath it. Suffocating, he felt the unremitting torture of drowning without the release of death. The gray waters became darker and warmer as he succumbed to this new hell. Fighting the return of the pressure in his chest over and again, he began to feel a rise in the temperature of the water he was descending into. Initially the growing warmth was no competition for the agony he was feeling in his lungs, but at some point the focus shifted. Descending into the dark, the heat of the waters began to burn his legs, cooking the flesh off his bones as he drifted deeper and deeper.

Through the onslaught of the boiling waters, Fin began to feel a tugging at his feet. At first he blindly reached toward this phantom sensation, finding the curling sheets of skin and muscle with his fingertips as it all now hung, boiled off his lower limbs. The minute taps became firm grasps that drew him deeper still into the scorching blackness. Hands clawed at him, pulling him hungrily into their midst. Fin could see shapes around him, rubbing up against him as he lost his sensation of movement entirely. Below him, he saw the glow of a tiny orange cinder emerging from the blackness. This ember grew as the shapes all around him became recognizable as bodies. They grasped at him, either in fear of descending further or in a tormented attempt to climb out of this hell. He could see the light growing, its center now white hot. The limbs and fingers that tugged at him propelled him toward this light, pushing at him, rather than pulling as they had before.

Looking upward toward the starting point of his descent, Fin saw the faces of these godforsaken souls, eerily pale in the green water. Grimaces and silent screams distorted the countless tortured faces as they sank into the depths. Behind him, through the vortex that had drawn him here, a clear channel remained. Fin could see brief glimpses outside this place, but the lake and trees he'd just left were gone. In their place was a metallic tunnel, lined with gold. At the end of this tunnel, Fin could see eight arms rising from the center, like a massive metallic starfish. Squinting, he tried to see more detail, but his view was obstructed by the bodies around him, as well as his own flesh as it was pulled from his legs back into this void. Eventually this channel disappeared completely from his view, swallowed by his new reality.

The ember beneath him grew larger, taking up more of his view. This light beckoned Fin toward another reality. Another brane to his torment, one through which he might find Eva. The pain he had felt in his legs faded as the broken limbs and cursing mouths hauled him up to the surface of the roiling water. Carrying him in some perverse procession, they passed him onward, hand over hand, tearing at him as he traveled over them. Fin no longer felt the pain in his chest, but the throbbing in his back had returned with vehemence.

As the horde deposited him on the bank of this fetid body of water, Fin noted his legs were bleeding but were otherwise uninjured. Dry heat blasted him in the face as he sat barefoot and shivering on the scorched and barren shore. From his shoulder blades protruded small nubs like antlers, and from around them trickled tiny rivulets of blood, which ran down the broken skin of his back. Contorting his arm he was able to awkwardly run his fingers over his left scapula. There was no pain, only a firm rocky nodule that stuck out. Off in the distance, a stand of mountains broke through the sulfur yellow haze that hung above the land. Their peaks extended up into a fiery orange sky and the black clouds that hovered there. He was alone, but away from the setting sun he could feel a warmth that pulled at him. She was somewhere in that direction. His little GOTU was here, and Fin felt closer to heaven than ever.

CHAPTER 29

The young female post-graduate dressed in her white waist-length coat looked more like a medical student than a budding world-class particle physicist. Edvard stood on a wooden gantry overlooking the main collider room 300 feet below the surface. "Dr. Krunowski! Sir, I'd like you to come to the auxiliary control room to see something."

There'd been coolant problems with the collider's magnets, and without them the beam wouldn't follow the prescribed arcing path of the circuit. If not for the strong, steering magnetic field, the beam would head off on its own wild tangent away from the circular path of the accelerator. Once it got through the walls of the tube, the annihilation it would bring about was unimaginable.

"There's something on the monitors that I think you should see, something that I'd like your input on." She hurried on ahead of him, her heels clicking on the gantry walkway. Like an excited school girl, he thought.

The last few weeks had been difficult ones. Despite mourning the loss of one of their own, the scientists in the core group were still putting in long hours weekly. It was a lot to ask, and it was adding to the difficulty of keeping this goliath up and running. The staff had diminished from the initial two thousand workers who converged here from around Europe over the past decade. After this initial contraction however, an ensuing big bang had forced their numbers to grow again as the facility came on line. The early manual labor for the site's excavation ultimately gave way to a far more technically oriented assembly of the pieces. Large numbers of skilled workers had been recruited from the oil drilling and roughneck industry, the civil engineering industry, and the European Space Agency. In between these large niches, all the gaps were filled in by handfuls of individuals with unique skills in such areas as fiber optic communications, metallurgy, disaster planning, and the small but growing magnetic levitation transportation firms from Germany and Japan. This place had developed into a bustling city, one whose collective emotions periodically bounced between the great highs of discovery and the lows of technical difficulties. The technical difficulties were currently pinning spirits to the mat.

Edvard made his way across the maze of gantries, following the intern toward the auxiliary control room. The initial plan had been to dismantle all the wooden supports to clean up the collider area, but with the frequent shutdowns it seemed a better idea to leave the scaffolds in place, at least for the time being. This area of the construction had come to be known affectionately as the bat cave because of the way it looked during the excavation. The tall arching dirt ceilings and the tunnels leading off in either direction had given this place the appearance of a subterranean habitat. Its current look, however, was one of clean ceramic tiles—tan and grey tiles covering the arch of the roof and the walls and white ones covering the six-foot-thick aviation-grade concrete that supported the machine's massive weight. The glistening five-story gem that sat in the middle of all this was their jewel of modern science.

Edvard had been to the auxiliary control room, or ACR, as it had come to be known, quite a few times in the last several days regarding "new discoveries." All of these discoveries, to his frustration, had ended up being software glitches and nothing more, likely a result of the failing coolant system. He was beginning to miss Fin for new and increasingly technical reasons.

The ACR was a rudimentary wooden shack sitting twenty-five feet above the main chamber floor atop its own spindly steel legs. It served as a makeshift waypoint to be used during periods of repair, permitting adequate testing control of the collider and its subsequent systems without requiring workers to travel all the way up to the main control room on the surface.

Three hundred feet above them, the main control room resembled something one would expect to see at a NASA facility, only grander. Its towering main wall of LCD screens fed vital information to the controllers. At the center of these smaller screens was mounted the mother of them all, the main display that conveyed the actions and interactions taking place within the main reactor chamber. The individual controllers sat at their respective desks around their own flat screen displays, monitoring numbers that embodied their life's passions. The data displayed included the collider's internal variables, such as temperatures and pressures, collider chamber mass, mass spectrometry preliminary data, beam velocity, vacuum integrity, and all aspects of the magnetic control systems. Overlooking this mural of data were rows of booths resembling the tiered galleries of a classical opera house. The booths were initially built for oversight control, but the top management had quickly realized what an untapped resource for PR they represented. These plush booths had been modified for use by dignitaries and VIPs who came to offer up their money for the cause. They were shown the cutting-edge, Hollywood-esque computer control arena, and then they were taken down below for the real show.

At the top of the ladder, Edvard pushed open the wooden door and climbed into the ACR. The inside of the room was as sparse as the outside. A large sheet of Lexan framed in raw two-by-fours served as their window down onto the ant farm of workers scrambling beneath them. "What am I looking at?" He moved closer to the main screen, squinting as he did so.

"Well, sir, it's not so much new information, but rather a new way of looking at the information that we've been collecting all along." The graduate student turned her attention to the screen as she took her seat. She performed a tight ballet with the mouse to navigate through its myriad windows.

"Where did you acquire this program?" Edvard was a little startled at the images he was seeing.

"It's one I found buried in a subset of folders. I believe it's one of Dr. Canty's. It was labeled . . ."

"I know what it's labeled, please go on."

"Sir, if you look at the composite images rendered, the vast majority of the mass being generated is coming straight out of the center of the chamber. There are still offshoots from that, but it seems to be an increasingly coherent beam over time. If I select this option . . .," she clicked on the rudimentary icon of a clock in the bottom left corner of the screen and the simple binary colored still image came to life. "There. You can watch the geometric progression of the matter we've been measuring as a function of time." She pointed at the screen while looking up over her shoulder at him. "See, over the last few months it slowly progresses from random bits and pieces being emitted in all directions, into this rather coherent beam-like emission. And, if you look at the entire progression, the beam has gained a tremendous amount of its focus just within the last day."

The thousands of swirling green and red dots, that previously seemed random in their motion, slowly coalesced. This new image formed a fountain of matter streaming outward from a central point. Emanating from a glowing halo, this beam struck the side of its container before scattering again.

"I see, and what do you make of that?"

"Initially it reminded me of a jet of material exiting a black hole or a blazar."

"Well it's not." Edvard's statement was surprisingly blunt, even to him. "What I mean to say is that we're not detecting any other phenomenon associated with the like, such as increased gravity, or radiation. It's a good thought, but . . ."

"I agree, sir, but if I may finish . . ."

His jaw tightened.

"What it does remind me of is a white hole." The small wooden hut fell silent as her gaze landed in his.

"It was only a matter of time, I suppose," he groaned under his breath. Then he said aloud, "That's impressive, my dear, but how do you figure that?"

"Well, as is the basis for most equations that we use, every action has an equal and opposite reaction. A black hole is seemingly in possession of near infinite gravity. It swallows up all matter to include light. In accordance with Einstein's theory, the opposite of this end would be a white hole. An object of equal mass to its sibling that spews matter outward."

"That is all very interesting, and impressive," Edvard continued on coldly. "However, this astrophysical unicorn has never been seen, nor has its existence been mathematically proven in any theorem. It only looks good on paper."

"Yes, but many of us still support the theory that these white holes do exist, only on the opposite end of the rip in space-time that these super massive black holes create." She paused for a minute, carefully continuing on. "What if the wormhole that connected these entities were a passageway for matter, no matter how small, between dimensions. And what if these white holes served as a kind of exit from this black hole destruction, spewing forth creation at the other end of the funnel?"

"That's a beautiful sentiment, but how do you explain that we've never seen one in the tens of thousands of galaxies we've found black holes in. Or in the billions, if not trillions, of light-years of space we've combed. No one has shown that an Einstein-Rosen bridge, or wormhole as you called it, truly exists. However, despite this preponderance of evidence against it, you're suggesting that we've accidentally created one here?"

"What about the Big Bang?" she added sheepishly. "The birth of our universe and the beginning of time and space as we accept it? It was the very moment of our own creation. What if the Big Bang were the last time that this universe has seen one? The very essence of communication from beyond."

Edvard stood staring at this unassuming twenty-eight-year-old graduate student. Her long brown hair was drawn up in a bun, and with each word she spoke her glasses slowly inched their way down closer to the tip of her nose. She looked as if she'd not seen the light of day in weeks, but was wearing two different colored nail polishes that alternated between black and white with each finger. He was speechless. "Who else knows about your theory?"

"No one. I was just sitting here staring out the window and saw you as this all gathered form in my head. So I came and found you. Why?"

Edvard stood with his hands resting comfortably in his

pockets, shaking his head from side to side. "Amazing, absolutely amazing. He motioned toward the door. "Please. This is a phenomenal theory, but it is just a theory at the moment. This needs to be formalized." He stepped back a pace, all that the small shack would allow, providing his newly discovered star pupil first passage toward the door.

As she slid her body between him and the console, she allowed her eyes to meet his. He placed his hand softly on her shoulder, her firm young muscles obvious beneath her thin garments. In the heat of the cavern, she had left her lab coat agape and he caught a fleeting glimpse of her unencumbered breasts beneath her thin silk blouse. Edvard had noticed her before; she was naturally beautiful, but inconspicuous. His hand slid up to the soft curve along the nape of her neck as he moved with her one step closer to the open door.

For too long she had toiled away as just another scientist in training, fit to digest and spit out numbers without any recognition. Edvard was an older man, but not an unattractive one. The female students spoke of him in Indiana Jones fashion, someone who both excited them as women and simultaneously comforted them like a father. This line of work seldom came with a thrilling social life.

With their two bodies approaching the portal, Edvard set his jaws firmly together. He turned her to face him and, pulling the clip from her tight coil, allowed his fingers to comb up through her thick soft hair, momentarily gripping a handful tightly. Their eyes met briefly as she nervously licked the corner of her mouth. Catching the heel of her flats on the subtle rise before the entrance, her mass left his grip and she struck her head with all her weight against the frame of the door. The crack of the two objects echoed throughout the small corrugated shack. Her body slumped downward and her momentum ushered her out the open door. Unconscious, her body fell unhindered to the floor twenty-five feet below. Edvard peered out over the landing. A few workers had already begun to move toward the body. He quickly turned, grabbed the radio on the desk, and depressed the button.

His voice cracking, he barked, "I need help at the ACR. There's been an accident!" Crossing himself in prayer, he exited the shack. Edvard descended to the project's lowest level and joined the growing crowd as they waited for help.

The soles of Salvador's feet were fissured and cracked from the rocky ground he had been forced to travel over. Panting heavily as he ran, this tortuous crossing had torn them open, leaving his wounds to be packed full of stinging sand. The unbroken vector of blood had long since dwindled, but the trail he was leaving them to follow had remained.

Sal's banishment to Hell was inevitable. The sins he had committed in life were unforgivable, even if his intentions toward the end of his days were good. It felt like he had been running for weeks, trying desperately to stay ahead of his demons. After Eva's murder, everything had changed so quickly. How long had he been here? His mind was clouded, confused. No matter how hard he tried, this place seemed to steal his focus. The thoughts of being back home in his parent's house, or in Todos Santos with Eva, were now fading memories beneath the intensity of this new place.

The sound of his own claws clicked against the rocks as he tried to gain purchase on this unforgiving terrain before sinking back into the scorching sand. It made perfect sense for him to be here, but why was Eva here, or her father for that matter? Sal's mind whirled as he tried to make sense of it all.

Off in the distance he could make out dry trails of dust wafting up into the acrid air. Whatever, or whoever, moved across the dry valley floor ahead of him appeared to have the same goal. He had to get to him before they did, to warn, or to help. His own grotesque disfigurement was testament to the power of this place. If Eva really was the bait, then there was no telling what these creatures had in store for them all.

Sal's thighs burned as he churned through the deep sand, dragging one emaciated limb after another from its grip. He would not fail her. He had made a promise to protect Eva in life or in death, and he would not fail her again.

Coming to rest half way down the slope of a large dune, Sal peered out over the scorched valley. The shifting winds brought the scent of decaying flesh, a smell he had been grateful to avoid for several days now. Turning to face those who were condemned before him, their howls stung his ears as their decrepit forms crested the dune.

The creatures began cascading in his direction, hunched over and moving like a pack of wolves. Sal could make out their luminous eyes in the failing light. He felt the hemorrhage of his humanity as he again prepared for battle. Every interaction was drawing him deeper into this place, and he didn't have much left before he would forget himself . . . and his real purpose for being here.

CHAPTER 30

Graves sat on an uncomfortable worn wooden bench in the corner of the precinct. The Mexican officials here seemed resentful of his intrusion into their business, not to mention their country. "I'm glad you're here. They haven't even let me see her yet!" Graves was noticeably overheated, but he couldn't help feeling better as his partner approached. Dana had her long, thick black hair drawn up in a single pony tail today, and her her dark eyes made her high cheekbones seem more pronounced than he remembered. Graves had come down to Todos Santos at the request of the FBI because of his involvement with the investigation, but he had accepted the assignment for other reasons. Rising to his feet to greet her, he continued, "We were promised by the local law enforcement that we'd get total cooperation in this investigation. Don't they understand this is an open case we've been working on for over a year now? There's been no sign of any collegiality."

"Relax, you're not going to get anything accomplished here with that hurry up attitude. Besides, you know things here are not like they used to be. The extradition treaty President Jimmy Carter signed in '78 became Mexican law in 1980. In 2001 the Supreme Court of Mexico ruled that extradition would be governed by the corresponding punishment established by the United States penal code. If they think we're going to put her to death, they have the right not to give her to us."

Dana sat with him. She placed her hand on his arm to calm

him down. "They're refusing to extradite her on the grounds we can't guarantee she won't get the death penalty."

"So all the lobbying the US State department has been doing for the continued involvement of the Bureau has gone to waste?" Graves's frustration still percolated beneath the surface.

"In the last few years, despite all the 'free trade' agreements, gang related crime has become a sticking point between our two governments. MS-13 activities aren't foreign to folks south of the U.S. border, and most Central American countries blame the United States for pushing this species of organized crime into their backyards." She looked up as she spoke. Offering a friendly smile to the man who was approaching, Dana finished quickly in a hushed voice. "Relax, let me talk with the local magistrate. I have a card to play that they're not yet aware of."

Dana rose and greeted the well-dressed, older gentleman. They exchanged what seemed to Graves to be pleasantries in Spanish before taking a few steps away into a private office.

As Dana walked off, Graves could not help but notice the growing number of elderly women gathering in the lobby of the precinct. They were clothed in traditional funeral attire with long loosely fitting black dresses, some of them complete with veils that covered their faces. He walked closer to see if he could get a better feel for what was happening.

The women were keeping primarily to themselves in a tight group, all carrying rosary beads, and most were softly chanting. He assumed they were praying, but one woman seemed to be leading the group. She was pleading openly with the local official behind the gated desk. Graves stopped one of the officers as he passed, "What is she asking?" He gestured toward the rustic bars of the dimly lit front desk.

The officer looked him up and down disapprovingly before answering him. In a thick Hispanic accent he said "She wishes to see de' one that found de' signs."

It had already been three days since the murders, and the scene at the home had been trampled to a state of uselessness dozens of times over by what Graves considered an incompetent local police force. He had gone to the house earlier when he realized he wasn't going to make any headway at the precinct without his obligatory FBI chaperone. He'd found dozens of tire tracks in the sand from the multiple police cars that had driven through the crime scene, innumerable footprints of all types, and the house unlocked with most of the contents already removed or looted. Graves had appreciated early on that any hope of accomplishing his goals here in Todos Santos lay with the young woman now locked up in this seaside Mexican jail.

Dana finally returned with the older gentleman. As they passed, Dana announced her success to Graves with a wink, while attempting to muster some sort of overt appreciation for the gesture they were about to receive. "Señor Valenzuela is the local magistrate. He will allow us the time we need with our prisoner."

"That's wonderful." Graves made deliberate eye contact with their host. "Please tell him T H A N K Y O U." He pronounced the last portion of his sentence slowly and slightly louder than the rest.

Señor Valenzuela turned sharply on his heels after unlocking the cell door. He looked Detective Graves in the eyes and answered "Y O U ' R E W E L C O M E" with a slow and deliberate sarcasm before departing. Without turning back to face his guests as he left he announced in impeccable English,

"My guard will be watching through our closed circuit monitors. Before you leave, please close her cell and let my man know that you are finished."

Dana looked at her partner before entering the cell. After staring at him for what seemed like an eternity, she closed her deep brown eyes briefly and shook her head from side to side in contrived disgust. "Nice . . ." Holding the door open, she gestured with a deep sigh for Graves to enter before her. Carrying in two chairs from the hallway, they entered the darkened cell.

The room was abysmal. The once white walls wore stains that ranged from the rusted-colored tributaries running from the pipes above to the urine patchwork that surrounded the unshielded toilet mounted to the crumbling stucco wall. The light in the single cell came from the flickering overhead lamp and the sunlight that shone through the bars of the sole window located high on the south wall. In the corner of the cell, on the floor, curled up with her arms around her knees, Maria sat softly crying. As the two approached her, she looked up.

"I think I could'a stopped him. He killed that little girl, didn't he? He killed her." Her sentence dissolved into her tears as she continued to rock in place. "Did you catch him?"

The two detectives exchanged subtle glances. Dana spoke first. "He's dead sweetheart. They're all dead. Why didn't you call me?"

Graves looked at Dana in bewilderment. "You know her?"

"I did. We'd been following the movements of a few prostitution rings in the area when one of their big-time pimps turned up dead near the interstate. Maria had been working for him, and we brought her in for questioning. She thought it had been this Azazel who'd ordered the execution, and she'd already been indoctrinated into the gang. She was looking for a way out too. We didn't want to tip Salvatrucha's hand, so we had Maria act as our mole. She deposed Sal in the van that first night, the gang got their traitor, and we got our financial information."

"What happened?" Graves was still stunned.

"The faction thought she was a star, and we were going to get a look at the gang's books, thanks to her. We never got a chance to get our hands on them though. Two nights later, Dr. Canty was killed, and Salvador crossed the border, disappearing with all the information she'd risked her life for. We had nothing to pin on the high-ranking individuals, and Maria vanished back into MS-13 after that."

"Why didn't you run?" Graves was impressed with this girl's fight.

"To where . . . and with what? Everything I'd promised the FBI was gone, and I was an accomplice to murder. Azazel should've died that night, that bastard. I prayed more than once that he would. He nearly bled out in that front seat, but somehow he managed to recover. They had everything on me, and I had nothing to take away."

"What can you tell us about the last few weeks?" Dana looked like she actually felt badly for her. All the anger and loathing was easily replaceable with pity in this place.

"Is the priest still alive?" Maria asked desperately.

"How did you know about the priest?" Graves was confused.

"After that night, after Sal fled, I got to thinking about the man John killed. He was concerned about all of us that night in the rain, he came right up to the window and asked if we were all ok. Why would they kill someone like that? When that man's name was released in the paper a few days later, I set up a meeting with the priest at the church the article said his funeral would be at. I went in as an FBI agent again." Her lower jaw started to quiver, and she covered her face in her hands again.

Dana crouched down and placed her hand on Maria's shoulder. "It seems local officials have allowed Father Moriel to leave the country. Albeit temporarily, but he's fine."

"What?" Graves blurted out, turning in surprise toward Dana again.

"They've already cremated the little girl's body, and the priest is taking her ashes to meet Canty's family overseas for a joint ceremony . . . we'll talk about it later." Turning her attention back to their informant, she continued. "This is detective Graves of the LAPD. Please, continue."

"It was a hit. All of it, it was all a contract. I just never thought they'd find her."

Graves stood with his mouth agape. "The little girl was a contract? Are you shitting me? You're saying this four-year-old was killed because someone wanted a toddler dead? How in the hell . . ."

Dana shot him a look as she placed a hand on his arm. Taking the cue, Graves sat down.

"I'm sorry Ms. Ramos, please continue." Dana offered her the seat she'd brought in. Rising from the floor to accept the offer, both officers took note of the tattoos emblazoned across Maria's upper back as they showed through the straps of her tank top.

"It was all a hit," she continued as she sat, "even starting with her father a year earlier."

"Was it the same individuals who ordered both?" Dana asked.

"It was the same person, I think. He called himself Job

and said he represented a group called ARCH." Her crying had slowed, and she was pausing in her sentences now, except for the occasional involuntary sob. "Azazel just thought that the whole friggin' thing was divine." She breathed deeply and closed her eyes before allowing her head to sink to her chest.

Dana prodded gently, her voice taking on a nurturing quality as she continued. "What else? What do you mean divine?" Dana had learned early on that empathy, even if feigned, was a powerful tool in getting important witnesses to open up. In cases where they were already distraught and looking for a connection, it made it even easier.

"Azazel was having these . . . these visions, or something. He kept saying his prophet wanted this to happen, and that his dreams and these instructions from Job were no coincidence. He felt this was all part of some bigger plan and that we needed to find the girl, too."

"How much money are we talking about here?" Graves rejoined the conversation, this time with a little more humility. "The contract, how much was it for?"

"A few hundred thousand . . . three, I think." She sheepishly made eye contact with him as she spoke. "We never saw a penny of that though." She paused, unsure of what they would think of her if she concluded her thought. "Both the little girl and her father were supposed to have been killed that first night last year. We failed, and they've been looking for her ever since."

"Who's they? You keep saying 'they,'" Graves pressed.

"Azazel and John . . . and Job. John was new to the gang, around the time that this whole thing began. He seemed to be tied into Job just as much as Azazel was."

"Tell us more about John." Dana encouraged.

"He was some new recruit Azazel brought in the night of the hit. He seemed to run things after that, he and Job. He was calm, and smart. He was the one with all the plans, finding Sal's house, deciphering the computer information, understanding what to call Job with and when not to bother him. Azazel never seemed to figure that out. It was also unusual for us to bring a non-Hispanic into the faction."

"What do you mean? He was white?"

Maria looked up at Dana. "He was white, with blonde hair. I think he was older than he looked, but I'd guess he was twenty-eight or so."

"Where or how can we find this John?"

"I threw my cell phone beneath the kneeler, under the pew where I found those symbols. After Father found me I got scared. It was the only identifying thing I had on me, I left it there when the police came. He's called that number before. So has Job."

Graves rose to his feet. "You finish with her, I'll go find that phone and get the numbers."

"I changed my phone's SIM chip for this region before we left the States. All those old calls were on the other chip."

"And where's that chip now?" Graves asked as politely as he could, as he stood over her.

"I don't know. Azazel took it from me. I never thought it would get this far. Salvadore was a better man than Azazel. He was smart too, you know. I thought for sure he'd played the game better, and that the girl was safe somewhere."

"It's ok, hon, you did well by us. That'll help your case once we get you back to the States."

"But what about the extradition rules we talked about?"

Dana turned to Graves. "That's my card. She was working

with us on this case, at least in the beginning. She risked a great deal to help the Bureau. She may still get a long prison sentence, but it certainly won't be a death penalty. They'll release her to us now that they're aware. As for the cell phone, find it please," Dana added.

Graves excused himself and departed the room. "Always one step ahead . . . ," he muttered to himself. As he closed the door behind him he heard Dana say, "Now, tell me more about these symbols."

Father Moriel walked quickly through the arrivals terminal in Geneva, paying little attention to the large glass walls and clean metal facade of his surroundings. Intending to be on time at the agreed upon location where he'd meet Dr. Edvard Krunowski, Father's strides lengthened to make up for the plane's late arrival. *Thank goodness I packed light*, he thought as he passed the baggage carousel. With his single duffle bag full of clothes and the holy items he'd need for the ceremony slung over his shoulder, he stepped out into the forty-degree morning air. From across the three-lane taxi driveway, a man looking over the roof of a darkly colored sedan called his name.

"Father, Father Moriel. Please, sir, this way." Edvard waved him across the street.

CHAPTER 31

Pulling up to the small church at the top of the hill, Graves was struck by how many cars were outside this tiny building. The gravel lot that formed a half moon around the stark white chapel was overflowing, but despite the overabundance of vehicles, the scene was otherwise desolate. Exiting his car, he could hear only the sound of the waves far below and the wind as it washed up over the small plateau. He walked over to the church's large wooden front doors and paused, listening for any sounds that might betray the numbers he was about to encounter.

Graves pushed hard to open the heavy doors of the church. To his surprise he was met with the curious faces of a hundred worshipers, all crowded around something in the far back corner of the room. At first he was not sure whether he should enter, but from the crowd came a meek voice that called to him.

"Sir, please come. Are you the American police?" A boy of not more than twelve or thirteen years old, dressed in a long white robe, was delivered from the parting crowd.

Striding toward him, Graves could see at the base of this boy's holy garment the trailing ends of a pair of jeans that were capped off by black Nike sneakers. "You have come to see the symbols, yes? I will show you." The crowd that had formed encompassed locals of all ages. Near the center of the congregation were the elders of the group. They were kneeling on the bare floor where the pews and kneelers had been cleared out of the way. In front of them, Graves could barely make out tracings in the dust that had collected there. Behind them stood the rest of the community, growing younger in age as they spread back in concentric circles.

Graves was led to the middle of the group.

"See, you see." The young man pointed excitedly at these oddly drawn shapes that were already becoming difficult to make out in the shifting light of the late afternoon.

"I'm not sure what I'm looking at," he said with a small degree of embarrassment. "They look like . . . like something a kid would doodle." Graves remembered what he'd come for. "I'm sorry to interrupt, but I'm looking for a phone, a cell phone, that may have been here." He held his thumb and little finger up to his head. "A phone, did you find it?"

The alter boy's eyes grew large, he held up one finger and then moved on into the crowd, leading detective Graves away from the worshipers. "It rings. That is why I find the symbols," he added with a bit of self-satisfaction. Walking into the priest's private office, the young man grabbed the simply constructed phone off the desk and handed it to him. "You call Father Moriel, ask him of the symbols. He tells you." He smiled and politely excused himself to return to the extended family that had gathered.

Graves stood there looking at this phone. "It rang huh?" he said out loud to himself. Opening the flip cover he noted one missed call. The number wasn't one he recognized, it had too many digits to be from within the United States. He hit redial and waited. After several oddly toned rings his effort was met with a recorded voice speaking in some Germanic dialect. The voice paused briefly before repeating the phrase in

English. "The Geneva switchboard is full at this time. Please try your call again." Graves thought about the young man's advice. Removing his own cell phone from his coat pocket, he dialed the number that the local police had given him for Father Moriel. After the fourth ring the line went quiet, and then a male voice answered.

"Father Moriel. Hello?"

"Father, I'm sorry to bother you, this is Detective Tom Graves . . . with the San Diego police department. Do you have a few minutes to talk?"

"Detective, how are you? In Mexico, I gather by your calling prefix. How was your trip?"

"It was fine, sir, I'd like to ask you a few questions about what I'm experiencing here in your church."

"Ahhh . . . are there still crowds gathering? Folks there are Catholic in ways that Americans have long forgotten. Anything that fosters a connection with divinity is an important cultural event, they'll come from miles just to see and experience. What would you like to know?"

"Well, I gather that Eva had drawn these . . . these markings. Why are the locals finding them so intriguing?"

"That's a loaded question my friend. She did indeed draw them, on the morning of her death, sadly enough. However, that is only the first reason that those folks there find this so spiritually intriguing. What's more intriguing is the symbol that she drew."

"How so? It just looks like a pineapple to me." Graves could hear the sharp bursts of wind from Father's laughter into the receiver.

"Very good, I hadn't thought of that one. Actually it has some meaning, both there and elsewhere, to many Catholics, believe it or not. To start with, the overall pattern is that of the Square of Saint Peter in front of Saint Peter's Basilica in Vatican City, not to mention the kiva."

"What's a kiva?"

"They were religious rooms that the Indians of the Southwest built . . . the Hopi as well as many Mexican tribes. The folks there have ancestral ties to these peoples and believe that this shape is one of both cultural and religious relevance. These structures, or rooms, were designed to offer welcoming arms, and in the case of the Vatican, the arms of the Mother Church, to the throngs that gathered. However, that's not all." The line crackled under the strain from the distance.

"Father, are you there?"

The priest's thought picked up mid-sentence as the line reacquired itself, " . . . has some other ancient correlations as well. It would seem that the symbol is also suggestive of the Greek letter phi, which has its own relationship with the golden ratio. Perhaps you've heard of this marvel? There are stories of the ratio's tie to all sorts of natural phenomenon, but in reality this number is most often found in the worlds of art, mathematics, music, and architecture because of its religious connotations. It's also believed that this number has some occult origins."

"How do you mean, Father?" Graves sat as he listened.

"There are some in the Church who believe strongly that despite these possible manmade origins, the symbol and the Greek number are linked biblically to the number of the Beast, 6 6 6. Following this line of reasoning, many also believe the pagan pentagram to be a symbol of the Beast. The ratios of the various lines that comprise the ten individual triangles of the pentagram again follow the golden ratio. In all of these triangles, the ratio of the longer side to the shorter side is again phi."

"As an undergrad I took a theology course," Graves interjected. "If memory serves, I believe that some ancient cultures saw the encircled star of the pentagram as a symbol of the four directions of travel, and not anything mystical."

"That's true, detective. This symbol is credited to the Babylonians, as it was initially discovered in their pictographs. They did indeed view it as a compass of sorts. They saw the various points of the star as representative of the four directions in space, with the remaining fifth upward point denoting time. Modern scientists have used two or more of these symbols in their computations, often shown passing through one another at their central axis to represent multi-dimensions. A coincidence which I find particularly . . . interesting, in light of Dr. Canty's profession."

"This all seems very loose Father. Especially in light of the fact that there is a large group of devout Catholics out there and you're telling me that they're here because this rudimentary symbol, one that a four-year-old scrawled on the floor in the dust, either has ties to something evil or scientific?"

The line was briefly silent again before Father Moriel continued. "Regardless of these endless conjectures, my parishioners there are quite aware of these religious inferences, both divine and evil. This brings the entire topic back full circle. If this child was unknowingly putting forth a message just minutes before her death, one complicated by a mortal sin that was not reconciled in the eyes of the Lord, then there may be deeper meaning in all of this. These religious implications in and of themselves have sparked quite a bit of mass prayer for her, as you're now witness to. That group you see there with you is only the tip of the iceberg, detective. For every one of those praying Catholics, there are dozens more who have or are yet to come to that hill to see and believe. You can be sure that there will be thousands upon thousands of prayers for her in the days and weeks to come."

Graves still didn't know what to say. "I'm not sure I buy all this, Father. I mean, not to sound disrespectful, but . . . really?"

Moriel laughed. "Really. Those that are there believe that this is a sign, and a very important one at that. A sign that the little one whose death we mourn may have left us by means of a divine passing. She may yet show us the light, but of course we'll have to wait and see about that. For now it has provided strong reason for Catholics to reconcile her violent death and hope, for a larger meaning to all of this horrible violence."

"When you return Father I'd like to ask you more questions. I realize that the local police released you, but we still have some things to discuss." He hesitated, hoping that he'd made his point without sounding threatening. "I'd like to catch all those responsible for this crime. Please don't disappear, Father."

"I understand. I look forward to our meeting. Thank you for the call, detective. It's nice to know that everyone there has taken up this cross for Eva. Please keep her in your prayers, Tom." There was a faint click before the line went silent.

Graves looked back out into the shadowed church. The crowd remained, silently huddled around the pictograms. He shuddered at the thought of this beautiful little child and all that she'd been put through over the last year. He'd call back to the precinct to have them run a quick trace on this mystery number—0 1 1—he had a funny feeling that he knew exactly where this call had come from. Taking his own cell from his pocket, he scrolled through the last few calls made and hit redial.

"Dana, it's Tom. Jot this number down." He waited a minute before passing on the fourteen-digit number. "This needs to be passed back to the Bureau. We need to have this line traced and monitored as well."

"You are needing more help?" The young man returned from the church.

Graves looked up from his call. "No, thank you. I'll only be a few more minutes." Hanging up the phone, he exited the tiny office and returned to the single room of worship. He had no idea how to do this. Before he left, he knelt before the statue of Mother Mary to offer a prayer for Eva.

The brightly colored banners advertising the zoo's visiting panda exhibit fluttered against the terminal wall in the breeze. As John stepped onto the moving walkway, he noted that the one from the opposite direction was broken and some of the frustrated patrons were jogging to make their connections. His side, however, was functioning as it was supposed to. John had over ninety minutes to make his gate, and he'd already checked his baggage with the porter outside at the curb. Before he left this City of Angels for good, he had one last phone call to make. Ducking into an unoccupied kiosk, John dialed the eleven-digit number.

Six thousand miles away Job politely excused himself from his conversation. Walking into the hallway outside the hotel room, he answered his cell. "Is it done?" His voice seemed on the verge of anger.

"Yes, sir, it's done . . . it's *all* done." John's voice was confident but hushed. "I'm leaving to meet you now. I should be there in eighteen hours. Is there anything more you need from me, Father?"

"Give me the prostitute's number. You've done well Iän, now I'll finish this myself." Job hung up his phone and dialed the number he'd been given.

"Hello?" A soft female voice filled the phone this time.

"Your services are no longer needed, Maria. You did very well and we're all pleased. The money you are owed will be delivered when the time is right for us, and no sooner. Do not attempt to contact me or there will be no payment. Do you understand?"

"Yes, sir . . ." was all Maria was able to add before the call ended.

Sitting in the dank cell, Dana removed her Bluetooth earpiece as Maria closed her phone. "The numbers are a match. It seems you were right, Tom." she added with an encouraging smile. "I think we need to take a trip and pay our priest a little visit."

Graves couldn't stop an answering grin from creeping over his face. Resting his hand softly on his partner's shoulder as he stood, he asked, "How do you feel about cold weather?"

CHAPTER 32

Every breath burned Fin's chest. He had been walking for days, ever since he'd left the rest of his family behind and chosen to come into this place, and the scenery had barely changed. It was an acrid expanse whose stinging wind blasted Fin's skin to bleeding with the sand it threw up. The glaring sunlight was so bright that, together with the bitter sulfur air during the day, it brought him to the point of blindness, beginning what would prove to be continual suffering throughout the night's brief hours of darkness. These hours, filled with an anguish the murkiness demanded of his battered vision, brought nearly endless tears that resolved just in time for sunrise to start the process all over again. The throbbing in his back continued, though it had become more diffuse. The pains now seemed to begin around his shoulders and cascade in waves toward his tailbone. The boney nubs that grew from his were larger now and the flesh around the bases had begun to peel away in thick rolling folds that left thin trails of blood streaming down his back. His back had become broader, wider between his shoulders, and more swollen beneath his skin overall.

The mountains Fin saw when he arrived were only slightly closer than they were days ago, but his view of them was clearer now. There were three distinct peaks in the chain; each was black and appeared scorched in most places, as if from some massive fire. He could see nothing growing on them, only a faint plume of smoke or maybe dust rising from the tops of their charred and deeply fissured surface. He assumed that these rising columns were the source of the black clouds that occasionally produced electrical storms.

Especially when the strength in his legs waned, the ground here would become soft, making it difficult to step quickly enough to keep from sinking, and he would grow too tired to lift his feet fully. But then, when he found his wind again, the terrain would change, becoming hard and rocky, cutting his bare feet further. The cuts on the soles of his feet—initially suffered when he ran through the forest at the cabin—had opened wide. The sand had ground its way into these lacerations and the pain now gripped him clear up into the center of his calves. Whatever minor aches he had previously had were now a focused misery that lanced his muscles with every step.

When Fin stopped briefly, leaning against a rock or outcropping to rest, everything he placed his hands on was burning hot. But all the while, the wind that scoured his body raked a chill through him, demanding constant shivering.

Fin continued to feel an emotional pull in the direction he'd chosen, clearly over the mountains, away from the river where he'd started. Despite his physical pain, he was unable to keep from imagining his daughter being tortured, both before and after her death. Fin felt responsible for Eva's imprisonment here, though he realized he may never understand the reasons fully. Here especially, the guilt of leaving her consumed him. He hoped that it would serve to take the focus off his physical pain, but it only added to his suffering.

As he came to the rise before the foothills of the mountains, he began to encounter rougher land. The rocks, initially small, rose erratically from the sand like blackened razor blades. These outcroppings eventually grew to create steeply walled igneous alleyways. It was growing dark now and Fin found himself standing at the entranceway to one such narrow passage, the tall vertical walls of which were burnt to a charcoal grey. He paused, resting his hand briefly on the jagged rock that bound the entrance. With his chest heaving, Fin looked up at the mountains. Another storm had begun, and with each lightning strike the path before him was lit up like full daylight. His exhaustion was total. His legs were burning from the bottom of his feet to the bulk of his thighs. Dropping one foot in front of the other, he moved on toward his initial goal of the foothills.

"This is like one of those bad movies where they show people wandering through the Sahara alone, with their pants on their head and a blistering sunburn." Fin murmured to himself with a bittersweet chuckle, realizing that he might be losing his mind, but at least here there weren't any vultures circling.

"There's nothing," he said out loud as he squinted and looked up toward the blackening sky just to reassure himself.

With fatigue, his thoughts had become rote, allowing him only the ability to focus on his next step. Struggling to stay up, he put his left foot forward, failing to find purchase on a loose stone. With an initial wiggle beneath his foot, the rocks shifted, upending his mass and sending him tumbling down a sharply walled ravine. Sliding toward the bottom, he grasped wildly at the rock wall, every jagged edge tearing at the pads of his fingers and the palms of his hands as he fell. With his back down, Fin was pitched up and over the uneven land, feeling the flow of blood increase from his wounds. Still trying to slow his steep descent, he grabbed haphazardly at the sides of the crevice as they flew past him until his hand found a single vertical ledge on which he could anchor himself. Wincing in pain, he looked up over his shoulder and saw small pebbles beginning to give way beneath from his support. As he began to plummet again, the last thing he remembered was a flood of rock pouring down toward him.

Fin awoke some hours later in a world of almost total blackness, free of all debris, and lying on his back. The rock wall, not a body length in front of him, was visible only in its uneven black silhouette against the faint light that still radiated from beyond the mountains. Stretching his neck and rubbing the back of his head as he lay there, he wondered what the hell he was doing. But there was a peace to being here—a knowledge, or rather a feeling, that Eva was here too. But how was he ever going to find her?

These thoughts were still lingering in his consciousness when a faint noise caught his attention. It sounded like small rocks tumbling off in the distance, but it had occurred so unexpectedly and was so brief that he couldn't be sure which direction it came from. Lying still, he waited for several moments. He could hear only the sound of his own breathing, which seemed to echo back at him in the near blackness he sat in. Then he heard it again, and this time it seemed to be coming from much closer than before. Still lying on his back, Fin slowly propped himself up on his elbows. Craning his neck, he attempted to see over the few large stones just beyond his feet. Peering into the dark expanse, he continued to wonder to himself if these impressions of "direction" were an illusion— possibly one impressed upon him by this evil place? He shook his head to clear his thoughts, thinking back to what Father Moriel had said to him just a year ago.

"We're all destined for something. You just need to be spiritually ready to recognize it when the time comes."

As Fin tried to peer through the surrounding blackness off into the distance, a terror he'd not yet felt in this place gripped him. The remainder of Father's pronouncement was finished aloud for him in a gravely insistent voice.

"Never be afraid of your faith . . . especially in yourself." The voice had a disturbing quality that seemed both forced and unnatural.

What Fin had believed to be a boulder, blackened by the dim light beyond, was slowly raising itself onto long spindly legs right in front of him. This grotesque creature had been huddled quietly along side him in the ravine this entire time. Set against the dimming light, with its boney appendages punctuated mid-length by bulbous joints and its crooked midsection undulating as it rose, it revealed its horrifying proportions to him, although the dimensions of its head were indiscernible in the dark. The voice seemed to resonate from all around him.

Fin froze in shock, uncertain whether he'd been seen. The darkness that had protected him was abruptly sliced into long stark shadows, cast outward by the glow of the creature's gaze as it opened its eyes. In the harsh radiance, fine particles of dust drifted upward as Fin, scraping his back along the ground, began to frantically scramble away from this new threat. Unraveling its limbs, the creature reached its full height in front of him, allowing Fin to make out its dark crusted outlines. Its emaciated legs ended in elongated talons, each with four digits that bore sickle-like claws. It walked on its toes, like a dog, with its swollen knees bending backward. As it advanced toward Fin, the light from its eyes intensified, giving off a more radiant yellow. With his heart pounding in his chest, Fin continued to push himself backward until he felt cold stone against the back of his neck. Any courage stoked by the onslaught of adrenaline froze beneath his overwhelming horror. His blood running cold and barely able to move, Fin sat hunched with his back against the unforgiving stone.

The creature continued to advance. First one cautious step, then several seconds later, another, as if it, too, was uncertain of what it found. Fin sat pressed against the wall. His fear gave way to images of his little girl, first her eyes, then her smile. With each step the creature took toward him, Fin felt a renewed sense of purpose. The chill of his panic evaporated in the heat of his growing rage.

Dropping its head between its widened shoulders the beast quickened its pace. A chill ran up Fin's spine as the rapid clicking of its talons resonated off the stone surroundings.

"Fuck you!" Fin's frustrated rage spit through his clenched teeth. Rising to his feet, the thought of Eva alone with these things drove his anger to a new level. He clenched his fists and prepared for a fight. In the near blackness of the ravine, the beast came to a stop. It remained motionless, standing just a few feet from Fin's reach. He could hear the rasp of its breathing as he watched the silhouette of its chest rise and fall in the faint light, the heat from its breath rising in the air above them.

"Come on!" Fin screamed with all his anger. "What are you waiting for, you son of a bitch!"

Lowering its head again, the beast descended to its knees. The light from its eyes faded. "I am to be your guide," it said in an unnatural child-like growl.

Fin's urge to run nearly overwhelmed his curiosity. *What the hell's going on?* He could hear his pulse surging in his ears as he stood there, uncertain if he should be preparing for an attack. "What?" was all he could come up with as he searched the beast's featureless face in the dark.

"Forgive me, I had to know if you were her father." It remained kneeling in front of him.

Fin's anger surged again with the mention of his daughter. "How the hell do you know who I am . . . or why I'm here?" His fury took him a step closer to the creature.

"You are the one who chose us, the one without sin."

With a cold chill Fin realized his uniqueness. He suddenly felt like other eyes were on him too.

"I will help guide you to her."

"I don't need any help!"

The beast bowed more deeply, closing its eyes and casting the gulley into darkness again. "They all know who you are, and you should beware." With this, its voice seemed to split into many. "He waits for you." The cacophony of varying octaves wilted Fin's bravado.

Fin's mind raced. He retreated one more step. *They all know? Who are they, and who's waiting for me?* "I know where I'm going, I don't need your help." His gut was telling him not to trust anyone or anything here. He needed to get in, find Eva, and then get the hell out . . . somehow. "Leave!"

"You have seven days, three have already passed you by." The creature rose and turned to leave. Stepping up onto the precipice, it twisted its head to the side, revealing its sunken profile. "The day of reckoning approaches." With little effort it jumped off, and the faint clicking of its talons echoed in the darkness as it fled.

There was a slight breeze, but otherwise everything seemed still. Fin stood shaking, this time not with cold but with unspent adrenaline. Unsure what to believe, he now knew his time was limited, and if he wanted to see Eva again he needed to pick up the pace. Tomorrow he'd make it over the mountains.

CHAPTER 33

"Only a pure soul can cross over. I will have his when he comes for her." The demon seemed uninterested in Job's presence tonight. His sleep, which he had thought would remain uninterrupted after their agreement had been honored, had once again been violated. Standing in the void, Job continued to listen, unsure if this monologue was intended for his ears.

"You have done well." The demon turned, casting up clouds of choking dust as it moved swiftly toward him. The ground shook with the immense weight beneath each heavy hoof as it strode closer. "The little girl is with us, and the blasphemer draws nearer still. His trials, in her name, will strip him of his humanity. The purity I will steal from him will rend the bonds that hold me here."

"When will I see what you've promised me? When will the evidence you've promised reveal itself to me?" Job had never been so direct. Throughout their dealings, he'd been patient and obedient, averting his eyes, all in the name of his own religion. But Job had grown tired of the sacrifices, the pain, and above all the continual danger he'd placed himself in.

The demon towered over him, its voice booming. "Do not mistake this world for a dream, nor my influence over you as subject to this place alone." Lunging at him, it thrust a cloven fist deep into Job's belly.

The agony was overwhelming. The pain besieged his senses and Job found himself praying aloud for his release into unconsciousness. Instead he remained awake and fully able to appreciate every facet of his suffering.

"Your obedience to my desires will tie you to this place for eternity. Do not think yourself the wiser of us for playing the false prophet." Standing upright, the monster lifted Job high into the pungent air above its head. Job could feel the pressure of his own body weight in his spine and shoulders as his blood streamed downward over the crusted limb that suspended him there. Bending at the knee as if to set Job back where he'd stood, the demon seemed to offer a brief smile before letting out a deafening howl.

Grimacing in pain, Job could feel the extremity that filled his abdomen tense, the rock-hard forearm that suspended him now straining at his ribcage with acceleration. Spinning wildly, the beast cast him off, hurtling him toward a rocky mount. Job's pain intensified with his release. Flying upward, he struck high up on the face of a cliff and slid to a rough perch, out of view of his attacker. He could feel the slick trail of blood that followed him downward, pooling around him where he sat. Through his staccato breathing Job looked at the wound made by the demon's fist, terrified to see the carnage. The gaping wound was massive, its edges bursting outward from the explosive pitch that had flung him here. His anxiety was evident in the rapid pulsations of crimson that spewed over his entrails, which were now delivered from his belly. He covered his wound loosely with his hands as he tried to remain vigilant against another assault.

"My imprisonment here is perpetuated by your kind." Job could hear the baritone notes of the demon's voice as it trailed off into the distance. "You worthless creatures, with all your self-ascribed knowledge, do not yet understand your own role in this reality."

The darkness that had surrounded their small enclave slowly gave way to a light beyond where he sat. With dawning awareness, Job saw a vast hell opening before him—one that until now he had not known. The light that filled the gorge was not peaceful. It was projected outward by the fires that consumed this place. The valley before him, awash with both rock and beast, seemed to move in unison with the shadows. The walls that hemmed in the gorge ran red with the blood of the damned, who were strewn across the rocks, with their bodies impaled on the jagged outcroppings and wailing as they continued to move. Job could see an army of demons patrolling like soldier ants all across this massive expanse of wasteland, protecting something at the far reaches of the basin. The cries and screams, which had been muffled on other nights, now seemed amplified a thousand times. From the rock where he was perched, Job could make out an area down the middle of all this chaos, a path that led to whatever was being protected beyond his sight. Midway through the valley ran a gully that cut across its bowl. Its breadth was lit up with the fires from below, with molten rock bubbling to the precipice, then bursting as it cooled before settling back down again. On the opposite verge of this rift stood the demon, towering over his minions as they ran about below him in his shadow. Bellowing commands, he spread his massive arms outward, his leathery wings increasing their span threefold. From the escarpments that surrounded them came the decaying carcasses of the lost, hurtling into the flames. Willing the wretched closer, the demon pulled them into the fire, igniting their souls in fleeting sparks as they breached the void and vanished into the bowels of this place.

As Job sat there, it became clear to him that he was witnessing the final path as it had been laid out for the friend he'd betrayed. At the far end of what would be Fin's valley of death, lay the little girl he sought, the little girl whose soul held the fate of all of their vile plans. Job sobbed uncontrollably with the thought of what tortures Eva suffered, what violations she endured as her father marched through this desolate and forsaken existence, determined to rescue her.

A deep concussion resonated through the valley, drawing Job's attention back to the center. With one massive beat of its wings, the demon thrust itself into the air. Rising high above, it landed with deafening force just feet from where Job rested, again shaking the ground to crumbling. With the arc of its wings blocking out the light from beyond, Job could only make out the searing orange light from the master's eyes as he sat in the darkness of its shadow.

"My eternity here nears its end. You will find your proof of the afterlife in the remains of my savior."

"I don't understand . . . his remains were cremated . . . there's nothing left of him."

The demon crouched closer and Job could smell the brimstone churning in the beast's gut. "My use for you has ended. If we meet again, it will be your damnation."

Job's regrets flooded his mind. They were beginning to pile onto his already burdened soul. "What will become of the girl?" he asked as he instinctively raised a protective arm before his face.

"Arrogant fool!" Out of the corner of his eye Job caught a glint of light off the demon's claw as it reached its apogee before crashing down toward him. In a single blow he was thrown again, this time leftward into the air, tumbling head over heels as he flew.

With a massive thud he landed, his head crashing backward into his nightstand, sending the ceramic lamp to its demise on the hardwood floor. With his chest heaving, Job sat motionless, moving only his eyes at first to take in his surroundings.

He was back, awake in his bedroom, alone and sitting on the floor next to the bed. Moving to stand, he was brought back to his crumpled position by the crippling pain in his abdomen. His night shirt was drenched in blood, seemingly from the wound he'd suffered at the demon's hand. Job paused, unable to bring himself to look under his clothing. In a fearful desire to know, Job began to cry. In a fit of self-loathing and anger, he tore wildly at his shirt, ripping it away as he grasped at his expected stigmata. But he found none, no wounds at all to help quell the guilt from his sacrifices.

The phone rang, startling him and again sending more raw adrenaline rushing to his quivering muscles. Allowing the moment to mature, he answered only after several rings. "Hello?"

"Father," the voice was both a familiar and soothing one. "It's John. Are you up? Have you forgotten? Today's the ceremony. The Canty family's going to be waiting for you."

Clearing his head, Job stood, still grimacing in pain. "With me, use the name I baptized you with, Ian." He groaned as he finished getting to his feet and shot a glance toward the clock that now lay on its side next to him. "I have some time." Remembering his station, he continued with what poise he could muster. "I don't want you there. We don't need any questions. We need to . . . to *finalize* his last payment. Take the organization's helicopter, but be back today."

"I understand. What have you decided about the tour?" he

asked, referring to the planned tour of CERN's Large Hadron Collider that had been scheduled for later this week. "Have you decided on a date for the event?"

"We'll just have to see how everyone feels at that point, now won't we?" Job collected the contents of the table from the floor. He thought of what the demon had said to him, *"You will find the evidence you seek for your cause from his remains."*

"Before you go," he said, "I have one more chore for you. . . ." Then, clutching his belly, he headed for the bathroom.

"We're at thirty thousand feet, and those passengers on our port side will get our first glimpse of the Western shores of Ireland." The radio crackled before an electronic thump signified the pilot had taken his thumb off the intercom. "We should be arriving at Heathrow within the hour."

Graves shifted uncomfortably in his seat, waking slightly as he did.

"*Please* stop fidgeting. Every time you move like that you shake the entire row." Dana was not one for sleeping on planes, no matter how long the flight. There was something about being unnaturally suspended this high up that kept her awake.

"I'm sorry, my ass is killin' me. I can't get comfortable in this friggin' seat. You know what I'd like?"

"I'm not rubbing your backside for you, if that's what you're about to suggest."

"No, although that would be nice. What I'd like is for this damn seat to go back just two more inches." Graves peered over toward her computer. "What are you reading anyway? You've been buried in that laptop for hours."

"It's all the newspaper files on the hearings that Canty was part of. You know, the ones regarding that CERN collider and the wackos in Hawaii." Dana remained fixated on the LED screen, and its dim glow lit up the soft features of her face like a kid under the covers. "It's interesting stuff. This guy was the man, I mean he pulled the entire project back on line." Dana had spent the better part of the previous afternoon performing a data search in the archives at the Bureau. She'd cross referenced CERN with Canty's name and ARCH.

"Are you finding anything useful in there?" Graves sat his seat up, sliding himself again to one side.

"There's a lot of talk just about CERN and their scope of research. But what I do find interesting is that there are numerous references to the large amount of money this lawsuit required."

"I thought some Christian group funded that?"

"Yeah, I did too. But if you read between the lines, it seems that they paid for the lawyer and nothing else. The court costs, initial document preparation, travel costs for the small legal team, and even financial compensation for the plaintiff's time away from work, were paid for out of an entirely different pool of monies. One article mentions a witness called for their cause in the initial hearing who required travel from Europe, and that couldn't have been cheap. They even called in the Justice Department's Environmental and Natural Resources Division, based in Washington!"

"Who paid for it then?" Graves was looking over her shoulder sharing into the glow of the screen as he placed his arm on her rest. Their fingers brushed against one another's, lingering briefly as they occupied the same space.

"It doesn't say, it just says ' . . . all at a cost of hundreds of thousands of dollars.' The two individuals who started the suit are quoted as saying they 'paid for most of this out of their own pocket,' but I find that hard to believe."

"I dunno, these last few days have shown me that people will do pretty amazing things in the name of their religion." Graves dropped back into his semi-reclined seat back as the lights in the cabin began to come up.

"I don't buy the whole story. The two guys that brought this claim before the court were a local school teacher and the building's custodian. We're not exactly talking world renowned physicists here. These are the two yahoos that called themselves ARCH apparently." Dana raised her eyebrows in sarcasm. "I mean, there's a great deal of science that backs up these initial claims, not to mention the money that was needed to pull this off. And get this last part," she pointed at the screen. " . . . although the suit was dismissed, an injunction was filed two weeks later that did result in a court order to secure satellite facilities to monitor all powered spins of the collider." Apparently to be able to remotely shut down the whole system should certain emergent conditions arise."

"What conditions?" Graves was rubbing his eyes forcefully. Half listening now, he was mostly just being polite as he tried to wake up.

Clicking through the articles, Dana found what she was looking for: "'an increase in local radiation production, an increase of greater than five percent on the internal gravitometer,' whatever that is, 'or an increase in the local gravitational field.' Oh, I guess that last thing measures the field strength."

"Is there anything there about the Collider itself? I mean, why are these nuts so worried about it anyway?"

Dana continued, " There's one article about the formation

of an Einstein-Rosen Bridge."

"What's that?"

"It's a wormhole." She flipped through a few screens before continuing, "'Central to the LHC is the ATLAS detector. One of two general-purpose detectors, it will search for theoretical particles, extra dimensions, and the makeup of dark matter. Some speculate this detector could form vacuum bubbles, microscopic black holes, or even a theoretical passageway between dimensions known as an Einstein-Rosen Bridge. These creations could change the universe as we know it, rendering our existence impossible.' I guess that answers that question, huh?"

"Ladies and Gentlemen, please return your seat backs and trays to their upright and locked positions as we are preparing for our approach. Those continuing on to Geneva will remain with us tonight . . .," the captain's voice trailed off, melting into the growing din in the cabin.

Graves let out an audible moan, "Great, I get to sit in this ass buster for another couple of hours."

CHAPTER 34

The last part of the flight had proved less painful than Graves and Dana had expected. With a decent tail wind their flight arrived in Geneva a full fifteen minutes ahead of schedule. Walking through the airport toward the baggage collection area, Graves could feel exhaustion settling into his bones. His knees and hips ached just from bearing the weight of his carry-on bag as he strode through the open terminal.

"Who's meeting us again?"

Dana had been quiet up until now. Staring straight ahead as they walked, she seemed a thousand miles away in thought. "Huh? Oh, uh, one of the senior FedPol agents, an Inspector Goll. He seemed like a very pleasant man when I spoke with him a few days ago."

"Well, I just hope he checked the arrival times so we're not sitting around here forever. What time is it anyway?" Graves stared at his watch as he followed his counterpart, trying desperately not to trip and fall while he did so.

"We're six hours ahead of the East Coast, nine hours ahead of the West Coast." She looked over her shoulder as she finished. Graves was still staring at his watch. "Look, just add nine hours to whatever time your watch says and that's the time here. It's nine AM on Sunday morning, Tom. Your watch should say midnight from back home. Who dresses you in the morning?"

"Oh yeah, you're right." He said as he followed closely

behind her, peering down at his wrist.

Riding the descending escalator leading to the baggage area, Dana could see two professionally attired gentlemen in dark suits waiting at the landing. As they rode closer, the larger of the two men approached holding out his hand.

"Agent Pinon? I am Inspector Goll . . . Bastien Goll. We are with the Federal Office of Police." He took her hand gently in their introduction. He was a physically imposing man, with an accent nearly as thick as his wavy blond hair. Dana guessed he was probably six-four and at least two hundred and twenty pounds.

"This is my partner, Inspector Aldo Baumgartner." Bastien gestured toward the other suit standing behind him.

Graves snickered aloud, then quickly dropped his head. Wiping his nose on his sleeve, he hoped to pass off his immaturity as a sneeze. "Excuse me, these long trips always irritate my sinuses," he said sheepishly, offering a weak smile before shaking hands with both gentlemen.

"Let us find your luggage. We'll continue our conversation on the ride out." Bastien turned toward the cavernous hall humming with a multitude of baggage carousels. Please, retrieve your bags and meet us outside. We will be waiting in the black Audi." As the men walked away, the two Americans moved to their baggage claim carousel to collect their bags.

Dana elbowed Graves in the ribs. "What the hell's the matter with you?" She scolded under her breath.

"I'm sorry! Look, I'm exhausted . . . and that guy said his friend's name was 'Bum-Gardener.'" He laughed again, his shoulders rising and falling quickly with each stifled chuckle. "Sorry, really. It's just that I pictured this pudgy Swede raking over a crop of bare asses sticking out of the soil with a hoe." He snorted one last time. "Sorry, it was the word hoe that time."

Dana shook her head in disgust. "His name is Baumgart-ner, not Bumgartner," she said. "Nothing's changed. You're still just a big kid." She stifled a smile. His offbeat sense of humor was one of the reasons she'd initially fallen for him. He always found a way to break down her guard and make her feel relaxed. As their years had wound on however, this hadn't been enough to overcome their differences. Now she was tired too, but she was beginning to wonder if bringing him was such a good idea after all. He was an excellent police detective when he wanted to be, serious and very bright. She knew how much he cared for her, and he would be a distraction if he wasn't focused. "Look, until you get some sleep, just keep your mouth shut. Ok?"

A few minutes later, their bags slid into view. They col-lected them and made their way through the sliding doors out into the cold sunlight.

The car was immense, dark and muscular in its stance. Its 6.0 liter V-12 purred idly at the curb waiting for its occupants to task it. The porter placed their bags into the trunk while Graves and Dana sank into the leather thrones in the back seat. With Inspector Goll driving, they moved off with nearly silent acceleration.

"I will first take you to the hotel. There you can place your belongings before we get started, if you'd like. I am told that you are here regarding suspects for several murders that have taken place in your country. This is correct?"

Dana placed a firm hand on Graves's arm before answer-ing, hoping to keep him quiet. "We have some evidence linking a suspect to the murders, yes. We are here hoping to question an American and possibly make an arrest. If it's all the same to you, we can go to the hotel later, Gentlemen. We'd prefer to just get started." She paused before continuing. "Inspector Goll, what is your office aware of regarding ARCH?"

The two men in the front seat exchanged knowing glances. Inspector Goll spoke first. "Please, call me Bastien. You're referring to the Activists Rebuking CERN's Heresy, the group out of America that is seeking to shut down the collider at CERN. We know quite a bit, actually, and I think that you should wait before your questioning. There is more that you do not know."

"It seems there's been quite a lot of money used for their cause, and not much explanation as to where it comes from." Dana watched Graves fidgeting with the controls for the small LCD screens embedded in the leather headrests of the front seats. "I'm curious, Bastien, what is it we don't know?"

"Well, including the death of Dr. Canty one year ago, there have been two deaths associated with CERN. In the last week here, a young woman, a doctoral fellow, fell to her death within the reactor room. Also, after you and I spoke the other day, I began first tracing and then monitoring that mobile number you gave to me." Bastien glanced over his shoulder at his guests. "Did you receive the transcripts from the calls that afternoon? There were a few very interesting comments made by our friend John, don't you think?"

"I did receive them, thank you. They're one of the more convincing pieces of evidence in this case. Evidence that helped persuade my director in allowing us to come out here."

"Your superiors know of this?"

"They do."

"The priest, 'Father,' as this John called him, is your target?"

"He is. Father Moriel's presence here concerns us greatly, especially at a time when the facility's functions are in their infancy and with the entire Canty family here."

"They held the ceremonies for the two deceased members of the family this morning. It was actually quite nice, I am told," Bastien interjected. "The ashes were thrown about the hillside where Dr. Canty lived while working here . . . just outside the home of his friend, CERN's director, Dr. Edvard Krunowski."

"It would seem that our Priest is not just a friend of the family, but another of these right-wing Catholic believers bent on stopping CERN in its endeavors. I just hope that he won't be given access to the collider any time soon." Dana's comment was met with another knowing glance between the two Swiss agents.

"Actually, he is supposed to have a guided tour sometime this week."

Graves couldn't hold his tongue any longer. "So I'm confused. Why should we wait to question Father Moriel, or even to take him into custody for that matter? It seems like we should get Father before he and his group have any further chances to do more harm."

"Well, you see, he's not the only link to the Catholic Church." Inspector Baumgartner broke in.

Graves and Dana exchanged surprised looks. "Where did you learn to speak English so well, Inspector?"

"Please Detective Graves, call me Aldo. I was born and raised here, just outside of Geneva, but spent the years of my higher education in England. I later moved to Rome, where I finished my education. I moved back to Switzerland after several years in service with the Swiss Guard at the Vatican."

Dana knew the Swiss Guard was not a position that people just fell into. Their host was obviously no slouch, he was someone of formidable background and education.

"So you were able to track that cell number then?" Graves asked as he continued to finger all the knobs and gadgets around him.

"No, we were not," Aldo added.

"You see Detective Graves, our cell system here in Europe is not as it is in your country. In order to allow for full roaming throughout the EU, most phones are sold shrink-wrapped over the counter as pay-as-you go items. They are not linked to a specific individual account. Additional minutes and a corresponding coded phone number are purchased on cards separately. These minutes are then added to the phone's online debit by calling that number. There is often nothing that ties a particular phone or its number to an individual."

"So how is it that you are aware of another member of the Church involved in this case?"

"Well, this brings me to my next point, Inspector Pinon," Aldo continued. "It seems that ARCH has a major financier." He briefly turned to face his guests. "We, too, wondered how this small group was funding their endeavors, so we attempted to trace the bearer bonds that were used to fund the tickets of those flown to Hawaii to testify. Many of the witnesses that ARCH called were locals from this region who also had per- sonal issues with this 'monster' buried beneath their homes. Most of these bonds were untraceable—Swiss I might add. But toward the end of the trial there was one last transaction that involved the testimony of a Cardinal Antonacci. His travel was paid for with a bond traceable back to the Vatican."

"Cardinal who? I don't think I've heard that name before." Dana was sitting a little more erect in her seat now.

"Cardinal Giuseppe Antonacci is the Vatican's senior

astronomer." Bastien added, making eye contact with her in the rear view mirror. "We think there are much bigger fishes here."

"The Vatican has an astronomer? That seems a little, well, counterintuitive," Graves added, raising his eyebrows.

"On the contrary," Aldo added. "The Vatican has their own observatory just southeast of Rome, as well as having exclusive scope time at the University of Arizona. The Catholic Church still suffers the stigma of their mistreatment of Galileo four hundred years ago. But to be fair, they have been on the forefront of a great many astronomical discoveries in the last century. The Jesuits who run the facility pride themselves on their fund of scientific rationality in light of their religion."

Graves was beginning to see a connection between Moriel and this group. "So what about this money and Cardinal Antonacci?"

"It seems that his testimony took place days after the others were finished and excused," Aldo replied. "He was the last witness called by the defendants."

"By the defendants!" Graves jumped in. "Why would The Vatican spend their money to bring this Priest out just to testify *against* their cause?"

"We don't' know. But the fact of the matter is that Cardinal Antonacci was there on behalf of the CERN to lobby for their collider, despite the fact that his trip was covered by the same money as the others from ARCH. The Cardinal argued that scientific research and the Christian faith are not mutually exclusive. Using the words of Galileo Galilei himself, he closed his statement by saying that scripture is intended to teach us how to go to heaven, and not how the heavens go." The big sedan shuddered slightly, betraying their travel across a small bridge overlooking a snow-covered ravine below.

"Well, if the Catholic Church was fronting the bill for ARCH, the Cardinal's testimony must have made him a few enemies in Rome. So where are we headed then?" Graves asked politely.

"To the local cantonal police department. We will coordinate their participation in whatever else is needed. I have arranged for a FedPol helicopter to take both Inspector Baumgartner and Detective Graves to talk with the Cardinal."

"To the Vatican!" Graves leaned forward and placed his hand on the shoulder of his supposed travel partner. "No, Aldo, I just got off one airship, I'm not entirely sure my rear end could take another. How do we even know that this Cardinal is going to be there?"

"I've already had a discussion with the Swiss Guard regarding our intended interview. I've got some pull there, remember." Again, Aldo glanced briefly over his shoulder. "Don't worry, Detective, the flight is not a long one. We should be there within two hours. While we're there, Bastien and Agent Pinon can begin to locate your Father Moriel to *discuss* matters with him."

"What about this planned tour of CERN's facilities? We need to make sure that we put a stop to that before we question anyone."

"I couldn't agree with you more, Agent Pinon," Bastien chimed in. "I will call the director at CERN and let him know of our plans. He needs to be aware of the danger that he and his facility may be in."

The sedan pulled up to a snow-covered lot just outside a single-story building. High overhead, the sun shed its midday light onto the ice, casting a blinding glare off the glistening roof of the police station. About 300 meters west of the complex sat a brightly painted 532UL Cougar, its main rotors already spinning.

"Is that our ride?" Graves pointed sheepishly at the green and yellow helicopter as he exited the black sedan.

"That it is, sir. Leave your bags here. You can freshen up quickly inside the station before we depart." Aldo was already crunching through the remains of an earlier snow as he headed for the front door of the drab grey building.

Graves raised his voice above the growing din. "Are you sure that it's safe? I mean, helicopters seem so unnatural. I've never seen anything in nature that has spinning wings."

"Maple trees have seeds that twirl to the ground. That's natural," Aldo said as he reached for the door. They were already feeling the draft of the four massive blades spinning in neutral pitch above the behemoth.

"Great, trees . . .! How foolish my fears now seem. Thanks, I feel better already."

CHAPTER 35

The caves that had loomed ahead of Fin for the past hours were now finally within reach. Their details had become more evident to him as the day progressed. Earlier in the morning it had appeared he was walking toward a land lightly quilted in fallen snow. Instead, it was covered with ash that fell gently from the black clouds above. Like everything else here, the discovery of this illusion only increased his suffering. The flakes of this hot oily veneer, unlike their icy brethren, did not melt on Fin's skin. Rather, each flake stuck like napalm, burning as it bled into the ones that fell before and after it. At first, Fin tried to mitigate their sharp sting by hastily wiping away each chip as it landed. But in their overwhelming numbers, and his growing fatigue, he'd long since lost that battle. When he looked back through the thickening curtain of ash, the expanse of the sloping desert he'd crossed seemed endless. His perception of the hot land, with its immense burden of rocks unfolding as far as he could see, rippled in the air thinned by the rising heat.

Fin had to stop more frequently now, as he hauled his bleeding body up the cragged mountainside. There had not been any vegetation to speak of, and since his trip across that river of decay, there'd been no sign of any water. His lips were cracked and fissured down to what was once pink and bleeding muscle. Muscle that had long since dried up, though his pain flowed on without diversion. His tongue was deeply crevassed.

Swollen and dried out like cotton, its bloated mass burning in his mouth.

Looking up at the approaching caverns, Fin noted they were far larger than he had thought. Their open mouths were lined with the charred teeth that this hell had wrought in them. Fin entered the first cave he reached. Stumbling into the shade, he draped himself across a wide rock just inside the brim of the enclosure. The relief from the heat above, though slight, was a welcome one.

Lying there in the relative cool, he began to think about Eva again. He could picture her laughing and running in their back yard, climbing on the cedar swing set he'd built for her a few summers back. He pictured her soft eyes and her enthusiastic smile. But despite his best effort to cheat this place, his attempt to feel the warmth of her hugs failed him. His ability to feel her had been decreasing all along as he made his way through this godforsaken place.

Maybe this isn't the right direction. His eyes burned as he began to tear up. Fin blinked forcefully in an attempt to conserve fluid and realized for the first time that, with the thought of Eva, his twitching had stopped.

Allowing his vision to adjust to the darkness, he noticed what had seemed like shadows and natural features on the walls were now taking a different form. Sitting up, Fin squinted in the sheltered light to make out his new surroundings. Rising from where he lay, he walked over to the flat cavern walls and ran his fingers over the smooth rock. He could hardly believe what he was seeing.

Stretched out over the entire length of the cave wall before him were primitive drawings, scrawled in all their faded glory like those found in the American West by archeologists. The stick figures of prominence resembled the beast that had engaged Fin two nights ago. Their disproportionate limbs and gnarled claws an unmistakable likeness for what were apparently more ubiquitous creatures than he thought. These larger creatures were chasing the smaller ones, which looked like humans—humans with spears and headdresses made of feathers. Fin made his way down the pictogram from right to left. He noted that with each successive installment, the numbers of these creatures grew, while those that looked like natives dwindled. What struck him most was the fact that, as this story evolved, some of the beasts drawn wore the feathers and carried the spears of those who were disappearing. In the last frame only one individual remained, alone and cornered against the rocks by a multitude of the creatures. Fin dashed back to the far right and counted all the human figures that wore feathers. Returning to the last image again he counted all those wearing the feathers, both human and demon alike. The numbers matched.

"These things were human."

In disbelief, Fin backed away from the mural. He, too, hoped to hole up here in this cave for a bit. It had obviously given shelter to another at one time, and for long enough to create this primitive fresco. Fin dropped back onto the rock on which he'd been lying. Still staring at these images, he rested his head against the cold wall behind him. The daylight had begun to fade and the darkness in the cave was being replaced by the long cascading shadows of the falling ash outside. Backlit, their silhouetted forms ran over the walls and floor like some abstract disco ball. In his exhaustion, Fin found himself amused, almost mesmerized, by the phantom images that danced all about him. Staring at them, his focus began to shift. His appreciation of his surroundings softened. Unable to fight his fatigue any longer, he closed his eyes.

When Fin finally woke he had no idea how long he'd been out. As he lay there, something moved at the brink of his vision. Fin's heart pounded, the cold pressure in his chest reviving his fatigued muscles. Jumping to his feet, he saw it again. What he'd seen was not inside, but outside the cave. Standing in the archway, their shadows commingling with those cast by the falling ash, were eight or nine creatures like the one he'd seen last night, and none of them looked as if *they* were here to give advice. They approached him slowly, the raspy sound of their breathing broken by shrill screams and demonic growls. Fin frantically searched for a weapon. Pouncing on two softball-sized rocks, he hurled one at the creature closest to him. His shot glanced off the wall and landed harmlessly in the falling ash outside. One by one they entered the dark cavern, their eyes glowing a now familiar orange. Fin slowly backed away. Although he couldn't see them well, he could hear their claws scraping on the unforgiving floor as they closed in. In his terror, Fin threw the second rock at the head of the creature now within a few feet of him. Jerking quickly to avoid being hit, it lost its balance. Fin grabbed another rock off the ledge next to him and lunged, driving the rock into the creature's head with all of his weight. The creature fell against the wall before slumping to the ground. Standing over his quivering prey, Fin raised the rock above his head and again smashed it into the creature's already fractured skull. Then he quickly withdrew further into the darkness of the cavern.

The creatures stopped their advance. With their breath now visible in the declining temperatures, they quietly regarded their fallen brethren from a distance. As Fin waited for their retaliation, he got his first close look at them. There were subtle differences in appearance between them. Some were shorter than others, some more rotund. There were variations in their coloring as well as their postures. Their faces, although grotesque and disfigured, showed characteristics that set them apart from one another. They were individuals, not clones from some satanic overlord.

Fin flinched and took a nervous step back as his would-be attackers suddenly rushed the fallen carcass. In horror, he watched as they tore the body limb from limb and devoured it, fighting and scrapping amongst themselves for the pieces. In a matter of minutes, all that was left were the scattered boney remains and a dark collection of fluid on the rocky floor. With their feast over, the creature's attention once again turned to Fin.

Petrified, Fin turned and ran, frantically racing down the cave's pitch-black tunnel hoping to find an escape. The harsh glow from the creatures' eyes shed some light on his course. The echoing wet growls and unnatural screams that pursued him drove Fin faster and further than he had imagined his legs could run. But rounding a corner, he slipped and crashed onto his side. He slid across the loose rock and slammed into the opposite wall of the cave, shattering his right leg just below his knee. The bone jutted out through his thinning skin, tearing a bloody hole in his already tattered clothes. Panicked and not sure what to do first, he clutched the rock above him and raised himself in agony. Gingerly placing his weight on his good leg, he felt the first razor-like slashes into the flesh of his back. Spinning wildly in defense, Fin brought his elbow down hard against the side of the creature's head. His attacker stumbled back, allowing two more to heave their weight onto his broken frame. With his own blood flowing down his arms, Fin clutched the throats of the two creatures as their weight drove them all to the ground. Tilting his head back and looking over the inverted floor, he could see a faint light in the distance. Holding their snapping jaws at arms' length, Fin knew his demise could be seconds away. Their talons dug into him repeatedly, ripping huge jagged tracks into his flesh. Fin's arms began to quiver and his strength faded beneath the immense weight of these creatures. As they drew nearer and nearer to his face, his unexpected salvation came from his remaining pursuers. In their competition to feed, they tore wildly at the backs of those who had led the pack. In the midst of the mêlée, Fin managed to pull himself out from beneath them. Unable to stand, he dragged himself toward the growing sliver of light at the end of the tunnel.

It was a fracture in the rocks through which daylight shone. Fin could hear the howls and fervent grappling of talons from the approaching horde as he reached it. Blindly throwing his hand up against the cave wall, he found a shallow ledge at arm's length. With his macerated limbs coursing blood across the rocks, Fin lifted his body off the floor. Turning sideways, he forced himself into this slight opening.

Already turned from his pursuers, he was unable to fit through the narrow portion of the crevice within reach. Having run out of room, he found himself pressed up against the cold jagged contours of his fate. With the hope of finding Eva sinking, Fin suddenly realized all the noise had stopped. Against the back of his neck, Fin could feel the pulsing hot breath of his pending doom. As the creature's jaws clamped down over Fin's neck, he felt his flesh separate from his body. He was being eaten alive.

Fin drove his fist into the back of the creature's throat, gagging it as it held him. Pulling back, it released him, and Fin was able to place a foot on the creature's shoulder for leverage. Before he could reach a higher opening on the wall, Fin felt another aggressor clamp down on the back of his left thigh. With its teeth sunk in to the bone, it shook its head like a junkyard dog, tearing off a chunk of muscle the size of his fist. Frantic to get away Fin did the only thing he could. He continued to climb up the side of the cave. His fear coursing through his body, he could see the damage they were inflicting, but he was no longer able to feel the pain.

The pressure against his back gave way as he rose above the pack and slid backwards toward the light. Their bites were now like small annoyances, tugging at his feet as he retreated from them through this wider gap. Emerging into a steep tunnel, Fin slid downwards toward a large opening, Overwhelmed by loss of blood, fatigue, and pain, he could hear only muffled sounds as he reached the opening and briefly went weightless, reentering the dim light before crashing to the ground several feet below. Hoping his attackers were too large to follow, Fin lay in the sand, shaking from the cold and his mounting blood loss, and drifting in and out of consciousness.

Suddenly the light of the dying day was blotted out. Fin rolled his head to the left and found himself staring into a looming shadow. The last remnants of Fin's will bled into the surrounding sand. Peering into another pair of burning orange eyes and too fatigued to defend himself, he passed out.

CHAPTER 36

Graves clutched the cargo seat that had been tearing into the back of his shoulders for over two hours now. This pain and the resonance of the airframe coaxed him forward out of his seat, forcing him to concentrate just to keep from falling on the floor. The passenger bay of this particular "bird" had been rigged for carrying twelve passengers, not inexperienced VIPs. Graves found himself sitting in aviation's version of a woven lawn chair with its bare aluminum frame digging into the back of his thighs, while his head had been continually banging into the risers that guided the hydraulic lines around where he sat. Now roughly twenty-five kilometers southeast of Rome, he could see the green Alban hills flowing beneath them as the aircraft rolled to the right. Descending sharply, Castle Gondolfo and the small Italian city of Albano Laziale came into view.

In their steep approach, the yaw of the helicopter brought the afternoon sunlight into the cabin, casting a dizzying array of shadows through the arc of the main rotor. This rapidly alternating light and dark pattern forced Graves to close his eyes to avoid the reflexive vertigo it created.

Tall grasses leaned away from the wash of the blades like a shimmering crop circle as they touched down. Their pilot gestured for them to stay put until all motion had stopped, but Graves found that between the heat of the cabin and the lights, he was beginning to feel nauseous. He removed his belts and headset and peered out the side troop door. He could see several guards in brightly colored uniforms awaiting their arrival. Their attire looked as though it would be more fitting in the company of pachyderms and peanuts than here at the summer residence of the Pope.

He could see of them, all in pantaloons and bloused long sleeve shirts. Their white collars and red folded cuffs were outdone by the royal blue and gold stripes that ran length-wise over their entire uniform to their boot covers. The ensemble was topped off with a black beret, cocked ever so gently to the left. Each one of them wore a golden saber on his left hip as they stood at parade rest awaiting their guests.

With the brake taking its final effect on the spinning blades, their air crewman removed the bolt and lowered the stairs to the ground. Two of the Vatican Swiss Guards appeared on either side of the ramp as a very Italian looking man with a large smile walked toward the aircraft.

Aldo exited first, grasping the hand of their host firmly as his feet touched the lawn. "Detective Graves, I would like you to meet a dear friend of mine, Sergeant Clavius of the Swiss Guard."

Graves reached out as his foot touched the last step, noting the golden lappet on the sergeant's sleeve. "Pleased to meet you, sir."

In clear English, with only a hint of a French accent, the man answered politely. "Please, call me Sergeant, I work for a living. "Sir" is to be reserved for my boss." The three men smiled before turning away from their ride toward the impos- ing castle ahead.

As the two friends chatted ahead of him, Graves hastily took in his surroundings. Lake Albano glistened a thousand feet below to his left as a sweet jasmine-scented breeze swept up over the hillside. In front of them, positioned just to the south of the immaculate grounds, was the enormous four-story brick and stucco structure capped with twin white domes on its northeast and southwest corners. Turning from his conversation with Aldo, Sergeant Clavius attempted to draw Graves into the discussion.

"So, Detective, what do you know of our castle." He swept an extended arm gracefully toward the residence.

With wide eyes, Graves shrugged his shoulders. "Not much."

"Well, it has been here since the twelfth century, and passed from family to family over many generations until coming into the possession of Pope Clement the Eighth. But it was Pope Urban the Eighth who had it redesigned in the seventeenth century. The great telescopes you see perched atop the roof were not here originally." He pointed toward the great white domes as they strode across the courtyard. "They were originally in Rome, behind the dome of Saint Peter's Basilica. Pope Pius the Eleventh had the Specola Vaticana moved here after the surrounding city lights became too great to appreciate the dimmer stars in the early part of the twentieth century."

Graves continued to listen, but despite the beautiful surroundings, the incredibly interesting history lesson, and the delicate French accent it was all being told in, he still found himself overly focused on this very professional man's outfit. All these serious words were coming out of the mouth of someone who, despite his best efforts, reminded him of the entertainment at his six-year-old birthday party. At any minute he expected these very somber men guarding this castle to offer him some cake and a pony ride.

Aldo interrupted his derailed train of thought. "Will the Cardinal be waiting for us?"

"He should be by now. He was with another visitor. You are to be Cardinal Antonacci's second guest today."

"Is it normal for him to have several guests in one day?" Graves thought he remembered Aldo mentioning in the helicopter that it should be very quiet here, as it usually was when the Pope was elsewhere.

"No, sir, not usually."

Graves's cell phone buzzed a tune, informing him Dana was sending a text. Unsnapping it from his belt clip, he pushed the unit's single button and slid the graphic to unlock his device. The text read, "Found this map of Castle Gondolfo." Attached was a schematic of the structure they were walking toward. With a single tap, it opened. *Christ. Like I can see a damn thing on this little screen.* After a few pinches and swipes, Graves had blown up the portions he found most interesting. "Hey, this place has a few blind stairwells that don't seem to go any . . ."

Aldo stopped them where they stood. "Who else has asked to see the Cardinal today?" His hand rested firmly on Graves's chest, arresting both his thought and his movement.

"I don't know, he did not say." Clavius looked puzzled. "The Cardinal only expressed that we were to leave him in the Northeast observatory."

"Did you see anyone come in or out?" Aldo was again moving quickly toward the large dark wooden doors off the courtyard.

"No, sir, I did not. I was here awaiting your arrival." The Sergeant hurried to keep up with his guests. "If the Cardinal relieves me of a duty, I follow his wishes. I have no reason to suspect anything further." Their pace quickened. "What is it that you are worried about?"

Aldo's words, jarred loose by his growing stride, were now coming sporadically. "I'm worried that this holy man may be tied to a scandal, and that one by one those who seem central to it are dying, or rather being killed."

The three men were running full out now, covering the last hundred yards or so to the immense doors in only a matter of seconds. Sergeant Clavius pulled hard on the brass loop that hung from the door at chest level. As the massive single slab of oak swung open, a solitary drop of crimson fell to the pavement between them. All three men looked down, then reflexively upward. Directly above them, four stories up, was the observatory.

Bursting into the marble foyer, Aldo took the lead. With their footsteps echoing loudly throughout the cavernous entrance, the men hurried toward a red-carpet-lined staircase. Clavius snatched his radio from his belt as they ran up the first flight.

"Beitrag Wachen auf Jede Etage!"

"No, Clavius, that won't be enough! Don't instruct them to just post guards. Send all those available to the observatory!" Aldo was several steps ahead of them now, jumping two to three stairs at a time.

As the sergeant relayed the changes to his previous instructions, Aldo drew his weapon and took a sharp left at the next open landing. Heading for the first elevator Graves had seen thus far, he noted a guard already standing at every choke point on the floor. The Sergeant continued up the stairs while the two men boarded the elevator up to the observation level.

"No act of aggression has been committed in this castle in over three hundred years, and even then it was not occupied by the Vatican. I intend to keep it that way." Aldo pulled the slide back on his firearm, chambering a round as he spoke. "I suggest you make yourself ready, Detective, but I strongly encourage you to hold your fire, if possible. This is holy ground." Graves was becoming uncomfortably used to surprises today. First a helicopter flight, then jesters with swords, now loaded weapons inside the Pope's vacation home.

It was eerily quiet as the mechanical doors of the elevator opened onto the top floor. In the distance they could hear the sound of the approaching guardsmen's heavy footsteps as they echoed off the marble walls of the stairwell. Ahead of the two men, the glass doors to the observatory were shut tight. The highly polished marble floor reflected the enormous telescope and its dome just beyond. With his weapon raised, Aldo crossed the hallway and pulled hard on the handle—with no luck.

Pressing his temple up against the glass Graves could make out the security panel on the wall adjacent to the entryway, its red warning light blinking intently in the dim room. "I think they're locked, and it looks like the alarm is armed from the inside."

The sergeant arrived breathless. "No sign of anyone on the stairs, what's the matter?"

"It would appear that whatever has transpired inside this room is still contained within." Aldo pointed at the alarm.

Removing a set of keys from his pocket, Clavius unlocked the doors and hastily disarmed the system. The men took opposite paths around the circular antechamber. The room was lit only by the afternoon sunlight cast through the tele-scope's open hardwood-lined roof panels. The soft hum of the targeting computer and its electronics ebbed and flowed as the system continually cooled itself. With the cherry panels on the inner walls of the dome reflecting the light, the giant Schmidt telescope seemed more like an offering than a scientific instrument in this holy house.

Aldo pointed toward the wooden doors that led out onto the balcony. The sergeant stood guard at the entrance, leaving Aldo and Graves to prepare for what, or whom, they might find out there.

"The balcony goes equally in both directions." Aldo informed Graves in a hushed voice. "It's about five meters deep and ten meters wide. As we open these doors we need to clear both directions simultaneously or one of us could get shot. Capisce?"

Graves nodded his understanding.

With that, Aldo threw open the doors, delivering both men into the daylight. Graves cleared the right side, leading his vision around the balcony with his weapon. With every muscle in his arms tensed, he fully expected a brief and violent fire fight. In Graves's direct line of sight, at the edge of the terrace, lay the Cardinal. On his back with his arms outstretched at his sides, his bloodied left hand hung over the parapet beneath the rail.

Seeing evidence of life still in the Cardinal's moving chest, Graves rushed to his side. "He's still alive!"

The Cardinal's hands were both torn deeply across the palms. The serrated edges of the wounds suggested efforts defending himself against a sharp instrument wielded by his assailant. In his neck, behind the angle of his jaw, was a deep and jagged stab wound. With each agonal effort, the Cardinal's breath bubbled from the gaping wound. Holding up the thumb and index and middle fingers of his right hand, he moved his lips in a desperate effort to communicate.

With his hand sliding about in the blood-soaked folds of the Cardinal's neck, Graves forced his fingers into the open wound in an attempt to squeeze off the offending vessel. Looking up, he found Aldo frantically inspecting the escarpment beneath the balcony. "Call for help, he needs an airway now!" Turning his attention back to Cardinal Antonacci, Graves lowered his ear to the dying priest's mouth as he continued to apply pressure to the wound. "Who did this? What did you see, Father?"

"It was de sun," he sputtered, coughing up gelatinous clots of blood. "Per favore, forgive me my role."

With confusion on his face, Graves withdrew. He held eye contact with the cardinal as he felt the pulsations beneath his fingers begin to fade.

Aldo returned with the Sergeant. "Help is on the way." His voice trailed off as he realized it may already be too late.

"He said he saw the sun." Graves looked up at the two men as he continued to hold the Cardinal's head in his lap. "What the *hell* does that mean?"

"I don't know. Who knows how long he's been lying here bleeding like this." The Sergeant crossed himself. "Maybe he's delirious from all the blood loss?"

"Who did this? The room was locked from the inside with the alarm system armed. Even if the perpetrator had keys, he couldn't have left with the system on." Graves could hear their helicopter begin to spin up in a hopeful attempt to medevac the Cardinal.

With the arrival of the local paramedics, Aldo pulled a towel from their flight bag and handed it to Graves, allowing him to leave the Cardinal in their care. "So how did our perpetrator escape?"

"Wait a minute . . . ," Graves pulled his phone from his belt again. "This," he said, pointing to the graphic Dana had sent him. "This is what I was starting to show you before. The observatory is one of the chambers that seem to have a blind-ending stairwell in it."

"No, Detective, that is impossible. Where this leads is known only to the Swiss Guard. But if it is so, it cuts down our suspects significantly." The sergeant turned and quickly headed into the gallery again.

"Over here!" A hand shot up above the control desk for the main telescope. As Graves and Aldo approached Clavius, they realized that he had been partially swallowed by a porthole in the floor.

"Why is this here?" Aldo asked, as he quickly made his way around the desk, still wiping the Cardinal's blood from his hands.

"The structure of the castle was unable to tolerate the increased weight of this newer telescope, so this support silo was constructed beneath it twenty years ago. In doing so, the sitting Pontiff decided to install a secret passageway out of here." Clavius began to descend the spiral ladder that lay below him. "He felt it not only provided an added layer of security, but also was in keeping with the mysterious passageways that line the catacombs of the Vatican."

"Where does it lead?" Graves asked, as he placed a tentative foot on the first rung.

"It connects to the rest of the sewer system of the castle." The sergeant's words faded as he quickened his pace and bowed his head to clear the lip of the hatch. "This castle enjoys the same extraterritorial rites as the rest of the Vatican's properties, at least since the treaty with Italy in 1929. Because of that, its systems of communication and utilities are tied directly to Vatican City."

"I need to call Dana to let her know what's happened." Graves pulled out his cell as he followed Sergeant Clavius further. "How the hell would an assassin know about this?"

"As I said before, Detective, the knowledge of this route reduces the number of possible suspects significantly." Reaching the bottom of the steep metal staircase, the men were faced with a decision.

"This tunnel goes in both directions," Clavius announced, his voice echoing off the dank walls around them. "Each direction opens up onto a different road, each leading to a different town. I suggest we split up."

Graves held his phone up again, shedding a bit more light on this darkened place. My map doesn't show anything down here, we've got nothing to go by."

Clavius took the device from Graves's hands. Rotating the phone sideways, he punched a new URL. "The Vatican has its own servers, and its own suffix, but you need the codes to access the information." He furiously punched in text before handing the phone back to Graves. Filling the small three by two inch screen were three-dimensional images of the tunnels. "As long as you have even the slightest signal, the GPS should guide you to the exit." Sergeant Clavius pulled a small flashlight from his belt. "Good luck." Turning from the two men, he disappeared into the darkness of the tunnel.

"Ok, I guess we go this way then." Aldo turned, pausing for a moment. "Since you have the map, why don't you go first?" He politely gestured for Graves to take the lead.

The tunnel was not a large one. Graves could feel the hair on top of his head brushing along the curved ceiling of the passageway. More oval than circular, it had a little room on either side of the men as they advanced. What started out as dry ground soon became wet. "We must have been at the high point where we started." Graves whispered over his shoulder. "Watch your step." He widened his stance with each step to avoid submerging his feet in the foul-smelling fluid that ran beneath them. Up ahead, the cinder-blocked walls showed a faint reflection of light from beyond. Approaching it, Graves stopped. "The map cut out, I'm not getting a signal any longer. It looks like there's a fork in the tunnel up ahead."

After a few more steps, the men paused. Waiting quietly, they listened for any sounds that might guide their decision. "I don't know." Aldo finally said, unable to tolerate the silence any longer. "This way seems to be brighter. Let's go right. Besides, all this sewage seems to be running the other way."

"I think I feel a breeze on my face. Does it look brighter to you, Aldo? Aldo?

Turning around, Graves saw his partner was holding up his index finger and listening intently behind them. "Did you hear that?"

"Hear what?"

"It sounded like footsteps behind us." They stood frozen again. "There. Did you hear that?"

"I did." Graves was slowly drawing his weapon. "It's passing the fork in the tunnel, toward us."

Crouching down in front of Graves, Aldo drew his weapon too. The two men took aim up the tunnel they'd just traversed.

Around the corner, the sounds stopped. Whoever, or whatever, was approaching knew they were there, too. Both men could make out a glint off the muzzle of a gun as it slowly advanced into the growing light.

CHAPTER 37

Their tour had begun outside, overlooking the rolling green hills surrounding the main facility along the southwest aspect of the collider's seventeen-mile loop. Walking across the empty tarmac and past the towering bronze statue of Lord Shiva that adorned the entryway, Father Moriel and Edvard entered the Globe of Science and Innovation. This enormous steel and glass structure served the institution both as an awe-inspiring welcome to Europe's preeminent scientific achievement and as the portal to the main control room for the Large Hadron Collider or LHC. They descended the wide ramp circumnavigating the Globe's perimeter.

Moriel again thanked his host for this tour. "I'm concerned about my parishioners. They've suffered much with the loss of Eva and I feel like I should be back there with them now that the ceremony here is over."

The two men continued on, passing through several large heavy metal doors that opened only after Edvard obligingly submitted his retina for review to the wall-mounted scanners adjacent to these access points. After the pattern of blood vessels lining the back of his eyeball was matched with the information archived in the facility's security computers, each door opened, granting them passage with a hefty but satisfying mechanical whir. Every checkpoint was arranged like an airlock, with two sets of similar doors bordering an elevator-sized antechamber. This setup provided each authorized individual the physical assurance that desired parties alone were granted entry. Only after the first set of doors had closed was the second set activated, subsequently allowing passage into the restricted area beyond.

"I understand, Father, and I appreciate your interest in what Fin helped to accomplish here before he died." Ahead of them, a wide set of stairs led down into a darkened chamber beyond. Edvard escorted Moriel into a small observation room on their right, just before the stairs.

"I certainly didn't want to leave without seeing the facility that Fin spoke so passionately about." Father added as he continued to follow his guide.

"I apologize for the gadgetry and lack of lights," Edvard chuckled as he again submitted his retina to the security system's scrutiny, opening the green sliding doors. "We've had to shut most of the operations down temporarily. We've been having some issues with the internal environmental control of the main detector."

"What sorts of issues?"

"We've been finding some sort of buildup on the internal walls. It's been accumulating there in increasing amounts over the last few days, and we're not sure why." Walking around the two empty high-backed chairs between him and a series of displays, Edvard turned on several of the smaller monitors in the control booth, taking care not to bring up the image of the main reactor chamber. "We're also not sure what this stuff is." He sat down, briefly taking a hiatus from their private tour of the facility.

Father stood over him in the darkened room looking at the images on the multiple screens. The room was small, but warm and inviting. Its floor was covered wall to wall with a chocolate colored carpet of thin pile, this was complimented on the walls with an organic green paint. A single massive glass window, framed in richly stained hardwood, hung in front of them looking out over the main control room, now dark and deserted. From where he stood he could see the entire theater of individual control pods as they lay beneath the inactive main display wall. Father stared at one small LCD screen in particular. Something looked vaguely familiar to him. "You say that this residue has been only on the inside of the reaction chamber and not the rest of the system's tunnels?" he asked.

"That's correct," Edvard said. "Over the last few weeks, like we spoke about on the phone before," he added as he looked up over his shoulder toward his visitor, "The matter generated out of the collisions has become increasingly complex, with increased mass, as you might remember." Edvard turned back to stare at the screens in front of him. "But only in the last few days have we had this *situation* arise," he added as he gestured at the multicolored display of peaks and valleys on the screen in front of them. "We've had to shut nearly everything down in our effort to get the chamber cleaned off and determine where this film is coming from."

"Where are these images from?" Father pulled back the remaining empty seat, making his way to a monitor on the far right of the bank. "This one," he said as he pointed to the black and white image on the screen.

"That's from one of the scanning electron microscopes . . . SEM number eight . . . inside the collider's main chamber, I think." Edvard glared at the screen with a hint of uncertainty before looking over his left shoulder toward the sole CERN technician who shared the booth with them

Feverishly tapping away on his keyboard, the post-graduate

student had been uninvolved in their conversation until now. Mr. Tong offered a confirmatory nod without looking up from his work. "That's correct, sir."

"The internal milieu must remain pristine, just like the rooms in which they make computer chips," Edvard continued. "If there were to be any contaminants, the vacuum inside the system would be violated and the proton beams would scatter unreliably, not to mention that our interpretation of their prodigy would be less than accurate."

Edvard leaned forward and touched the screen nearest to him. Sliding images around the large touch-sensitive monitor, he quickly worked through an icon-driven menu until he arrived at a collection of images similar to the one that Father had in front of him. "We don't intend to dismantle this monstrosity every few weeks to test the inner walls . . . nor could we. Instead, what we've done is build in a series of small scanning electron microscopes throughout the chambers, with a few in the tunnel networks as well. These take roughly one to two hundred images each over the course of a regular operational day, which can last up to twenty hours or so. As long as we continue to see the crystalline structure of the wall's inert ceramic coating and nothing else, we're good . . . but as you can see, that's not what we have." Frustrated, Edvard slumped backwards into his seatback, causing it to rock slightly beneath his weight.

By now Father's interest had been piqued. It had been too long since he'd had a chance to have a real scientific discussion with anyone. *It's been over a year*, he thought, *since Fin's death*. "Where's the mass spectrometer?" Father pointed back to the screen where a multitude of colored spikes rose up from a digital horizon.

Edvard raised his brow. "Impressive, I'd forgotten you had some science in your background, no wonder you were so interested in seeing all this before you leave tomorrow morning."

"Well, it was in genetics, and theology, of course, but not a great deal of physics. My interest in particle physics was mostly just a hobby for me, one that Fin nurtured. I'm just interested in seeing everything you've accomplished here."

Edvard scanned back and forth, viewing each monitor briefly. He stopped at each of them for an indication as to which tier of computers was feeding the data. "That mass spec is also from within the main reaction chamber . . . actually it's from the primary vent tube. Why?"

"That pattern is familiar. What was the last atomic speciation you had? Was it still carbon 14?"

"No, sir, we've had newer results as of yesterday afternoon," interrupted Mr. Tong. Both men turned toward the darkened corner of the room. "Sorry, Dr. Krunowski, sir, you were unavailable. I had every intention of telling you before you left today." The dutiful graduate student offered a weak smile.

"Please, continue Mr. Tong," Edvard said with a deep baritone voice, his displeasure evident.

"Well the most recent results show that *this* material is more complex." He nervously shuffled through a stack of printed reports. After dropping a few of the ticker tapes on the floor, he found the one he was searching for. "It consists of chains of carbon atoms, some of them combining with the remaining hydrogen to form basic amino acids . . . "

Moriel suddenly shot forward in his chair. "At what magnification is this SEM operating?" He was briskly tapping the screen that had caught his eye when they first walked in.

"I believe it's at two hundred fifty thousand times." Edvard paused and said, "down to about ten angstroms."

"Can you pull back to about half that?" Father excitedly scooped the air back toward himself with anxious fingers, gesturing to the young post-doctoral physicist.

Punching in new instructions, the terrain dropped away like that from a departing hot air balloon. As the men stared at the developing picture an image began to magically come into focus.

"Heilige scheisse," Edvard muttered under his breath in disbelief as he sat forward in his seat. "Has that been there this whole time?"

On the screen in front of them was the sharply contrasted impression of several delicate necklaces lying atop a crystalline bed. The sandy backdrop beneath these jewels served as the canvas for their shadows, cast long in the light of the bombarding electron gun. Many of these rings were broken, scattered about the topography like fragmented pieces of spaghetti, but one perfect ornament lay just within the lower boarder of their field of view.

This one would be the proof that *He* had promised.

"Those aren't just amino acids son," Father said, now sure of where he'd seen that spectral pattern before. "That gas chromatograph is of the nucleotide adenine. And that," he said pointing proudly at the twenty-inch LCD screen in front of him, "that is an intact strand of double helical DNA."

"You will find the evidence you seek in what remains of my savior's form to be conjured from this place."

"The question now is where the hell did it come from?" the graduate student asked, his face still lit from staring into the ambient light of his monitor. "That chamber has been sealed up for weeks, way before all this began, and with no loss of integrity in the vacuum either."

The pager on Edvard's hip began to vibrate. He reached down and blindly removed it from his belt, never taking his eyes off their discovery. Raising it up to his face he glanced at the tiny backlit screen before reaching for the phone on the desk in front of him.

"Dr. Krunowski here." He listened for a few moments before covering the mouthpiece. "Father, you'll excuse me. It's my secretary, this will only take a moment." Edvard turned to his graduate student, who was now combing through the digital archives of electron photos stored from the previous days. "Why don't you take Father down onto the main floor and give him a brief tour of the remainder of our topside facility." After the two men exited the room, Edvard returned to his phone call.

"Continue please." Dropping his head, he rubbed his eyes deeply with his thumb and index finger as he continued to listen. " . . . and they said that they're on their way here to talk with me now?" Cloaked in the darkness of the booth, Edvard stood back from the massive window watching the two men walk about the amphitheater below. "Please call him back and let him know where we are, and tell him that I'm busy with the priest." He softly placed the receiver back on its hook.

Keeping a watchful eye on his collared friend, Edvard approached the glass and politely offered an approving nod as his graduate student motioned that he and Moriel were going to head toward the elevators to continue the tour below. Edvard opened his phone and dialed one last number. After two soft digital pulses, the line was flooded with the sound of whirling blades.

"Where are you now?" Edvard asked in a deep voice.

Five hundred feet below the main control room, Father Moriel and the grad student entered the reactor chamber. The power level surged within Atlas, serving the strong coherent stream of matter that grew inside its pristine vacuum.

CHAPTER 38

The fading light shone pink through Fin's closed lids as he lay, feeling every rock and crevice on the ground beneath him. In the quiet heat, he slid his hand beneath his legs, suffering mounting pain in his back to explore the wounds he had received while in retreat from his demons. Keeping his eyes shut, Fin found himself increasingly uncertain about how he would react to the absence of flesh where he had been attacked. He ran his fingers down his leg little by little until he could feel the dried blood caked on his skin. Advancing his hand slowly, expecting his fingers to curve into the sickening void where he'd been bitten, Fin hesitated. Where he expected an absence, he found something else. His fingers brushed up against a coarseness rising up in place of his wounds. What he at first had thought was a small and insignificant change soon filled his palm. Sitting up quickly, with the pain in his back beating a moaning grimace out of him, his terror returned.

Twenty paces in front of him sat another of the beasts. Fin froze, quietly abbreviating each breath in pain. The creature kept its back to him, seemingly unaware Fin was there as it sat motionless facing the dying light. Fin could see its slow breaths rising and falling in the pronounced ridge running the length of its back, across which he could almost make out words, like a faded tattoo. Over its left shoulder, on the tented dark flesh that thinly veiled its bones, there were three distinct dots arranged in triangular fashion. Fin's eyes followed the beast's hypertrophied spine downward to where its terminal spike pierced its burnt hide. He let his own fingers blindly explore his new wounds, keeping an eye on his foe. Fin planted his open palms onto the rocky ground around him. Painfully, he tried to raise himself to a crouching height as he lowered his gaze to search for a weapon. With a cold flood of horror, his eyes fell on his own legs. Covering every deep gash he'd received was a thick black scab, its rough matrix flowing over his limbs like some saprophytic vine. The skin around these areas peeled away from the fungating masses as they coursed toward his feet in broken heaps.

"The light grows. It's not dying."

Again Fin froze, raising only his eyes to meet the eerie voice that addressed him.

"What?" Fin asked in alarm.

"You slept all through the night while I sat watch over you." Its voice was still shrill and breathy.

Fin was unsure of what to do next. Clearly this creature had passed up the opportunity to harm him, but his instincts still made him anxious with suspicion.

"I told you I would watch over you, and I have." It turned to face him, dragging its claws across the rock as it slid its thin woody legs over the ledge. "It's important you find her."

"What's happening to me?" Fin looked up, a cold chill running up his spine as his eyes fell on the burning sockets of his self-proclaimed guardian.

"Your soul is pure. You are alone amongst sinners who crave what you have, hope. They will fight and tear it from you if you let them."

Again, Fin looked down at his legs.

The creature drew closer. Sensing his fear, it moved like

a serpent as it crept on all fours over the ground. Crouching within feet of where Fin sat, it continued.

"With each act of defense, each act of violence, you give yourself to them, to this hell. You are becoming one of us." It sat back down in the dust. Dragging its talons across the ground, it scooped up a handful of dirt and poured it out again.

"Will I look like you?"

"I don't know. Those of us who are not here by choice look much this way when we arrive. This place, its existence, its very substance, is made from the evil of those who are condemned here. One cannot remain here without succumbing to its will." The creature paused and looked over its shoulder before continuing on. "*He* needs her, and it is their job to stop you. You must find your daughter before this place consumes you fully."

With the warmth of the day still in its infancy, Fin could feel the heat of Eva's love pulling him toward the valley beyond where they sat, but his thoughts seemed more clouded now. Although he could imagine a faint light burning from the place where he headed, he had grown too focused on what was happening to him than to Eva, his true purpose in this place.

"You can't escape their sight. Yours is a soul that commands their attention, calls to them, to us all. It's an unrelenting beacon that reeks of a comfort only vaguely remembered in this place." He leaned in closer, dropping his head as he spoke, as if to conceal his words. "He will continue tearing at you until you fall."

"Who is he?" Fin asked.

Fin's guide stood. "We've been here too long. They'll be back again soon."

"Who is he? Does he have my daughter?" Fins anger drove him swiftly to his feet. "Answer me, goddamn it! Who is he?"

"He has no name." In the growing light, Fin could almost read the remnants of the tattoo on the creature's back as it walked away from him. "He's the strongest amongst us, the one who punishes. He's many."

"Does he have my Eva? Why does he need her?" Fin's fury was overtaking the pain he felt previously. Tears streamed down his bloodied face as his eye began to twitch again. Fin grabbed the demon by its gnarled shoulder and spun him back. "Answer me!"

The creature shoved him, driving its blackened claws into Fin's already scarred chest, knocking him to the dirt. "He does have her, and he'll soon have you too!" The creature lowered its head again. "He keeps her to draw you in, she's the bait and you are the sacrificial lamb. Save your anger for them, you'll need it." He seemed saddened.

"My God would never desert me here." Fin's words echoed off the cold rocks around him as the creature stared at him in disbelief.

"Your god is not here, only you are." Its eyes burned with more intensity as it answered.

"Do not be afraid or discouraged," Fin muttered as he began to regain his footing. "For the Lord your God is with you wherever you go." He continued struggling to his feet, citing what little scripture he could remember. "I know the Lord is always with me. I will not be shaken, for he is . . ."

Lunging at him, the beast grabbed Fin by the throat and pinned him to the cliff wall beside them. "Where is your Christ now! Your bravery is outweighed only by your ignorance! There is no God, no creator, only you and me!" The beast's voice was different now, deeper and angrier. It propped its insurmountable heft into the claw around Fin's neck, choking him against the rocks.

Struggling against its unexpected weight, Fin found himself lofted into the air by his bleeding throat before being thrown over the precipice. Tumbling down the dune to the bottom, Fin scrambled to face his attacker. He could hear its voice booming after him as he continued to stumble.

"Enough with your incantations and wasted efforts! No one is listening to your useless prayer, no one has *ever* been listening!"

With fear swelling in his chest, Fin could feel the blood begin to pour again from the growing wounds in his back. Before he could right himself, the creature was on top of him again.

The beast seemed enormous, swollen far beyond its size from just moments ago. Fin quickly shuffled backwards up against an outcropping, holding his hands in the air to protect his turned face.

Several moments of quiet passed before Fin lowered his hands to watch as the beast, slumped to the ground before him, knelt with its head bowed. Its stature seemed to have returned to what it was before. Continuing to breathe heavily, it kept its distance.

Fin leaned forward off the rocks and reached around behind his own shoulders. Running bloodied fingers over the growing appendages there, he offered a lone olive branch as he spoke again. "What do you mean no one has ever been listening?"

The beast stood and turned as if to leave, then stopped. "There is no God, there is no Satan, there is just us."

"Bullshit!" Fin's frustration spilled from the chalice of his Catholic upbringing. "Why would you know that and I wouldn't? How *could* you know that?"

"That place you came from, what was it like?"

Fin hesitated, afraid of being beaten again if he gave the wrong answer. "It was perfect, it was Heaven!"

The creature sat back down in the dirt, and its voice softened just a bit as it spoke. "And what type of Heaven do you think you'd suffer if those there knew they were alone? If they knew only self-doubt and loneliness would accompany them until the end of days?"

Fin stared quietly at his counselor with a growing sadness for Eva burning in his chest.

"You'd suffer this Hell. That place would not exist as an alternative to this if you knew you only had each other to pray to, your own weaknesses to depend on." The creature raised its voice, its emaciated arms held up toward the blackening clouds that collected above them as he screamed his words. "This, this is Hell! The knowledge of these things consumes every creature here, look around you. This secret is shared with all who are condemned to suffer, and all who know this secret to be true, suffer because of it. Only here, in this forsaken hole, are we made aware of life's greatest secret . . . we're alone."

Fin felt nauseated. The burning in his chest was beginning to sicken him. "That can't be." He could feel the heat of his tears washing the dirt from his face. "Who created all of this? Where did all this come from then?"

"From us, you and me. It came from us. Life itself creates it all, man's will, his prayer. This mass belief molds our realities, not some all-knowing being. Our conviction that there is a better place makes it so, and this better place, Heaven, gives you something to hope for." Its face seemed softer, more human than before. "Eons of devotion to these rituals, these notions of the afterlife, inseminated the dream."

Fins head was swimming. The desperation of this place was overwhelming. "I don't understand." He could feel the dual pains of his chosen purgatory, the pain he endured bodily, and now the notion of the supreme good this place had robbed him of. He had come so far and borne so much, all to feel more alone and unsure of finding Eva than ever before.

"You *do* understand," the creature continued, "you always have, but you just don't want to accept it. Human will is the most powerful force the universe feels. It has shaped and bent everything."

Fin dropped his head into his hands. He could feel his sorrow washing over him. "I don't believe you."

"Your savior referred to himself as the son of man. Why then is it so hard to believe that his conception, during the most religious time on earth, was brought about by the focused will of the masses? The same will that forges *this* existence from nothingness. With all the evil man is capable of, we have no need of a fallen angel to guide us."

Thinking back to the drawings on the cave walls, Fin asked one last desperate question. "How long has this place been here?"

The gravelly voice grew distant. "As long as it's been needed." The creature paused, staring intently at his audience. "Focus on her, Fin Canty. Do not lose sight of your true purpose here."

As the light and heat continued to rise, Fin sat crying with his back pressed against his cold rocky shelter. With blood and tears flowing from his broken soul, the dirt around him began to congeal into a deep red mud. Weeping uncontrollably, Fin finally looked up. His companion was standing. Sitting alone and hopeless, Fin could hear a faint whisper again, or maybe it was several whispers all at once.

"Wait, what's your name? If you're supposed to guide me, I need to know what to call you."

"Salvador. My name is Salvador."

Graves pulled back the hammer on his weapon, the click resonated off the algae-covered walls around them.

"Inspector Baumgartner? Is that you?" a familiar voice called from just around the bend.

"Clavius? My god, man, we nearly shot you."

The Sergeant lowered his weapon, a well maintained SIG Sauer 220, and walked into the lit tunnel before them. "I'm sorry, sir. I reached the other end and there was no sign of our perpetrator, so I figured I'd joint back up with you. How did you know not to choose the left tunnel back there?"

With Aldo standing again, Graves looked over his shoulder to answer. "It was a guess, why?"

"There's a ten-meter drop off not three minutes' walk down that way. There used to be a gate there, but it rusted out and fell down the opening a few years back."

"Maybe our suspect chose that route and met his fate." Graves suggested.

"Not likely, Detective. Whoever came down here knew their way around."

"There's just a locked gate with nothing beyond it back that way. I suggest we try your dead end Sergeant."

Hiking back up the tunnel to the fork, the men traversed the sewage filled alternative to its end. The tunnel was shorter, but infinitely more polluted than the previous one. They each crouched down, trying hard not to allow any part of their bodies to touch the walls or ceiling around them. At the far end, tied to the embedded remains of the once substantial iron gate, was a rope.

Clavius leaned out over the opening. Holding onto the slick remains of the gate's hinge with one hand, he shined his light down the shaft. "I can almost see the bottom." He said, straining to lean out even further. Putting too much faith in the tired bolts that held the metal to the surrounding rock, Sergeant Clavius suddenly found himself holding a metal hinge in one hand and a flashlight in the other. Spinning his hands wildly in the air, he dropped both objects into the shaft before being grasped forcefully from behind by both Graves and Aldo. The light and hinge plummeted, following the knotted line all the way to its coiled terminus on the slick ground thirty feet below.

"I'll be dammed," Clavius added, still leaning far out over the open pipe. After bouncing several times, the flashlight had come to rest with its beam shining off what appeared to be an exceptionally clean metal object.

"What? What do you see down there?" Aldo asked, gripping a fist full of brightly colored uniform that now held the Sergeant's weight.

"I'm not sure, but we'll know once we get down there."

"I'm not climbing down that smelly pipe. Not on that rope, anyway." Graves said.

"Don't worry," Clavius reassured the two men, as they hauled him back to safety, "I know another way."

CHAPTER 39

The trip back had been as jarring as the one out. Start to finish, the whole thing had taken them about six hours, and the sun was beginning to set now.

"Dana? Dana, can you hear me?" Graves was sitting on a black padded stool with his feet resting comfortably on its circular bar below. The FedPol lab was of typical Scandinavian style, sparse and simple in design with all the lab equipment spaced evenly across the two parallel laminate benches that ran the length of the room. While Graves talked, the techs busied themselves with what he and Aldo had brought back with them.

"Are you back yet? How's the Cardinal?"

"Not well." Graves turned away from the lab techs as he continued. "He was flown to the Holy See's closest medical facility, the Regina Apostolorum Hospital . . . he's still in surgery."

"What did you find in the tunnel?" The Audi carrying her and Bastien crested the hill approaching the sprawling CERN facility visible in the distance.

"After we spoke, things didn't go as well as we'd hoped."

"What do you mean, what'd you find?" Sitting in the passenger seat, Dana swung the mouthpiece of her cell away from her face as she informed Bastien of the men's return.

"After Aldo and I climbed down to the sewer, we followed it out to the end . . . and by the way holy shit smells the same as the regular variety."

A small smile crept across her face in the darkened car. She was beginning to appreciate his sense of humor again. "What did you find?"

"Well, the tunnel ran on for probably a half mile and then ended at a seaside road that ran along the cliff. At the end, there was a heavy, and I mean heavy, wrought iron gate . . . which was locked."

"So the killer didn't go out that way?"

"No, but that's not all we found. Down a separate shaft we discovered what appears to be the weapon."

"Tom, that's a big assumption. How can you be sure at this point whatever you found was the weapon the Cardinal was attacked with?"

"It was covered in blood, first off," he added with just a hint of condescension. "It's a screwdriver, an industrial flathead screwdriver." Graves stood up and walked over to a window overlooking the helipad. "We think this may have been an inside job, possibly one of the Swiss Guards."

"Is there anything *about* the tool that would give us a lead?" Dana was getting impatient.

"Maybe. It's a red-handled PB Swiss Tool, an ElectroTool screwdriver." Graves held up the bagged instrument in his hand, lifting it from the bench under the window as he described it.

"What does that mean?"

"I'm told that it's used for jobs that require significant electrical insulation, like big industrial jobs. Its shank is about six inches long and the rest of it is completely insulated with a rubberized red coating that continues up into the handle."

"Were there any prints or anything on it?"

"No, but there was a lot of blood, and as of right now it

looks like it is the Cardinal's. But . . ."

"How long until the lab guys know if the blood is the Cardinal's?" She could see the Globe lit up at the facility's entrance in the distance now.

"They're saying about an hour or so. Listen . . ."

"Good, then get over here. We're headed to CERN to talk with Father. Edvard Krunowski never answered our calls today and they're in the middle of a *private* tour that Moriel asked for before he leaves tomorrow morning, at least that's what Krunowski's secretary told me over the phone about twenty minutes ago."

"Stop interrupting me Dana! Man, some things never change. I have something to add to what you think you already know. Listen, and allow me to help you. The techs here are running a PCR on the samples now."

"Sorry." She knew she could be very strong willed, so much so it had served to drive a wedge between them before. "You mean *sample*, right?"

"No. There was more on that tool than just the blood. Covering the flat head of the screwdriver there was this . . . *material*. It kinda looked like the crud you get on the shower door, you know, the hard water deposits. The guys here at the lab say that this stuff is more DNA, more *human* DNA."

"Are they from the same source?"

"That's just it. They're telling me the blood and this other material are from separate individuals. The material on the tip of the tool is not of Cardinal Antonacci's DNA. It's odd . . . it's in some strange petrified form. There's one more thing too. We were able to lift a single partial print off the gate. Aldo's already told them to call him with any results. We'll be on our way shortly."

With a soft click they were disconnected.

In the distance the lights of the globe illuminated the grounds as Dana and Bastien approached. She had pictured a warm visage. Instead, tonight the abandoned CERN complex gave her the creeps.

Slipping his badge back into his coat pocket, Bastien piloted the big sedan into the CERN complex. "That's a good sign, don't you think my dear? They seemed to be expecting us at the gate." The usual series of formal questions that had granted him access in the past had been summed up in one nonchalant wave of a gloved hand this time. Their car moved confidently through the serpentine network of tree-covered lanes leading to the facility's entrance.

"What exactly did Dr. Krunowski's secretary say when she called back?" Dana had been skeptical about the entire day's events. This whole arrangement tonight felt forced, like it had been orchestrated to end here.

"She said that Edvard and Father passed by the entrance gate to the Globe about two hours ago and they were down below now, but she didn't know where exactly." The Audi came to rest in a vacant "staff only" spot just outside the sphere. With the sun setting, the two exited the car and stepped out into the cold.

At the front desk, the night security staff gave the Inspector an official swipe pass to open the doors that would allow them into the antechambers below. The lights in the great sphere had already begun to shut themselves down at the end of the long work day. Only those that illuminated their legs remained on as they descended the circling ramp and continued toward the LHC.

"Who's still here?" Dana removed her 40 mm Glock from

its holster inside her fitted dark blue coat. She liked the feel of the heavy carbon fiber up against her ribs. She released the resin composite magazine and quickly reassured herself it was loaded. "Are we expecting a greeting of any sort?"

"I do not think so, but there could be a few of the graduate scientists still about." Bastien regarded his counterpart as she returned her weapon to its resting place beneath her coat. "You know, this is probably not the best place to be firing hot lead willy-nilly into the air . . . there are a lot of things that go boom down there."

"Well, let's just hope that this is a friendly conversation then," she added with a smile as she snapped the holster shut.

The inspector slid the card through the first reader, initiating the sequence of events that parted the heavy steel doors at the bottom of the ramp.

"What are you planning to ask him . . . the priest, that is?"

As the first set of doors closed behind them, the second set of doors slid open. The two could see a dim blue light emanating from an open room to their right. Hurried shadows escaping the silent doorway flitted across their path, repeatedly breaking its silent threshold and lighting the darkened hallway.

Dana ignored Bastien's inquiry and moved quickly toward the room. Peering around the corner, she could see a young Asian man in a white lab coat frantically pulling switches and pushing buttons while quietly muttering profanities under his breath.

"What seems to be the problem here?" Dana ushered herself through the open doorway and into the room.

The young man jumped, nearly falling over the scattered chairs that he'd hastily arranged behind him. "Who the hell are you, and what are you doing down here?"

Dana could see sweat beading around his brow and above his upper lip.

"I'm agent Pinon, with the United States Federal Bureau of Investigation, and this is Inspector Goll with FedPol. We were told to meet Dr. Krunowski and his guest here to ask them some questions tonight."

"I'm Dr. Tong, one of Dr. Krunowski's graduate assistants. I think your interview is going to be placed on hold for a bit." He wiped his forehead as he returned to the terminal overlooking the now partially lit main control room below. "As a matter of fact, please close the door behind you and come in. It's for your own safety," he added, briefly looking up at his confused guests.

"Our own safety . . . what are you talking about?" Bastien pushed the wall mounted pad that closed the green lead-lined doors behind them.

"This is not supposed to be happening, not like this anyway." The graduate student nervously continued to occupy himself with the data that was streaming across the various screens, ignoring the policemen who now shared this limited space with him.

"What's going on here? And where are the Doctor and the Priest?"

"The radiation level, it's way above anything that we've seen *here* before," he added, without turning to face his audience.

"How can that be? This facility is linked to several stations outside the grounds that monitor the same thing." Bastien turned toward Dana. "This facility was linked by government mandate to our headquarters, not to mention to all the surrounding monitoring stations. If it was truly that high, they would have shut it down by now."

"You don't understand." The look of panic on his face was highlighted by the flashing monitors in this dark room. "It's not even on!"

"What do you mean it's not on?" Dana moved closer to the bank of computers running across the desk in front of them. She could see data streaming across the screens in front of their host.

"It's off!" He pointed frantically toward the main screen hanging over the empty room in front of them. "It's off, the whole damn contraption has been off for days now. Dr. Krunowski discovered some buildup on the inside of the chamber the other day. I've been trying to reach them down there."

"I'm sorry, what did you just say?" Her attention was forcefully pulled back inside the room.

"The buildup, the problems with the vacuum, the whole thing is off! There's no reason that any radiation should be coming from anywhere in here. And as far as the topside facilities shutting things down, they only know that there's nothing to monitor now because we're offline." He turned to face Bastien. "No one is monitoring us right now."

"No, no, who's down where?" Dana pushed.

Their graduate student continued to type away furiously at the terminal in front of him. "What? Look, just sit down while I try to raise them on the radio . . ."

"They are down there?" Bastien turned and headed for the door.

"Sir, please. Just give me a minute. If I can reach them on the two-way then we can just have them return topside. Besides, Dr. Krunowski is wearing a dosimetry badge. It should begin to change color under even the most diminutive levels of exposure. As long as he notices, he should come up on his own."

"How did they end up down there anyways?"

"Dr. Krunowski asked me to show Father the control room." He pointed absently out the window without lifting his head from his chore. "After he joined us down below, he 'excused' me from my duties," he added, making quotation marks with his fingers in the air, "and the two of them disappeared into the tunnel."

"What's this buildup you're talking about in the collider?" Dana was looking at all the different screens that were vibrantly displaying their wares.

"The priest thinks that it's some sort of crusted DNA residue or something." He punched a few buttons, bringing up the latest SEM photo on an idle screen for Dana to view as he spoke.

"Father Moriel?" Dana's puzzlement was mounting.

"No one's answering. Maybe their battery's dead or something."

"Or maybe they are?" Bastien snatched one of the radios off its charger. "We're going down there! What channel are they on?"

"Sir, I don't think this is a good idea."

"It's not up for discussion, Mr. Tong." Bastien paused, staring into the graduate student's eyes impatiently.

"They're on channel three."

Dana grabbed a radio off the rack before following the Inspector out into the darkened hallway.

Mr. Tong hastily grabbed two plastic dosimetry badges off the desk beside him. "Wait, you'll need these," he said as he handed them to Dana. "If there's enough radiation down there, these'll begin changing colors. If they get to purple, you need to get out of there fast."

"Is that the highest color?" Dana asked.

"No, green is." Mr. Tong added as the two detectives headed down the stairs and into the darkened control room toward the elevators. As he watched the doors closing, another sound grabbed his attention from behind him. Standing in the light of the observation room was a tall man with blond hair.

"Hello, I'm Iän, your relief," he said, holding up his security badge.

"How did you pronounce that, Yahn?"

"That's right, but you can just call me John if that's easier for you."

CHAPTER 40

Sliding into the spot next to the big German sedan, Graves and Aldo followed in the footsteps of their counterparts from over ninety minutes ago. They'd been delayed by the questioning that Bastien and Dana had avoided. Having spent over twenty minutes at the front gate defending the legitimacy of their evening visit, they finally arrived at the Globe. They made their way toward the entrance as a young Asian man hastily crossed the parking lot.

"He's likely a graduate student heading home for the evening," Aldo reassured Graves. "Try again, they should be able to receive calls in the upper rooms." Aldo held his badge up against the glass as the night guard within the Globe came closer. "Öffnen Sie die Tür. Machen Sie schnell!"

The two men entered the dome. "Dammit!" Graves closed his cell phone. "She's still not picking up. They're walking right into it!"

"Maybe." Aldo asked for the badge off the night guard's chest as they passed. "Danke, we'll need this to get in." He took a brief moment to inform the guard that there may be a hazmat team arriving shortly before they hastily made their way down the circular ramp to the entryway below.

After passing through several series of doors leading toward the topside control room, Aldo and Graves entered the last airlock. The solid doors thudded closed behind them. The two men found themselves waiting an unusually long time for the opposing hatch to open. After several seconds of inactivity Aldo swiped the magnetic strip through its slot without any results.

"Shit!"

"What's the matter?" Graves stood behind him looking over his shoulder at the scanner's blinking red LED.

"We're stuck. The radiation level inside must be high enough that the security system has locked the doors down already." Aldo began to look around the tight booth, running his hands up and down the walls.

"What the hell are you looking for?" Graves began mimicking his friend, unsure of what he might find before catching his finger on the head of a screw sticking up out of the brushed stainless steel panel. "Ow!"

"Move," Aldo nudged him aside. Pulling at the screw he opened a near seamless panel. Inside was housed a small series of unlabeled buttons and a speaker, countersunk into the blackened metal housing.

"Don't tell me, you used to work here as a security guard as well, right?" Graves added with good-humored sarcasm, briefly sucking on his bleeding finger.

"No, my cousin does. You're in my light." Aldo shot a disdainful glance over his shoulder. With a grin on his face he spoke into the speaker. "This is Inspector Baumgartner with FedPol. My partner and I are stuck in lock number . . . ." Glancing around the small chamber his eyes fell on the plate above the retinal scanner. Taking his finger off the speaker button, Aldo returned his attention to the speaker in front of him. "Is anyone there, hello? Never mind."

Graves looked at him in disbelief as Aldo closed the small metal flap. "'Never mind?' Are we just gonna wait here for the cavalry to arrive or is it time for the standard European siesta?"

"Hand me the card we lifted that print with."

Graves reached into his pocket and removed a firm white piece of cardboard. About the size of a baseball card, it had a clear plastic film on one side that was hinged to its backing with tape at the upper edge.

Aldo took it from him and moved to the scanner. He opened the flap and held the plastic film that was ripe with the perpetrator's oily print up against the blank panel.

"What the hell are you doing?"

"In these facilities, there's always the potential that someone will need to get in or out in an emergency, whether that's a radiation event, a fire, a terrorist attack, whatever. An electric blue beam slid silently over the print as he spoke. "In these situations, the retinal scanners can be rendered useless. They have to think of everything nowadays, especially since nine-eleven and the Madrid bombings. In the event of a biological attack, like with a nerve agent, those attempting to get in or out may have suffered severely constricted pupils, effectively preventing the imager from getting a clear shot of one's retina."

"Of course, anyone would know that," Graves said sarcastically with a nod.

Aldo continued to hold the plastic film up against the reader as its beam panned up and down. "Or in the case of a fire, if there was enough smoke, the scanner may not get a clear shot at all. If that were to happen here, people could die. So the security software allows the panel to double as a fingerprint reader for those entered in the system." The small screen above the pad displayed the words 'LOCATION FAULT' in green type before the doors opened. "Voila!"

"How did you know that print was gonna work?" Graves remained briefly where he stood before quickly scrambling to follow.

"Call it a hunch," Aldo replied as they moved toward the carpeted stairway leading into the main control room. "What concerns me," he continued "is that 'location fault' code."

"How so?" Graves hurried to catch up as they moved into the poorly lit hallway.

"Well, it usually means that someone with that security clearance is already checked into the system, somewhere else."

Entering the darkened hallway, both men could hear anxious mutterings from beyond closed doors just ahead of them. Again Aldo held the print up against the scanner, and the panel rapidly blinked the same message, "LOCATION FAULT." The green doors slid open.

Inside was a young man in a white lab coat seated at a terminal on the far side of the booth. Glancing up from his work, he looked surprised to see them. With blond hair coiffed in a Marine Corps high-and-tight, and his fingers poised above his keyboard, he seemed out of place. "Can I help you gentlemen?"

"Where are the other two detectives?" The two men entered the room as the doors slid closed again behind them.

"I was told they're down below at Atlas, the main detector." The young man turned his attention back to his computer terminal.

Regarding him suspiciously, Graves continued into the room, his voice taking on a more authoritative tone. "What do you mean you were told? By whom?"

"I'm the twenty-one hundred relief. The off-going grad student's pass-down was that there were two officers here to talk to some priest that the Director's giving a tour to. Why?"

"With this growing radiation you let them go down there?" Aldo's anger was apparent in his tone.

The student's fingers, which had been tapping wildly, now hung, poised motionless over his keyboard. He slowly turned back to his guests. "I didn't let them. As I said, I've only just arrived. The doctor and the priest . . ."

"I'm sure they took two-way radios down with them." Graves gestured toward the now half empty charging rack over by the door.

The student stood up from his seat and walked over toward the bank of charging handhelds. With an air of deliberate nonchalance he asked, "How did you gentlemen know about the radiation?"

"We called a few of the tier-two centers and asked them to check their readings . . ."

"Oh my God." Graves was standing at the far side of the room staring into a monitor as its light blinked wildly across his face. "What is this? Where is this image coming from?" On the big screen in front of him was a fountain of moving lights, digitized particles streaming from the center of a glowing circular base.

"That's the inside of the main chamber, Atlas." The postgrad student walked over to where Graves stood and switched off the monitor. "Why?"

"That pattern—I've seen it before." Graves stood in quiet wonder before finishing his thought under his breath. "My God, I think they were right, she *was* telling us something."

Aldo's cell phone broke the silence. Pulling it out of his pocket he flipped open the cover. "Hello . . . ok, send it." He mouthed the words, "It's the lab," to Graves as he stood, dividing his interest between the monitor and his conversation. "I see, and the other?" Listening intently, Aldo's brow furrowed tightly. "What! Are you sure? How's that possible! And the print? Ok, call me when you know." Shutting his cell, he stared at Graves. "The blood on the tool was Cardinal Antonacci's..."

"That's what we expected."

"I know," Aldo looked back at the monitor briefly before returning his gaze to Graves. "But you're never going to believe whose DNA was on the tip."

With a firm clank, the green lead-lined doors of the observation chamber closed behind them. Startled, both men turned to see their large blond host standing between them and the door.

Graves was no longer in the mood to discuss the matter. "We need to get down there. What's the fastest way to do that mister . . ."

He leaned in to read the small plastic name tag on the student's left pocket. "Mister Tong."

CHAPTER 41

Fin stood looking down the valley, its high rocky walls set at vast distances from one another. The heat and dust that funneled toward him felt as though it would incinerate any effort put against it. In his head the whispers were growing louder, and although none dominated the others, they pulled him on toward a growing fire he could feel far beyond, toward the end of the basin before him. His facial twitches were worsening again, their propagation aborted only by the fire lines the growing scars had etched in his face.

The pains in his limbs and back were almost unbearable, and every minute they grew worse. Where only a faint rash had appeared a lifetime ago, spines now punctured his back. Still others had crept up between his fingers and toes. Insidiously spreading his digits away from one another, these buds made it nearly impossible for him to close his grip fully. The encrusted keloids that blanketed his wounds were beginning to coalesce, forming a thick husk that slowly replaced his own skin.

"Why are you sad Daddy? Are you dying?"

Eva's voice hung heavy in his mind, echoing and fusing along with the tormenting whispers. Fin shook his head wildly, trying to clear his thoughts. This all felt like a horrible nightmare, one in which the darkness kept him from seeing what he watched for, but knew to be just beyond his weakened grip. His feet moved more slowly than he commanded them to, sticking in the dry sand, which held him fast with the weight of wet mud.

"Am I dying? Then we're fine and you shouldn't be sad anymore."

Fin's exhausted panic was becoming palpable. He knew that he'd lost something, though at times now he couldn't remember what it was. He was changing faster now, less the man he'd been when he came into this place, and more a product of it. In lucid moments, he'd see Eva's face and remember what he was here for. In this hell, however, the farther he went, the further he felt from her. Fin shook his head again, desperately trying to focus. Eva's face, her smell, her touch . . . as these fragmented delusions consumed his thoughts, his vertigo returned, shifting his focus again. Fin could feel the blood running down his back, oozing from around the two robust dactyls that had grown there. All the while, around him spun this unrelenting hell.

"Where are you?" Fin screamed in frustration, looking up toward the sky as his muscles strained against his frustration. With the dust blotting out the growing light, Fin's small voice was sucked up into the wind and gone before it reached his own ears. "Where are you?" He fell to his knees, catching himself on all fours.

As he crawled along, Fin's attention was caught by the sight of his hands, sprawled out and partly buried in the sand before him. The ring finger and thumb of his left hand hung from their base, painlessly torn off like discarded scabs. Fin could see jagged bones protruding from their stumps, but there was no pain. Pushing his fingers out as they grew, the advancing sickles were the knurled claws of the beasts. Fin continued to stare at them. Unable to comprehend what was happening to him, he pushed himself up to a kneeling position. Turning his hands in the air, he regarded his limbs, not as his own but as another's. Slowly Fin grasped the loose appendages and tore them from where they hung. As the rivulets of bright red blood trickled down his arm and around his blackened scabs, he opened and closed his new claws, rejoicing in the misshapen digits as they coldly ground against one another.

At the verge of his vision on the far end of the dried ravine, Fin could make out what seemed like a ruined city, its walls crumbling in the blasting sand and heat. Rising high above the valley floor were spires, possibly once majestic but now in shambles as the wind and sand ran through them. Squinting to make out these new features, he became acutely aware of the shrill growls being carried to his ear by the shifting winds. As Sal had prophesied, they'd found him again. Staring at the walls in the distance, Fin hoped that he could make it that far before the great beast's legions closed the gap.

Fin tried to stand. A tightness he'd not felt before squeezed him about the knees. His pain increased with every effort he made to rise fully. He stumbled a few feet before falling again. Fin struck the sloping ground and felt something pop with a sound that pierced the air. Hesitating for a moment, he felt the discomfort begin to recede and for the first time in its place he felt the warmth of relief flooding over him. Returning to his feet, he wobbled for a moment before witnessing the inhuman hyperextension of his own legs. With a sickening crunch, his full weight settled into his knees as they buckled backwards, splitting the dead husks that surrounded them. There was no blood, only an invigorating absence of pain in his legs as they assumed their hellish posture.

Fin swiftly covered the distance to the ruins, his knees flexing in the same perverse fashion as those of his pursuers. Ahead of him, small fault lines opened as the day prematurely gathered its light. From within these fissures came a faint glow, similar to the light that had welcomed him here days ago in that putrid river. Looking down, he could see the burning silhouettes of the damned within these crevices as he passed, all the while fighting the fear that fueled his panic.

"I've got to make it . . . focus . . . just make it to the city!" he told himself as he prodded, trying to block out the increasing noise that followed him. It was a symphonic disharmony of growls that grew louder no matter how fast he moved. The dust around him had nearly choked out the light from above as he reached the first stone in near darkness. Fin's terror-stricken imagination had painted the beasts at his heels. He dove for the protection of the decaying wall, landing hard on the jagged rocks that rimmed its border. Rolling onto his stomach, Fin noted amidst his panic that he was able to move the bony projections from his shoulder blades like the wings of a mantis.

In the winds that accompanied the early demise of the day, Fin was still unable to rid himself of the whispers in his head. Though one seemed finally to rise above the others, he was unable to discern any of its meanings. In a desperate prayer, he hoped he'd soon hear the clear voice of his mother or the warm encouragement from Rachel above these howling winds, offering a way out of this place and to a path to Eva.

"Where are you?" a soft female voice called. "Daddy! Daddy, where are you?" Eva's ghostly voice encircled him.

Fin leapt to his feet, the sound he'd been craving surrounded him as he stood. Peering over the crumbling waist-high wall, he could barely make out innumerable pairs of orange glowing eyes within the storm's churning blackness, relentlessly searching this desolation for him. The remaining whispers fell away and he could clearly hear the sobbing of a child through the tempest about him. Fin made his way carefully along the barrier and down a partial stone corridor that stemmed its terminus. Determined to avoid discovery, he ducked through several fallen archways, making his way toward the towering dark outlines of a ruined structure that lay on the other side of this city.

As he approached the decaying edifice, Eva's voice was growing louder, and he could hear her words more clearly. Cautiously placing his hands on the entryway pillars, Fin blindly entered the quieted hollow, guided only by his daughter's voice.

"Daddy, please! Daddy, where are you? Are you there?" Her pleading grew louder, and he could hear the panic in her voice.

As he moved forward, Fin could smell her now, an astonishingly fresh scent that openly repudiated this place. The blowing sand drifted like snow all about the stone barriers, catching his feet as he recklessly moved from room to crumbling room.

Eva's sobs grew louder and he was able to hear her stammering breaths as she tried to sooth herself. Passing through the next entryway, Fin's heart leapt. In the far corner of this room, shivering in the shadows, sat his little girl.

Cast in her own light, Eva crouched, her pale white skin looking as though it was lit from within. Fin could see the fear in her eyes as she waited for the only salvation she knew, him. Leaving the crumbling doorway, Fin sprinted toward Eva, his vision of her consumed by the joy in her face. Before he could reach her, the glow she lent this hell was blotted out by a blackness that fell from above. With his dread and anger at equal odds, Fin lowered his head and tried to drive his way through the curtain of demons that kept them apart. Their numbers were overwhelming, and the flood of hatred cast him back with ease.

The creatures were on top of him in an instant, biting and kicking him. Fin struggled beneath their numbers. Reaching for Eva in vain, he could feel his daughter's heat fading under their onslaught. Driven back out into the storm, Fin was forced to the ground. With a heavy hand forcing his face into the dirt, one of them spoke.

"We rape her," hissed a single voice of thousands just beyond Fin's ear. The words dripped with hatred, and Fin could feel the pleasure this thing derived in torturing both him and Eva. Fin had found her, he was closer to Eva now than ever, and this wretched beast represented all that kept them apart now.

Before the creature could lift its head, Fin reached back. Grasping its face, he drove his untried claws into its glowing sockets and pinned the beast's skull to the ground. Despite his continued beating, Fin lifted his head. With every muscle in his body strained against their oppressive weight, he let out a demonic howl rivaling the din of the storm. As his prey writhed beneath his grip, he felt his remaining fear melt away, like a retreating tide set to reveal the black volcanic sand beneath.

As they forced his face back into the soil, Fin's anger grew until black was the only color he could see. Then somewhere in his mind it all became red. He felt aimless in a sea of rage, able to sense only the undulations of his uncontrollable anger. He could feel the searing heat of Eva's retreating cries as he lay helpless beneath these monsters. The pounding mass of their hatred drove this place deeper into him with every moment. His memory of Eva's touch went cold as he shattered what remained of his hands, crushing his captor's skull against the rocks and leaving only his advancing talons to finish the work. The smell of this godforsaken place filled his head with each putrid breath, all of it rushing at him with an intensity that devoured his consciousness. All of it with an evil he now longed to face.

Fin's level of pain soared beyond what he had known, as an excruciating ecstasy ran the length of his back, splitting his thickened skin wide open and delivering his greatest advantage yet. Fin opened his eyes. All that had been black and clouded by the storm was now made crystal clear to him through an orange hue. Turning his head, he could see his attackers quickly backing away. The air about them felt charged with the smell of fear as he rose unhindered to his feet.

Fin spun, arms spread wide with his talons outstretched. His grotesque agile wings sliced through the air on edge, finding the throats of his closest protagonists. Their heads fell to the burnt ground. Freed from their demonic bodies, the severed heads tumbled about, giving Fin a sense of power that, until this very moment, he'd not felt here. Facing the remaining horde, he offered them the first view of their fallen angel transformed. Its metamorphosis nearly complete, Fin's once human shape was nearly unrecognizable. His posture had taken on a naturally aggressive stance owing to his canine hind limbs and huge wings. Leaning in toward the enemy, Fin saw their deformed faces clearly for the first time; long, uneven, yellowed teeth scattered erratically throughout their decaying mouths. Their faces were strung together with sparse fibers that exposed massive gaps, leaving their salivating holes visible. Most with sunken and rotting cheek bones, they all wore on their deformed faces an expression he'd not expected, fear.

Whatever humanity remained, he'd tear it from them. His daughter's heat was gone, leaving only that of his anger. Fin lunged at the horde, driving the boney spikes now adorning the tips of his wings into the throats of the two beasts unlucky enough to be within reach. Lifting their lifeless bodies off the shifting sands, he forced them backwards into the crumbling wall and held them fast, burying his wingtips into the rock. The translucent membranes of his huge leathery wings unfurled to the ground, trapping several of the demons within their sinister arc. The creatures backed away in fear, trapped between Fin and the wall behind them. Pulling his new appendages from the towering rubble, Fin collapsed the entire structure down upon his daughter's captors, crushing them where they stood.

Through this orange clarity he could see others as they escaped far out into the clearing beyond. "You sons of bitches!" he cursed through his split and blackened lips.

With a single powerful beat of his wings, Fin rose up through the dust over the ruins and fleeing dead and dropped with his full weight onto the largest number of them. Shattering the bones of those who had led the retreat, he spun to face what remained.

As they descended further into the valley, away from the fallen city, many of the creatures slid in the loose sand as they frantically scrambled to remain free from retribution. Folding his wings behind him like a mayfly, Fin ran headlong toward the group using his talons to slash through the throats of its leaders as he passed between them. With their combined blood splattering from his claws onto the beasts following in close ranks, Fin rapidly drew his wings around in front. Never slowing his attack, he drove the spikes of his wingtips into their chests before ripping them in two, then continuing up the slope to meet the rest of the pack.

Their numbers were immense. Fin could have faced twice as many—but not all of them at once. Their ranks closed, and the massive cloud of dust cast up by the advancing horde swallowed his view of the crumbling city. He could hear the sounds of their talons clicking and scraping over the bare rocks as they drew closer, the finer details of their hatred only becoming visible in their expressions as he parted their advancing numbers with his outstretched wings. Their sheer numbers overwhelmed him. They forced him to the ground, kicking and biting at him. Fin was no match for this many, and the weight of evil piled on him blotted out the light. His world went dark.

He could feel the warmth of blood across his face and chest, though there was no pain. The sounds of their snarls were replaced with screams of torment as the heft of their burden was pulled from on top of him. Fin heard a familiar voice from behind him. "I'm with you brother." Rising to his feet, Fin found himself face to face with Sal.

"We're not brothers . . . !" Fin winced in pain as his thoughts were cut short by slashing talons from behind him. Wings outstretched, he spun to face those who remained. With another powerful beat of his wings, Fin left the ground.

Reaching down with his feet, Fin snatched one of the beasts like a raptor. Forcing his talons through the animal's skull, he dragged his prey high up over the legions. Stalling above the waiting crowd below, Fin inverted his path. Folding his appendages across his back, he plummeted, with his kill in tow, toward the unforgiving desert floor beneath them. Fin released his quarry, hurling its carcass into several of its brethren as he arced high above them again.

Beneath him Sal continued to dispatch one creature after another, while those who were able to escape with their lives did so.

Fin slammed down onto the shoulders of his would be-guide. Left alone now in the valley, he repeated, "We're not brothers. I don't owe you anything, and you certainly don't owe me." Fin used the sharp tips of his immense wings to pin Sal's shoulders to the ground.

"It's not you I owe. It's your Eva."

Pressing harder, Fin's wings began to pierce Sal's burnt hide. "Explain yourself."

"I was there that night in the rain, the night you were killed. Your death gave me my escape from that life. It also gave me Eva."

Fin stood motionless over Sal, his fists clenched. "Go on."

"She was my salvation, my muse, my reason for change. I never meant any harm to come to her. I did everything I could to protect her from the life I'd left behind."

Fin released Sal, folding his wings behind him. "How did she die?"

Sal sat up. Rubbing the places where he'd been pinned, he continued, "Protecting me from the one who helped put us all here. He and his master are waiting for you, and Eva is the bait. It's your soul they want. The more you fight, the closer you get to her, but the more of yourself you'll lose to this place."

"I don't need your help, stay away from me." In a cloud of dust, Fin rose, momentarily hovering above his counterpart.

"Don't lose your will," Sal screamed after him. "His name is Azazel, and his only purpose now is to finish what he began a lifetime ago."

With the ravaged bodies of his foes strewn across the valley wasteland, Fin turned and continued on. Leaving Sal beyond the walled city, soaring toward the fires that lit the mountains ahead, he found solace in the expectation of the carnage that awaited him there. More of these creatures would die at his hands, wings, or teeth . . . whatever it took, he would destroy them all before it was over.

CHAPTER 42

Thirty stories beneath the control booth, Dana and Bastien were exiting CERN's main LHC elevator. The ride had been a slow one as the magnetically shielded cabin rode deep into the earth on its tandem cables. Under the guidance of a leisurely turning drive, the motor's ferocious torque kept the box from swaying in its shaft as it descended along its eleven-minute trip. Only two button choices were offered—up and down. There was nothing in between.

Stepping out into the main chamber, Dana was dwarfed by the dark form of the fifteen-million pound Atlas detector towering eighty feet above her. Sprawling across the cathedral-like room, its eight massive superconducting magnets stretched outward from its solenoid core like some titanium squid. The dim blue glow of the safety lights was cast all across the arcing metal, reflecting off the gold and silver surfaces that lined the machine's shielding, giving the room an eerie sci-fi feel.

"Where do we go from here?" Dana asked, trying to keep her voice low.

"I'm not sure. I've never been down here before. I was expecting more lights on than this." Bastien moved off to the right, toward a white wooden gantry that led up to a walkway above them. "I'll see if I can find some central control area down here. There must be somewhere to turn on the lights."

The only appreciable noise was a constant soft drone coming from the vents in the ceiling, which hung a staggering hundred feet above them. At this secluded depth, the ventilation and purification systems needed to run twenty-four hours a day to keep this buried city supplied with fresh air. Without these systems, just a handful of workers would render the air at this depth stale and unable to support life within just a few hours.

Dana continued forward slowly, allowing her eyes to adjust to the darkened environment. She approached the base of the main reactor near the primary shielding, just barely able to make out the myriad waist-high objects that were scattered randomly beneath this circular behemoth. With the recent environmental control issues the facility was having, the supercooled liquid helium tubing for the magnets had allowed the chamber's temperature to drop, and along with it the dew point too. Moving through this alien environment, a thin fog had begun to collect above the floor. It enveloped the visitor about her ankles as she moved through this alien environment. Lifting her knees high in order to avoid tripping, Dana proceeded awkwardly through the ghostly blue mist that flowed around her.

"What *are* these things, Bastien?" Her voice echoed off the hard surfaces that surrounded her. With no reply, she turned to see where her Swiss equivalent was. The iridescent blue glow that enveloped this place cast everything in a low-contrast haze that made it difficult to discern objects more than a few feet away.

A sharp metallic clang came from behind her, or possibly in front of her. It was difficult to tell as everything reverberated off the high ceilings.

"Bastien? Is that you? Bastien?"

Continuing just a few feet further, Dana was able to discern the objects before her as rolling tool trays littered with hand tools. Tilting her head as she approached them, her black hair fell briefly into her eyes before she pulled it back behind her ears. She shuffled her way around to read what was written across the handles of the tools, relying on the faint azure light that surrounded her.

"PB Swiss Tool / ElectroTool," each label proclaimed.

Dana quickly scanned across the multiple trays that adorned the chamber floor. To her far left was a nearly complete set of rubberized screwdrivers, almost identical to what Graves had described to her just hours ago. In this light it was nearly impossible to make out their true color, although the handles on the tools looked to be a rich black and not the red that Graves had detailed over the phone.

She could feel a faint tingling on her skin, although the dosimetry badge on her blouse had not yet begun to glow. Off in the distance, toward the collider's afferent tunnel, Dana could hear men's voices. They were faint, but growing closer.

Three hundred feet up, Graves and Aldo squared off with the increasingly agitated graduate student.

"Gentlemen, I think you should leave! It's becoming dangerous here." His attitude had undergone a rapid departure from its initial unremarkable tone to one of dire concern. "I will see to it that your friends and our director exit the facility safely."

"Thanks, but I don't think so, pal!" This was getting strange, and Graves was not about to leave this kid in charge of Dana's safety. "I'll need one of those radios and a badge to head down there." He held out his hand without breaking their locked gaze. "Or do we need to have a more informal discussion about this?"

The tech handed him his two-way. "They're likely on channel three, though I've not been able to raise Father . . . ." He paused nervously for a moment before continuing, "either gentleman at all." He turned and sat back down at his desk.

"Look at this!" Aldo had been scrolling through images from the closed circuit cameras located throughout the tunnel system. "Where are they now, where is this?" He seemed almost frantic, pointing with an increased sense of urgency toward a monitor at the far end of the metal rack. "What part of the loop is this image coming from?" Aldo's eyes doubled in size as he continued to watch the little black-and-white picture.

"I don't know, sir."

"What the hell do you mean 'you don't know'? How long have you worked here?" He didn't wait for an answer to his rhetorical question. Aldo motioned to Graves, catching his eye briefly. "Krunowski and the priest, they're heading right toward Dana and Bastien." He pointed stiff-armed toward the screen. Aldo drew closer to the screen, screwing up his face to sharpen the screen's image. "What the hell is Moriel doing?"

"He's got his hand inside his pants pocket." Graves squinted at the grainy image now too. "What's he got there?" Their voyeuristic view of the developing situation was visibly agitating Graves as the two men continued to watch their worst nightmare unfold. "He's still walking with his hand in his pocket . . . wait, shit, he's got something in his hand. What is that?" Graves quickly dialed in the frequency and depressed the button to talk, hoping to hear Dana's voice on the other end. "Dana, are you there? Bastien? Can anyone hear me?"

A soft crackle spilled from the speaker, followed by a single short tone before Bastien's voice came through. "We're here, we only just arrived in the main collider chamber. The Doctor and . . ."

"I know, I know, listen." Graves interrupted him. "The radiation level is increasing down there, and the tech is now telling us that there's an increase in the gravitometer within Atlas as well. I don't think it's a good idea for you two to be down there."

"Dana and I are split up. I'm not sure where she is."

"What! You need to find her and get up here. Now!"

Aldo's cell rang, briefly pulling their focus back to the little dark room.

"Inspector Baumgartner here." Closing his eyes as he listened, Aldo bowed his head in exhalation. "Scheisse! . . . ok, thank you." He replaced his phone on his hip. "He's dead," he said quietly.

"Shit! I'm going down there before he kills someone else . . . or blows the whole goddamn place up!" Graves turned toward the door, striking its wall plate as he raised the radio to his mouth. "Dana, it's Tom. They've killed the Cardinal. Did you hear me? Cardinal Antonacci is dead." The heavy green doors rushed shut behind him as he made his way into the darkened main control room below.

As Aldo stood alone in the blue room with the graduate student, he could hear Graves continue over the radio.

"Move in and take him, we can't wait any longer. I'm coming down there."

Dana could hear the radio transmission coming from two different directions. One source came from down the tunnel beyond the detector and was far more distant than that which came from above her. She watched for the one closest to her and saw a shadow cut through the cobalt light as it moved across the gantry-way above.

"Bastien? Is that you?" There was still no answer. Reaching into her coat Dana drew her weapon from its holster. With the barrel down and her finger extended past the trigger she slowly made her way around Atlas.

She could barely make out two figures exiting from the darkened tunnel ahead as they passed the superconductor's exposed cryogenic tubing. One individual seemed to be walking in front of the other through the blue fog as they continued toward her.

"Put your weapon down and kick it toward me . . . now!" The deep male voice was distorted as it echoed off every surface around them.

Dana hesitated for a moment, unsure who was speaking or even what she was witnessing. The figure in the rear removed his hand from behind the other as a deafening concussion rang out, briefly casting light across the entire chamber. The errant round struck the ceramic wall behind her before finding a resting place amidst a flurry of sparks near the steel legs of the ACR.

During the split second of light provided by the discharge, Dana thought she made out a priest's collar on the man in front. She also caught a glimpse of Bastien poised above them all on the gantry way.

"I said put your weapon down and kick it toward me, or he will die."

Dana followed his instructions. Standing in the open, she hoped Bastien was in a good enough position to help.

"Ok, ok, take it easy. Here, I'm putting it down."

Placing her Glock on the smooth tile, she slid the gun

toward the shadowed figures, its motion stopped just before it departed the dim reach of the lights.

"Cute," was all she got in return.

"Bastien? Dana? Are you there?" Aldo's muffled transmission came from the gunman's pocket, while a much clearer version emanated from above them.

"I hear your radio up there, Inspector Goll. Please come down here immediately."

The request was met with silence. The two men took a few steps closer, remaining in the shadow of the reactor. Dana could only make out their legs as they broke the blue arc of the safety lights. The figure in front bent forward, picking up the gun she had forfeited. He then handed it to the other man before stepping back into the pitch black.

The radios chirped their simultaneous arrival of another transmission. "Tom's on his way down there, and Bastien . . . the lab called back. You're never going to believe this . . ." The hum from the transmission faded for an instant. "The DNA on the screwdriver was Fin's! Did you hear me?" Aldo's voice was beginning to take on a metallic quality as the signal changed beneath the weight of the growing radiation. "That substance crusted on the end of the murder weapon was Dr. Canty's DNA! And the partial print we lifted belongs to . . ."

There was another short burst of static and then a large crash over the radio. Moments after their communication was cut short, a small hum filled the room as the lights in the chamber began to come up.

Dana stood frozen, the shock on her face made obvious by its reflection in those she found herself staring at. "What do you think you're doing?" Her eyes fell for a moment on the tool trays that were now revealing the red handles in the growing fluorescent lights.

"It's Fin Canty's DNA." Edvard pointed at the machine behind them as he held a weapon against the back of the priest's head. "Inside the reactor . . . he's reaching back to us from the next life, from heaven!" He was ecstatic. "It worked! The singularity we generated inside Atlas needed a foci on the other side to anchor to. Together they opened up an Einstein-Rosen Bridge following the one thing stubborn enough to pierce the planes . . . Fin!"

Edvard raised Dana's weapon. Bringing it down swiftly, he struck Father Moriel across the base of his skull and dropped the priest's limp form to the floor. With a satisfied look on his face, he continued. "I'll be damned if you're going to turn off this miracle machine before we're done." He raised the familiar weapon toward Dana as she stood just a few feet in front of him.

The small hum that had begun to fill the room minutes ago was now rising to far more ominous decibels. From around the far side of the chamber, Bastien appeared.

"Drop your weapon Dr. Krunowski." He was slowly approaching the huddle with his firearm fixed on Edvard.

Edvard chuckled. "You know so very little, Inspector."

The noise that had been rising now settled into a rhythmic chant, giving life to every ferric object in the room. The weapon that Bastien had trained on the director flew from its owners' possession along with the myriad tools in the room. In a hail of iron, the immense chamber seemed to come alive with the glitter of flying debris. Hurtling through the air toward the five-story behemoth in the center of the chamber, they slammed into the Atlas's center. The shimmering mass that collected there, contorted and bent under the immense strength of the field, filled all the gaps in the machine's façade.

"It has the capacity to crush a city bus once the toroid magnets reach full strength," Edvard added as he held Dana's gun on her. "I do appreciate you lending me your weapon Agent Pinon. I rather enjoy the carbon fiber variety, don't you? They're lighter, and pay no mind to the magnets, eh?"

Edvard waved the barrel of the weapon rapidly toward Bastien and then in Dana's direction, indicating his desire to have the two agents standing together.

"You see, together Fin and I have accomplished what no other human being has ever been able to. Not even Christ himself was able to offer definitive proof of the afterlife," Edvard said, raising his free hand toward the roof in a self-aggrandizing gesture. "Do you know what this means for Catholics and Christians everywhere? No longer will we have to defend ourselves against this fictitious rift between science and religion. As of today, particle physics *is* religion."

"That DNA could be from any source, his buried corpse for God's sake!" Dana moved subtly toward him as she spoke.

"Wrong detective. Nothing remains of the good doctor, only a pile of incinerated ashes. Certainly not a viable source of either carbon fourteen or DNA, wouldn't you say Father?" Edvard chuckled as he gazed down at Moriel's limp body.

"His cremation took care of that loophole for us. The white hole that churns within that vacuum has revealed to us the *real* God particle." Again, he gestured at the multi-spoked machine above him. "Proof that we're not alone, and that heaven exists!"

"You're insane!" Bastien moved closer to Dana, positioning his body in front of hers. "You've committed murder. That is a mortal sin. Your god will never absolve you of that."

"You killed your friend! You killed a four-year-old little girl, you sick son-of-a-bitch . . . and for what? Dana was growing angrier, and making Edvard visibly uncomfortable. "You're going to hell just as sure as you stand there. There is no for-giveness for what you've done."

"That's enough, this machine stays on! My effort has given mankind the only physical connection we've had with God since the First Coming." He trained the Glock on Dana as he crossed himself. "I'm not going to tell you again, back up or someone will die!"

"What are you going to do, Doctor, kill another innocent person in Christ's name?

Behind them all, announcing its arrival with an old-world chime, the elevator doors began to slide open. From within this slowly moving box, Graves had been witness to the last of the radio transmissions, an anxious silence that followed, and the concussion of a single gunshot. As the door opened, a second shot reverberated off the aluminum walls around him.

Graves exited, briefly holding his weapon out in front of him before it was ripped from his hands to join the compressed ball of metal at the field's center. With his mouth and eyes wid-ening, he stood in the open doorway, dumbfounded.

Crumpled on the floor in front of the colossal reactor were the bodies of Dana, Edvard, and Moriel. Standing over them all was Bastien.

CHAPTER 43

Finding respite on top of a rocky ledge, Fin perched, over-looking the rest of the valley. Off in the distance, standing on the far side of a rift in the valley floor, stood a creature more massive than anything he'd seen here so far. It appeared to be directing the demonic traffic that scurried about beneath its cloven feet. This army of worthless souls busied themselves around something that was beyond Fin's focus. They moved in and out of the glow of a beautifully dim light, the only one of its kind in this entire basin, causing it to flicker through their tireless numbers. Like an equatorial bird drying its wings, the demon's enormous appendages opened and closed as if under their own will. Spread wide, they cast a stark shadow with edges drawn crisp from the firelight of the surrounding canyon walls.

The light from beneath the hoard flashed from between the rocks. The demon's long shadow slithered across the black clouds above, stretched to tearing as the dark canvas billowed past.

Fin's eyes lit his own path as he focused on the ringmaster conducting this vile circus. Fin's very reason for being here, Eva, was now all but lost because of his own transformation.

Fin could feel the demon's awareness of him. Standing boldly, allowing his full span to drape about him, Fin cast his own shadow up the valley floor. All those who sensed what little remained of his soul stopped what they were doing and prepared, waiting hungrily for his arrival. Beyond the creature, the beautiful light glared through the void.

Leaping from the vantage of his ledge, Fin pushed off, dragging his outstretched limbs behind him. Open fully, Fin could feel his growing power coursing through his body, his metamorphosis culminating in the fear of those he now battled to control. The translucent skin of his open wings, interrupted only by the throbbing vessels that nourished it, carried him toward his final victory.

Fin landed confidently, cutting down the fragile few who dared to stand in his way. Slashing and tearing, he left dozens of the creatures decapitated and halved, as he slowly made his way toward the towering demon who awaited his soul on the other side of the crevasse.

Fin caught glimpses of this demon now and again above the legions. In his unrelenting effort to topple their master, every decimating act of hatred was rewarded with the strength of the one he felled. With each violent act, what remained of his threadbare humanity was thinned further. Fin continued to burn through their masses, gaining strength as his encrusted talons and charred limbs ran red with the glistening blood of these pawns.

When the dust settled, Fin stood on the edge of the precipice, opposite the beast. Behind him lay the long path of the journey of destruction through which he'd been led. It had served its purpose well. Blind now to Eva's presence, Fin's chest heaved in anticipation of the battle before him.

Fin could clearly see the creature, massive in form and nothing like the beasts he'd battled to reach this point. Heavily muscled, it was built more like a bull than the emaciated rats that had hunted him before. Its eyes burned with the same ferocity beneath its shelved brow, though the bridge of its nose had a more humanoid shape. Flattening as it went down, the edges of its nose melted into a face without punctuation. The evil of its appearance was heightened by its lack of mouth as the light from below cast an unbroken shadow clear to its brow.

Stabbing forcefully upward, Fin freed himself of gravity's hold. He rose above the crevasse and the swirling dust of his own wings. The creature rose to meet him, climbing quickly toward him as Fin closed the gap. Striking Fin mid-flight with its massive forearms, the two met at their apogee. Bouncing across the jagged landscape, Fin twisted awkwardly in his wings before landing hard on a short wall of rock.

The faint scent of strawberries flooded Fin's head, and a delicious panic ran through him.

Eva! She was here! Fin's senses tingled with the reawakening of his hibernating emotions. He could see the demon settling back again on the edge of the crevasse. Staggering to his feet, Fin was knocked to the ground from behind as a childlike hissing filled his ear.

"My first failure in the city only sharpened my resolve. I won't fail this time."

Fin spun, thrashing his wings and staggering under the increased burden of this creature clinging to his back.

"I'm only a soldier, an miserable wretch in his army, but I'll claim my victory before he takes your soul"

This creature was different. It was personally interested in destroying Fin himself —not just in corrupting his purity. Its hold on Fin's throat was choking, and with the smell of Eva and the reawakened purpose it gave him, Fin had momentarily changed his focus. He dropped to one knee and then the other, as this new foe tightened its grip. In desperation, Fin inverted his wingtips and drove their stakes through the creature's back, piercing his enemy's body as well as his own flesh beneath. He lifted the dying weight off and thrust his attacker forcefully onto the ground in front of him.

"EME ESE" read the tattoo across the beast's back. The deep blue letters gave Fin vibrant flashbacks to that last night with his little girl. Fin recalled standing outside that crumpled vehicle in the rain, seeing the same tattoo. Slumped over the wheel just before the flash of light, the vehicle's driver had the same marking beneath his tattered shirt. Sal's words of warning rushed back to him. "Azazel." With the return to his purpose in this hell, the warmth of hope flooded in.

From behind the demon, Eva emerged from the haze. Her white glow overtook the decay surrounding them.

"Azazel . . . Goddamn you!" The guttural shriek of Fin's changing voice startled even him. With newly spilt blood staining the ground around them, Fin stepped heavily onto their murderer's skull, holding the side of Azazel's head firmly against the dirt. Bleeding from his puncture wounds, Azazel flailed in desperation as he tried to break free of his fate.

An enormous fist gripped Fin's throat and lifted him into the air, nearly liberating Azazel from under him. Fin quickly drove his wing's dagger into the muscle belly of the demon's arm. The piercing strike forced the release of its grip, and with Fin's full heft returned to Azazel's skull, he drove his opposing spike up into the soft throat of the demon towering above. The creature staggered backward, releasing Fin to refocus his wrath.

"You led us here from the beginning!" Fin screamed at Azazel, as he tortuously slid a bloodstained spike between the vertebrae of his exposed neck. Piercing through to his throat, Fin pinned him to the ground beneath. He bent forward, lowering his head enough to see the blood pour from Azazel's mouth.

"The collisions of our fates end here," he whispered into Azazel's ear.

Withdrawing his weapon, Fin raised his hell-spawned appendages into the winds above him. In one massive strike, he leapt back from his nemesis, knees flexed back and feet drawn to his chest. Rising above his quarry like a bird of prey, he thrust his wingtips into Azazel's head, splitting his skull open and spilling its contents leaving his antagonist's defeated husk quivering in the dust.

"Eva! Where are you, Baby?" Fin called as he settled back, folding his wings against his exhausted body.

He could feel her near as the sound of her breathing filled his head. Eva's heat burned his charred skin as her presence grew stronger with each moment. Turning toward her warmth, Fin realized Eva was behind the demon as it rested in the dust before him.

Barely reaching the height of his enemy's chest, Fin unfurled himself wholly. The stalks of the wings exiting his back were now the thickness of his arms. Heavily muscled, they tripled his once human span. Extending beyond his outstretched hands, they spread into broad flat blades. Fin's limbs were gnarled and black, their ends punctuated in the sickled four digits that had dispatched his fingers days ago. His chest and neck dripped with the molted shreds of flesh that clung desperately to his new shape.

The demon towered over him as it spoke. "Your soul will now be mine. I will leave you and yours here to rot for eternity."

Fin stood his ground, dwarfed by the demon's mass. "Like hell you will, you son of a bitch!"

Forcing his wings downward, Fin climbed. His chest swelled and his thoughts cleared as the fog of this place evaporated beneath Eva's warmth.

"We are stronger together than you could ever be!" Her love infused him with the strength that brought him here.

But Fin's rising focus was interrupted by a sudden insurmountable weight pulling him downward. Snatched by his ankles like a chicken for the slaughter, Fin twisted and his world twisted and spun as the demon hurled him in an arc and slammed him into the rocky walls surrounding them.

"Insignificant insect! For millennia I have been here, hoarding my strength and biding my time."

With each impact against the jagged cliffs, Fin's mass broke loose an avalanche of rock. He folded himself into the cocoon of his massive wings, trying to protect himself. As the assault continued, the centripetal forces drew him out. Fin's outstretched form was crushed again and again against the rock, and his wings were left wilted, torn, and shattered beneath his broken body. With its anger at full tilt, the demon directed its efforts now solely toward the goal of extracting the soul that would foster his escape from this hell.

The beast held Fin up before him. "Your journey has been scripted from its inception, right down to your destruction before *her* eyes."

Grasped by his wrists and the crux of his wings, Fin hung facing his destroyer, with his arms outstretched, his legs hung limp beneath him. "Most would have crumbled beneath this place, but not my prize. The strength of your will, my sacrificial lamb, has been impressive."

The demon's massive arms tensed, pulling hard at Fin's wings.

Tilting his head toward the blackening sky, Fin let out a demonic howl that echoed off the canyon walls around them.

With a sickeningly soft crunch, the demon tore the wings from his captive fly, dropping Fin to the ground in a crumpled and bloodied heap.

"It will be your forfeited soul that grants me passage from this place." The demon clutched Fin's broken body, raising him above its head before slamming him down into the sharp rocks below. "You have nothing more that I need, and nothing to compare with what I have."

As the creature crouched to quell its hunger, Fin caught a glimpse of Eva's face through the swirling dust. Her large brown eyes rained tears over her dirty soft cheeks. She ran toward them, stretching out her hand toward the beast as if to defend her father. With the aura of her presence on Fin's face, the demon turned on her.

Fin lunged one last time, sacrificing the last of his humanity for his daughter.

As Fin strained after the demon, the blurred form of another crusted and burnt soul split their view. For one brief moment this new combatant drove the demon to the ground.

In the absence of the demon's mass, Eva's soft fingers touched the hardened and bloodied talons of her father. The heat of Eva's touch drew out the purity of Fin's soul. For an instant, Fin looked upon the face of their savior.

In the end, their salvation had come from one whose promise had long since been made. Fin watched as the eyes of his guide, surrounded by rotting skin and sunken cheek bones, lost the orange glow that came with this damnation. One blue and one brown, Sal's eyes were now alight with the colors of his own redemption.

. . . and then they were drifting.

CHAPTER 44

Edvard's unconscious form lay draped across the plastic tool dolly. With his right arm trapped awkwardly beneath his body, a pool of blood grew slowly on the elevator floor as it dripped from the dependent fingertips of his left hand. The cabin shuddered as it rose slowly toward the surface, sending ripples through the sticky mess where it grew.

"What the hell happened down there?" Graves was looping his fingers through the holes in Dana's lapel while she leaned against the aluminum wall of the elevator.

Standing with her arm slack at her side, her weapon once again in her possession, Dana slowly answered him. "I dunno. I heard . . . felt, a pop as the bullet grazed my coat." She rubbed her forehead and looked up at him.

"How'd you get hit twice? You've got two holes in this coat!" He held it up for her to see. "And who shot him?" Graves loosely gestured towards Edvard's body where it lay, loaded on the tool cart in the middle of the elevator.

"He shot himself." Until now, Moriel had been unconscious, lying in the corner.

Dana jerked her weapon up and aimed the barrel at the head of the priest.

"Whoa, Agent Pinon." Propped up on one elbow in the corner of the elevator Moriel held out an open palm in objection. "I was the one attacked, remember? Relax, please."

"I'm not sure what's going on anymore, and I'm certainly not going to trust you at this point." She left her weapon where it was.

"What do you mean he shot himself?" Bastien enquired.

Dana's eyes strayed briefly from her rapt target to Bastien and then back again. "Yeah, what do you mean?" she added.

Moriel was sitting now, rubbing the back of his head where he'd been hit with the butt of the very gun now pointed at him. "The ceramic gun, your ceramic gun, Detective Pinon, along with the brass and zinc casings of its bullets, probably shielded the lead rounds in the clip from the growing magnetic field down there. Once they were fired, the lead bullets followed the same path that all the other metal objects in the room did, right to the reactor." He grimaced a bit as he adjusted his position. "Maybe Dr. Krunowski assumed the short range and high initial velocity would be more than the field could overcome."

"You're saying the bullet turned midair and hit him?" Graves's voice rose in disbelief as he again pointed at Edvard's body.

"It would seem so, Detective."

The elevator groaned as it approached the surface. The monotonous drone of the cables above had been overwhelmed by a metallic clicking noise, one that had been growing louder over the last few minutes.

"What the hell?" Graves looked around the elevator cab, running his hands over the walls. The stainless steel screw heads in the panels had begun to dance in their holes.

"Are we slowing?" Bastien was staring up at the indicator arrow as it slowly arced its way from "Atlas" towards "Surface."

"I think so." Graves's eyes narrowed and his voice trailed off. "Your badge is changing colors." He was staring at Dana's coat where he'd laid it on the floor.

"Oh shit, yours is, too." She gazed around the group. All the dosimetry badges had begun to lose their dull black finish and were showing a deep purple. "We need to get the hell out of here." Dana kept her weapon trained on the priest as she nervously tapped the button for the surface.

As their collective concern focused on the glowing badges, the lights in the elevator flickered twice before going out, leaving the occupants in the blush of emergency lights.

"What the . . .?" Graves muttered. "How the hell are we still moving?"

"I think that the power sources are from different places, the lights being from below, if I'm not mistaken," Bastien added.

The rattle of the steel screws increased, as a few from the lower edges of the walls flew forcefully from their perch, landing on the floor and sticking without so much as a single bounce. Graves kicked at one.

"Christ, it's like it's welded to the floor. Look at this!" Graves bent down to grab at it. The elevator shuddered again, this time violently sparking a shower of threaded metal from the ceiling above.

As the crew pinned themselves against the walls to avoid the metal hail, they watched Edvard in horror out of the corners of their eyes. Small spurts of blood, accompanied by shreds of clothing, leapt from his body as it was pierced again and again by the screws. Waking to this reality, Edvard let out an agonizing scream. He made a pleading grasp for Father, before his eyes closed again and his body went limp.

The panels above them began to bend under the magnetic forces from below. Their ride lurched to a stop and the doors began to open slowly. A growing shaft of brilliant blue light cut the fluorescent air, revealing a viewing chamber awash in a swirling brilliance.

Running bent over to avoid the metal storm, the crew covered their heads and burst from the elevator. From the back of the small cab, Graves shoved the tool cart carrying Edvard, trailing what little liquid blood remained.

"Jesus Christus." Bastien stood, circling in place with his mouth agape.

The entire chamber shimmered with an electric blue light emanating from a rippling image on the room's massive viewing screen.

"Isn't that image from the inside of the reactor chamber?" Dana managed.

The group stood frozen, focused on the chaotic image before them. Dana raised her radio to her lips and depressed the button.

"Aldo, can you . . ." Dana's words died to a whisper. Her transmission was echoing from somewhere off in the dark corner of the room. From the top of the stairs leading down from the control booth, she thought she made out the hiss of another radio.

"Aldo?" Dana took a tentative step toward the concealed source. "Are you . . ."

With a loud snap, a quick burst of light filled the room. Something stung Dana's forearm, causing her to drop the gun.

Graves moved quickly to cover her and retrieve the weapon. Another bright flash of light burst from the shadows, followed by several more, which left the room ringing with the rico-chets of bullets as they glanced off the heavy metal surfaces all around them. Graves changed his course mid stride and brought Dana to the carpeted floor behind one of the room's long arcing rows of vacant desks. The remainder of the group scrambled for cover.

"Father!" From the shadows, a man Graves recognized as the gruff grad student they knew as Mr. Tong was striding quickly down the stairs with his weapon held out rigidly in front of him, his high and tight blond hair almost as unwavering as his scowl. "What have you done?"

The room's flickering iridescent light shined off the gunman's weapon as he continued further into the control room. From behind him flashed a figure. Covering the distance of the five stairs in a single cartoonish dive, Aldo drove their attacker to the floor. A brief struggle ended with two shots that echoed through the chamber. Rising to his feet, the fair-skinned young man's focus returned, this time directed fully toward Father Moriel.

Father stood. "Whatever sins you've committed, my son, the Lord will forgive you."

With his anger finding new motivation, their attacker continued, "Sins! You talk of sins. Those who have died at my hands have done so for a greater cause, one that will return the Church to a glory not seen since the coming of Christ. It was you we were after, holy man. You were our target that night. My father chose you after his last conversation with Dr. Canty. He savored the sweet irony. But divine guidance chose a messenger far more capable."

"But why the girl?" Moriel pleaded.

"Dr. Canty gave us hope, but the little girl's death was necessary to bring the Church back to its former grandeur. His search for her now in the afterlife will secure our very faith. Cardinal Antonacci shared my father's vision—a Church once again united with its followers in Christ. The Cardinal's last act in your reassignment to Mexico was supposed to draw their attention to you, but instead you've brought them here . . . to us!"

"I would gladly have died for them," Moriel said, the sadness evident in his voice.

The young man raised his gun. "As you wish. The Cardinal outlived his usefulness, just as you have. My father was the only true holy man, sacrificing everything to stay true to physics, the one great religion."

Moriel glanced back over his shoulder toward the body that remained slumped over the tool cart. "Dr. Edvard Krunowski was your father?" he asked incredulously.

The young man's scowl tightened. "You don't deserve our Lord's mercy either!"

A single shot ripped through the chamber, spinning Father Moriel wildly to his left. Falling to the floor, he lay awkwardly, face down and motionless. The gunman turned and continued forcefully through the control room toward the elevator.

Stopping beside the motionless body on the tool cart, the young man knelt. He took Edvard's bloodied hand into his own and kissed it before pressing it firmly to his forehead as he wept. "Father, forgive me. I have failed you."

Edvard's eyes opened. Mustering what earthly strength remained, he reached across his torn chest to take his son's hand. "Iän, our proof lies in the reactor. Save the machine." As his life faded, Edvard's grip failed, and his eyes closed for the last time.

"No!" The young man's scream filled the room. "What have you done?" Extending his arm, Iän rose, showering the room with an arc of metal. "You've killed him! You've destroyed all my father slaved for!"

Graves and Dana lay behind their cover. From their vantage point they could see the body of Father Moriel, his head turned grotesquely to the left and his chin tilted upwards, his arms both trapped beneath his rotund frame. Graves thought he could still make out the subtle rise and fall of the priest's chest.

Graves rose to his knees peering over the rows of desks that separated him and this, until now, unknown son of Edvard Krunowski. The brief quiet was surreal. The undulating waves of blue light rippled across every surface in the room. Graves bent to retrieve Dana's fallen weapon as Iän brazenly stepped toward him.

"You have nothing left to harm me with," Iän continued. His knuckles white with anger as he gripped the weapon pointed at his father's pursuers. He backed away from them, retreating slowly in the direction of the waiting elevator. "We will prevail. You've not won, the proof is there." He pointed at the open elevator.

As Iän wheeled the cart and his father's body into the darkened box, Graves noticed his dosimetry badge begin rapidly shifting its colors. With a grinding whoosh, the heavy metal doors closed, and both Edvard and his son were on their way back to the reactor floor.

After a moment Graves stepped away from his blind, motioning to Dana it was safe to stand. Quickly walking past Moriel, he reached down and grasped Aldo's shoulder. Still conscious, Aldo clutched at his belly. With each shallow breath blood oozed between his fingers.

Graves gently coaxed Aldo's hands from his abdomen. "It's not bad," he called out as he looked over his shoulder in Dana's direction. "It's not," he reiterated to Aldo. "It's through and through in your left flank, we need to get you outta here." Smiling at his friend Graves continued. "How did he fit into all of this?"

"That was Dr. Edvard Krunowski's son, Iän, or John, as we

all knew him." Aldo's words were strained, forced out through breaths while keeping his stomach muscles tightened.

"He was our MS-13 contact, the one whose cell phone conversations we'd been tracking?" Graves asked. "Then how did Moriel figure into all of this?"

"I don't."

All heads spun in the fallen priest's direction. Rising to a knee in the room's intensifying light, Moriel reached into his coat.

Graves raised his weapon toward the priest.

"No!" Aldo grasped Graves's ankle from where he still lay. "He's right. He has nothing to do with this."

"How are you alive? We all saw you get shot, fall . . . you should be dead!" Dana was standing with her back to the flickering screen in awe of what she was witnessing.

"Ein Wunder," Bastien whispered to himself, crossing his chest in disbelief.

"I believe you're right, Inspector, it *is* a miracle." From his inner lapel pocket Moriel pulled a flat bronze pin, roughly the size of his palm that was cast in the shape of a badminton birdie. From the center of its circular base, several small rays were etched, which projected upward to the top of the pin. Embedded in its center, was the shattered 9 mm projectile.

"Since Eva's disappearance I've kept this with me to remind myself of what a gift her life was to me." Tears filled his eyes as he continued. "I never imagined it was actually intended to save my life."

"I'm totally lost." Graves was standing with the weapon hanging limply at his side.

Dana walked over to assist Moriel to his feet. The dizzying kaleidoscope of blue light intensified as she went. She staggered slightly under its disco ball affect.

"The favor that our previous FedPol director did for the late Dr. Krunowski, or Job as your MS-13 had known him, was to facilitate his son's placement in the Swiss Guard years ago. That is, after he completed his formal schooling in the States." Aldo grimaced as he continued. "Right before Iän knocked me out, I received a call from our lab. That single print we lifted, the one in your pocket Graves, was traceable only to records held in two locations . . . the Vatican and CERN."

Graves was shaking his head. "The Cardinal told us, only at the time it didn't make any sense to me. I thought he was referring to the sun, but what he said was 'I saw the 'son,' Job's son . . . Iän."

The quiet of the room was interrupted once again, this time with the groan of bending metal. From behind the group, the elevator doors had begun to warp inward. The group's dosimetry badges changed from deep violet to a brilliant emerald green as the gap between the elevator doors continued to widen.

"We definitely need to get out of here." Dana was helping to collect the disheveled priest as light metal objects throughout the room began flying toward the growing gap. Paperclips and other tiny objects flew to their new collection point inside the elevator shaft. The light on the room's monitor from the reactor chamber began to change.

Retreating to the back of the room, the group stood mesmerized by the image on the main screen. Warped at first, as if viewed through a lens held too far from its subject, the picture slowly coalesced in the center and began to take recognizable form.

As the room emptied of its smaller debris, the metal lining of the elevator shaft collapsed. The immense doors broke loose, leaving a gaping hole to the chamber 300 feet below. A strong breeze began blowing toward the elevator. The crescendo was joined by a deafening rumble of myriad larger objects in the room as they lurched erratically toward the growing forces that drew them in. The screen's light no longer cast shifting shadows; rather, its once erratic nature now became a constant bright light hurling long unwavering shadows.

The wind increased, moving all the nonmetallic objects toward the expanding mouth. With all the noise in the room, Dana could barely hear her own voice as she yelled.

"It looks like two figures . . . like two silhouettes." She backed closer to Graves, their arms gently rubbing together. Without taking her eyes off the screen she grasped his hand, lacing her fingers with his.

In front of a bright blue background were two ghostly images, out of focus at first but becoming recognizable as the chaos in the room violently approached its crescendo. The faces of an adult and child embracing melted into focus, translucent as if cast in ice.

"My God!" Bastien dropped to one knee amidst the maelstrom. "It's the Holy Mother and Child"

"No." Father Moriel's jaw quivered. He swallowed hard to continue, yelling above the din. "It's Fin, and he's holding Eva."

The noise in the room had become deafening as the combined forces from the growing white hole threatened to tear the facility apart. Objects that were once firmly fixed to the floor ripped from their moorings, meeting with ear shattering noise as they were devoured by the growing black abyss where the elevator shaft once existed.

Transfixed by the proof of his faith, and with tears streaming down his face, Father whispered to himself. "Sapientone, you found her."

Eva's soft fingers touched the hardened and bloodied talons of what she still knew to be her father . . .

As if a switch were thrown turning it all off, the chaos ended. With a collective thud, all objects fell to the floor and skidded to a halt. A deafening silence filled the room. When the violent movement of air ceased, the screen flickered, and the image faltered, leaving only a brief glimpse of a glowing halo with a single brilliant ray of light streaming outward from its center, then it all went dark.

With the aura of her presence upon Fin's face . . . they were drifting.

CHAPTER 45

One year later . . .

"Welcome back to the show, where our guest tonight is Father Daniel Moriel. Father, before the break you were saying that it's the religious community that's offering caution in taking your findings at face value."

"They're not my findings, Anderson, they're the findings of the scientists who operate the most sophisticated scientific piece of equipment ever constructed."

"I understand that a few of those scientists died in the process of making this discovery. Is that true?"

"Yes. CERN's director and his son perished the night the images were received. It's unfortunate the way it worked out, but in their absence, the remainder of the community has rallied to comb through the data collected. Everyone else, the religious establishment included, can say what they wish, but it's difficult to dispute the accumulated evidence collected from CERN and its machinery."

"Come back to bed, Tom. I can't see anything with you standing right in front of the TV." Keeping her eyes glued on the screen, Dana flipped the covers back and gently patted the mattress.

"He looks good. I think he's lost some weight." Graves walked backwards toward his reserved spot as he spoke.

"We've got recorded video of a deceased man and his daughter embracing, video that was streamed directly from CERN's main reactor chamber, ATLAS, from what has been proven to be a briefly existing white hole."

"The experts are arguing that it may be a hoax, a ruse played by . . ."

"By whom, Anderson? Me? The Church? CERN?"

"Maybe the Church. Some say that this is a new millennium stunt pulled to increase numbers in your congregations, and to add to the coffers of the established religions."

"We have DNA samples taken from the inside of ATLAS that are from Dr. Fin Canty, the man obviously in the footage . . ."

"Yes, Father, but DNA that could have been taken from any source before his death, and several leading experts argue that they could have been samples replicated in huge numbers using PCR."

"Anderson, let's take this one page at a time. First we're talking about phenomenal amounts of genetic material—proteins and nucleotides measurable in amounts that would take decades to amass. Second, the so-called 'experts' are indirectly suggesting that a scientific machine, one costing tens of thousands of dollars per hour to operate, one that conjured man's first-ever dimensional rip, was hijacked by the Catholic Church and used as an April Fool's prank to increase attendance. This would be a conspiracy theory of the grandest magnitude."

Graves was sitting up in bed now, smiling ear to ear while Father continued to defend their point of view. "Good for him. It's about time somebody said publicly what we've all been thinking for months."

"Okay Father, I for one do believe what I've seen. But what

does this mean for us, for the human race?"

Father grinned before continuing. *"I think we're seeing what it means, Anderson. The number of people worldwide who have returned to religious services, of every denomination, is unprecedented. We're seeing increases of more than 200% in attendance. Our discoveries at CERN—this revelation, if you will—is changing the face of religion as only Christ's presence on Earth had done previously."*

"But what does it mean for us? . . . for me?"

"It means that people no longer feel alone, or disconnected." Father had his eyes closed now and was talking vigorously with his hands. *"Folks move through their day with a greater purpose and sense of belonging. There's a feeling that there's more to this existence than what we see here. We're destined for something, somewhere greater, and we've seen it."*

Father sat forward in his chair and rested his arms on the desk as he continued more slowly. *"Crime rates in New York City, Chicago, and L.A. have declined by over thirty-one percent in just the last six months . . . and that's all crime, violent crime included. The current peace talks in Gaza were begun a little over five and a half months ago, a period of relative peace that has lasted longer than any in their history. Prison populations have begun to shrink for the first time in decades, traffic tickets are on the decline, and in general people are just friendlier. And why not . . . most of us again believe that God is watching us, and waiting for us."*

Father paused and sat back in his seat. *"I think it means that we've found our faith again—in our God, in ourselves, and in our fellow man to great extent."*

"What would you say to those who don't believe?"

Father sat quietly for a minute before continuing. *"In a*

way, this man, Fin Canty, died because of the collective sins of our society. Our drug wars, our Internet, our addictions, and self-promotion have all fostered the culture that so easily swallowed him and Eva. . . . In a way, he rose again to show us the light. Even if this is not the second coming, as some have suggested, we're unlikely to see another miracle of this magnitude in our lifetime. I guess I'd ask the nonbelievers, 'If not this, what are you waiting for?'"

"I want to thank my guest . . ."

Graves turned off the TV and the light. Placing his hand on top of Dana's as it rested on her stomach, he kissed her cheek before closing his eyes. "I love you."

"I love you too." She said softly.

The two fell asleep to the noises of the city.

The seasons were changing again, but the fall warmth stayed on at the lake. Fin sat with his father by the water while Eva played with her mother and grandmother in the shallows of their shorefront. It was late in the afternoon and the gold and brown colors saturated their mood.

"You haven't been up on the roof much in the last few months. Have you found something more important than solving the mysteries of our universe?" Jack asked, in a good-humored, teasing voice.

"It's funny how it all works out, Dad. I've just been enjoying Rachel and Eva so much, but then Fin's words stalled as he sat staring out at the water.

"Then what, Son?"

"There was that cave where I first really encountered those creatures. That mural, I've been unable to get it out of my thoughts. All I was told while I was there . . . it's all had me thinking. This process—life, death, heaven, hell—it's been ongoing since we've needed it. But there's something that's been occurring a whole lot longer than that."

Shielding his eyes from the setting sunlight reflecting off the lake, Jack turned toward his son. "What's that?"

"Life."

"What's that got to do with it all, Fin?"

"Life began about four billion years ago, right around the time the strength of dark energy overtook the forces of dark matter. Life has been spreading and diversifying ever since, but it all started right at the point our universe began to expand faster and faster . . . the point at which Einstein's cosmological constant became relevant."

Rachel sat down beside Fin as he continued.

"There's an energy stronger than anything else around us, and until recently I didn't know what it was, or why it was." Fin turned briefly toward his wife, grasping her hand where it rested between them in the soft grass. "It seems life is the one thing that refuses to abide by the boundaries our universe sets. It's the one thing that pushes through each one of them. I think we're all part of this dark energy."

"Are you referring to all of us, our family, here in this place?"

Fin could feel the smile growing on his face as Rachel's stare warmed him. He sat for a brief moment watching Eva. Silhouetted against the setting sun, her dark figure splashed and danced as she giggled.

"We're not alone, you know." Fin continued quickly, "I

don't know if what I was told was true, if there's a God or not, but I was never alone there . . . she was always with me." He nodded subtly toward his daughter where she played.

"Son, what do you mean life expands through each boundary?"

Fin sat contentedly for a moment, leaving the fall air pregnant with his father's question as he listened to the noises of the lake. "I love you," he said quietly, turning his head in Rachel's direction.

"I love you too," she whispered.

Placing his hand on top of Rachel's as it rested on her stomach, Fin smiled before closing his eyes. He breathed deeply and slowly, savoring the rhythmic kicking of the new life that thrived in Rachel's womb.

— THE END —

CHRISTOPHER JOHN HEJMANOWSKI

Dr. Chris Hejmanowski is a science fiction writer who has a passion for medicine, physics, cosmology, and the mysteries of religion. Military trained in Emergency Medicine, Hejmanowski began his career as a flight surgeon.

Throughout a career that spanned over a decade, he spent time overseas with both the United States Navy and the Marine Corps. As an ER physician, Hejmanowski deployed with the United States Marines to Al Taqqadum, Iraq from the summer of 2008 to the spring of 2009.

For several months, within a mobile surgical unit, he led a Shock Trauma Platoon, moving with the Marines along the Syrian boarder. It was here, during quieter moments in a tent, that he began to write his first full-length novel, "Collider."

Dr. Hejmanowski is currently an emergency room physician in the Southeastern United States. When not working or writing, he enjoys spending time with his family, as well as woodworking and restoring classic cars.

Watch for the new book "JESUS ROCK"
coming soon from Chris Hejmanowski

In December 1945, the Dead Sea Scrolls were discovered. Dated as early as A.D. 40, these manuscripts were regarded by historians as the earliest account of the living Jesus' words. Not accepted by the Catholic Church as canonical, they were excluded from Catholic teachings. The text, when made public, was understood to have been divulged by the Catholic Church in its entirety, until now...